SIRI HUSTVEDT

Siri Hustvedt is the author of three novels, *The Blindfold*, *The Enchantment of Lily Dahl* and *What I Loved*, as well as a poetry collection, *Reading to You*, and three collections of essays, *Yonder*, *Mysteries of the Rectangle: Essays on Painting* and *A Plea for Eros*. Born and raised in Minnesota, she now lives in Brooklyn with her husband, Paul Auster.

'[An] astonishing family drama ... a lyrical investigation into the way memories are communicated and transmuted within families, and the lengths to which people go to preserve or deny them ... Hustvedt is famous for writing positively thrilling prose. But she is on fire here. Not a single word is wasted or wrong, and to each of her diverse characters there is a seasoned, utterly believable vernacular. This passionately conceived, coolly delivered work is almost certainly the best American novel you will read this year.'
Melissa Katsoulis, *Sunday Telegraph*

'This novel is easily described as wonderful, although, like a lot of great novels, it doesn't sound so good in the retelling. You have to read it to believe it. *The Sorrows of an American* does have a lot of plot, but that is not the main attraction: its beauty lies in the ability of the narrator to reveal the frailties of the human mind ... her skill lies in convincing the reader that we have seen right inside someone's soul'
Viv Groskop, *Observer*

'A mystery story that develops into a subtle and complex novel ... Hustvedt switches gracefully between her characters, involving them in each other's webs of grief and secrecy, confession and anger, lust and need. She weaves together family saga, comedy of manners and gothic horror ... With great skill she shows inner and outer worlds colliding with and penetrating one another.'
Tom Deveson, *Sunday Times*

'A profound analysis of how loss and the fear of living are the roots of Erik's depression. What begins as a baffling puzzle ends on a movingly optimistic note ... Warmly recommended'
John Harding, *Daily Mail*

'A masterful semi-self-portrait by turns abstract and realistic, intimate and alienating, effulgent and bleak, concise and blurry, straightforward and elusive – but the author couldn't have it any other way'
Sarah Emily Miano, *The Times*

'For all its cerebral riches, this novel is composed with superb artistry. Hustvedt handles the numerous interlocking narratives with immense skill. From the rural farm during the Depression to urban New York, every life is revealed with precision and love … It is a proof of Hustvedt's talents that the terrors of this novel feel real.'
John de Falbe, *Literary Review*

'Satisfying and emotionally rich … Hustvedt's cerebral characters are tenderly drawn, wise and realistic. With a sure hand, she communicates both the intellectual dynamism of New York – where "talk is a form of play" – and the blank endlessness of the Minnesota landscape.'
Economist

'A kaleidoscope of intellectual and emotional ideas, dancing with philosophical speculation, neuroscience and an ongoing enquiry into the relationship between the self and creativity. Rather than drift into abstraction, these ideas are pinned to characters who are intriguingly flawed and damaged, and who, in trying to confront that damage, throw some light on the mystery of what makes us who we are'
Claire Allfree, *Metro*

'An intriguing novel of suspense beautifully combined with a melancholic treatise on memories and loss.'
Psychologies

'It brims with luminous, unknowable characters ... a book about memory and loss, about how we reconstruct our pasts through our families and how we continue to rewrite them for our present selves. It's also about the gap between what we think we know about someone close to us, and how much more there is that we can never know'
Chitra Ramaswamy, *Scotland on Sunday*

'Hustvedt's gifted story-telling crams five generations into a compact, elegant story ... She navigates the past and present better than many of us manage our day.'
Helen Greenwood, *Sydney Morning Herald*

'Siri Hustvedt is a modern master. Her works belong among the most exciting and insightful of contemporary novelists ... *The Sorrows of an American* is the kind of book that spoils you for other novels'
Age

'Complex and contemplative ... a thought-provoking book that offers pleasures across many different registers ... Hustvedt's descriptions of the immigrant experience and the Minnesota landscape have a spare Scandinavian elegance, while her account of the life of a Brooklyn psychoanalyst feels quietly authentic ... a writer deftly able to weave intricate ideas into an intriguing plot'
Sylvia Brownrigg, *New York Times Book Review*

'One of the most profound and absorbing books I've read in a long time. Hustvedt pushes hard on what a novel can do and what a reader can absorb, but once you fall into this captivating story, the experience will make you feel alternately inadequate and brilliant – and finally deeply grateful ... I reached the end emotionally and intellectually exhausted, knowing how much I'll miss this book'
Ron Charles, *Washington Post*

THE SORROWS
OF AN AMERICAN

SIRI HUSTVEDT

SCEPTRE

First published in Great Britain in 2008 by Sceptre

An imprint of Hodder & Stoughton
An Hachette Livre UK company

First published in the United States in 2008 by Henry Holt

First published in paperback in 2009

1

A CIP catalogue record for this title is
available from the British Library

ISBN 978 0 340 89708 9

Typeset in Janson Text

Printed and bound by Clays Ltd, St Ives plc

Hodder & Stoughton policy is to use papers that are natural, renewable
and recyclable products and made from wood grown in sustainable
forests. The logging and manufacturing processes are expected to
conform to the environmental regulations of the country of origin.

Hodder & Stoughton Ltd
338 Euston Road
London NW1 3BH

www.hodder.co.uk

For my daughter,
Sophie Hustvedt Auster

Don't turn away.

Keep looking at the bandaged place.

That's where the light enters you.

— RUMI

THE SORROWS
OF AN AMERICAN

M̲y sister called it "the year of secrets," but when I look back on it now, I've come to understand that it was a time not of what was there, but of what wasn't. A patient of mine once said, "There are ghosts walking around inside me, but they don't always talk. Sometimes they have nothing to say." Sarah squinted or kept her eyes closed most of the time because she was afraid the light would blind her. I think we all have ghosts inside us, and it's better when they speak than when they don't. After my father died, I couldn't talk to him in person anymore, but I didn't stop having conversations with him in my head. I didn't stop seeing him in my dreams or stop hearing his words. And yet it was what my father hadn't said that took over my life for a while—what he hadn't told us. It turned out that he wasn't the only person who had kept secrets. On January sixth, four days after his funeral, Inga and I came across the letter in his study.

We had stayed on in Minnesota with our mother to begin tackling the job of sifting through his papers. We knew that there was a memoir he had written in the last years of his life, as well as a box containing the letters he had sent to his parents—many of them from his years as a soldier in the Pacific during World War II—but there were other things in that room we had never seen. My father's study had a particular smell, one slightly different from the rest of the house. I wondered if all the cigarettes he'd smoked and the coffee he'd drunk and the rings those endless cups had left on the desk over forty years had acted upon the atmosphere of that room to produce the unmistakable odor that hit me when I walked through the door. The house is sold now. A dental surgeon bought it and did extensive renovations, but I can still see my father's study with its wall of books, the filing cabinets, the long desk he had built himself, and the plastic organizer on it, which despite its transparency had small handwritten labels on every drawer—"Paper Clips," "Hearing Aid Batteries," "Keys to the Garage," "Erasers."

The day Inga and I began working, the weather outside was heavy. Through the large window, I looked at the thin layer of snow under an iron-colored sky. I could feel Inga standing behind me and hear her breathing. Our mother, Marit, was sleeping, and my niece, Sonia, had curled up somewhere in the house with a book. As I pulled open a file drawer, I had the abrupt thought that we were about to ransack a man's mind, dismantle an entire life, and without warning a picture of the cadaver I had dissected in medical school came to mind, its chest cavity gaping open as it lay on the table. One of my lab partners, Roger Abbot, had called the body Tweedledum, Dum Dum, or just Dum. "Erik, get a load of Dum's ventricle. Hypertrophy, man." For an instant I imagined my father's collapsed lung inside him, and then I remembered his hand squeezing mine hard before I left his small room in the nursing home the last time I saw him alive. All at once, I felt relieved he had been cremated.

Lars Davidsen's filing system was an elaborate code of letters, numbers, and colors devised to allow for a descending hierarchy within a single category. Initial notes were subordinate to first drafts, first drafts to final drafts, and so on. It wasn't only his years of teaching and writing that were in those drawers, but every article he had written, every lecture he had given, the voluminous notes he had taken, and the letters he had received from colleagues and friends over the course of more than sixty years. My father had catalogued every tool that had ever hung in the garage, every receipt for the six used cars he had owned in his lifetime, every lawnmower, and every home appliance—the extensive documentation of a long and exceptionally frugal history. We discovered a list for itemized storage in the attic: children's skates, baby clothes, knitting materials. In a small box, I found a bunch of keys. Attached to them was a label on which my father had written in his small neat hand: "Unknown Keys."

We spent days in that room with large black garbage bags, dumping hundreds of Christmas cards, grade books, and innumerable inventories of things that no longer existed. My niece and mother mostly avoided the room. Wired to a Walkman, Sonia ambled through the house, read Wallace Stevens, and slept in the comatose slumber that comes so easily to adolescents. From time to time she would come in to us and pat her mother on the shoulder or wrap her long thin arms around Inga's shoulders to show silent support before she floated into another room. I had been worried about Sonia ever since her father died five years earlier. I remembered her standing in the hallway outside his hospital room, her face strangely impassive, her body stiffened against the wall, and her skin so white it made me think of bones. I know that Inga tried to hide her grief from Sonia, that when her daughter was at school my sister would turn on music, lie down on the floor, and wail, but I had never seen Sonia give in to sobs, and neither had her mother. Three years later, on the morning of September 11,

2001, Inga and Sonia had found themselves running north with hundreds of other people as they fled Stuyvesant High School, where Sonia was a student. They were just blocks from the burning towers, and it was only later that I discovered what Sonia had seen from her schoolroom window. From my house in Brooklyn that morning, I saw only smoke.

When she wasn't resting, our mother wandered from room to room, drifting around like a sleepwalker. Her determined but light step was no heavier than in the old days, but it had slowed. She would check on us, offer food, but she rarely crossed the threshold. The room must have reminded her of my father's last years. His worsening emphysema shrank his world in stages. Near the end, he could barely walk anymore and kept mostly to the twelve by sixteen feet of the study. Before he died, he had separated the most important papers, which were now stored in a neat row of boxes beside his desk. It was in one of these containers that Inga found the letters from women my father had known before my mother. Later, I read every word they had written to him—a trio of premarital loves—a Margaret, a June, and a Lenore, all of whom wrote fluent but tepid letters signed "Love" or "With love" or "Until next time."

Inga's hands shook when she found the bundles. It was a tremor I had been familiar with since childhood, not related to an illness but to what my sister called her wiring. She could never predict an onset. I had seen her lecture in public with quiet hands, and I had also seen her give talks when they trembled so violently she had to hide them behind her back. After withdrawing the three bunches of letters from the long-lost but once-desired Margaret, June, and Lenore, Inga pulled out a single sheet of paper, looked down at it with a puzzled expression, and without saying anything handed it to me.

The letter was dated June 27, 1937. Beneath the date, in a large childish hand, was written: "Dear Lars, I know you will never ever say nothing about what happened. We swore it on the BIBLE. It can't matter now she's in heaven or to the ones here on earth. I believe in your promise. Lisa."

"He wanted us to find it," Inga said. "If not, he would have destroyed it. I showed you those journals with the pages torn out of them." She paused. "Have you ever heard of Lisa?"

"No," I said. "We could ask Mamma."

Inga answered me in Norwegian, as if the subject of our mother demanded that we use her first language. "*Nei, Jei vil ikke forstyrre henne med dette.*" (No, I won't bother her with this.) "I've always felt," she continued, "that there were things Pappa kept from Mamma and us, especially about his childhood. He was fifteen then. I think they'd already lost the forty acres of the farm, and unless I'm wrong, it was the year after Grandpa found out his brother David was dead." My sister looked down at the piece of pale brown paper. " 'It can't matter now she's in heaven or to the ones here on earth.' Somebody died." She swallowed loudly. "Poor Pappa, swearing on the Bible."

AFTER INGA, SONIA, and I had mailed eleven boxes of papers to New York City, most of them to my house in Brooklyn, and had returned to our respective lives, I was sitting in my study on a Sunday afternoon with my father's memoir, letters, and small leather diary on the desk in front of me, and I recalled something Auguste Comte once wrote about the brain. He called it "a device by which the dead act upon the living." The first time I held Dum's brain in my hands, I was surprised first by its weight, and then by what I had suppressed—an awareness of the once-living man, a stocky seventy-year-old who had died of heart disease. When the man was alive, I thought, it was all here—internal pictures and words, memories of the dead and the living.

Perhaps thirty seconds later, I looked through the window

and saw Miranda and Eglantine for the first time. They were crossing the street with the real estate agent, and I knew immediately that they were prospective tenants for the ground floor of my house. The two women who lived in the garden apartment were leaving for a larger place in New Jersey, and I needed to fill the vacancy. After my divorce, the house seemed to grow. Genie had taken up a lot of space, and Elmer, her spaniel; Rufus, her parrot; and Carlyle, her cat, had occupied territory as well. For a while there were fish. After Genie left me, I used the three floors for my books, thousands of volumes that I couldn't part with. My ex-wife had resentfully referred to our house as the Librarium. I had bought the brownstone as a so-called handyman special before my marriage when the market was low and have been working on it ever since. My passion for carpentry is a legacy of my father, who taught me how to build and repair just about anything. For years, I was holed up in one part of the house as I sporadically worked on the rest. The demands of my practice squeezed my leisure hours almost to nil, one of the factors that led to my joining that great legion of Western humanity known as "the divorced."

The young woman and the little girl paused on the sidewalk with Laney Buscovich from Homer Realtors. I couldn't see the woman's face, but I noticed that her posture was beautiful. Her hair was short and cut close to her head. Even from that distance, I liked her slender neck, and although she was wearing a long coat, the sight of the cloth over her breasts triggered a sudden image of her naked, and with it a wave of arousal. The sexual loneliness I had felt for some time, a feeling that had on occasion driven me to the voyeuristic pleasures of cable porn, intensified after my father's funeral, mounting inside me like a keening storm, and this post-mortem blast of libido made me feel that I had returned to my life as a slobbering teenage onanist, the tall, skinny, practically hairless jerk-off king of Blooming Field Junior High School.

To interrupt the fantasy, I turned to look at the girl. She was a spindly little thing in a bulky purple coat who had clambered up onto the stoop wall and was balancing there with one thin leg out in front of her. Under the coat she was wearing what looked like a tutu, a pink concoction of tulle and net over heavy black tights that bagged at her knees. But what was most noticeable about the child was her hair, a pale brown mass of soft curls that enveloped her small head like a huge halo. The mother's skin was darker than the child's. If these two were mother and daughter, I decided, the girl's father could be white. I drew a breath as I watched her leap from the wall, but she landed easily on the ground with a little bounce in her knees. Like Tinkerbell, I thought.

LOOKING BACK AT our early life, the most astonishing feature must be how small our house was, my father wrote. *A kitchen, living room, and bedroom on the first floor came to 476 square feet. Two lofts on the second floor, which were used as bedrooms, provided the same amount of floor space. There were no amenities. Our plumbing consisted of an outdoor toilet and a hand-operated pump, each at its own location about 75 feet from the house. A teakettle provided hot water, as did a reservoir attached to the kitchen range. Unlike better-equipped farms we had no underground cistern to store rainwater, but we did have a large metal tank which caught rainwater during the summer. During the winter we melted snow. Kerosene lamps provided light. Although rural electrification began in the thirties, we did not "hook up" until 1949. There was no furnace. A wood-burning range warmed the kitchen and a heater cared for the living room. Except for storm windows, the house had no insulation. Only during the coldest spells was fire maintained in the heater overnight. The water in the teakettle was often frozen by morning. Father was up first. He built the fire so much of the edge was gone by the time we crawled out of bed. Even so there was shivering and huddling around the stoves as we got dressed. One winter in the early 1930s we ran out of wood. Not enough had been put up in the first place. If one must burn green wood, ash and maple will serve you best.*

As I read, I kept waiting for a reference to Lisa, but she didn't appear. My father wrote about the refinements of piling "an honest cord of wood," plowing with Belle and Maud, the family horses, clearing the fields of dreaded weeds like Canadian thistle and quack grass, the farm arts of dragging, seeding, cross-dragging, corn planting and cutting, haying, collective shock threshing, silo filling, and gopher catching. As a boy, my father killed gophers for money, and from his later vantage point he understood the humor in this occupation. He started a paragraph with the sentence: *If you are not interested in pocket gophers or how to catch them, move on to the next paragraph.*

Every memoir is full of holes. It's obvious that there are stories that can't be told without pain to others or to oneself, that autobiography is fraught with questions of perspective, self-knowledge, repression, and outright delusion. I wasn't surprised to see that the mysterious Lisa, who had sworn my father to secrecy, was missing from his memoir. I knew there were many things I would leave out of my own story. Lars Davidsen had been a man of rigorous honesty and deep feeling, but Inga was right about his early life. Much had been hidden. Between *Not enough had been put up in the first place* and *ash and maple will serve you best* was a story untold.

It took me years to understand that although my grandparents had always been poor, the Depression had ruined them entirely. The sorry little house my father described is still standing, and the remaining twenty acres of what was once a farm are now rented to another farmer who owns hundreds upon hundreds more. My father never let the place go. As his illness progressed, he willingly decided to sell the house he had lived in with my mother and us, a lovely place built partially with wood from trees he had chopped down himself, but the farmhouse of his childhood he gave to me, his son, the renegade doctor, psychiatrist, and psychoanalyst who lives in New York City.

By the time I knew my grandfather, he was mostly silent. He sat in the small living room with the wood-burning stove in a stuffed chair. Beside the chair was a rickety table with an ashtray on it. When I was young, that object fascinated me because I found it shameful. It was a miniature black toilet with a gold seat, the only flush toilet my grandparents would ever have. The house always smelled strongly of mildew and in winter of burnt wood. We rarely went upstairs, but I don't believe we were ever told not to go there. The narrow steps led to three tiny rooms, one of which belonged to my grandfather. I don't remember when it was, but I couldn't have been more than eight. I sneaked up the stairs and walked into my grandfather's room. A pale light was shining through the small window, and I watched the dust specks dance in the air. I looked at the narrow bed, the tall stacks of yellowing newspapers, the torn wallpaper, a few dusty books on a beaten dresser, the tobacco pouches, the clothes piled in a corner, and felt a muted sense of awe. I think I had a dim idea of the man's solitary existence and of something lost—but I didn't know what. In this memory, I hear my mother behind me, telling me that I shouldn't be in the room. She seemed to know everything, my mother, seemed to sense what other people didn't. Her voice wasn't at all harsh, but it may be that her sanction made the experience memorable. I wondered if somewhere in that room was something I shouldn't have seen.

My grandfather was gentle with us, and I liked his hands, even the right one, which was missing three fingers, lost to a circle saw in 1921. He would reach out and pat me or lay his hand on my shoulder and hold it there before returning to his newspaper and spittoon, a coffee can that said "Folgers." His immigrant parents had eight children: Anna, Brita, Solveig, Ingeborg, another Ingeborg, David, Ivar (my grandfather), and Olaf. Anna and Brita lived into adulthood, but they were dead before I was born. Solveig died of tuberculosis in 1907. The first Ingeborg died on August 19, 1884. She was sixteen months old. *Our father told me that this Ingeborg died shortly after birth and was so tiny that a cigar box was used as a coffin. Our father must have confused Ingeborg's death with some other local tale.* The second Ingeborg also came down with tuberculosis and spent time at the Mineral Springs Sanitarium, but she recovered. David fell ill with tuberculosis in 1925. He spent all of 1926 in the sanitarium. When he recovered, he disappeared. He wasn't found again until 1936, and by then he was dead. Olaf died of tuberculosis in 1914. Sibling ghosts.

My grandmother, also the daughter of Norwegian immigrants, had grown up with two healthy brothers and inherited money from her father. She was entirely different from her husband, a female spitfire, and I was a favorite of hers. Entering the house became a ritual. I would throw open the screen door, run through it, and bellow, "Grandma, my sword!" This was her cue to reach behind the kitchen cupboard and pull out a two-by-four onto which my uncle Fredrik had nailed a short crosspiece. She always laughed then, a loud cackle that sometimes made her cough. She was fat but strong, a woman who hauled heavy buckets of water and carried a bushel of apples in the folds of her skirt, who peeled potatoes with a fierce stroke of her paring knife, and overcooked every comestible that came her way. A woman of moods, she had her smiling, chatty, storytelling days and her days of gloom, when she muttered asides and squawked out dubious opinions about bankers and rich folks and sundry others who were guilty of crimes. On her worst days, she would say a terrible thing: "I never should have married Ivar." When his mother ranted, my father stiffened, my grandfather remained quiet, my mother tried humor and negotiation, and Inga, sensitive to every emotional wind change, whose face registered pain at even the hint of a conflict, drooped. A raised voice, a retort, a sullen expression, an irritable word stuck her like needles. Her mouth tensed and her eyes filled with tears. How often I had wished in those days that she would toughen up just a little.

Despite the occasional outbursts from Grandma, we loved it there, the place my father called "out home," especially in summer, when the broad flat fields with growing corn ran to the horizon. A rusting tractor, overgrown by weeds, a permanently parked Model A, the old pump, and the stone foundation of what had once been a barn were all fixtures in our games. Except for the wind moving in the grass and trees, the sound of birds, and an occasional car passing on the road, there was little noise. I never gave a moment's thought to the fact that my sister and I were climbing, running, and inventing our stories of shipwrecked orphans in an arrested world, but at some point, the world of my grandparents, of those second-generation immigrants, had ground to a halt. I see now that the place is a scar formed over an old wound. It's odd that we're all compelled to repeat pain, but I've come to regard this as a truth. What used to be doesn't leave us. When my great-grandfather Olaf Davidsen, the youngest of six sons, left the tiny farm high on a mountain in Voss, Norway, in the spring of 1868, he already knew English and German, and he had his teaching credentials. He wrote poetry. My grandfather would finish the fifth grade.

The diary was one of those small five-year volumes with only a few lines allotted per day. My father kept it from 1937 to 1940, and there were some sporadic entries from 1942. Lars Davidsen's prose had undergone a revolution since 1937, and I puzzled over his peculiar use of the verb *to be* and his mutating prepositions.

There were several entries that simply stated, *Was to school.* It took me several minutes to realize that this odd construction was a loose translation of the Norwegian *Var på skolen,* literally "Was on school." His syntax and a number of the prepositions were English versions of the family's first language. I guessed that he had received the diary for Christmas and began writing in it on January first. He recorded visits from and to neighbors: *Masers were up for dinner. Neil was along, too. The Jacobsen boys were over in the afternoon. Was to Brekkes today. Was on a party at Bakkethuns.* Weather conditions: *There was a snowstorm today. The wind is blowing very hard. The weather was nice and melting. Today there was a hard snowstorm. From morning till now. There is a drift four feet high outside the house.* Winter illnesses: *Lotte and Fredrik were not in school, but Fredrik was up today. Was in bed all day because account of a cough.* Animal troubles: *Daddy and I was up to Clarence Brekke. He was having bad luck. 4 of his cattle was dead. Daddy was up at Clarence helping him skin the seventh cow. 4 heifers, 1 steer, 1 cow, and one calf have died for him inside a week. Jacobsen's horse, Tardy, died. Ember's dog was driven over.* On January 28, I found a mention of David. *Today is a year ago since dad was up in the cities to identify uncle David after hearing he was dead.* By spring there were several gopher entries: *I caught 6 gophers today. Caught four gophers. I caught 7 gophers in all at Otterness.* On June 1, my father wrote, *Today there was a row between Harry and Daddy.* June 3, I found the first mention of the world beyond that small rural community. *I plowed and dragged today. King Edward and Mrs. Wallis Simpson.* On the fifteenth of that same month, my father recorded an emotion. *I hoed potatoes all day. Pete Bramvold was here and wanted to hire me. I am so doggoned disgusted because I can't go.* On the day before Lisa sent the letter to my father, June twenty-sixth, I found this entry: *We plowed in the potatoes. Daddy was to town. Harry was put in jail.*

Who was Harry? When I spoke to Inga, she said she had no

idea. I agreed to write to Uncle Fredrik and ask him. Tante Lotte was beyond asking. She was in a nursing home with Alzheimer's.

THE FIRST THING Eglantine ever said to me was, "Look, Mommy, he's a giant." After opening the door for my new tenants, I was somewhat relieved that when I looked at Miranda a second time, I shook her hand without going to pieces. Her eyes were unusual. They were large, almond shaped, the color of a hazelnut, and tilted upward slightly, as if someone in the family had come from Asia, but her intense gaze was what held me during those initial seconds. She then lowered those remarkable eyes toward her daughter and said, "No, Eggy, he's not a giant. He's a tall man."

I looked down at the child and said, "Well, I come pretty close to being as tall as a giant, but I'm not like the ones in fairy tales." I bent over and smiled encouragingly, but the little girl didn't smile back. She looked at me without blinking and then narrowed her eyes as if she were weighing my comment with great seriousness. Her grave expression made me even more self-conscious about my height. I'm six feet five inches tall. Inga is six feet, and my father measured in at just a hair under six-three. My mother is the shrimp at five-nine. The Davidsen family and, on my mother's paternal side, the Nodeland family, tended toward the thin and towering. The genetic combination had been predictable, and Inga and I grew and grew and grew. We had endured the bean-pole and how's-the-weather-up-there jokes throughout our lives, as well as the mistaken assumption that our jump shots were superb. Not a single seat in a movie theater, playhouse, airplane, or subway, no public toilet or sink, no sofa or chair in lobbies and waiting rooms, not one desk in the world's libraries has ever been built for the likes of me. For years, I have felt that I inhabit a world a few sizes too small, except at home, where I raised the counters and built high cabinets that, as Goldilocks put it, are "just right."

As we sat at my kitchen table, I felt a strong reserve from Miranda Casaubon, a proud distance that I rather admired, but which made conversation difficult. She could have been anywhere between twenty-five and thirty-five, was conservatively dressed with the exception of her high boots that laced up the front and tightly followed the line of her calves. I knew from Laney that she had "a good job" as a book designer for a major publisher, could afford the rent, and had insisted on Park Slope so her daughter could attend P.S. 321, the local elementary school. There was no father in the picture. Miranda told me that she had grown up in Jamaica and left with her family when she was thirteen. Her accent had been blunted, but she retained some of the musicality of Caribbean English. Her parents and her three sisters were now all living in Brooklyn. Miranda kept her hands on the table as we spoke, one laid over the other. They were slender with long fingers, and I noticed that there was no tension in them or in the rest of her body for that matter. She was still, relaxed, and alert.

If not for Eggy, I wouldn't have discovered anything more. She had stayed silent after our greeting, and when we sat down she hugged her mother's arm, buried her face in her shoulder, and then began a game with the back of the chair. She held it with one hand and leaned outward until she could go no farther and then pulled herself back again. After this gymnastic routine, she abruptly skipped away and began to dance around the room with her arms out, pale brown curls flying. She hopped over to the bookshelves and began to sing, "Books, bookers, books, and more bookerees! Book-a-book, book-a-book. I can read today."

I turned to Miranda. "Can she read?"

Miranda smiled for the first time, and I saw her even white teeth, which protruded just slightly. The overbite sent a shudder through me and I looked away. "A little. She's in kindergarten and is learning."

Eggy leaned her head back, threw out her arms, and started to spin on the floor.

"You're getting wild," Miranda told her. "Calm down."

"I like to be wild!" She grinned at us, and her wide mouth seemed to take up the whole bottom of her small face, for a moment giving her an elfin expression.

"I mean it," Miranda said.

The little girl watched her mother, then spun again, but more slowly. After a short rebellious tap with her foot, she shook her curls and skipped over to me, eyeing her mother with a touch of resentment. She moved close to me and in a conspiratorial way said, "Do you want to hear something private?"

I looked at Miranda.

"Maybe Dr. Davidsen doesn't want to hear it," Miranda said.

"Erik," I said.

Miranda glanced at me but said nothing.

"I'm happy to hear it if it's all right with your mother," I said, striking a compromise.

Eggy regarded her mother fiercely. Miranda sighed and nodded, and then I felt the child's hand on my head as she pulled my ear toward her mouth. In a loud, excited whisper that felt like a blast of wind on my eardrum, she said, "My daddy was in a big box, and it got very sticky and wet in there, and so he dis"—she paused—"peared. 'Cause he's magic."

I wasn't sure whether Eggy believed these words were inaudible to her mother or not, but I saw Miranda grimace for a moment and lower her eyelids. I turned to Eggy and said, "I won't tell any-body. I promise."

The young Eglantine gave me a flirtatious smile. "You have to swear and hope to die."

"I swear and hope to die," I said.

This seemed to delight her. She beamed at me, closed her eyes, and then inhaled loudly through her nose, as if we had just ex-changed smells rather than words.

When I turned back to Miranda, I found her regarding me with a shrewd expression, as if she were penetrating my depths. I have a weakness for smart women, and I smiled at her. She smiled back, but then stood up, effectively ending the interview. The abrupt gesture provoked a sudden desire to learn her story, to find out all about this woman, her five-year-old, and the mysterious father the daughter had assigned to a box.

Before they walked out the door, I said, "Please let me know if you need anything or if there's anything I can do before you move in."

I watched them walk down the steps, turned around in the hallway, and heard myself say, "I'm so lonely." It shook me be-cause this sentence had become an involuntary verbal tic. I seldom realized I was saying it or perhaps didn't know that I was speaking the words out loud. I had started to experience this unbidden mantra even while I was still married, mumbling it before sleep, in the bathroom, or even at the grocery store, but it had become more pronounced in the last year. My father had it with my mother's name. While he was sitting alone in a chair, before he dozed off, and later, in his room at the nursing home, he would utter *Marit* over and over. He did it sometimes when she was within hearing distance. If she answered the call, he seemed not to know that he had spoken. That is the strangeness of language: it crosses the boundaries of the body, is at once inside and outside, and it sometimes happens that we don't notice the threshold has been crossed.

AS WIDOW AND divorced man, Inga and I found the common ground that mutual loneliness offered us. After Genie left me, I realized that most of the dinners, parties, and events we had attended were connected to her rather than to me. My colleagues from Payne Whitney, where I worked at the time, and my fellow psychoanalysts had bored her. Inga lost friends, too, people who had been attracted to the shine of her famous husband and had accepted her as his charming second, but who then disappeared after Max was dead. Although there were many among them whom she hadn't much cared for to begin with, there were others whose precipitous absence deeply pained her. She did not, however, pursue a single one of them.

Inga met Max when she was a graduate student in philosophy at Columbia. He gave a reading at the university, and my sister was sitting in the front row. Inga was a twenty-five-year-old blond beauty, brilliant, fierce, and aware of her seductive power. She held Max Blaustein's fifth novel in her lap and listened intently to every word of his reading. When he was finished, she asked him a long complicated question about his narrative structures, which he did his best to answer, and then, when she laid her book on the table to have it signed, he wrote on the title page, "I surrender. Don't leave." In 1981, Max was forty-seven years old and had been married twice. He not only had a reputation as a major writer but was also known as a profligate seducer of young women, a carousing wild man who drank too much, smoked too much, and was, all in all, too much, and Inga knew it. She didn't leave. She stayed. She stayed until he died of stomach cancer in 1998 when he was sixty-four.

Only a month after she defended her dissertation on

Kierkegaard's *Either/Or*, Inga was pregnant. Although Max had no children from his earlier marriages and had declared himself a "nonparent," he became an almost comically enthusiastic father. He bounced Sonia and sang to her in his rasping, altogether tuneless voice. He recorded her early utterances, photographed and filmed her at every stage of her growth, taught her to play baseball, faithfully attended her school conferences, recitals, and plays, and bragged shamelessly about her poems as the verbal gems of his "wonder girl." Still, Inga did most of the everyday work, the feeding and comforting and dressing, and a good share of the nighttime reading. Between mother and daughter, I saw a tie that reminded me of the connection between Inga and our mother, an unarticulated corporeal closeness that I call an overlap. I have seen many versions of the parent-child story in my patients, people suffering from the intricacies of a narrative they are unable to recount. Max's death wrenched Inga and Sonia off course. My niece was twelve, a precarious age, an age of inner and outer revolutions, and she retreated for a while into compulsive orderliness. While my sister sank, shuffled, and wept, Sonia cleaned and straightened and studied far into the night. Like my father's labels and files, Sonia's perfectly folded sweaters organized by color, her radiant report cards, and sometimes brittle response to her mother's grief were pillars in an architecture of need, structures built to fend off the ugly truths of chaos, death, and decay.

Max was emaciated at the end. As he lay in the hospital bed, no longer conscious, his head looked like a skull with a thin covering of gray, and his arm, inert over the sheet, reminded me of a twig. By then, the morphine had carried him off into a twilight reserved for the dying. After the agonies that had gone before, I felt resigned. I'm still haunted by the image of Inga lifting the IV and crawling in beside him. She pressed her body against him and rested her head on his shoulder. "Oh, my darling, my darling, my own darling," she repeated. I had to turn away and walk into the hallway, where my tears fell more freely than they had in a long time.

It was only after Max's death that I truly became Uncle Erik, the all-purpose fix-it man, science paper advisor, speedy pot washer, and general consultant to Inga and Sonia on matters grave and small. I had failed as a husband, but I succeeded as an uncle. Inga needed to talk about Max—to tell me about the ferocious daily stints of writing that left him limp and depleted, his nightly communing with a whiskey bottle, Camel cigarettes, and old movies on TV, his irascible moods that were followed by regrets and declarations of love. She needed to talk about the cancer, too. Again and again, she told me about the morning when he vomited and vomited, and then, white and shaking, how he had called out to her. "The toilet was full of blood. The seat was splattered red and the bowl was full of it, blood and more blood. He knew he was dying, Erik. I hoped, and I kept hoping. But later he said to me that when he saw what was coming out of him, he knew it, and he thought to himself, 'I've done a lot of work. I can go now.'"

I had always sensed that theirs had been a passionate marriage, but not an easy one. The two had been mutually dependent, a couple locked in a long love story that never became stagnant but churned and boiled until it was finally cut short. "There were two Maxes," Inga likes to say, "My Max and the one out there—the literary commodity: Mr. Genius." Writers come in every form, but Max Blaustein represented some idealized cultural notion of the dashing novelist. He was handsome, but not in an ordinary way. He had gaunt, delicate features, a full head of hair that had turned to an even white early, and signature wire-rimmed spectacles that Inga thought made him look like a Russian nihilist. The Max Blaustein *out there*, the author of fifteen novels, four screenplays, and a book of essays had inspired devotion and fanaticism in his readers and, from time to time, all-out hysteria. At a reading in

London in 1995, the author was nearly trampled to death by a hopped-up crowd that surged forward to get close to the idol. The memorial service had brought out hundreds of weeping fans, people who despite their demonstrated sorrow, pushed and shoved one another as they pressed into the hall. "He inspired adoration," Inga said, "that sometimes bordered on sickness. He always seemed bewildered by it, but I think his stories scraped on some darkness in people. I'm not sure anybody could or can explain it, Max least of all, but sometimes it frightened me—what was *in* him." I remembered these words because when Inga spoke to me, her voice broke, and I felt there was more behind them. Later, I wished I had asked her what she had meant, but at the time something had blocked me. I know that what I choose to call reserve or deference may be a form of fear—an unwillingness to listen to what comes next.

IN ORDER TO pay off the interest on his mortgaged land, my grandfather sawed lumber for a man named Rune Carlsen: *He received one dollar for each 1,000 board feet that was sawed. When they moved to a new site, there was much heavy work but no pay. The same was true if the machine broke down, and there was much of this. The rig was old. Our father worked the fields from four to six in the morning and from 7:00 p.m. until dark in the evening. The American shibboleth that hard work guaranteed success became in this case a crass lie. After some years of this, just when things began to improve, came foreclosure.*

The lost forty acres hurt my father for the rest of his life. It wasn't that he pined for the missing land but that the effort to keep it had broken something in his father. He never said this, but I've come to believe that is what happened. *A depression,* he wrote, *entails more than economic hardship, more than making do with less. That may be the least of it. People with pride find themselves beset by misfortunes they did not create; yet because of this pride, they still feel a pervasive sense of failure. Bill collectors earn their living by demeaning and humil-iating people with pride. It is their ultimate weapon. People of character become powerless. If you have no power, all talk of justice is just so much wind. The consoling argument that everyone was in the "same boat" had only partial validity. Farmers who entered the depression free of debt may, in fact, have increased their assets by buying up cheap land and farm ma-chinery at dumping prices. During these years farmers went up or down. We went down.* Those bill collectors had faces. Perhaps there was one man in particular who took pleasure in shaming Ivar Davidsen in front of his oldest son. Perhaps Lars had watched the man badger his father repeatedly for money he didn't have, and perhaps Lars waited for his father to clench his fists and throw a left to the bastard's jaw, followed by a swift right to the gut. Those blows were never delivered, not then, not ever.

UNCLE FREDRIK'S LETTER arrived less than a week after I had written to him. His mother had mentioned Lisa, he wrote. She wasn't from one of the neighboring farms but had traveled from Blue Wing to help out at the Brekkes when their son came down with appendicitis and was then laid up for a while. The girl had disappeared, and his mother had worried that something had hap-pened to her. Then he retold the story of the lost land.

> Before the Depression, my grandfather Olaf made a loan from
> Rune Carlsen and secured the loan with forty acres of land.
> During the Depression Rune foreclosed, and Dad, who had
> purchased the land from his father, lost the land to Rune. Dad
> suffered emotionally from this loss and often had nightmares
> during this period. When it happened, Mother would ask either
> Lottie or me to wake him up.
>
> Rune was sawing wood on the forty acres and hired Dad.
> This was humiliating for him. Harry Dahl also worked for

Rune. One day, the sawmill broke, and Harry was sent to Cannon Falls to buy parts. He returned late and intoxicated to face a hostile crew at the rig. I remember Dad talking to Mother about it. He had been angry and told Harry to go jump in a lake. I don't remember Harry's time in jail. But there was a great deal of talk about Chester Haugen's drunk driving charge and arrest in Blue Wing. Had he only been more cordial to the police, he would not have received thirty days in jail. He was missed by all of us during his sentence, and when he was released, we gave him a festal reception that included small gifts.

With love, from Fredrik

As I folded the neatly written letter and returned it to its envelope, I imagined the eight-year-old Fredrik standing in the tiny room with its narrow single bed. I saw him lean over his father to shake him from the dreams that made him cry out in the night.

IN THE EVENINGS, after I returned from the office and had eaten my dinner, I would go over my patient notes for the day. This had been my routine since my divorce, when the hours I spent at home grew longer, and I knew I had to fill them. As I surveyed the words I had recorded during a session, insights would sometimes come to mind unbidden, and I would make further comments or write down questions to bring to a colleague whom I might need to consult. After my father died, I began to fill another notebook, jotting down fragments of conversations that had taken place during the day, my fears about what looked like an imminent invasion of Iraq, dreams I could remember, as well as unexpected associations that arrived from the recesses of my brain. I know that my father's absence had prompted this need to document myself, but as my pen moved over the pages, I understood something else: I wanted to answer the words he had written with my own. I was talking to a dead man. During those hours at the dining room table, I would often hear Eggy's high shrill voice and Miranda's much softer one, although I could rarely make out what they were saying. I smelled their dinners, heard their telephone ring, their music play and, from time to time, squeaky cartoon voices from their television. Those solitary winter evenings seemed to spawn fantasies. I recorded some of them. Others never found their way into the black-and-white journal I reserved for my private thoughts, but at some point Miranda began to appear as a character in this disjointed record of my life. She kept hours different from mine, and I rarely saw her. When I did, she was polite, reticent, and well-spoken, nothing more, but I began to dream that I would someday crack her coolness. Her distant eyes, her imperfect teeth, her body hidden under layers of warm clothing had become part of a life I wished for.

One night, I returned rather late after a meal with a colleague, and as I approached the house, I noticed that a shutter on the middle window of the garden apartment had swung open. A light was on, and I saw Miranda seated behind a table in the front room. She was wearing a bathrobe that had fallen open at the neck, and I saw the curve of her breasts as she leaned over a large piece of paper, her hand moving as she drew. Beside her were scissors, pens, inkpots, and chalk. At first I thought she was working on a book design, but when I glanced down, I saw a large female figure with a gaping mouth and sharp teeth like a wolf's. There were other figures, too, smaller ones, but I couldn't identify them. Afraid she would catch me spying, I walked on, but that momentary view of the bestial woman remained with me. That evening, I recalled the first time I saw *Los Caprichos* and how the pictures had made me queasy as I shuttled between fascination and repulsion. The single glimpse of Miranda's picture made me think of Goya and of monsters in general. What's frightening is not their strangeness, but their familiarity. We recognize the forms, both human and animal, that have been twisted, contorted, elongated, or mingled together until we can't say they're one thing or the other. Monsters burst the categories. I went to sleep thinking of Mr. T., my old patient, who had been occupied by the jangling voices of the famous and infamous dead, male and female, and of poor Daniel Paul Schreber, whom Freud wrote about after reading the man's memoir. Tortured by supernatural rays that were tied to celestial bodies, Schreber suffered from "bellowing miracles" and "nerves of voluptuousness" that were filling him from head to toe and slowly turning him into a woman.

WHEN SHE WAS little, my sister had spells. Her eyes would become unfocused and then, for an instant, she would lose herself. Only once did it last long enough to frighten me. We were playing in the woods behind our house. I was the pirate who had captured her and tied her with imaginary ropes to a tree while she begged for her life. Just as I was relenting and about to invite her to become a girl pirate, she opened her mouth to speak and stopped abruptly. I saw her eyelids flutter strangely as a thin line of saliva trickled from her bottom lip. The sunlight caught the string of spit, and it gleamed like silver as I looked at her. I remember that there was some motion in the leaves above us and that I could hear the noise of the water from the creek, but otherwise everything seemed to have stopped with Inga. I don't know how long it went on, only seconds, but those seven or eight beats of waiting and watching terrified me. I imagined the game had somehow hurt her, that my villain fantasy had paralyzed my sister. After an unendurable pause, I howled her name and threw myself into her arms. All at once, she was comforting me. "Erik, are you all right? Are you hurt?"

I'm convinced now that Inga was suffering from absence, what used to be called petit mal seizures, which resolved themselves spontaneously as she grew older. What has remained with her are migraines and their auras and something fragile in her personality. As a boy, I knew that Inga had a quality that separated her from other children and that it was my job to take care of her as best I could. Inside the family, she was safe, but once we boarded the school bus, her vulnerability became a target. I can still see her walking down the aisle to her seat, holding her books against her chest, long blond braid trailing down her back, brown glasses on her nose, trying to look as if she didn't hear the rude whispers that followed her: "Weirdo" and "Inga, dinga-bat." She quivered. This was her fatal error. Her shuddering encouraged the verbal assaults, and because from early on she had decided to live a life of purity and goodness, she never answered her tormenters. This gave her a feeling of inner superiority but did little to ease her trips on the bus or her suffering at recess.

Neurological debilities always have content; this is something that hard science has been loath to recognize, just as psychoanalysis has often disregarded the physiology of various forms of mental illness. The stuff of Inga's early seizures and auras turned on our religious education. Neither my mother nor father was particularly devout, but out there in the American heartland just about everybody went to some church or other. We attended a Lutheran one, and our Sunday school teachers fed us stories about God and Jesus and that third and most distressing deity—the Holy Ghost. Because I felt that my parents were relaxed about the God problem, and I was not prone to "funny lifting feelings" or seeing "sparklers" the way Inga was, my connection to the divinity was more abstract. I worried about an invisible God looking inside my head and listening to my thoughts. Sometimes, before going to sleep, I'd cup my penis in my hand and think I heard him speak harshly in my ear, saying single words like "No" and "Don't." My sister, however, had angels inside her. She heard wings rustle in her ear and felt flaming hands touch her head and lodge themselves in her chest cavity and pull her upward toward heaven, and sometimes they spoke to her in rhythmic verses. She didn't like their ministrations one bit, and when the seraphim paid her a visit at night, she would sometimes come to me. If I wasn't sound asleep, I would hear a soft knocking at my door and her voice say, "Erik, Erik, are you awake?" A little louder. "Erik?" When it was late, and I was completely unconscious, I would feel her tapping my shoulder. "Erik, I'm afraid. The angels." I would turn over then and hold her hand for a while or let her hug me until she had the strength to return to her own room. Sometimes her courage failed, and I would find her curled up at the end of my bed in the morning.

Occasionally, my mother woke to Inga's short cries or to the sound of her restless feet padding down the hallway and would get up to lead her back to her room and sit by her bed, soothing her or singing to her until she fell asleep. She would always step quietly into my room afterward and put her hand on my forehead. I would pretend to be asleep, but my mother knew I wasn't. She would say, "Everything is fine now. Sleep." Inga and I didn't talk about the visitations except when they were happening, and it never occurred to me that my sister was either sick or crazy. Over time, doubt infected Inga, and she came to recognize that her nervous system had probably played a role in calling the spirits, but the experiences are a part of who she is and their influence can't be ignored. In another era, I might have been the brother of a saint or a witch.

A COUPLE OF days after I saw Miranda through the window, I noticed a paper clip with a rubber band attached to it lying just inside the inner door that separated my part of the house from the rental apartment. I thought little of it until a Q-tip bound with red thread was slipped under the door the next night, followed by a piece of green construction paper on the third, which had been inscribed with three large teetering letters: a W, an R, and an E. After that cryptic message, it seemed clear that these offerings had been made by Eglantine. On the fourth night, as I sat with my notebooks open before me, I heard scratching from the hallway. I walked toward the sound and saw that a key tied with a piece of yarn was being pushed under the door.

"A key," I said. "What a surprise. I wonder where these presents are coming from?"

From the other side of the door, I could hear the child breathing loudly, then Miranda's voice. "Eggy, what are you doing up there? It's your bedtime."

THAT SATURDAY, I saw mother and daughter on Seventh Avenue, walking hand in hand down the street as I was leaving the hardware store with the nails I needed for the bookshelf I was building. I quickened my step and called out to them.

Miranda nodded at me. Then she smiled. The smile made me absurdly happy.

Eggy stared up at me. "Mommy says you're a worry doctor."

"Yes," I said. "I went to school to become a doctor, and I help people with their worries and other problems."

"I have worries," she said.

"Eggy," Miranda said. "Everybody has worries."

This wasn't what Eggy wanted to hear. She looked at her mother and frowned, "I'm telling Dr. Erik."

She remembered that I had asked her mother to call me Erik. "You know, Eggy," I said, "you're welcome to knock on the door and come in and visit me. I like presents, but I like to talk, too."

I heard Miranda sigh. In that sound was a world. I thought of her long workdays and the evenings alone with her energetic five-year-old. I realized then that I had never seen her with a man. When I turned to look at her, Miranda met my eyes for a couple of seconds, pressed her lips together, and looked down at the sidewalk. I didn't know what to make of it. For a second I saw the ferocious drawing again.

"Are you walking home?" I asked her.

She looked up, apparently recovered from the small spasm I had just witnessed. "Yes, we were at the park and then picked up some groceries." She lifted the bag in her hand.

Just minutes later, we found the photographs. There were four lying on the house steps when we returned. At first I mistook them for the flyers or menus that appear regularly outside Brooklyn houses. Prepared to discard them, I bent over and saw four Polaroids of Miranda and Eggy in the park. Miranda was tying Eggy's shoe near the swings at the playground. Across Miranda's bent torso someone had drawn a black circle with a line through it. I muttered some low exclamation and picked up another picture, which must have been taken only minutes later. Miranda was pushing Eggy on a swing, and this time the crossed-out circle was drawn across the mother's face. The two others were similar recordings of the innocent outing, each one marked by the peculiar sign on another part of Miranda's body. My first impulse was to hide the pictures from both of them. What good this would have done, I have no idea. I felt a desire to protect them from whoever the photographer might be, but it was too late. Miranda was beside me, looking down at the pictures, and Eggy was jumping up and down asking to see what we were looking at.

"Just throw them away," Miranda said in a low voice.

"Do you know who took these?" I asked.

She looked me straight in the eyes, her mouth tight. "Put them in the garbage."

"I'll throw them away inside," I said. "Miranda, have you found any other pictures—or things?"

"What are they? Let me see! Let me see!" Eggy said.

"They're nothing," Miranda replied. She gave me a warning look, and I understood that I had stupidly launched into a subject not to be discussed in front of Eggy.

The four photos were in my right hand. I closed my fist and crumpled them on the spot. Before we parted, I said again that if they needed anything, they should let me know. I gave her my hand, and when she took it, her fingers felt ice cold against my skin.

I DISCOVERED LISA'S last name through Ragnild Ulseth, the second daughter of old Mrs. Bakkethun, a close neighbor of our grandparents. When I dialed the number, I felt some trepidation. Although Ragnild would certainly remember me, I recalled the sympathy card she had sent my mother after my father's death. The note had been written in a shaky hand explaining that her current health made traveling to the funeral impossible. She must have been well into her eighties. She answered the phone with a creaky but determined voice. "You're Lars's son, how nice. How nice." I made small talk for a couple of minutes before getting to the point. I didn't mention the contents of the letter but told her that my sister and I wanted to identify my father's correspondents if we could. "Do you remember a girl named Lisa? Fredrik thinks she worked for the Brekkes."

"Oh, dear me, yes. I remember. I'm as right as rain in my mind, you know, it's the rest of me that's falling apart, and better to ask me about the old days than about yesterday. Yesterday can fly right out of my head, but not times from way back. You must mean Lisa

Odland from Blue Wing. Was with the Brekkes maybe a year and came to us time and again. I was a little sorry for the girl, had a scar on her neck, but otherwise wasn't bad looking really, a bit on the heavy side. They said she was wild, but I wouldn't know about that. I never saw it. She was stubborn, if you ask me, and sad. Didn't say much. Her parents came from somewhere in the Dakotas, I think, and moved to Blue Wing. There was some talk of trouble back where they came from. She disappeared, oh let me see, it must have been sometime in the summer of thirty-seven, but she turned up again in South St. Paul at Obert's Lunch to see your dad. He was working there on Sundays as I recall."

"To see my father?"

"I had it from Obert himself," she said. "It's funny. I didn't know that Lisa was close to your dad. We all knew her, but she hung back, so we couldn't count her as a friend, if you see what I mean."

"Obert, my grandfather's cousin."

"Yes." Ragnild's voice softened. "They're all gone now. Hardly anybody left. With your dad's passing, well, it was sad, that's all. He was a good man."

"Yes, he was," I said, almost in a whisper. It wasn't the words she spoke as much as their sounds that moved me. The rhythm and music of another language haunted her speech, just as it had haunted my father's.

"Do you know anything about Harry going to jail?" I said.

Ragnild made a noise into the phone. "Poor man, he drank. It might have been on account of the drinking."

EGGY BEGAN TO pay me visits. She knocked at my door about once a week, and our encounters were quickly ritualized. She would open the lock from her side, and then lead me to the sofa for a talk. I heard about dragons and dinosaurs and a cat named Catty that ran away and never came back and about her Wendy doll, a bad girl, who needed regular punishing. On occasion, she gave in to scatology and unleashed an excited barrage of it into my ear. "The witch." She paused and breathed hard. "The witch, when she wasn't looking, ate her broom. It tasted awful. Then she found two people dancing on her hat so she pooped on them, and cooked them up in a sandwich." This was followed by hoots of laughter. I heard about her nightmares, a monster with "long, biting, angry teeth" that invaded her kindergarten classroom and a windstorm in the garden behind "our house" that crushed the chairs to bits and pulled off her arm, but she put it back. "Mommy works in an office with books," she said, "but she's really an artist. Shhh, she's working. We have to be very, very quiet." She talked to me again about her father. "My daddy is away in a special place. He took his car there when I was little and he can't come back anymore. It's too far." Eggy wagged her head back and forth and then fluttered her fingers on her chest. "Ahhh!" she wailed, then stopped abruptly and squinted at me. "He's so tiny now I can't even see him."

I recognized the oddness of the friendship. Eglantine had sensed that I was a man who would listen to her. It was my job, after all. As "Dr. Erik," I served as a worry closet. *Worry* spelled WRE. At the same time, I was careful to avoid the trap of ad hoc therapy. Eglantine was not my patient.

"DATE!" INGA YELLED. "I'm almost fifty years old, and you want me to date? The word itself is offensive. I have a *date*. I'm going on a *date*." She turned her pale face to me. "I've had *dates*. What I want is a man. My body aches because it's hardly touched. I'm starting to feel rigid, wooden. But the idea of gussying myself up and having dinner with a stranger just seems awful to me now.

How am I going to arrange it anyway? Put an ad in the *New York Review of Books*?" Inga raised her palms to stop me from speaking. "Six-foot, cranky, hypersensitive, aging, still mourning widowed writer with philosophy degree seeks kind, brilliant man, twenty-five to seventy, to love and be loved." Near the end of the sentence, she looked down and I saw a liquid gleam in her eyes.

"Oh Inga," I said, and opened my arms. She fell forward into them but didn't cry. She let me embrace her for a little while and then pulled away.

"Don't die," she said to me. "That's all I can say to you. Don't you dare die. When Pappa died, I thought about Mamma right away. She's not so young. I want her to live to be a hundred, a hundred and five, and be just as good as she is now . . ." Inga paused. "You know, I've been reading both Max and Pappa these days, trying to find them in the words, trying to explain my husband and my father to myself, but there's something missing, and I don't mean their bodies. They had a quality in common, something obtuse and unknowing. I think that's what drew me to Max—that hidden and oblique shadow I recognized without ever knowing what it was." She paused. "Do you remember when it started, the walking? Do you know when he disappeared for the first time?"

I heard the door click softly shut in my mind and felt the ache and fear that accompanied it—a memory in my body. "When we were small," I said. "I don't remember that he did it; it was later. I think I was twelve or thirteen the first time I realized—the time when he didn't come back until morning."

"Mamma didn't want us to know. He never took the car. Do you think he just walked and walked for hours?"

"Maybe," I said. "I think he had to flee. Emotions would build up in him, and then he couldn't stay. I don't know where he went."

Inga looked at me. "I remember hearing him leave. I was lying in bed wide awake because I'd seen it at dinner, that brooding, cut-off, distressed look in his face. It's strange," my sister continued. "Taking a walk, even at night, even if you're upset, is such an innocent thing, and yet it was so secretive, so thick with feeling that it became terrible. I never knew what caused it. It never followed an argument with Mamma or anything like that."

"There was a moment in medical school when I thought Pappa might be a fugueur."

"A fugueur?" Inga said smiling. "On a fugue?"

"Yes, it got a lot of attention in the nineteenth century, and it's still diagnosed as dissociative fugue. I've never heard of it happening to a woman. It's always men, who suddenly run off and vanish for hours or days or weeks, even months, and then wake up somewhere without remembering who they are or what happened to them. It's extremely rare, but I did see one case years ago when I was a resident at Payne Whitney. A man was brought in after a bad fall on the street. He had broken his elbow and had several contusions, but no head injury. They fixed him up, but he didn't have identification and told the staff he couldn't recall anything prior to a month earlier, and he didn't seem to care. They sent him over to us in psychiatry. Eventually, they discovered that his wife had filed a missing persons report in South Carolina four weeks earlier. When she came in, he didn't recognize her."

"What did you do for him?"

"There aren't any drugs for it, just talk. His wife had taken the long bus ride up to retrieve him, and although she'd been warned, she took it hard. It turned out that he had been humiliated. The owner of the garage where he worked had forced him to crawl out the door in front of his co-workers while the man held a wrench over his head. It seems it was a repetition of his father's brutality. When he went home to his wife, she called him a coward. He left the house in a rage and disappeared."

"He came back to himself?"

"Yes, within a week."

"My brother, the genius."

"I wasn't the attending physician. I just followed the case, and even without therapy most people have spontaneous recoveries."

"But Pappa knew who he was."

"Yes, but I can't help thinking that it was another form of fugue, one we haven't named."

She nodded. "He always wanted to be so good to everybody."

"Too good," I said.

"Too good," Inga repeated. It was a Saturday evening on White Street. The overhead light illuminated my sister's delicate features. I thought she was looking a little better than she had. The lines around her mouth looked less deep, and the skin under her eyes had lost its blue tinge. The conversation took place after dinner. Sonia had gone out with a group of schoolmates. We sat in silence for some time after that, an intimate, ruminating silence that is possible only with very old friends, and we drank another glass of wine.

"Well, here we are," she said finally. "Erik and Inga, a couple of kids from the boons living in New York City, full-fledged, card-carrying urbanites who've nearly lost our Minnesota accents. Our father was born in a log house on the prairie. It's positively mythical."

I didn't answer for a couple of seconds. There was a blazing image in my mind—a picture of something I'd never seen. "It burned," I said.

"What?"

"The log house. It burned to the ground."

"Yes, that's why they moved to the house that's still there, *your* house." Inga's smile was ironic. "Out there, standing empty."

THE PHOTOGRAPH WAS lying outside the gate that led to the garden apartment when I returned from work. It had been a long day, and on the way home in the subway I had finished reading an article and was musing over its implications when I saw the image, which was lying face up on the ground. As I leaned over to look at it, I recognized Miranda's face at once, but the black-and-white photograph had been altered. The irises and pupils in Miranda's eyes were missing. I looked into the blank spaces and suffered an uncanny feeling of recognition, then lost it. I turned the paper over, wondering if there was a message. I noticed the sign I had seen on the earlier pictures, a circle crossed with a line, nothing else.

When I laid the image down on the dining room table, I had a visceral memory of one of my patients hurling a photograph at me as he yelled at the top of his lungs, "Fuck them!" I hadn't thought of Lorenzo for a long time, but looking down at the empty eyes in the picture, I recalled his tirades during sessions and how I had braced myself for the verbal assaults before he arrived. I left those sessions feeling as if I had been physically battered. Lorenzo was twenty-three. His parents had brought their son to me and were paying for his treatment. There were several cases of bipolar disorder in his extended family, and I worried that he might be showing signs of it. I considered prescribing lithium, a very low dose, but when I mentioned it, he objected violently to taking any drug, and not long after, I realized that Lorenzo was lying to his parents and using me as a pawn to justify his behavior: "But Dr. Davidsen says it's all right." I ended the treatment. Lorenzo had sent the picture he threw at me to his parents with a single change. He had taken a razor blade to the photograph and scratched their eyes out.

Someone was stalking Miranda, and I guessed it was a person she knew. Unlike the earlier Polaroids, which were probably taken surreptitiously, this was a full-face portrait, the kind of photograph people usually *pose* for. The mystery person had either taken the picture or had somehow gotten access to it. The only thing I felt certain of was that the sender wanted to disturb the recipient. It was an overtly aggressive act, and this made me think the perpetrator was a man, but I knew I could be wrong.

I had to show it to her, of course. If the image came through me, the unpleasantness might be softened somewhat. Wiping out eyes is a cheap trick, a cliché borrowed from horror movies, but the lack of originality didn't make it any less effective. As Inga once pointed out to me, since Plato, Western philosophy and culture have had an ocular bias: vision is our dominant sense. We read each other through our eyes, and anatomically they are an extension of our brains. When we catch someone's eye, we look into a mind. A person without eyes is disturbing for the simple reason that eyes are the doors to the self.

FROM HIS TINY room in the Coates Hotel on Concord Street in South St. Paul, my father looked down on a brave new world, the heart of which was Obert's Lunch. He worked two grueling janitorial jobs during the week, took some night classes, and peeled potatoes at Obert's on Sundays. His cause: college tuition. *During the week Obert's was a bustling place. Regulars who worked in the stockyards or at one of the packing plants came in for breakfast and left with their lunch buckets and thermoses. They returned for a leisurely evening meal. Many luxuriated over one of Obert's giant T-bone steaks. Nothing fancy: a mountain of fried potatoes, four slices of bread, and all the coffee one could drink for 45 cents. Beef or pork roast with mashed potatoes and gravy was a 40-cent option. Harry O'Shigley was the chef, a man with a massive torso placed on a pair of short legs. Oscar Nelson, a thin small-boned man, ate little else than hot milk and toast, known cheerfully at Obert's as Grave Yard Stew. The Wee Cook lived at the fire station, but drove a city truck. Some years back his daughter had refused to let him see his newborn grandson because he came drunk. He had not touched a drop since that day, but the ravages of an earlier life were evident. Billy Muir, better known as the Windbreak because of the primitive shelter he had built for himself on the Mississippi flats, was a general handyman and a homespun philosopher. Persons who wanted his services made contact through Obert's. A Reverend Christianson, known for his conservative views, came by one Sunday to talk to Billy about some repair work.*

"What's cook'n in the parish?" asked Billy.

"We need a hundred good new members," said the parson.

"Why don't you get a hundred bad ones and make good ones out of 'em?" said Billy.

My father took warmly to the splendid riffraff he found himself among, to Happy Kramer, Push 'Em Up Tony, Jerry the Dip, and Putsy Schultz, characters who would brighten his inner landscape for the rest of his life. They are the creatures of a young man's perception, preserved forever in the glow of his first steps away from home. My Concord Street was New York City, a town loaded with the vibrant, the eccentric, and the outré. In the first two months after my arrival, I met Boris Izcovich, a homeless, alcoholic former cellist; Marian Pibble, the cheery one-eyed cashier at Bubba's Bagels; and Big Rita, the first drag queen I'd ever laid eyes on. Only a couple of inches shorter than I am, she liked to stop me on the street, lean her head on my shoulder, and coo, "I just love a big man." My first super was a character named Dumpy Gonzales, who repeatedly dared me to heal him. "Hey, young doctor man, I got a pain in my knee. Take a look down my throat, will ya?" An ambulatory catalogue of complaints, from imaginary tumors to fantasy hair loss, Dumpy was a medical student's nightmare, but I remember him and all the rest of them fondly nevertheless. They were so vividly *un*-Minnesotan, so *un*-Lutheran, so *unknown* to me and, as such, they have lingered as the radiant symbols of my urban initiation. I am less impressionable now, more prone to tune out the mad diversity of human life that confronts me every day on the subway and in the streets. I am inhabited by my patients, who have spoken every language and come from every walk of life. They have provided me with as much variety and color as I could possibly want.

My father was unhappy that I decided to go east to medical school. He never told me this. He told my mother, who mentioned it to me many years after the fact. He had wondered aloud why the University of Minnesota wasn't good enough, or the University of Wisconsin, where he had earned his Ph.D. I think he viewed my choice as surreptitious criticism of him and, although I knew nothing of it then, it created an unspoken cleft between us, one that grew as the years passed.

While he was living in South St. Paul, my father met a young woman whom he took out a couple of times. *Poor Dorothy was about as inept at the art of dating as I was. We may have shared educational aspirations, but our backgrounds could hardly have been more different. Everything I said sounded stupid and contrived and in all likelihood was. What does a farm lad tell a history professor's daughter? How to psych out a mean Holstein bull?* Lars Davidsen became a history professor, but he also remained a "farm lad," and I don't think he ever reconciled the two. *The worst of the regulars at Obert's were perhaps only steps away from skid row—has-beens, moral and physical wrecks, family disgraces, and each in his own way a failure in life. Nonetheless, there was goodness among them and little hypocrisy.* All his life, my father freely distributed his tenderness to the downtrodden, the misshapen, the sorry, and the sad. He never judged the powerless. That was his goodness. It was also his misery. Success, his own, but mine as well, was colored by a feeling of betraying those at home and the ghosts they had left inside him. The irony is that my ambition, if you measure the distances traveled, was finally not as great as my father's.

I SEE LISA walking into Obert's Lunch on a Sunday afternoon. It's a fall day in 1941. Pearl Harbor is yet to come. I imagine a heavy-breasted blonde with blunt features, wearing a trench coat and those short boots to the ankle I've seen in period movies. Then I see her and my young father (with a full head of hair) outside on a nearly empty, muddy street. She has her hand on his arm and is speaking to him urgently, but I am too far away to hear what they're saying.

WHEN I TOOK the photograph to Miranda that same evening, Eggy was already asleep. I didn't want the little girl to see the altered picture of her mother, but when I looked into Miranda's closed, tense face, I realized that I missed the child's piping voice, her energy, her affection. Miranda opened the pocket doors to the front room and waved me inside. I stepped into the once familiar space, now changed by its new spare furnishings—the large worktable I had seen through the window, bookshelves, a small sofa, and a box of toys. I glanced at the table, hoping to see more drawings, but none were visible. On the wall above the mantel was a large ink drawing, a full-body picture of a younger Eglantine, her soft hair lit from the right so the curls on that side of her face formed a partial nimbus as she looked soberly at the viewer with the intense expression I had come to know, her arms folded across her chest. She was standing in an empty, featureless room, wearing a one-piece bathing suit, and she looked rather grubby. Her bare knees were smudged with dirt, and there were dark spots around her mouth, perhaps from candy. Despite the child's firm stance on the floor and the grime on her body, the image had an ethereal quality, as if the little girl were indeed an enchanted creature rather than a mere mortal. Was it her expression? Was it the emptiness of the room? Although the picture's luminosity conveyed a feeling of transcendence, I found it unsentimental, not one of those pictures that turn children into the objects of an adult's false romantic projections.

"That's a great drawing," I said, rather stupidly.

"I did it as an exercise in likeness," she said. "Sometimes it's harder to draw a person you're close to than a stranger."

"Eggy told me that you're an artist, not just a graphic designer."

"Yes," she said. "I needed to be able to do something practical that I also like." She looked at me for an instant before she moved her eyes away. "I make money from one. My heart is in the other. You said there was something you had to speak to me about?"

I had noticed Miranda's conscious, slightly formal diction from the beginning, but her curt tone took me aback. "Yes, another photograph was left outside the door. It's rather unsettling."

Miranda rubbed her face with one hand. It was an oddly masculine gesture, I thought, like a man feeling his beard. She sighed. "Let me see it."

I handed the picture to her. She looked at it for an instant and then put it on the coffee table. She didn't invite me to sit down.

"You're being harassed," I said. "Stalking is something of a professional hazard in my business. A woman who has an office near mine went through it last year. Have you thought of notifying the police?"

"What are they going to do?" she said.

"Do you know who it is?"

"If I did," she said evenly, "why should I tell you?"

She hadn't spoken in a harsh tone, but the words cut me, and I felt a hot rush come to my face. In that instant I was hurt far beyond what I knew to be reasonable. The words *because it's my house* appeared in my mind, but I suppressed them. "I'm sorry to have bothered you," I said. "I'll leave now."

I let myself out without looking at her. She would have to lock the gate from the inside, but I didn't bother to remind her. Upstairs, as I made myself some chicken sausages and mashed potatoes, I replayed the encounter over and over again. Why should she tell me? What was I to her? The landlord. The shrink upstairs who had befriended her kid. A really tall white guy with the hots for her, or worse: a busybody, an old woman butting into the neighbor's business. I knew I was vulnerable to these blows, even when they were minor. In analytic-speak, my narcissistic balance had been thrown off, a wound reopened. Pride, I thought, the Davidsen curse. That hurt stayed through the evening and reappeared for days afterward when I had a moment to remember. I blessed the commute, my full days of patients, the hundreds of articles I was behind on reading, the Empathy Conference the following weekend with its good papers and bad ones. I blessed Laura Capelli, fellow analyst and Park Slope neighbor who had flirted with me over doughnuts before the first speaker that Saturday and given me her card. "If we run low on empathy," she quipped, "we can always refuel on guilt. That's next month." And I blessed Ms. W., one of my patients, because she had started to pain rather than bore me. The pangs I felt as I listened suggested that something was stirring in Ms. W., and after months of attending to her precise, uninflected dissections of her co-workers' habits at the advertising agency and her intellectualized versions of her childhood, I had welcomed the slight but definite color of anger in her voice. "He looked at me as if I didn't exist," she said.

I BECAME DESPONDENT, my father wrote, *when Roger began to unpack his wardrobe: suits, sports jackets, slacks, sweaters, neckties, pajamas, etc. He mounted each garment on a hanger, held up each piece for viewing, and then hung it in his closet with the solemnity of a religious rite. When he ran out of closet room, I said he could fill out my unused space, hoping that visitors might take his clothes for mine. In this new environment I was ashamed of my poverty and did what I could to disguise*

it. Least of all did I talk about it. Today I am ashamed that I was ashamed.
My first impression of Martin Luther College? A grand style show.

A WOMAN I didn't know was shutting the door to Inga's apartment just as I arrived. I saw her hunched body and rust-colored hair
on the landing as she turned and, with her head lowered, proceeded
slowly down the stairs. When we neared each other, she abruptly
looked up into my face for a fraction of a second. I backed off to allow her to pass, but she didn't move out of the way, and we
brushed arms for an instant. "Excuse me," I said, although I felt I
had done nothing that called for an apology. She jerked her head
toward me, looked me in the eyes for an instant, and then, before
she moved away, she smiled. It was a grim smile, an uncomfortable
mixture of self-satisfaction and shame. It reminded me of a child
who has just kicked a dog and enjoyed it, but who, when discovered, is also keenly aware of adult disapproval. She said nothing.
She turned away immediately and continued down the steps, but
the expression I had seen lingered in my mind like the aftermath of
a pinch.

I greeted Inga with the words "Who was *that*?"

Inga looked shaken. Her face was drained of color, and I could
see that she was making an effort to control her voice when she
spoke, "It was a journalist from *Inside Gotham*."

"You did an interview about your book?"

Inga nodded. "That's what I thought, anyway. It was supposed
to be about all my books. I even went back to *Essays on the Image*
and *Culture Nausea* to make sure I was fresh. The magazine editor
must have lied to Dorothy. I thought publishers were supposed
to protect you from sleaze. For the first half-hour I was confused
about what she wanted, but she kept asking me about Max, insinu-
ating all kinds of things. . . ."

"What kinds of things?"

Inga made a face. "Let's sit down. I feel sick, Erik."

"Your hands are shaking."

Inga clasped them in front of her.

Once we were seated, I asked what on earth the woman had said to her.

"It wasn't anything she said directly, it was what I smelled coming from her, something rancid . . ."

I stared at her. "Smelled?"

Inga straightened up in the sofa and took a breath, "You know what I mean. She wasn't interested in my writing or my ideas. She wanted gossip about my marriage, and I refused to say anything. She said, 'It's only fair to warn you that lots of people are talking, and it might be better for you to go on the record with your story than keep quiet.' She's writing a piece for the magazine. I'm sure it will be one of those gossipy articles that make you want to climb in the shower after you've read it." Inga put a trembling hand on her forehead.

"Is there something you're afraid of, Inga?"

"I loved Max with all my heart. He never left me." I could see that Inga was thinking about how to phrase what came next. She looked at me with open, earnest eyes. "The truth is he was fragile, sensitive, and a little volatile. He threw things across the room a few times. He roared like a lion when he was angry. He could be cut off, too, hard to talk to sometimes, but she used the words 'physically aggressive,' a euphemism, I presume, for wife beating or something. You can't respond to that; it sounds like denial. You can't say anything. There's no recourse at all. She also mentioned Scotch with a little sneer, asking me which label he preferred, and then she brought up the time he punched that stupid reviewer at a PEN dinner. Max drank, but he worked hard every day of his life until he was too sick and that was only near the very end. Even in the hospital he kept notes. All the time I knew him, he got up in the morning and wrote. The difference was that when I met him, he wasn't sad. He was so hungry for everything, but as he got older, he got sadder. After his mother died, he suffered, and I suffered with him. He was my best friend, but did I know everything about him? No, I didn't, and I didn't want to either. This awful woman will round up Adrian and Roberta. They were both married to him for exactly three years. Adrian won't say much, but Roberta will be delighted to crap all over him. God only knows how many of his ex-lovers and one-night stands are out there. She'll talk to the ones who continued to like him and the ones who hated his guts. She'll listen to the envious yakking of this third-rate novelist and the next one, and she'll write some garbage that will all be accurate, not a word misquoted, and then she'll parade it out there as the *real* story. That's how it goes, Erik. I know that. What sickened me was what I felt in her—something intrusive and ugly that made me feel polluted, no, not just polluted, frightened. I was scared."

"Of what?"

"I had the feeling that she knows something . . ." She paused. "She mentioned Sonia too, in an unpleasant way. She said something about all those women and just one child—it was so . . ."

"Mom." We both turned to see the girl herself standing in the hallway. "Who was talking about me?"

"A creepy journalist."

"Did she have red hair?"

"Yes," Inga and I said in unison.

Sonia took a few steps forward. "I was at the Bowery Poetry Club with some friends, and she came up to me, 'You're Max Blaustein's daughter,' blah, blah, blah. I tried to be polite and blow her off, but she kept pushing. I'm afraid I got kind of angry. I told her to piss off."

I laughed. Sonia smiled at me, but Inga shook her head. "Next time, just say you have nothing to say."

I don't know why the picture of Sonia at that moment has fastened itself in my memory. She was wearing a pair of sweatpants and a ragged T-shirt with words on it. I've forgotten the words, but I remember her face very well. She was so lovely, my niece, just eighteen, standing in the hallway with her fine face, her large dark eyes, and that long lithe body. She looked like both her mother and her father, but that evening I saw only Max in her. God, I missed him. God, he could write. He tapped the underground in his stories—the harrowing nether regions of human life, articulated in a language we all understand. But Inga was right. He did get sadder, and he had a rough time sleeping. I remembered making a delicate suggestion to him once that psychotherapy or an analysis might be an adventure for him, and if that seemed impossible, an antidepressant might lift his low spirits, but he'd have to lay off the booze. Max had leaned close to me and clapped me on the arm. "Erik," he said, "you mean well, but I've got a self-destructive bent, in case you hadn't noticed, which I very much doubt, since you do this for a living, but people like me don't go in for salvation. Crippled and crazy, we hobble toward the finish line, pen in hand."

THAT NIGHT I dreamed that Inga and I were in a long corridor. Sonia was locked behind one of the doors. Inga was walking in front of me. Something was wrong with her legs, and she was limping. On her head she was wearing a red wig, which I found unsettling. I called Sonia's name, walked to a door, opened it, and was greeted by a blast of light that illuminated, not Sonia, but Sarah, my patient Sarah, who committed suicide in 1992. "Sarah," I said.

"You're here." Her eyes were huge. She shuffled toward me with her arms open as if she wanted to embrace me. "Dr. Davidsen," she said in her quaking, too-loud voice. "Dr. Davidsen, I can see!" I jolted awake, waited for my racing heartbeat to subside, and then walked downstairs for a glass of milk. I put on Charlie Parker, sat down in my green chair, and listened for a while until I felt able to return to bed.

SECOND-SEMESTER ENGLISH INCLUDED *the ordeal of writing a proper research paper. I no longer remember why I selected Savonarola, the Italian reformer and martyr who drove the Medicis out of Florence. I had no problem with the subject matter. But I lost my way in the mechanics of research—endless note cards, each one with a special function that had to be filled out just so. More confusing was footnoting, with mysterious terms like* ibid. *and* op. cit. *Note cards were scattered in sorted piles throughout my room. As a temporary reprieve from my mental chaos, I checked on my mail. At the post office I opened a letter that instructed me to report to Fort Snelling on March 16, two days before the term paper was due. I returned to my room, swept up every wretched note card, and tossed them into a trashcan. After I went to bed that night, panic struck. What would I do if I failed the army physical?*

. . . We moved from doctor to doctor assembly-line fashion. Our last hurdle was a psychiatrist. "Do you date?" he asked me. Thanks to Margaret, I gave him a confident yes. He waved me on. Ah, such are the refinements of my profession: We'll take anything standing, but weed out the queers. Lars Davidsen was nineteen. Unless there had been something between him and Lisa, Margaret Lien was the only girlfriend he'd ever had. Before he left Minnesota for the first time in his life, he called her at her dormitory on the campus of Martin Luther College to say good-bye. *I did not tell her of my dreary state*

of mind. We just chatted. But, if I have anything resembling a soul, Margaret's voice of that evening will certainly be part of it.

WHEN I ASKED Inga about the *Inside Gotham* article, she said it hadn't appeared, and she was hoping it had been dumped. "I'm sure they're not really interested in what I had to say, and maybe they didn't get anything juicy from other people, so it probably won't come out—too boring. It's ironic, though, because in my book I try to talk about the way we organize perceptions into stories with beginnings, middles, and ends, how our memory fragments don't have any coherence until they're reimagined in words. Time is a property of language, of syntax, and tense. But then, that woman isn't interested in the problem of consciousness and reality. She doesn't give a jot about philosophy. These journalists actually believe they can get the *real* story, the objective truth, or tell *both* sides, as if the world is always split in two. At the same time, 'reality' in America has become synonymous with the rank and sordid. We've fetishized the *true* story, the tell-all confession, reality TV, *real* people in their *real* lives, celebrity marriages, divorces, addictions, humiliation as entertainment—our version of the public hanging. The crowd gathers to gape." After this speech, Inga paused. "You know who she made me think of?"

"No."

"Carla Screttleberg."

"Your tormenter in the sixth grade."

Inga nodded. "The ache has never gone away. She got all the girls in on it. No one would speak to me, or, if they did, it was to say something hurtful. I hadn't done anything to anyone. I found it incomprehensible, and yet those months are blurry now. I see bits, not wholes, parts of the school building where something cruel must have been said, a stairwell, a hallway, the classroom, my desk, chalk drawn on the cement to play foursquare. All saturated with general misery. It's as if my sadness soaked the architecture. I can tell you a story about it, and I wouldn't be lying, but would that reconstruction of events be real or true?"

"No—just true for you now."

"When it happened to Sonia, I felt desperate."

"But it ended for both of you."

"Solved by a new school. It was like becoming another person. Sonia said the same thing: 'One day you're a pariah, and the next day you're a regular person again.'"

"How is Sonia?"

"Still too neat."

"And the nightmares?"

"Fewer." Inga swallowed. "She doesn't talk much about her father, you know. I worry about it. She writes a lot of poems."

"Does she let you read them?"

"Sometimes. They're good but rather frightening."

"Adolescence is frightening," I said.

Inga smiled. "I wonder what she would have been like if there hadn't been September eleventh."

I remembered walking into Emergency that morning. I heard myself explaining that I was a doctor and wanted to volunteer my services. Countless people must be injured, and the numbers would be more than the city hospitals could handle. The memory hurt. "Your description of that day is the best thing in the book," I said out loud.

In *American Reality: Examining a Cultural Obsession*, Inga devoted one chapter to the media's version of September eleventh and its almost instantaneous construction of a heroic narrative to gloss the horror. She noted the use of cinematic devices in television reporting, the footage of firemen set to music with American flags waving on a split screen, the spectacular images, the pious announcements that irony had come to an end as the bitter ironies multiplied one on top of another. She wrote about the cheering crowds in other places in the world, who had manufactured their own fiction of heroic martyrdom, one so powerful it snuffed out empathy. And to counter the hackneyed pictures and dead words, she told her own story of that day as she remembered it, a fractured account. She heard on the radio that a plane had hit the tower eight blocks south. She decided to get Sonia out of school and began to walk downtown when she saw the second plane ram the other tower. She had started to run then, against the crowd streaming toward her, but she didn't register what had happened, not really, but raced to Stuyvesant, where she was stopped by a guard. There was another mother, too, whom they wouldn't let in, a woman whose voice reminded her of a squalling cat at night. Inga remembered the woman's contorted mouth, her saliva hitting the man's collar as she wailed, "Let me in! I want my son!" and how the sight of the woman's face had made her strangely quiet, calm, and distant, and how she had waited for them to find her daughter, standing numb in the lobby, and that when she finally saw Sonia's face, she felt it must match her own, a mask of pallid emptiness, and how when they left the building the towers were gleaming red like burning skeletons, and Inga had said to herself, "I am seeing this. It is true. I must tell myself this is real," and then they ran north to White Street without saying a word to each other, running with hundreds of other people pushing forward away from the fires. A man on his hands and knees, vomiting. Another man seemingly frozen, turned the wrong way, as he looked upward, a hand over his mouth. Her feeling of urgency, fear, but not panic. No tears, no screaming. And then the strange impulse that came over her just before they turned onto White Street. She said to Sonia, "Okay, turn around and look." They did.

In the days afterward, I couldn't get in to them. The area had been cordoned off and most of it evacuated, but somehow the police never arrived at 40 White Street to tell its residents to leave. The first weekend, Inga and Sonia managed to travel to Brooklyn, and I cooked for the two of them. We talked a little. Inga told me about the ruined cars piled up on Church Street, the smoking pit a few blocks south, the pale dust that had covered everything like a toxic snowfall, her worry about poisons in the air. And then they slept. They slept and slept and slept, the sleep of exhaustion and perhaps relief to be away from there, the place where it had happened. But on Sunday, when Inga asked Sonia what she had seen from the classroom window that morning, the girl just shook her head, her eyes blank and her mouth tight.

FOUR DAYS AFTER the United States invaded Iraq, Eggy slipped a drawing under my door. In the foreground two people held hands, a large person and a smaller one. The hands resembled overlapping balls and were attached to skinny arms. Because the shorter figure had a mass of scribbles on its head, I guessed it was a self-portrait. The other figure with a straight line for a mouth was probably Miranda. In her free hand the child held what at first looked like a kite, but when I examined it more closely, I noticed that attached to the long curving line was a tiny airborne man at the very top of the picture. When I looked down at Eggy's rendering of herself and her mother, I couldn't help wonder what children might witness or suffer in this new military nightmare.

And yet, my grim thoughts of war didn't prevent other thoughts. Sometime after Miranda uttered the sentence, *If I did, why should I tell you?* I had tried to avoid taking a mental image of her to bed with me. I substituted other women, Laura Capelli, for one, with her voluptuous body and broad smile, and I perused pornography: always effective, but the tawdry pictures left me depressed. I was dreaming of companionship, too, of dialogues and walks and dinners as well as sex. Miranda and I had hardly spoken to each other, and I had to admit that my attraction might be killed by a conversation that revealed a pedestrian mind behind those bewitching eyes. I rationalized that what had happened was just another rejection among many, and I should accept it, but there were three images that had now taken hold of me: Miranda's drawing of a monster, her portrait of Eggy, and Eggy's own picture—a girl's rendering of her family, perhaps? Was the floating man an image of her missing father? Perhaps Eggy wanted to tell the worry doctor what her mother didn't want to tell me. Miranda's words had made me think that she knew the identity of the mysterious messenger. Further, I guessed that the connection between the two of them probably had something to do with photography and art, and that it was plausible other pictures had arrived without my knowledge of them. I wrote Eggy a note and pushed it under the door.

Dear Eglantine,
    Thank you so much for the drawing. I like it very much, especially the little flying man.

Your friend,
Erik

I HAD SEEN too many veterans during my years at the hospital to fall for the moronic patriotism they were offering the public on television: cameras and tanks rolling, flags and dust flying, eager journalists decked out in combat fatigues sputtering in excited tones about our brave troops, the sturdy families back home, sacrifice, duty, America, homeland. Inga's book had spoken directly to this kind of grotesque spectacle, and yet I was certain that her words would be met by deafness. History is made by amnesia. In the American Civil War, they called it soldier's heart, and over time it changed its name to shell shock, then war neurosis. Now it's PTSD, post-traumatic stress disorder, the most antiseptic of the terms for what can happen to people who witness the unspeakable. During World War I, in the barracks of field hospitals French and British doctors saw them coming in droves—men blind, deaf, shaking, paralyzed, aphasic, catatonic, hallucinating, plagued by recurring nightmares and insomnia, seeing and re-seeing what no one should see, or feeling nothing at all. Clearly, they weren't all suffering from brain lesions, so the physicians began to tag their patients NYD (not yet diagnosed) or GOK (God only knows) or *Dieu seul sait quoi* (God alone knows what this is).

"Dr. Davidsen," he said. "It's come back now all these years later. It's not like remembering, no sir. It's the shock, same as it was, as if I'm goin' through it again. I wake up to the impact in my leg, no pain, just the blast, and then I see it." A chronic alcoholic, Mr. E. hadn't been hospitalized for trauma. He had had his ascites drained but was sent to me after he screamed at night and woke up the whole ward.

"What do you see?" I said.

He had a wrinkled red face mottled by brown spots. He rubbed his cheeks with both hands. His arms shook uncontrollably. "Harris on top of me. Rodney Harris, without his head."

Trauma isn't part of a story; it is outside story. It is what we refuse to make part of our story.

MIRANDA RETURNED FORCEFULLY to my consciousness that weekend. On Sunday morning when I retrieved my *New York Times* from the doorstep at around nine o'clock, I saw her on the sidewalk. Her back was to me, and at her feet stood a bucket of soapy water. To my surprise, she appeared to be washing the tree. When she took a step to one side, I immediately saw why. The stranger had left his mark in red paint on the trunk of the tall oak just beginning to bud.

I didn't walk down the steps to speak to her. I grabbed my newspaper and shut the door very quietly, but she heard the sound and turned. For a moment our eyes met through the glass door. She didn't smile, but I saw in her face something softer than the time before. I think I nodded before I returned to my coffee, my whole body electrified by the expression on her face.

IN AN UNDATED letter from 1944, my father wrote, *After a long time at sea, we hit land. The trip over was warm and crowded. I did not get seasick, but many were hit hard. The ceremonies crossing the equator were both cruel and fun. New to me are the natives: fuzzy-haired, small, black, and barefooted people with cloths around their waists. They sell wares in shells and bamboo—or try to. I can say we are somewhere in New Guinea. I write this by candlelight.*

INGA'S FACE WAS flushed with excitement when she opened the door. Her eyes were wide and she spoke quickly. "I found something through the Hall of Records in Blue Wing. I don't know what it means yet, but it's interesting. I've got a record of a marriage between an Alf Odland and a Betty Dettling in 1922. A year later they have a child, but the name on the birth certificate is not Lisa, but *Walter* Odland. There's no record of a Lisa being born to those two people at all. Pappa was fifteen and Lisa had to have been at least his age, probably older, if she was working away from home, so something's wrong about this."

"Maybe it's another Odland."

"The only one in town," Inga said. "She may have been a child from an earlier marriage. Maybe he divorced his first wife, or she died. Divorce was very common among immigrants on the prairie, of course this was later, but it still would be unusual for a girl to go with her father, not her mother, don't you think, so death is more likely. Alf Odland died in 1962. Betty lived on until 1975. The good news is that Walter is still alive. I called the listed number, but no one answered. He's an old guy without an answering machine, but I'm hoping to talk to him."

A sudden feeling of reluctance came over me, a sense that we were encroaching on something that might wheel around and slap us. I was aware that it was odd for me—who has listened to so many confessions of betrayal, misery, and cruelty—to shy away from the story hidden behind a few sheets of paper in a hall of records, but the analyst as a person who can hear anything is made possible because of the role played, the position occupied in the room. Outside that room, I occupy another territory: brother, son, friend. "Are you sure you want to pursue this?"

"Don't you?"

"I'm thinking of Walter Odland. What if your questions . . ." I was lying. I wasn't thinking of Walter Odland until that second. "No, that's not it. Inga, I think I'm worried about what we'll find."

"I keep thinking I'll mention it to Mamma, and then I don't. Something stops me, a fear of hurting her, I guess. She's suffering as it is. Still, I want to know. I think you do, too."

"Yes." I had a moment of guilt about my mother. I should call her, I told myself.

We spoke of other things then, about Sonia's project, a long rhyming narrative poem, her plans for college, her silences. "Half the time I don't know what she's thinking, even though she's nice to me most of the time."

"And she still doesn't want to see a therapist?"

"No, but I don't think she'd mind having lunch with her uncle Erik."

After I told Inga that I'd call Sonia and make a date, my sister informed me that she was writing a book unlike any other she had written. Stories of the philosophers, she said, stories of discovery, stories that demonstrate how feeling and ideas are inseparable. She talked about Pascal's carriage hanging over the water on the Pont de Neuilly, about his rescue, and the Memorial, written Monday, November 23, 1654, when he recorded the words of his ecstasy, which he sewed into his coat to keep with him always. She told me about a dream Descartes had as a young man, in which phantoms chased him as the wind blew, that he couldn't make any headway against those gusts but stumbled and then stumbled again, about Wittgenstein writing in his notebook on the Russian front in the summer of 1916, "There are indeed things that cannot be put into words. They *make themselves manifest*. They are what is mystical," and lastly of Kierkegaard's discovery of his father's secret. Kierkegaard sensed something in his gloomy, strict, religious father, and when his father was dying, he discovered it. He called it "the great earthquake, the terrible upheaval," which forced on him "a new and infallible interpretation of all phenomena."

"I'm burning, Erik," she told me. "I'm burning, and there's more, much more, and it's all very close to me, as if these stories of breakthrough belong to me, too. Real meaning, true insight is rarely dry. It's almost always accompanied by emotion. Of course, Schopenhauer was a cold fish, but I'll leave him out. It's not only philosophy. Think of scientists like Einstein. Think of artists like Max. He was so happy when he found them, his people and their stories. He loved his characters. He loved them, and they were just figments. We all love our figments." Inga's voice cracked with feeling, and her animated face seemed to be lit from within.

My sister had always passed through phases of writing hard, arcs of energetic production that were followed by migraines and the blues, what she referred to as her "neurological crashes." Had

I seen my sister at that moment as a patient, with her shining eyes and rapturous face, I would have jotted down that she presented as manic. As one of my colleagues once said to me, "Every person who walks through my door is a suspect." "You're pretty keyed up, Inga," I said. "I'd be a little careful."

She narrowed her eyes and grinned at me. "You think it's my epileptic, hypergraphic, euphoric, angel-feeling self coming out?"

"Something like that," I said.

"I live with it all pretty well, you know, considering," she said, and spread out her arms. "Give me a hug."

I moved closer to Inga on the sofa and put my arms around her. I could feel the tiny bones of her shoulders as I embraced her. When I let go, she turned her head to the window that looked out at the next building. After a few moments, she said, "Kierkegaard never recorded what his father's secret was. We may never know about our own father. I've had all kinds of fantasies about it, making up stories in my mind, thinking that they saw a woman die or found a corpse in the woods. I've even thought of murder, that they saw something terrible. . . . Pappa would never have stayed silent about a crime, would he? I can't believe that."

The small white house jutting upward from the wide fields around it came into my mind, and then I found myself closer, watching my grandmother pull open the flat door to the root cellar as we descended into the dark guided by her flashlight. I had always liked its smell of cold, damp earth. The odor of a grave, I thought suddenly.

"And then she looked him up again four years later at Obert's," Inga continued. "And then—there's Harry, and now the business of a stepmother. He would have burned the letter. That's what I keep thinking. He would have burned it, Erik. He might have left us a key to his past."

Unknown keys.

I left White Street around seven, and despite the cold rain that fell on the street, I took note of the lengthening day as I closed the heavy door behind me. That's when I saw a woman with red hair in the middle of the block. She was walking toward Broadway with a large bag over her shoulder. I paused to watch her, distinctly aware of my growing alarm that it was the same woman I had passed on the stairs, the journalist from *Inside Gotham*. But I couldn't be sure. She walked quickly with her head lowered, her umbrella poised at an angle for maximum protection, moving along at the brisk, determined pace of someone on a mission.

APPROACHING MY HOUSE, I saw Eggy through the illuminated window. Wearing pink pajamas with the saccharine image of a cat on them and a small towel draped over her head, she was bunny hopping across the floor of the living room. As she left the ground, she squeezed her eyes in concentration and her mouth tensed into a wide, flat grimace. She was jumping for her life. As I passed, I realized that I hoped she would see me, but she didn't. Trudging up the stairs with my briefcase, I suffered a feeling of intense sadness, and I was startled to feel my eyes moisten as I opened the door. I spoke to my mother on the telephone at some length that night. She told me that she was restless, unable to concentrate or read or organize her closet. She reached out for my father in her bed every night to check on him and was surprised to find no one there. She talked about his death again, how he had looked when he died, and about the kind of gravestone she wanted for him. She asked me some questions about bills she had to pay, and as I listened to her talk, I heard the vulnerability in her voice, a quaver that hadn't been there before. Before we hung up, she said to me, "And you, my dear Erik, how are you?"

"I'm hanging in there," I said.

The words echoed in my head—"hanging," a man suspended in space, "in there." In where? I thought. Not here, but there, somewhere else. The word brought back Dale Plankey, who had hanged himself one spring day in the tenth grade, the day he didn't get on the school bus. One of my old patients, Mr. D., had found his father hanging from a belt in the basement. He was seven at the time. My thoughts continued, jumbled and inchoate, along this macabre line as I ate alone, and then, rather than read an article on the neurobiology of depression, I drank an entire bottle of red wine in front of a movie I didn't watch and then listened to the cars passing on Garfield Place, the noisy laughter of teenagers wandering by in desultory groups, the distant sound of a television from the house next door. By the time I threw my woozy, tormented self into bed, I was pushing away thoughts of Sarah, hearing the voice of Genie screaming at me, "Mr. Perfect! Mr. Good and Perfect! You're an asshole!" and thinking of my father's fugues. As I dropped into sleep, I was walking with him, in him, aware only of my feet as one and then the other slammed into the gravel, moving fast into the blackness on Dunkel Road, our road, without a light anywhere, just the flat expanse of the cornfields on either side.

ON DECEMBER 6, 1944, my father wrote to his parents from New Guinea. *We have come back to where we landed for some rest. I write this letter in a tent and it is raining.* The next day the men of the 569th received their first mail delivery from the States. Among the letters was one from a friend of my father's at Martin Luther College. A high school football injury had kept Jim out of the military.

Lars,

Howard Lee Richards died of wounds received in action on October 17, 1944. He parachuted into Southern France on "D" day plus 2, after being in Italy for two months.

He leaves these eternal comrades: Lars Davidsen, John Young, and Jim Larsen. Write! Jim

I found a place to hide, my father wrote, *and I cried until I could do it no more*. In the same mail delivery, he had received a letter from Margaret. At the top of the page, she had penned Corinthians 12:9: "for my strength is made perfect in weakness. Most gladly will I rather glory in my infirmities."

There is no way I can now untangle the crosscurrents of emotions that assaulted me throughout the night that followed. I tend not to believe in stories about sudden changes in attitude due to this or that single event. I do, however, believe in preconditioning—explosives that accumulate bit by bit over time, and then along comes the igniting spark that claims all the credit. The news of Lee's death was by itself more than I could handle. Paul's definition of grace both mocked and comforted. "The death of each day's life," as Shakespeare called sleep finally came my way. I woke to a strange calmness. I had, with no conscious effort on my part, somehow divested myself of an endless accumulation of trivial concerns. There was a new sense of freedom. I became a better soldier, or so I like to believe. Lt. Goodwin, a college-educated officer, may have been the first to detect a change. Standing by as we clambered over the railing of the ship that would take us to Luzon, he had a cheering word for each. When he spotted me, he said, "Here comes the stoic." He called me nothing else after that. At the time, I had only a vague notion of what the term meant.

JANUARY 21, 1945. Somewhere in the Philippines. This is my second letter. Finding time for letters is difficult. During the day we are always moving—at night we have no lights.

MIRANDA WAS BREATHLESS, and as she spoke, she fixed her eyes on mine. "I need a favor," she said. She was standing outside my door at seven o'clock on a Wednesday evening. Behind her at the bottom of the stoop, I saw Eggy dressed in her pajamas and a heavy sweater. The girl was hugging a doll to her chest and her cheeks were shiny with still-drying tears. "I've called my sisters, and they can't. Something's come up," Miranda panted, "and . . . and I need someone to stay with Eggy." She turned her eyes away from mine. "I'm sorry to bother you, but it's urgent. I wouldn't ask otherwise."

I nodded and said, "Will you be gone long?"

"No, it shouldn't be too long. I, I have to take care of something."

I looked down at Eglantine, who seemed to have shrunk since I last saw her. It may have been her stillness that made her look smaller. The habitually bouncing child had frozen. "Do you mind staying with me while your mother is out?" I asked her.

She stared up at me with huge eyes. Her bottom lip was trembling uncontrollably as she nodded.

"You're unhappy that she's leaving."

Another nod.

"You and I have had some nice conversations before," I said. "If you don't want to talk to me, you could draw, and I have some books here you might like."

Miranda walked down the steps and knelt in front of her daughter. I didn't hear what she said, but Eggy took her mother's hand and allowed herself to be led up to the door. After giving the miserable child a quick hug, Miranda fled. As soon as the door was shut, Eglantine began to howl, "Mommy! Mommy!" The doll fell to the floor as she put her hands on either side of her small, contorted face and sobbed, jerking her head back and forth in a rhythmic motion that matched her desperation.

I squatted and reached out to touch her shoulder in a gesture of comfort, but the little girl batted my hand away and wailed more loudly, her voice rising to a scream as she rushed into the living room and threw herself onto the sofa.

I decided to wait. In a loud voice I told her that I would be very close—sitting at the table in the dining room if she needed me.

As I listened to the child weep, I stiffened myself against the sound, helplessly wishing she would stop. After several minutes, her sobs subsided into a lower register, and then they were replaced by a series of loud sniffs. A minute after that, I heard the sound of her light steps and then saw her standing in the doorway. With swollen pink eyes and two transparent lines of snot running from her nostrils to her mouth, she stared at me, and as she stared, she sniffed involuntarily. Her head and chin convulsed with each inhalation.

After several more seconds of silence, she announced in a small but dignified voice: "I don't like it when Charlie calls me Egg Yolk."

"And who is Charlie?" I asked.

"A boy in my class."

The turn had been made, and after that we were comrades united by that misfortune known as waiting. Eggy drank three glasses of juice, wolfed down a chocolate that was a month old, a banana, a blueberry yogurt, and half a bowl of cereal, retrieved Wendy, the doll, who was scolded harshly for numerous infractions, drew four pictures of very sad mice and then a big cheerier picture of a woman she identified as a Maroon and her great, great, great, great, great grandma, took a tour of the house that she pronounced "big as a house," listened rapt while I read three stories from Andrew Lang's *The Olive Fairy Book*, and chattered in every pause between activities. Her breath-filled flute of a voice kept me company with reports of kindergarten betrayals. "Alicia said she wasn't my friend anymore. I was sad, but guess what? She forgot!

Charlie's bad. He punched Cosmo. The teacher had to pick him up by his shirt." The evening was also punctuated by moments of worry about her mother. Several times I watched her face wrinkle into an expression that forecast tears, but they didn't arrive. Instead, Eggy let out a great sigh that was followed by an exclamation, which, despite its sincerity, was tinged by a theatrical quality: "Oh where, oh where could my dear mommy be? Oh where, oh where, Mommy, my dear?"

Where indeed? I began to think around eleven o'clock. By then, we had settled into the library in front of *Top Hat*, watching the gray figures of Fred and Ginger spin, waltz, and kick. I had given Eggy a pillow and a blanket, not because she was staying overnight, I stressed, but because it was more comfortable for the movie. At one o'clock, *Top Hat* had melted into *Kitty Foyle*, and I was still on the sofa, sleeping child beside me, growing increasingly agitated as I listened for the bell, hoping that I hadn't been derailed by those lovely eyes, that Miranda hadn't abandoned me for the night as she lay in the arms of a lover or, God forbid, that she had left Eggy altogether, but that seemed impossible. I didn't know much about Miranda, but I had seen her often enough with her daughter to dispense with this thought, and then I began to think of the sinister stranger and the photographs. How long do you wait before you call the police? But exhaustion defeated me and, when the doorbell rang I jerked to attention, noted the time, three o'clock, and ran downstairs.

Miranda stood in the doorway squeezing her right hand with her left as blood ran over her fingers. Without saying a word, I grabbed both of her hands, and after finding the gash on her right index finger, led her over to the kitchen to rinse off the blood, while she insisted it was nothing and I shouldn't bother, and where was Eggy? I bandaged the finger with gauze and tape, and then, emboldened by my hours spent doing *the favor*, I placed my hands on her shoulders and told her to sit. To my surprise, she did.

"It's late," I said. "I don't know what happened to you or what's going on, but the evening was hard for Eggy, and rather tough on me, too. You dragged me into this, and I think some kind of explanation is in order. If not now, then tomorrow."

Miranda sat with her bandaged finger lying on the table in front of her. Before we walked upstairs to remove Eglantine from the sofa, she turned to look at me. "It's a long story," she said. "Too long. But I want you to know that tonight I didn't have a choice. I really didn't."

"And your finger?"

"Collateral damage," she said with a weak smile.

"SOMETHING'S GOING ON with Mom," Sonia said, "something weird." The final word of her sentence was muffled as she bit into her sandwich. She gazed up at me for an instant and then studied her plate as she chewed. "I found her crying the other night when I came home, and she refused to talk about it."

"Your mother can cry," I said. "I mean, it doesn't always take so much. She's been working very hard, and I sensed she might crash if she wasn't careful."

Sonia nodded. "There's something else, though. I think it's about Dad."

"Really?"

"Last night she watched *Into the Blue*, but she didn't just sit and watch it to the end, she kept rewinding to a few of the scenes over and over again, and I could see she was all agitated and upset. The thing about Mom is that she's pretty open with me now. If I ask her what's going on, she tells me. This or that got her down or whatever, but she was really vague about why she kept looking at this scene between Edie Bly and Keith Roland. It didn't make any sense. . . ."

"Your father wrote the screenplay. Maybe she wanted to hear the lines."

"Five hundred times?" Sonia put down her sandwich and began twisting a long piece of hair with the fingers of her right hand. I'd seen her do it before, a tic, and as I watched her, I suddenly remembered her lying in her mother's lap, a large contented baby sucking on her bottle and idly turning her fingers in Inga's long blond hair. Sonia spun the strand of hair and talked on. "So something's going on, and she'll probably tell you. I'm a little worried about what's going to happen to her when I leave."

"Did you choose Columbia to be close to your mother?"

Sonia's face colored deeply and she released her hair. "Uncle Erik! That's not fair. I like the city. I love it, and Columbia's a great school. I don't want to spend the next four years in some backwater."

"You're both worrying about each other."

"Mom's worried about me?" Sonia regarded her half-eaten sandwich. She had her mother's beautiful mouth, the very same full lips Inga had when she was young. The boys must be going crazy, I thought, and felt some pity for those nameless adolescents who sat near her in class.

"She told me you have nightmares," I said.

"Everybody has nightmares," Sonya answered. "It's *normal*." She looked away when she said this, and I noted her reluctance to meet my eyes.

"That's a tough word, *normal*," I said.

She turned back to me and grinned, "I bet you say that to all your patients."

Sonia's evasions didn't surprise me, and yet I felt a new confidence in her. She spoke very intelligently about her long poem

"Bones and Angels," and about her ambition to write. She wanted to take Russian so she could read Marina Tsvetayeva and Anna Akhmatova in the original. When I asked, she confessed that there was no boyfriend in the picture. She had admirers but no one she liked, and although she sighed deeply, I sensed that she wasn't ready to love anyone, not yet. She, too, had silent ghosts inside her, and she guarded them carefully. I didn't say that I hoped I would find them in the poem, but I asked to see it when she was ready. My niece hugged me hard before we said good-bye on Varick Street, and as I watched her walk east on her way home, I noticed that she bounced a little. That lift in her step was new, and it made me glad.

As I walked toward Chambers Street and the number 3 train, I thought about Max and *Into the Blue*. I had admired the film, and it returned to me in bits and pieces throughout the subway ride and the whole of that warm, brilliant, budding Saturday afternoon. He had written the original screenplay for the independent director Anthony Farber and an unknown actress, Edie Bly. I wondered what had happened to her. She had appeared in a few small independent American movies, and then she had vanished. I remembered sitting next to her at a dinner Inga and Max gave before shooting began. She had short dark hair, a pretty heart-shaped face, and an insouciant, slightly reckless air that was well suited to the character she played: Lili. And then I saw her enormous face in profile on the screen as she tilted her head back for a kiss. Beautiful women kissing and being kissed. What would the movies be without them?

The story Max wrote was about a young man, Arkadi, who arrives by train in a nameless city that looks a lot like Queens—was Queens, in fact. He wanders into the streets and soon discovers that every time he turns a corner, the inhabitants are speaking another language. Some of the languages in the film are real; others are gibberish. He begins searching for work, but no one can understand his English, and they chase him away. Three men dressed in red shout nonsense at him and point to his clothes, howling with derisive laughter. He is wearing ordinary blue jeans and a T-shirt. Not long after that, he sees the back of a woman in the street. She turns her beautiful head, smiles at him, and disappears into a crowd of people in yellow. Seconds later, he is beaten bloody by a group of strangers in green. After a series of further misadventures, Arkadi is taken in by a friendly, deaf innkeeper, who gives him a room and work as a janitor. While he's there, the colors of the inn change slightly. One morning the carpet is bluish, the next day greenish, the following day a more yellow-green. He records his thoughts in a journal heard in voice-over while he goes about his days mopping, dusting, and changing linens in the dark and shabby rooms. Although the rooms contain objects, clothing, and papers that he presumes belong to residents, he never sees a single one. In the evenings, he studies a book on sign language, which the innkeeper has offered him as a gift. There is a shot I love of his hands in shadow against the wall, as he forms the alphabet of the new language. His daily shopping rounds in the streets, however, are inevitably punctuated by some menace. Gangs of young men in various colors roam unchecked by the police. He decides that there is a mysterious color code that must be penetrated in order to understand this new city. The other alternative is that he is going mad, and the viewer isn't sure which theory is correct. Arkadi spots Lili in a tenement window. She looks down at him, smiles, then pulls down the shade. He sees her from a distance buying oranges in a grocery store. Again, she meets his gaze and smiles, but when he nears the store, she is gone. He notices her photograph in a camera shop, buys the frame with the picture in it, and puts it on his bedside table. The photograph, however, is only one of her several incarnations. Each time Arkadi sees her, the young woman looks a little different: her makeup, her hair, her clothes, her posture change from one sighting to another. On his day off, Arkadi wanders into the streets and spots an art gallery. When he walks inside, he finds seven large paintings displayed not on the wall, but on the floor. He looks down at them, and the viewer understands that something momentous has taken place. When the camera pans the canvases, it becomes clear that all the paintings are identical: seven portraits of Arkadi himself writing in his journal. He looks up and sees the beautiful girl walking toward him. She smiles, and their strange love affair begins.

I think it's about Dad. Max had loved working on the film, and Farber had kept him on the set to write changes if and when they were needed. Inga has a framed photograph of Max and Tony with their arms around each other's shoulders, both beaming, with huge cigars clenched between their teeth. The spring air and light entered me as I walked home. The colors of red geraniums and purple pansies in pots on the Brooklyn stoops, the blooming deep pink crab apples and the white dogwoods I passed felt as strong as pains. Perhaps my thoughts of *Into the Blue* had sharpened my color sense. The elusive woman. Genie had been one, at least in the beginning. Miranda was another. I imagined Miranda leaning back and looking up at me, and I imagined kissing her. She had not called me after my stint of babysitting, and I had not seen her, but I knew she was there from the noise of the gate closing, her steps on the floor below me, and her voice rumbling at Eggy every once in a while.

That night, I watched the film again. In the gallery, the woman introduces herself as Lili Drake and explains that she is the artist. When he asks her how she could have painted him when they have only seen each other fleetingly, she says, "I never forget a face." She ends up in Arkadi's bed that same evening, but refuses to spend the night with him. Farber used the same scene three times, a cinematic déjà vu: Lili dresses quickly, tiptoes to the door while her lover sleeps, runs down the stairs and out into the city. And then one night, although she tells him she has to go, she falls asleep beside him. When she wakes up, he embraces her joyfully, but something terrible has happened: she no longer recognizes him. "Who are you?" she asks coldly. "Who are you?" Most of the film's action is silent, and the voice-over never corresponds to what the viewer is seeing on screen. Max gave his erotic fable an ambiguous ending. After searching for Lili all over the city, returning to every place he has seen her, Arkadi finally gives up and boards a train. His destination is unknown, but when he sits down, he sees a young woman sitting across from him wearing sunglasses, her head bent over a book. There is something familiar about her. She lifts her head and smiles at Arkadi. Farber searched high and low for an actress who resembled Edie enough to make the last scene work. The girl they found bore an uncanny resemblance to the young actress, but she wasn't an actress herself, and despite the fact that all she had to do was raise her chin and smile, the scene had required fifteen takes.

When the phone rang, I hoped it was Miranda, but to my surprise it was Burton, my old friend from medical school, someone I hadn't spoken to in several years. Burton had always been an odd duck, but over time he had become increasingly isolated and peculiar, and we had fallen out of touch. Brilliant but morose, Bertie, as he was called then (his parents had blessed him with the awful name Bernard or Bernie Burton) had left medicine and turned to scholarship—the unremunerative but honorable field of medical history. He now worked in some capacity at the medical library on 103rd Street. When he asked me if we could have dinner together, I told him that would be "great" and then felt a little uncomfortable afterward because I understood it was true.

As I busied myself getting ready for bed that evening, the old mantra escaped my lips several times. It came unbidden, as always, and I felt embarrassed, as if there were some stranger in the room listening to my refrain: I'm so lonely.

WE WERE BADLY *shelled for three nights*, my father wrote. *I and others were naïve enough to believe that the shells that screamed overhead the first night came from our own naval guns and that their targets were frighteningly close. We heard the patter of shrapnel as it fell in the sand. How wrong we were. The Japanese, who had captured our coastal guns in 1942, now used them against us. They were huge machines mounted on tracks and pulled out of caves at night. They pounded our beach in a systematic and repetitive manner. It did not take us long to learn the pattern. Like thunder each burst drew closer and closer. The terror you felt when you knew the next one might dig a cellar where you lay is war at its worst. The relief one felt for each escape hardly included proper concern for comrades farther up or down the line. The shelling went on all night, but stopped at dawn. The craters were enormous.*

A number of bodies washed ashore during our first night on the beach. Things had, after all, gone wrong for some on their way in. We were told to leave them be. Graves Registration men, they said, would comb the shoreline and they knew what to do. Henry Parker and I did fish one body out of the surf. We couldn't stand seeing it being tossed back and forth by incoming waves. Most of the other bodies were half imbedded in sand so in their case a burial of sorts had already taken place. Bodies continued to drift ashore the next two days but decreased in number. By the third day the beach was strewn with supplies: rations, ammunition, wooden crosses and stars of David, the basic needs of war. Incidentally, we all carried a mattress cover in our backpack. No one ever told us why we toted this extra pound, and when you figured it out for yourself, you yielded without protest to the army's one taboo. In World War II, you carried your own body bag.

We all dug deeper holes the second night, not foxholes but slit trenches. During the second night, because of my deeper trench, several inches of water seeped in. Strolling sand crabs tumbled in and added to my misery. Later that night I moved in with Henry Parker whose trench was on higher ground and because of a cave-in had room for two. Henry's fears were less than mine. Each time we survived an explosion intended for us, Henry laughed, saying repeatedly, "They missed us! They missed us!" Extreme fatigue had set in by the third night. With it came a kind of fatalistic indifference. Despite the pounding, I slept when the shelling was someone else's worry. On the morning of the fourth day we watched American dive-bombers demolish the entrances to the caves that housed the artillery that had given us so much trouble. A bit later we received orders to move ahead.

After reading this, I remembered my father in his study, rolling his chair away from the oxygen line that would get tangled underneath it, a constant irritant that made him swear under his breath. His head was lowered over the page, and I knew that he was writing against time. The urgency of his task made his muscles tense through his back and neck. I walked toward him and placed my hand on his shoulder. He turned and smiled, then clapped his hand over mine, a sign of camaraderie, of some vague masculine understanding between us. When he bowed his head and returned to work, I lingered in the room for a moment and stared out the window at the field beyond Dunkel Road, brown stalks protruding from the snow. Inga and I were home in Minnesota for what would be my father's last Christmas. I remember thinking I should say something. Words I might have uttered came to mind, and then I abandoned them. The memory holds the repetition of an old feeling. It's as if I'm avoiding something I dread, but don't know what it is. I've retained the moment because it troubled me and is swollen with emotion. I believed that in my own analysis with Magda Herschel, I had been able to articulate the distance I felt from my father and that my empathy for him had been the avenue to my acceptance of the gulf between us. As I looked through that window in December of 2001, I realized that I was deluded.

OVER DESSERT AND after a long talk about the book Burton was writing on theories of memory from the ancients to the most recent brain research on the subject, he abruptly asked me about Inga. There was a slight tremor in his voice, and I remembered the terrible crush he had had on my sister when we were all young. It was a sorry business, because even then Bernard Burton was a fat, waddling, red-faced person who had little luck with girls. His chief trouble, however, wasn't his looks, but his moistness. Even in winter, Burton had a steamy appearance. Bubbles of perspiration protruded from his upper lip. His forehead gleamed, and his dark shirts were notable for the great damp circles under the arms. The poor fellow gave the impression that he was humid to the core, a peripatetic swamp of a man with a single vital accoutrement—his handkerchief. Once in medical school I had suggested that there were some treatments for hyperhidrosis. Burton had informed me that he had tried everything known to humankind that didn't risk turning him into a vegetable, and his was a hopeless case. "My ur-reality is sweat," he told me. The first year of residency had marked the end of his career as a practicing physician. His melancholy, dripping face, his sticky palms and sodden handkerchief had alienated nearly every conscious patient, but aside from that, he wasn't cut out for that grueling initiation. To be frank, none of us was, but Burton flagged more than the others. The beeper madness, the emergency EKGs, the interminable bloodwork that meant poking into the veins, arteries, and spinal columns of screaming infants and demented octogenarians, combined with the chronic sleeplessness, felled him. When a patient howled, "You're a torturer, you're killing me," his face would crumple up in distress and, ever serious, Burton never cracked a smile when Ahmed and Russel, our two resident comics, juggled bagels, mimicked a difficult patient, or made jokes about "cold meat" or "circling the drain." Funereal humor. Burton didn't have it. The year had assaulted me, too, had worn me to exhaustion, and at night I dreamed of protruding veins that slid out of arms and fell to the floor spurting blood. My overwhelming desire was just to get it over with and go on. I found a way to keep my distance from the agonized expressions, the noise of weeping, the smell of urine and feces, the dying and the dead. It wasn't war, but I knew what my father meant when he wrote that if the shelling wasn't his worry, he slept.

"Inga's doing all right," I said. "She had a couple of rough years after Max died, and it's hard even now, but she's working well."

Burton took a long breath. "Last Tuesday, I left the library to have my lunch in the park. I pack it, you know, and well, as it happens, I saw her. Lovely woman still, beautiful, I would say. Exceptional."

Listening to my old friend, I remembered that when it came to anything personal, his speech was suddenly burdened with even more qualifications than usual. He wiped his forehead and continued, "I considered speaking to her. She was very close, sitting right there on the next bench after all this time, after that last dinner we had together, November fifth, 1981, but she was with someone, a woman, and they were deep in conversation. Fortunately, I had something to read. Actually, it was Shimamura on memory and frontal lobe function in the Gassinga collection. I'll send it to you, if you like." After a look from me, he returned to Inga. "I couldn't help but notice the fervency of it, the conversation, I mean. Your sister was very upset." Burton began to pat his wet forehead with his handkerchief, which during the course of our meal had turned from white to an unpleasant shade of gray. "She walked right by me," he said. "Didn't notice me, of course. She was distracted, overcome actually, quite beside herself." He fell silent then and observed his plate. "I called you that night."

"I see," I said.

Burton looked distraught. "I found myself in an awkward position. As a former friend, despite the unfortunate finale to our relationship, during which I disgraced myself rather badly, I hold, have always held, your sister in high esteem, and seeing her in that state unnerved me. I was eavesdropping, I'm afraid, and didn't know where to turn except to you."

"Well?"

"Well," he repeated. "I didn't quite understand it. There was talk of letters. I heard that word several times, and money." He uttered the word *money* in a low, hollow tone of voice. "I thought you might know what this was all about and relieve my mind."

I shook my head. "What did the other woman look like?" My thoughts ran to the redhead.

"She was small, very attractive, long dark hair, a little hard looking, I thought."

"Was there anything else?"

"Your sister screamed at her at the end: 'How could you? How could you do this? It's despicable!'"

I worked to hide my anxiety from Burton as I told him I would speak to Inga, that she was a woman of high feeling, and that her outburst might not have signified anything too awful, but I understood that I was speaking to pacify Burton, whose jowls were quivering with emotion.

THE SEVEN PHOTOGRAPHS I found the following evening had been left for me, not Miranda. They lay in a neat row outside my door, each one fastened to the step by a bit of masking tape. As I bent over to retrieve them, I instantly registered my own image in the pictures. The photos had been taken the day I walked home with Eggy and Miranda, the day we found the first Polaroids on the steps. They didn't include the discovery of the pictures, only our walk on Seventh Avenue and up Garfield. In each one Eggy had been wiped out—all that remained of her was a small white silhouette on the sidewalk. As I stood on the stoop and studied the images, I thought I heard the rapid sound of a camera shutter, but when I turned to look behind me, there was nobody in sight, only a woman and man strolling up the sidewalk across the street. As I turned my key in the lock, awkwardly clutching photos and briefcase to my chest with my left arm, the soft repetitive clicking returned. I spun around, but again saw no one. I pushed the door open in a single motion and then kicked it shut behind me.

Sitting down at the table, I laid out the pictures in front of me and felt myself grow calmer. I reasoned that suspicion could transform almost any low noise from a host of sources into a paranoid fantasy that I was being photographed on the sly. Park Slope is not a loud neighborhood, but it's never silent either. Living alone, I had become sensitive to the auditory mishmash that inundated my world—the stentorian racket of pipes, the sibilant whistling of radiators, the whirr of chainsaws, and the drumfire of drills. Distant traffic rumbled even when the local streets were still. Most nights in the spring, I listened to the muted drone of voices that floated from backyard gardens, the sporadic shouts, yelps, shrieks, and laughter that erupted in the street, the five or six lines of rap that burst from a passing car, the rock ballads, chamber music, and jazz that emanated from open windows down the block. In the mornings, various birds cheeped and called regularly, and sometimes a multitude came together in a loud, excited chorus. But there were countless unidentifiable sounds as well: clicks, soughs, crackles, wheezes, and various mechanical hums that throbbed in the background charivari of my life. I had been looking at photographs and therefore I had heard a camera. At the same time, if the stranger wasn't lurking outside at that very moment, he had certainly been hanging about earlier in the day, and the idea of his vigilance was enough to create a feeling of diffuse threat. The empty figures in the photographs where a five-year-old child should have been made it worse. I picked up the telephone and called Miranda.

If I had called her the morning after I sat up with Eggy, as I had meant to, it would have seemed a small, ordinary gesture, but with each day that had passed since then the act of phoning her had swelled in my mind until the gesture of punching eleven simple numbers had become so bloated with meaning, I found myself paralyzed. When I heard her voice, I felt instant relief, understanding immediately that I had feared she would snub me or even hang up on me. After I had explained about the pictures, she said she would call me as soon as Eggy was asleep and that we could talk downstairs.

I washed my armpits, put on a clean shirt, and then examined myself in the mirror on the inside of the closet door. Genie had hung it for herself, and I rarely used it, sticking to the smaller one in the bathroom where I shaved. The man who met my gaze wasn't ugly. He had strong, even features, large green eyes, and pale straight brows, but his body was thin and somewhat underdeveloped in the chest area. His skin was a whitish pink—on the transparent, veiny side. Not just a white man, a very white man. Was this body anything for Miranda? For good measure, I changed my socks.

THE PICTURES DIDN'T seem to surprise Miranda. When she saw them, she locked her jaw, narrowed her eyes, and, after taking a single breath, launched into her story. I noticed that when she spoke, her narration had a third-person quality, a matter-of-fact reporting style I had grown accustomed to in some of my patients. It kept emotion at bay. "I met him," she said, "when we were both students. I was in the graphic design program at Cooper Union. He was at the School of Visual Arts. He was very smart, knew a lot, and was kind of edgy, a few piercings, you know, considered himself an *artiste*." She dragged out the word slightly. "We were just friends then. I didn't see him at all for a few years after we graduated, and then I ran into him at a restaurant in Williamsburg where I was eating with a friend. He asked me to have a drink with him the next night, and I did. That was when he told me his parents had died in a car crash in California three years earlier. He was still recovering from the shock." Miranda looked across the room at the bookshelf and then lowered her eyes. "It all happened pretty quickly after that. I left my share, and we started living together in his apartment." Miranda paused. We were sitting on her blue canvas sofa, and I looked at her arms, which she had folded across her chest. They seemed to shine in the lamplight. "He'd inherited money, and so he didn't have to work at a job. He just pursued his art, which is photography—digital stuff, mostly.

"He was fun," she said, "a real entertainer, the kind of person who made everybody laugh, who liked to tell stories, dance, get high." Her voice had changed. The inflection was more personal. "I'm telling you this because you're involved now. He's put you in the photos." She turned her eyes on me, and I couldn't help noticing their size and shape again, how they defined her entire face. "He could be so kind and considerate. He liked to buy me presents, take me out to dinner, and he loved to talk about art. We'd go to Chelsea and walk around, and he was so sharp about it all, what was hot and why. He's as white as you are, but he comes from a mixed background. His grandmother was half black with some

Cherokee blood, which made him 'a black guy in disguise,' he said. You know, a single drop of blood." Miranda gave me an ironic smile. "That's the American way."

I looked at her, and she met my gaze. Her eyes held mine until I glanced away. It's a hard thing to continue to look a person in the eyes, and I felt her steadiness as a challenge. Rather than say anything, I waited.

"Well, despite precautions, I got pregnant."

"Eggy's father," I said.

"Yes." She looked at me again, and this time her eyes were mournful.

"He was happy at first, or said he was. And then, after a while, he started hinting about an abortion, not for his sake, you know, but for mine. And then, finally, he told me he didn't want the baby. I said fine, I'd have her alone. I was twenty-eight years old, and I wasn't going to stop it. My parents backed me up, and I moved in with them." She paused again. "Without them and my sisters, I couldn't have managed." Miranda brought her legs up onto the sofa and clutched her knees to her chest. In a low voice, she said, "He wants her *now*. He wants to see her now."

"And you don't want that?"

She shook her head. "He didn't sign the birth certificate. He abandoned her. That was it for me."

"He's changed his mind. But why does he do it this way, by leaving the photos? It's hostile."

"I'm not sure he sees it that way. That's how he is. My mother would say he's 'inappropriate.' That was part of his attraction—a spirit of insurrection. He never did anything in the normal way. He'd wear a clown nose to an opening or a T-shirt with a quotation from some art critic that would get people talking. When he was introduced to someone, he'd blurt out a wacky comment or do a little dance and then shake hands. Some people hated it; others were charmed. You know, he couldn't just walk into a room, he had to make sure people were looking at him. He liked to pretend that he wasn't ambitious, that doing his work was what mattered, but he spent a lot of time making connections and getting himself noticed without it seeming like that's what he was doing. And he always had a camera. He'd usually ask people, if he had no choice, but not always. He loved snapping famous people. Half artist, half paparazzo. He'd sell the shots, too."

"New York is full of people like that," I said. "In every field. In medicine, clown noses may be rare, but not self-promotion."

"I know," Miranda said. "After I got pregnant, I think I lost my prop value."

"What does that mean?"

"I felt that he didn't want to be seen with me anymore. I was his pretty, smart, *black* girlfriend. My pregnancy was bad for his image."

"Did he say that?"

"He didn't have to. Even after it started to go wrong between us, he took pictures all the time. I'd wake up and he'd have the camera on me. I'd be working, and he'd take pictures. We'd be fighting, and he'd grab the camera, a documenting maniac." She closed her eyes for an instant, as if to get her bearings, and when she opened them she looked directly at me. "That day, when you took care of Eggy, he showed up. Nearly every day for a month, I found pictures of me and Eggy or just me from when we were together, and I knew eventually he'd come in person. My number is unlisted, so he couldn't call. He rang the bell, and I found him standing outside with a gigantic stuffed horse. He looked kind of pathetic. It was awful. I pulled him onto the sidewalk and told him he couldn't just waltz in and say, 'Hi, I'm your dad.' I promised to see him at his apartment that night. Everybody in the family was busy, so I came to you. As soon as I walked through his door, he started taking my picture. I felt like he wanted those photographs more than he wanted to talk to me. Finally he put the camera away, and we talked. He says he wants Eggy in his life, but he doesn't say how. He doesn't want to talk about money or visiting or anything. It's all about *him*."

"What about Eggy? Does she know about any of this? What have you told her?"

Miranda lowered her knees and sat back in the sofa. "I told her the truth as gently as I could: that I was living with her father, became pregnant with her, and that even though her father is a good person, he wasn't someone who was ready to be a real father to her. It's like it didn't sink in. She makes up all kinds of stories. He's invisible. He's in another country."

"He's in a box."

Miranda shook her head and smiled.

"Are you afraid of him or just annoyed?"

Her eyes were fastened to the wall. "No, I'm not afraid. He's not a bad person, just immature. . . . I don't know."

"Is there something you're not saying?" I asked. The words popped out of me, and I worried that she would find them aggressive.

Miranda turned her head toward me. "Isn't there always something people don't say? You're a psychiatrist. Isn't that your job, figuring out what people aren't saying?"

"I've never thought of it like that," I said. "It's a process, a process of discovery."

Miranda fell silent. "Jeff was in therapy for a while. Then he stopped."

"That's his name?"

"Yes, Jeffrey Lane."

"Why do you think he took Eglantine out of the photographs?"

She shook her head, but I watched as her face convulsed slightly and two tears appeared at the inside corners of her eyes. They didn't fall. I reached out and touched her right hand, which was resting on her knee, and then withdrew.

"He took out your eyes, too," I said.

"He loved my eyes," she said in an unsteady voice. "He always talked about my eyes."

"You have beautiful eyes." I could feel my face flush again as I spoke, and I turned to look at the windows. The shades were drawn and there was nothing to see.

"You like me, don't you?" she said abruptly.

"Yes."

"But you hardly know me."

"That's also true."

We were silent for several seconds after that, and I realized that I didn't mind, because Miranda conveyed no awkwardness. We might have gone on talking if Eggy hadn't appeared in the doorway. With her arms extended and her fingers splayed, she had frozen in a bow-legged stance. The tragic expression on her face was worthy of Ophelia. She looked from her mother to me and then gasped out the words "I peed!"

"It's all right, Eggy," Miranda said calmly. "Don't worry."

"I'll go," I said.

Before leaving, I squatted in front of the little girl and said, "It used to happen to me."

Her eyes widened. "When you were a little boy?"

"Yup," I said. "Back in the olden days."

Miranda burst out laughing.

MEMORY OFFERS UP its gifts only when jogged by something in the present. It isn't a storehouse of fixed images and words, but a dynamic associative network in the brain that is never quiet and is subject to revision each time we retrieve an old picture or old words. I knew that, simply by coming into my life, Eglantine had begun to push me backward into the rooms of my childhood, which in spite of my analysis, I had kept closed—or rather left open just enough to see a crack of light or inhale a musty odor now and then. But that night I traveled into the boy's body, and I heard the crackle of the stiff rubber pad under my sheet when I moved in bed and woke to the warm urine flooding my legs, soaking my pajamas and bedclothes. I felt myself lapse into heavy sleep again, like a drugged person, brought to consciousness later by the chilly cotton against my legs and the keen, sour smell. Like Eggy, I had gone to my mother when I was five and six, but later I would bundle up my pajamas and the sheets and stuff them in the hamper. I'm too big, too big, I would say to myself. My father caught me only once as I scooted out of the laundry room. He was emerging from the bathroom, and I saw his looming figure in the half light. My shame made me want to run, but I froze in front of him. He placed his large hand on my shoulder for a moment, turned, and walked down the hallway without saying a word.

WHILE I WAITED for Mr. R. to arrive for his session, I noted my growing irritation with him. Mr. R. had been late five times in a row. As I looked out the window of my office at the building across the street, I remembered his term from the last session: *self-reliance*. I had thought of Emerson, but he hadn't mentioned the philosopher. The word had come up three times. Mr. R. had had an old mother and an even older father. They had both worked long hours, and Mr. R. had learned to *rely* on himself.

When he entered, he was breathless and full of explanations. Yet another person in the office had let him down right before it was time to leave. He grinned as he settled into his chair. When I pointed out that lateness had become a pattern, he held his hands up, palms toward me, as if he were warding off an attack, and said, "It was unavoidable." Then he began a minute description of his secretary's incompetence. He went on for quite some time in an agitated manner, but after about five minutes he seemed to talk himself out and grew quiet. He then asked me to remind him of the last session. He often forgot. After I had told him, he again stressed his independence as a child. He had even learned to make his own meals. Then he said, "What I'd really like to know right now is what you're thinking. You sit there calm, cool, and collected, but what are you thinking?"

"I was thinking," I said, "that while I was waiting for you today, I was feeling frustrated, a little angry as well, and then I thought about your parents' workdays and what it must have felt like for you to wait and wait for them to come home."

Mr. R. gave me a surprised look. He examined his hands, which were resting on his thighs. Then he let them drop limply onto the seat of the chair, his eyes on his lap. After a long pause, he lifted his face to mine. His mouth was stretched into a flat, tight grimace, and the skin between his brows bore two deep wrinkles of distress.

For the first time, I liked him.

He remembered his mother's exhausted face, her legs stretched out in front of her after she fell into a chair. " 'Not now, not now. I'm too tired.' She always said that."

Just before the end of the session, he was looking at the wall behind my desk and I saw his eyes stop on the small rug from Turkestan that hung there. "It's new," he said, "isn't it?"

"No," I said, "It's been there since we began almost a year ago."

"Well, what do you know?" he said. "What do you know?"

MY SISTER REFUSED to tell me what had happened in the park. All she said was that she felt sorry for Burton and that it made her sad to know that he was worried about her. When I mentioned that Sonia was worried, too, and that she had deduced the problem had something to do with Max, Inga fell silent. I held the telephone receiver for several seconds, waiting for her to speak. "Erik," she said, "I can't talk about it. I just can't. I promise you that as soon as I can, I will. But pressuring me won't help." I let the subject go. She launched immediately onto another topic, what I call voluble defense, explaining eagerly that she wanted to give a dinner party while our mother was in town, that she was fretting about the menu, that she had banished a potential guest on account of his vegetarianism, that she would never make "that damned eggplant thing again" if she could help it. "Mamma needs some fun, and she needs meat." And then, without hesitation or thought, I blurted out the sentence, "I'd like to bring someone, if that's okay." Inga naturally said yes. I asked her about Walter Odland then. "I never called back," she said. "I've meant to try again, but I've been distracted. You could try, you know."

"I'm ambivalent about the whole thing," I said. Before we hung up, I saw the small white house in the country again with its dark windows. I feel guilty, I thought. Is it my guilt or does it belong to someone else?

ABOUT TWO WEEKS *after our landing, I had an experience that I find difficult to recall or to discuss,* my father wrote. *It is the only wartime experience that returned to me in troubling ways by reliving it in dreams. Four of us were bouncing down a rural lane in a jeep. Lieutenant Madden was one of the four. We spotted a Japanese officer a distance away. We knew this because he carried a samurai sword. His manner was strange. When he became aware of us, he scurried for cover in an effeminate, short-step-tip-toe fashion. He then crouched down in some foliage, yet far better coverage was nearby. We boxed him in and then moved slowly forward. The poor devil was quite visible from all sides. He didn't move. I hoped that he would be sensible and rise with his hands up. He had taken on what seemed to me to be a position of prayer. In a matter of moments, four carbine barrels would be nudging him into action. That would bring him out of his trance. Then came two rapid shots. He didn't make a sound. He rolled over to one side, ever so slowly. There were a few twitches as if he wanted to stretch himself and that was all. Our lieutenant had done it. None of us had noticed that he had stopped and had taken up a cover position, which was the proper thing to do. "He was going for a grenade, for God's sake" was his explanation. There was no grenade. There was a pistol, a Japanese Luger, but the holster cover was firmly clasped shut.*

It is pretentious to claim to know what one was thinking in moments like this. I may have expected a humane outcome and then come apart when the reverse happened. I may have felt that you do not shoot people while they are praying. His praying position had a powerful impact on me. I became quite deranged and by soldier standards behaved badly. I lashed out at the lieutenant, saying he ought to be shot, too. I was led from the scene and slapped about a bit. I came to my senses and felt shame for what I had done. The lieutenant told us that he believed our lives were at risk. He himself might have survived a grenade, but not us. He could live, he said, with what had happened but not with what could have happened. The Japanese officer had surely become addled from earlier experiences and may have roamed for days without detection. How did he get separated from his unit? An officer at that? Why did he hide and yet not hide? The experience hardened me. About six months later, when I was in Japan, I began to relive the sorry spectacle, often just when I went off to sleep.

My father said the man "crouched" in the grass and then took on a position that made him think of prayer. I imagine him on his knees, beseeching heaven, asking for mercy. He may have had his hands clasped together. Then came the shots. *Harris, on top of me. Rodney Harris without his head.* Intrusive memories. Fragments.

These are the pieces that won't fit. Sonia's cries at night. My grandfather's nightmares. I knew that research was confirming what I had always felt was true in my patients: their memories of war, rape, near-fatal accidents, and collapsing buildings aren't like other memories. They are kept separate in the mind. I remembered the images from PET scans of PTSD patients and the colored highlights showing increased blood flow to the right brain and to the limbic and paralimbic areas, the old brain in evolutionary terms, and decreased flow to the left cortical areas, the language sites. Trauma doesn't appear in words, but in a roar of terror, sometimes with images. Words create the anatomy of a story, but within that story there are openings that can't be closed. By then, my father had seen many dead bodies, but this one was different. Beyond combat. I beg of you. Help me. The man had not fought back, had not gone for a grenade or a gun. I wondered if the frightened officer had reminded my father of another man who had fallen to his knees, begging for another chance, or maybe the man's humble, frightened position was itself a visual metaphor that summoned what Lars Davidsen couldn't put into words.

"THERE WAS NO wind the day Lars died," my mother said on the first night of her visit. "And it was snowing. It came straight down in large, slow flakes, hour after hour. For a while in the early afternoon, before Inga came, I was alone with him. He wasn't conscious anymore. I held his hand, rubbed his arms and his forehead. During that time, I felt someone enter the room behind me. I thought it was a nurse, but when I turned around, no one was there. It happened three times." My mother shook her head slowly. "I wasn't at all frightened by it," she said. "It was just a fact." Her pale hands were folded in front of her as she sat across from me at the table, her large blue eyes intensely focused. "Lars couldn't have gone on the way he was. I know that. He couldn't have. Still, it's strange. The strangest part about his death is that I can't tell him things. If I'm out and have a conversation with someone, I still think, Oh, I have to run back and tell Lars, or Lars will love hearing this, and then I remember he isn't there to tell." My mother smiled thinly. I noticed that her eyes had turned inward. A moment later, she reached for me and took my hand in both of hers. As long as I can remember, she has taken my hand like that, and once she has secured it, she strokes it a few times before she lets go.

THERE IS NO clear border between remembering and imagining. When I listen to a patient, I am not reconstructing the "facts" of a case history but listening for patterns, strains of feeling, and associations that may move us out of painful repetitions and into an articulated understanding. As Inga said, we make our narratives, and those created stories can't be separated from the culture in which we live. There are times, however, when fantasy, delusion, or outright lies parade as autobiography, and it's necessary to make some nominal distinction between fact and fiction. Doubt is an uncomfortable feeling that can quickly become suspicion, and under the intimate circumstances of psychotherapy, it may be nothing short of dangerous. I began to feel this uncertainty with Ms. L. in April, and I recognize now that it marked a turn not only in her, but in me.

For almost six months, the pretty, well-dressed Ms. L. had sat tensely in her chair, knees locked together, eyes lowered as she revealed a life of privilege, money, and neglect: her parents' divorce when she was two, her mother's serial boyfriends, her mother's long trips with them to houses and apartments in Aspen, Paris, the south of France, her mother's breakups, bouts of weeping, drinking, and shopping. Ms. L.'s serial nurses and nannies, her father's detested second wife and two children, his infrequent calls and sporadic gift-giving, the two hated boarding schools, her suicide attempts, her hospitalizations, her three weeks at a repugnant college, her abandoned lovers, both men and women, all repellent human beings, her abandoned therapists, all incompetent, the classes she started and then quit due to the professors' stupidity, her lost friends, her lost jobs, her periods of blankness and feelings of unreality, her grandiose daydreaming, her rages. The people in Ms. L.'s life fell into two camps only: angels and devils, and the former could quickly be transformed into the latter. "I came to you," she had said early on, "because I heard you're the best." I had said that words like *best* and *worst* aren't applicable to psychotherapy, that it is a work done together, but Ms. L. wanted a genius, a divine mother/father/doctor/friend. When I pointed this out to her, she smiled and said sweetly, "I think you can help me, that's all." Her idealization of me didn't last. She began to ricochet from one extreme to the other, and as I bounced from hero to villain, I felt increasingly fragile and hurt. It was difficult to keep my balance, but worse, she sometimes had a hard time separating the two of us, and her confusion began to cause me acute discomfort.

Ms. L.'s voice was shrill. "My mother says I should just forgive her and get over it! Can you believe it?"

"I thought you weren't speaking to your mother."

"I'm not. Last time we talked, she said that. I asked you if you could believe it. You interrupted me!" Her fury felt like a slap.

"Yes, I can believe that's what your mother hoped for. I'm interested in the fact that you haven't spoken to her for over a year but your anger at her is very immediate, as if she were here with us now."

For several seconds, Ms. L. said nothing. I watched her clench her fists. "So," she shot back. "What's next, Mr. Know-It-All?"

"I don't know," I said, "because I don't know it all."

"What's the point of all this, then, if I'm in here with an igno-ramus?"

"Your anger, perhaps. I think by holding on to your anger at me, you may be holding on to the story between you and your mother. There's always some hope in anger, I think, hope for things to be different."

"Hope?" She looked at her knees with trembling lips, and I watched her open her hands. "You're right, I need to be angry. It's like a drug. I crave it. When I'm not angry, I feel frozen out."

I had an image of Ms. L. standing outside the locked door of a house in a snowstorm, shivering on the step. The pain this men-tal picture brought was sharp as a knife.

We talked about her words *frozen out* then, and my picture of her locked outside in the snow, about feeling numb, empty, and unreal, about her revenge fantasies, and she grew calmer. I felt like a man who had managed to steer a ship out of a gale.

After the session was over, she walked to the door, turned around, and said calmly, "My mother tried to kill me, you know. I've been remembering it. It's all coming back to me now. I'll tell you about it next time."

I AM WALKING across the Martin Luther College campus after leaving my organic chemistry class, lost in thought about the re-mainder of the semester and all I have to do. It is late autumn and very cold. The memory carries a trace of dry, dun-colored leaves lifted by the wind and a few intermittent snowflakes, tiny and hard against my face. I look up. My father is striding toward me. I smile at him. Do I make a gesture, lift my hand? I don't know. He looks straight into my face but doesn't recognize me. It's as if he doesn't know me. He keeps on walking. I keep on walking. Why don't I stop him? Why don't I run to catch up with him, tap him on the shoulder? Dad, it's me, Erik. We missed each other back there. Are you on your way to class? Why don't I walk with you? I don't because there is something forbidding in that closed face, like a door that's better left shut. The idea of opening it creates the old dread. Frozen out. Ms. L.'s words come back to me. I've remembered the incident before, but without much emotion. I can see the sidewalk, recall my amazement, discomfort, but earlier, I read it differently: my father, the absent-minded professor. A fluke. With my elbows resting on my desk, I clutched the sides of my head with both hands and allowed myself to suffer. I remained in that position for well over a minute. Before I stood up, I understood that my vision of Ms. L. in the cold had also been an image of myself.

ON MY WAY home from work, I boldly rang Miranda's bell. When she opened the door, she was wearing tight jeans spattered with paint, a small white T-shirt, and a blue scarf, knotted at the top of her head. She said hello and then looked at me expectantly.

"I'm here," I said, using the phrases I had planned, "to invite you to a dinner my sister's giving for my mother next week, Friday. She's in town for a while . . ."

I interrupted myself because Miranda had lowered her eyes and was staring at her hands.

I pressed on. "I'd like to go with someone, that's all. It's nothing formal."

"I don't know if I can."

My disappointment must have been obvious. I knew I was clenching my teeth. Nevertheless, I persisted. The words came before I could stop them: "You could think of it as a favor."

She lifted her face to mine. "Yes," she said, a smile crossing her face for an instant. "In that case, if I can get a babysitter, someone other than you, that is, I accept."

I felt a moment of triumph, followed immediately by embarrassment and then guilt. I had stooped to coercion. We both knew it, and I stared at my shoes for several seconds until Eglantine came dancing down the hallway singing, "Skippity skip and jippity jip and liddy doo doo dah." She swung the piece of paper she was holding up and down, and when she reached me, she held it out proudly. I glanced at Miranda for a moment before turning to Eggy and was relieved to see that she looked amused, not irritated. The picture had been done in charcoal with big swaths of black blur in it. I made out five or six large rectangles, several crosses, and three figures below that appeared to be sleeping. When I asked Eggy to explain the drawing to me, she knelt down and beckoned me to lower myself beside her.

"It's dead people," she said, "under the ground in the clemitary. They're dead, really and truly. This one is my great-grandma, and this one is my great-grandpa." Eggy moved her pliable lips into a desperate and highly unconvincing pout. Then, to add to this exaggerated emotion, she sniffed a few times and ground her fist under one eye.

"And who's this very large person with all the hair?" I asked, tracing the lines of an elongated, prone body with my finger.

Eggy looked at me with wide eyes. "That's Grandy Nanny. She's the one who can get up and fight and be undead again. She has the science."

When I lifted my eyes to Miranda, she was smiling. "Nanny was a Maroon leader, an obeah woman. She fought the British and negotiated a treaty with them so Maroon territory remained independent. She's become *the* Jamaican heroine. My father's a kind of amateur historian of the Maroons, so Eggy's heard a lot of stories about her. She was a historical person, but she's also a legend. It's impossible to separate the two."

While Eggy was busy playing dead and then resurrecting herself as a thunderous Grandy Nanny, Miranda pulled me aside and said, "Erik, he's stopped sending the pictures." I think it was the first time she'd called me by my name, and it created a small stir in me. When I told her I thought that was a good sign, she said in a lower voice, "Yes, but he doesn't answer my calls. I've thought it over and think we should work out some arrangement for Eggy's sake, but he's disappeared. I've left messages at his apartment and on his cell, but nothing."

I suggested giving it some time. Before I left them, I took Miranda's hand in mine to say good-bye and suddenly remembered her bloody finger. "I've always wondered how you cut your finger that night," I said, realizing that it gave me a chance to continue to hold her hand. I examined the finger, which had a small scar.

Miranda didn't withdraw from me, and I felt a shudder of sexual feeling move between us. Not wanting to lose her touch, I squeezed her hand firmly and then pulled it to my chest. Miranda, who was clearly not expecting my impetuous tug, gasped, stumbled forward, and then started laughing. Reeling with embarrassment, I let her go.

She looked up at me with kind eyes and a small smile still on her lips. Then it vanished abruptly. She spoke slowly. "Jeff picked up a knife and said he'd slice his arm if I didn't let him see Eggy. I grabbed it away from him and accidentally cut myself."

Each story about Lane brought the man further into focus, but this last one, with its histrionic threat, magnified my unease. I knew perfectly well that any number of reasonably healthy people "fly off the handle," a phrase that never fails to bring to my mind the blade of an ax hurtling through the air. In a fit of rage, Genie had once flung a toothbrush in my face, a moment that might have been comic if she hadn't thrown the little weapon with considerable force. Lane hadn't waved the knife at his ex-lover, but I was beginning to fear that he was far more unstable than Miranda knew.

BY THE TIME my father left the Philippines, the boy who had joined the army at age nineteen as a private had been promoted to first sergeant and, during a late-night poker game, gained the nickname Lou. One of his comrades had decided my father resembled the actor Lew Ayres. Lew was transcribed as Lou. The name stuck, and his men called him nothing else. After the war ended, he served in Japan, and then after four years his service finally ended. The night before he left for the States, the company gathered to bid him good-bye in a ceremony that my father wrote, *mixed sincerity with levity*. In his memoir, however, he reported on the evening's levity.

Like most military units we had a small group that took up precision close order drill, tricky choreographed maneuvers as a hobby. The more sophisticated performers used rifles. Our team of five, geared to the comic, shouldered mops and brooms, which were more suited to the manual of arms than were our carbines. These drills were often done silently by counting a predetermined number of steps before a turn is made. That evening, however, four did the marching and one shouted the commands with a Minnesota Scandinavian flavor. They had developed a pattern where two obeyed the sequence and two did the reverse, or so it seemed, but through a chain of successive commands they somehow came back together. They could sing a bit as well. As a finale they marched to a snappy and well-known marching song which lent itself to name insertion. I recall the first stanza:

> *We're Sergeant Lou's troopers.*
> *We're raiders of the night.*
> *We're fightin' sons of bitches*
> *Who'd rather run than fight.*

My father had been told that as a farewell gesture at the evening formation the following day he would be asked to review the troops. *The squads would march by as individual units and then later merge with their platoons to form a company formation. The appropriate noncoms would report to my replacement who in turn would report to me and I to the company commander or the officer of the day, a simple ceremony that marked my final official function in the 569th. It turned out to be more than that.*

A crude bench that served as a platform for three to four oil drums in the motor pool had been set up as my reviewing stand. It was a full dress parade. Then came what I had not been told—a change in the chain of command. The corporals reported to the platoon sergeants, the platoon sergeants reported to the new first sergeant, who in turn reported to Lt. Noel. He reported to Col. Bass, and Col. Bass, like the reporters before him, made an about-face, saluted, and reported to me. No Olympic gold medal winner standing on his or her polished podium can have felt a greater rush of feelings than I did in that moment on my oil-bespattered stand. I have on occasion later in life been extended recognition from high places, but none somehow has been more satisfying than this one.

I HAD MEANT to return to Brooklyn, change my clothes, and escort Miranda to Inga's, but just before I was about to leave my office, the phone rang, and I heard a familiar voice talking at me: "The old bad brain came back, Doc, infra-red techtonic foibles up there under the cranium. The jabberdose chip, yak, yak, yak, wacked out, hijacked, multilingual, glottal, fricative genius gab."

"Mr. T.?" I said. "Is that you?"

"The river, Heraclitus, man. Death-rattle tattlers. I," he mumbled, "don't want to go."

After learning that my old patient was just outside the building,

I flew down the stairs, rather than wait for the elevator, and shot out the door. I hardly recognized him. The slender young graduate student in comparative literature I had treated at Payne Whitney ten years earlier had grown immensely fat. His clothes were filthy, and he had an oozing scab on one bulbous cheek. He kneeled on the sidewalk, his grimy black-and-white notebook pressed to his chest, his chin raised as if he were summoning the heavens. I also noticed that his eyes flicked back and forth. The voices were probably coming fast and furious. I offered him my hand, and he managed to pull his vast body into a standing position. "They're not happy about you," he said. "Watch out."

"I'm going to take you to the E.R. at New York Hospital. We'll get a cab together. Is that all right?"

Mr. T. looked at me, nodded, and kept talking. "Chip planters from the other side, channeling me, man, the great dead heads (not grateful, ungrateful), Goethe, Goering, God, Buddha, Bach, Bruno, Houdini, Himmler, Spinoza, St. Theresa. Rasputin. Elvis. Talkin' graves. Chosen from the other side. Nondimensional spaces, texts coming through, beating me hard up there. Mingus. Fear and trembling, fear and trembling. Repetition. Killer words. They want me over there." Mr. T. held the notebook close to his face. "The whole of life," he muttered. "Void and empty noise, boys."

After I had managed to hail a cab, get my hallucinating companion in beside me, and give the address to the driver, I watched Mr. T. open his notebook, take out his pen, and begin to write. Mr. T. wasn't composing. He was taking dictation from the dead. Poets, philosophers, prophets, tyrants, and sundry others spoke through him to produce a jumble of references, neologisms, and garbled quotations in at least three languages. I had treated him at Payne Whitney for five months and watched him slowly improve. Early on, he had jealously guarded his notebook from thieves who were after its "revelations." If understood correctly, these universal truths had the power to extend the reader's life. Mr. T. was a master of clanging. The vowels and consonants in his speech were generating machines that created such memorable sentences as "Lavinia in Slovenia is slipping into schizophrenia," a line that came from what Mr. T. had once described to me as a "meisterwerk en suite, Iggy's Insignia Divinia." But the voices had also nearly torn him to pieces. After his admission, he had stood rigidly beside his bed, a tortured but alert expression on his face, and moaned for hours.

As we walked together toward the psych E.R., Mr. T. continued his monologue. "Multi-vox." He closed his eyes. "*Vox et praeterea nihil*, *non*, no, *nein*, *nicht*, *nada*."

"Did you stop your medication?" I asked him.

"Couldn't stand the meds, Doc. Poison berries. Made me so fat and slow, so slow, bro."

Mr. T. lumbered forward. I hoped he wouldn't refuse the berries now. He had the notebook open. Then he paused. I felt a rush of anxiety that he would turn around. He was looking down at a smudged, crossed-out, barely legible passage written in lines, a poem:

> Where's the bar, Mr. Farr?
> Où est le scar, Désespoir?
> Wo ist mein Schade Star
> Mit la lumière bizarre
> Ich will etwas sagen,
> Monsieur Fragen.
> Krankheit. Blindsight.
> Strut Stage. Rage Page.

Mr. T. went willingly. I made sure he could keep his notebook. The last thing I said to the attending physician was "No Haldol. He doesn't tolerate it."

"I'LL MEET YOU there," Miranda said after I told her about my emergency. "No problem."

Rather than arriving late, as I had thought I would, I was the first guest. My mother, who was staying with Inga, hadn't yet emerged from the bedroom, and Sonia, too, was still in hiding. The loft was lit with candles. I smelled roasting lamb, basil, burnt matches, and my sister's perfume. Trying to push Mr. T. out of my mind, I told myself I would check on him in the morning.

My sister was in her diva mode, dressed in a tight-fitting silk jacket and narrow pants, her hair pulled up, her mouth red. I told her that all she needed was a cigarette holder to complete the picture.

"Gave it up, remember?"

With a mischievous smile, Inga raised her thumb and began to enumerate the guests, lifting a finger for each: "You and your mysterious Shakespeare heroine; Mamma, Sonia, me; Henry Morris, professor of American literature, NYU, knew Max a little, recovering after painful divorce from mad Mary. He's a wee bit stiff, but very smart. In fact, I like him a lot. We've had a *date*." Inga winked at me, then thrust up the thumb of her other hand to keep on counting, "My friend Leo Hertzberg, yet another professor, but a retired one, from art history at Columbia, lives on Greene Street, sees poorly, but he's very interesting and extremely kind. I met him through my friend, Lazlo Finkelman. I've been reading Pascal to him every week for an hour or so, and then we have tea. His great sadness is that his only child, a boy, died when he was eleven. Matthew's drawings are all over his apartment." She glanced at me. "And I invited Burton."

"You can't be serious," I said. "After that incident in the park you won't talk about?"

Inga's smile vanished. "Well, that's why I did it. I found him in the telephone book and called."

I wasn't able to continue the conversation because we were interrupted by the buzzer, and seconds later Miranda arrived. To say "Miranda looked beautiful that night" would be unjust. When I saw her come through the door, I felt choked with admiration. She was wearing a white sweater that exposed her shoulders, black pants, and gold loops in her ears, but it was her long slender neck and arms and gleaming eyes that crushed me, not to speak of the way she held herself. Her straight back and slightly elevated chin communicated an ineffable mixture of confidence and pride. Inga immediately engaged her in conversation. My mother and Sonia emerged from the back of the loft, arm in arm, both dressed up for the occasion, although in Sonia's case that meant a loose dress paired with motorcycle boots.

It wasn't the first time in New York City that a motley group of the divorced, widowed, bereft, or merely solitary gathered for a meal, but despite the fact that Inga had any number of friends who came in pairs, she hadn't included a single married couple on her guest list. It was an evening for our mother, whose mind didn't leave our father for long in that first year after his death, and Inga may have thought that the sight of intimate couples, old or young, might be painful. I knew that my sister regarded the dinner party as a ritual, organized around the idea that talk is a form of play. Like children at recess, the players must make an effort to resist the rough stuff and maintain respectful limits. She also felt that the combination of personalities was crucial to its success or failure, and so I paid close attention to the two strangers I was introduced to that evening.

Leo Hertzberg was a middle-sized man with thinning gray

hair, a beard, a small paunch, and glasses that hid his eyes. He steered himself carefully into the room with a cane. When he reached Inga, the two pecked each other twice, and after the kisses I overheard him say to her in a low voice, "Can you look me over to make sure nothing's out of place?"

Inga placed both hands on his shoulders, glanced down at his blue shirt, nondescript tie, gray sports jacket, and somewhat rumpled trousers, and said, "You look dashing. No tweaking necessary."

The man smiled then and shook his head as if to say, Although I take pleasure in the compliment, I know it isn't true.

The first thing I noticed about Henry Morris was his eyes. After looking at him for a while, I understood that he blinked less often than most people, a trait that was slightly disconcerting. The man was only a couple of inches shorter than I am, strikingly handsome, and I guessed a few years younger than my sister. When he shook my hand, he looked at me directly, his gaze cool but not unfriendly. His grip, however, was strong, almost combative, and I sensed that he might be one of those men who instinctively treat all other men as rivals. But it was what I witnessed a couple of minutes later that gave me pause. Morris was talking to Inga in the kitchen, and she was laughing at something he had said. As she turned away to pick up a plate of hors d'oeuvres, I watched him place his fingers around the upper part of her right arm and begin to squeeze it, exerting increasing pressure, or so it seemed to me. Inga stopped laughing and turned to look at him, her expression sober and compliant, her eyes shining. Then, with a small smile, she gently put her hand over his and made him release her. Their erotic connection was palpable, and I gathered that Inga's use of the word "date" had been a euphemism.

Burton arrived last. The rest of us were sitting with drinks near the front of the loft. When Inga opened the door for him, my friend looked bulkier than usual, as if he had overdressed for the spring night. As soon as he entered the room, he thrust forward a bouquet of flowers covered in plastic that he held in two hands, and began to apologize profusely for his lateness. As I studied his body more closely, I began to suspect that he had improvised some kind of sweat-catcher under his suit, a suspicion that was confirmed when Inga took the flowers from him and I heard a distinct rustling sound in the vicinity of his underarms. But it was his face that worried me. His expression when his eyes met Inga's was so unguarded, so plainly adoring, it brought to mind not a man in love, but a dog mooning at the sight of his mistress. My heart sank.

The conversation meandered that evening from the war in Iraq to the vicissitudes of memory and the character of dreams. The wine was poured freely, and exactly how we got from one topic to another is unclear, but I know that by the time we were seated and ingesting the lamb, I had discovered that Henry Morris was writing a book on Max—a large particular Inga had left out of her description of him—that he was vociferously opposed to the war, and also that he sliced and chewed his meat with a precision and delicacy that struck me as fastidious.

Burton's handkerchief seemed to have a life of its own that evening. Like a white flag, it unfurled itself, wiped and dabbed the face of my friend, and then vanished into its owner's waiting breast pocket. Burton looked elated, a combination, I suspect, of wine and proximity to the beloved, because when he smiled, which was often, his lips had a loose and flabby quality I hadn't seen before. He discoursed on some topic to Inga at the other end of the table as my sister, her cheeks flushed, nodded enthusiastically. My mother had a tête-à-tête with Leo Hertzberg, of which I heard snatches. He said, "After we left Berlin, my parents found an apartment in Hampstead. I remember it looked small and dirty to me, and I didn't like the way it smelled." "I was living outside Oslo during the occupation," my mother said quietly. "After the war, like a lot of Norwegian girls, I went to England and worked as domestic help. I was with a family in Henley-on-Thames for a year. Then I went back to university." Miranda was more at ease than I had ever seen her. She smiled more, used her hands more when she talked, and I thought to myself that whatever burdens were weighing on her, she had at least momentarily forgotten them. She was seated next to me at the table, and the presence of her body so close to mine seemed to activate my peripheral nerves. I could almost feel them tingling. She was wearing perfume, and I had a strong desire to press my nose to the hollow behind her ear and inhale the scent. Miranda spoke to me and Henry about the early Russian Constructivists and their book designs, a subject I knew nothing about, but then the conversation moved to the use of color for emotional effects, and Miranda said that a certain shade of pale turquoise made her shudder—as if she were getting sick with the flu. I brought up synesthesia then, and a man I had read about who would involuntarily see a color whenever he met someone. "I think he saw green for a withdrawn person, for example." "But colors always have feelings," Sonia said. "Red is completely different from blue."

Our talk was broken off by an exclamation from Inga. "You mean you're bringing together classical memory systems and neuroscience! That's wonderful!" Burton gave Inga a triumphant grin. His handkerchief leapt out of his pocket, snapped to attention, and made contact with his wineglass, which promptly flew off the table and shattered on the floor. Despite immediate protests from Inga, Henry's remark "What a trajectory," and Sonia's spontaneous applause, Burton, with a mortified expression on his face, threw his lumpy self onto the floor and, as his mysterious undergarment crackled, began picking up the glass.

The incident of the broken wineglass marked a change in the

evening. The eight of us settled into the living room. After asking permission, Morris smoked a cigar, and Burton, rather surprisingly, joined him. Cognac made the rounds, and the once tall candles shining in the room flickered low in the breeze from the open windows, their burning wicks hazy behind the rising smoke.

"Still," my mother was saying to Leo Hertzberg, a faint smile on her face, "there are many things in life that we don't understand, things that happen without any explanation at all."

I felt sure she was thinking of the invisible presence that entered the room on the day my father died.

Leo nodded. He looked meditative and a little sad, I thought.

Burton, apparently recovered, lurched in, and suddenly we were all listening. "Mrs. Davidsen," he said.

"Marit," said my mother.

"Well, thank you. I take that as an honor." Burton nodded at my mother. "Marit, I couldn't agree with you more. In my research, well, perhaps not in all my research, but in a good deal of it, certainly, it has become eminently clear that we, that is, not me, but scientists, don't know about a whole range of human phenomena. Take sleep." Burton wiped his face. "Nobody knows why we sleep. And dreams. No one knows why we dream. Back in the seventies, seventy-six, to be exact, yes, I can be exact, Daniel Dennett proposed that dreams may not be real, that they aren't experiences at all, just false memories that flood us when we wake up. Discredited now. Thoroughly. Also the REM theory."

"Really?" my mother said politely.

"Indeed." The handkerchief dabbed. "There are non-REM dreams, some of them entirely indistinguishable from REM dreams. Allan Hobson"—Burton took a breath and surged on—"'activation-synthesis' man, par excellence, big in the field, believes that pontine brainstem mechanisms, that's reptilian brain territory, way back"—the handkerchief flew to Burton's neck—"*cause* sleep and dreams.

In his model, dream imagery is loaded at random and the forebrain tries to make sense of it. Dreams have no rhyme or reason, according to him, no wishing, no disguises, no Freud. Mark Solms, psychoanalyst, brain researcher, and neurologist, passionately begs to disagree. Heard him speak not long ago. Excellent delivery. Patients with specific forebrain lesions stop dreaming altogether. He believes parts of the forebrain generate dream pictures, that complex cognitive processes are involved, so dreams *do* have meaning. Memory's involved, but nobody knows exactly how. Francis Crick, yes, the inimitable DNA Crick, argued that dreams are memory's garbage disposal, the leftovers, nonsense, if you will, churned up and spewed out in our sleep. David Foulkes thinks that semantic and episodic memories are *randomly* activated in dreams, but that dreams have predictable features. There's been a long-standing notion, oh, let me see, at least since Jenkins and Dallenbach in 1924, that when we dream we process and consolidate our memories. Then . . ." Burton's brain was ticking away. He began to recite. "There was Fishbein and Gutwein, Hars and Hennevin . . ."

Inga mercifully interrupted the footnotes with an exclamation: "Fishbein and Gutwein! That's wonderful. Laboratory broth: fish bones and good wine!"

Burton smiled sheepishly, his forehead wet and gleaming in the candlelight. "Never thought of that. In all events, just as many researchers say they're wrong, about memory, that is."

"I know dreams come from memories," Sonia said, her face grave.

I looked at my niece. "There are different kinds of dreams," I said. "I've had patients who have repetitive dreams about a single terrible event. They're more like reenactments than dream narratives. Your grandfather had them after the war."

Sonia's eyes were large and thoughtful, but she didn't answer me.

"In my dreams," Miranda said, "I mostly live in the same house.

It doesn't resemble anywhere I've ever lived. Part of it belongs to me, but then there's some doubt about the other rooms. They're all connected, you see, and sometimes I open a door to a whole new room, but who owns it is never clear." Her expression was pensive. "On the fifth floor there are three small bedrooms I've somehow forgotten about. I turn a key that's in the lock, and then I rediscover them one by one. They're falling apart, and I need to repair them, but somehow I never do. Do any of you go back to the same places in your dreams, I mean places that don't exist anywhere else?"

"I'm not sure," Inga said. "Usually it's a house or apartment that's supposed to be a particular place, but it doesn't look like itself at all."

"Yes, I have that, too," Miranda said, "but lately I've been recording my dreams, and I realize that what happens on the other side is a kind of parallel existence. I have a memory of what's happened there. There's a past, present, and future. I return to the same house, but it's"—Miranda squinted, as if to help herself remember—"it's like the rules of living are different. And the view from the window changes. Sometimes it's the United States, sometimes Jamaica. I've been drawing my dreams, and they might be strange, but they're not nonsensical."

"And the drawings you make look like the dreams?" Inga said. "When you're finished, you feel that they're accurate?"

Miranda leaned forward and gestured with her right hand. "No," she said. "Not accurate in the way you mean. I begin with the rough drawings I do after I wake up and then I fill them in bit by bit, finding my way forward to make sure it doesn't *feel* wrong."

"I've had the most curious dreams about my body," my mother said, "that it's deformed."

"Me, too," Miranda said, "that I've become a monster."

I thought of the female monster I had seen in her drawing—its immense mouth and fang-like teeth: a wolf woman.

"I've often dreamt that I have extra eyes," Inga said. "One or two more on my forehead or at the back of my head. That's monstrous, but in the dream, I just feel kind of unsettled."

"Before I'm really asleep," Miranda said, "I often see horrible creatures that keep changing their shape. I find them fascinating. I wonder where they come from."

"Hypnagogic hallucinations," Burton said.

"So that's what they're called. You'd think they'd have a better name." Miranda looked thoughtful.

"I get chased all the time," Sonia said. "I'm surprised I don't wake up exhausted from all that running at night."

"In my dreams now," Leo said quietly, "my vision is just as faded as when I'm awake. I dream in a blur with sounds and words and touch, and I run, too, from Nazi soldiers who have found their way to Greene Street and are banging on the door."

"The truth is," Henry said, "I rarely remember my dreams." He snapped his fingers. "They just disappear."

"You have to wake up slowly," Miranda said, "and make notes—or draw."

Henry put his arm on the back of the sofa behind Inga and moved it close to her neck. I watched my mother scrutinize the gesture.

"You're an analyst, Erik," Henry said. "You must interpret dreams. What's your position on all this? Do you follow the orthodox Freudian line?"

"Well," I said, asking myself whether there had been a hint of hostility in his voice, "a lot has happened in psychoanalysis since Freud. We know that Freud was right that most of what the brain does is unconscious. He didn't invent that idea, of course—you have to at least give credit to Helmholtz—but still, it wasn't so long ago that many scientists rejected the very possibility. I've come to think of consciousness as a continuum of states, from fully awake cogitation to daydreaming to the altered consciousness of hallucinations and dreams. Still, interpreting dreams can only take place when we're awake. I believe meaning is what the mind makes and wants. It's essential to perception and to consciousness in all its forms. But the important meanings in psychotherapy are subjective. There's a lot of research that confirms that dream content reflects the dreamer's emotional conflicts."

"Hartmann," Burton chimed in.

"Yes," I said. "By telling a dream, a patient is exploring some deeply emotional part of himself and creating meaning through associations within a remembered story. The nonsense theory of dreaming that Burton cited doesn't explain why dreams are narratives."

"Max used dream structures in his novels," said Morris, turning to Inga. "Sudden shifts and transformations. I'm thinking of *A Man at Home*. Horace wakes up, goes to work, comes home, has dinner, kisses his children goodnight, makes love to his wife, and the next day, he wakes up and they're gone. The house is empty except for the bed he's sleeping in. Nothing's there."

"Reading Max's work," Inga said slowly, "is like seeing him again in a dream." Her voice broke on the word *him*. "You know how you meet someone, but then the face is all wrong, and it's somebody else." Inga's hands began to shake. My mother gave her daughter a concerned look. Burton's handkerchief vanished between his palms, and Sonia turned her head to the window. *It's something about Dad.* Henry Morris, however, kept his steady eyes fixed on my sister's face.

"Don't worry," Inga said, grabbing her thighs with her hands. "I'm okay. It will pass." She made a wincing smile. "I think everybody feels that dreams are important in some way. The Egyptians believed in universal dream symbols. The Greeks thought dreams were divine messages; Artemidorus wrote the *Oneirocritica*, a kind of dictionary of dream interpretation. Mohammed dreamed most of the Koran, and on and on." Inga lowered her voice. "Last night, I dreamed I was home in the old house where we grew up. You, Mamma, and you, Erik, were there, and it all looked just as it was. We were in the living room, and suddenly Pappa was standing there, true to life, not at all different. But he didn't have his walker or the oxygen. I knew he was dead, and then he disappeared. In the dream, I said to myself, 'I've seen my father's ghost.' "

After a pause, Leo said, "It can't be accidental that we bring back dead people we've known and loved in our dreams. Surely that's a form of wishing."

Sonia was curled up in a chair. She glanced at Leo as he spoke, then hugged her knees and rocked herself a couple of times. She mouthed a word to herself, but I couldn't make out what it was.

We were all silent then. I watched a candle sputter for an instant before it went out. The party was all but over. Sonia whispered that she'd like to see me soon. Leo kissed my sister's hand, and the gesture looked natural. I'm sure Burton would have liked to do the same, but hand kissing wasn't in his repetoire. When Inga kissed both his cheeks good-bye, his face flushed to a deep red. My last impression was of my mother watching Inga say goodnight to Henry, her eyes both attentive and wary.

Miranda and I returned by taxi to the same house. I invited her upstairs for a nightcap. I actually used the word, which sounded strange coming from my mouth, but she turned me down. She kissed me politely on both cheeks, thanked me for a "lovely evening," and left me to my imaginary exploits, in which she, as usual, played no minor role.

MY FATHER RETURNED home on the S.S. *Milford* in early April of 1945, debarked in Seattle, where he ate *a small, tough, tasty piece of meat, that was indeed steak,* compliments of the Army, and was then hastily discharged from the service. *My last serious bout with malaria had started before I boarded the train for home. First comes a burning behind your eyeballs; the chills and fever come later. I shared a seat with a sergeant who was on his way to Camp McCoy in Wisconsin for discharge. From time to time he pulled out a letter, which he read. I could sense that it did not contain good news. Later, when I began to feel better, he told me that his wife had met another man and wanted a divorce. She said it was his fault. He was not pleasant company, but he wanted to talk. The rear car had a platform in back. I forget how we ended up there, but as we leaned on an iron railing and looked into the western horizon we were leaving, he declared—now without any fear of being overheard—that the first thing he would do when he got home was to kill his wife.*

My bewilderment was hardly as neatly packaged as I now explain it. Was this just army big talk? Was it a ploy to see how I would react? Should I find a way to report him? My feelings rose to defense of his wife. I first went through a "You can't really mean it" speech. I mentioned that at least once a week someone in our unit would get a "Dear John" letter. "Welcome to the club" was about the best my comrades could say. "We'll put in for a Purple Heart," said others. "You'll have to catch the next bus" also passed for army wisdom. I told him I thought his plan was stupid. By the time we reached St. Paul, he had decided first to visit his parents and then a married sister. He would confront his wife later. I made no efforts to report him.

My father took the bus to Cannon Falls. His father was working his shift at Mineral Springs Sanitarium, and Lotte was at her job in South St. Paul. My grandmother, Uncle Fredrik, and Ragnild Lund were waiting at the station. *My mother lost her composure completely when she saw me get off the bus. We had a public scene. Ragnild, whom I barely recognized because she had lost so much weight, looked on with mild embarrassment. There was something strange about Fredrik that at first I couldn't grasp. He had grown at least six inches since I last saw him. Then we got into Mother's 1935 Ford and drove home, where nothing had changed save for further deterioration of the buildings—the barn in particular. This was my homecoming.*

My grandmother must have burst into tears. I find this ordinary, but my father, usually compassionate, conveys in this passage irritation at best and shame at worst. Did she weep and wail? Did she throw herself on him? There is something missing. In the following paragraph, he attempts a further explanation: *Our mother's capacity for worry had no boundaries. Even though I knew this, I had failed to understand what she had gone through during my stint overseas. There had been war casualties in our community. As these dreaded telegrams reached families we knew, her fears mounted. Minister Adolph Egge had wept in the pulpit as he delivered memorial sermons over young men he had confirmed. This had caused Mother to wander around in the cellars of despair for days. Father did not know how to deal with it, nor did anyone else for that matter. I have often wondered what impact this had on Fredrik, on Lotte, too, for that matter, but she was older and did not live at home.*

I have a vague memory of my father dismantling the empty barn with Uncle Fredrik. I may be wrong. It's possible that my father only told me about it, and I provided an image for the story. What is certain is that he didn't want the dilapidated structure going to ruin on the property. The word *eyesore* comes to mind. He made sure it was taken down. A matter of pride.

AFTER TALKING TO Mr. T.'s mother, the attending physician on the ward discovered what I already knew: Mr. T. had stopped taking his drugs. Zyprexa had apparently worked well for his symptoms, but it had also made him obese, and after a year he had found the weight gain and what he described as "a slow head" intolerable. When he stopped suddenly, it had precipitated the psychotic break

I witnessed. They were trying risperidone, which seemed reasonable. Dr. N. was in a hurry, and when I asked him about Mr. T.'s writing, he alluded to "thought disorder," and that was the end of it. While he was my patient, Mr. T. had aroused my sympathy and later, my affection. His paternal grandparents had survived the Nazi death camps, but his father had never spoken of it. I returned to my old notes. The first words he had ever spoken to me were "The ground is screaming."

THE STORY MS. L. told me was that when she was very little, "about two," her mother had dragged her out of her crib in the middle of the night and had thrown her against the wall again and again "like a rag doll." The memory had returned to her all at once. She kept seeing it over and over. When she finished telling me this, she said, "It was attempted murder," and the trace of a smile appeared on her face.

I have treated many patients who were hurt as children—beaten, raped, sexually molested—but I immediately sensed that there was something wrong with Ms. L.'s tale. Infantile amnesia prevents explicit memories from such an early age, although sometimes people mistake later events for earlier ones. The words "like a rag doll" also disturbed me: they suggested that she was watching rather than participating in the scene. This kind of dissociated vision can happen when people are severely traumatized, but her following reference to "attempted murder" had the ring of a courtroom, and the tiny grin after relating the memory alerted me to its sadistic value for her. It was as if I, not she, were the rag doll.

When I articulated these doubts, she went silent for three minutes, staring at me with dead eyes. I reminded her that we had an agreement. If she had nothing in particular to say, she should say whatever came to mind. The words *I hate you* came to *my* mind, and I felt the pronoun slide between us. *You hate me*. What did I mean?

Ms. L. began stroking her thighs as she continued to look straight at me. Then she began to knead them. The effect was immediate. I felt aroused and had a sudden fantasy of slapping her hard and pushing her off the chair to the floor. She grinned, and I had the distinct impression she was reading my thoughts. Her hands stopped moving. When I told her I thought her seductive gestures might be an effort to control me, Ms. L. said, "Did you know my stepmother's been snooping around in my building and lying about me to my neighbors?"

When I asked her what evidence she had for thinking this, she barked, "I know it. If you don't trust me, what's the point?"

That was exactly the point, but my saying so led to another wall.

After she left, I felt disoriented. Ms. L.'s delusions, paranoia, and what I feared were lies affected me like a man lost in a poisonous fog as he desperately searches for a way out. At the end of the day, I called and left a message for Magda. I knew I needed help with Ms. L. On the subway platform, I found it hard to think, except in fragments, and as the train roared into the station, I had the terrible thought that its screeching wheels sounded human.

EXACTLY A WEEK after the dinner party, I was awakened by noises on the floor above my bedroom. I had been dreaming that I was building a contraption with a pulley that would facilitate retrieving books in my library. A lifelike hand was attached to the end of my device, but when I tried to use it to reach for a volume, the fingers withered into useless stumps. Half conscious, I thought at first that I was hearing my mother's footsteps above me, but then I remembered she was staying at Inga's. Perhaps someone was pacing next door. Sound is often hard to track in brownstones.

It wouldn't have been the first time I had been fooled. I sat up, held my breath, and listened. No, the steps were above me, coming through my ceiling. Someone was in my study. I had an intruder. As quietly as possible, I dialed 911 and whispered the information into the phone. The dispatcher said "I can't hear you" several times, but I finally made her understand the address and the situation. In the next moments, I weighed the consequences of action. If I lay still, the robber might take what he wanted and leave. But as I heard him moving upstairs, I remembered the hammer I had left in the closet after mounting an extra hook inside the door. It is terrible to try to move silently in the dead of night when every noise is magnified, but I managed to move to the closet, open it with a single squeak, and grab the hammer. Then I stepped toward the door, opened it slightly, and poised myself inside for a view of the hallway and stairs. I knew that if he tried to descend those stairs, each tread would creak. Motionless, I waited. The person came down slowly, pausing between steps. It seemed to go on for a long time. Finally, I saw a large sneaker, followed by a naked leg and the bottom of a pair of wide shorts, between the rungs of the stairway. This lower body was only dimly illuminated from the skylight above. My lungs had tightened into two nearly airless sacks, and I consciously took a single breath so as not to get dizzy. Then I saw hands, bearing no weapon, followed by a lean torso in a loose T-shirt. The man was inching cautiously down the stairs as they groaned loudly. He kept his hand on the railing until he finally reached the landing and then paused. Slowly, carefully, he continued down the hallway in my direction. There was a night-light shining from the open bathroom door, and it illuminated the face of a young man with black hair and tan skin, at least six inches shorter than I am. About four feet away from my door, I saw him put his hand in his pocket, and I leapt into the hallway, hammer raised. As I yelled, "What the hell are you doing in my house!" I noticed that the thing the man had taken from his pocket was a small digital camera, and in that same instant I understood that I was face to face with Jeffrey Lane. The revelation caused me to lower the hammer. Then I froze. He saw his chance, turned and ran, but had the gall to stop and photograph me. My rage reignited, I chased him up the stairs, howling that I'd called the police. He took the stairs two at a time, raced around the landing, thrust open the door to the roof and dashed up the steel ladder with me at his heels. As I mounted the ladder, I looked up and saw that the hatch was open. I lunged for his foot, but he was too fast for me. By the time I scrambled to the roof, he was racing past the neighbor's chimney; I watched, panting, as he flew down the row of houses and disappeared.

I told the police everything, except that I knew, or thought I knew, the identity of the intruder and that he had taken photographs. Lying to the officers made me feel uncomfortable. At the same time, I noticed how smoothly I did it, as if it were business as usual. Only seconds after the words were out of my mouth, however, I began to wonder whether my protection of Miranda had been misplaced. A man who breaks into people's houses and takes pictures should be arrested, shouldn't he? And yet I knew I had done something stupid. The Sunday before, I had gone up to check the condition of the skylight because I had noticed a small leak during a rainstorm. I had made several trips with sealant and brush to reinforce the cracked tar and must have forgotten to lock the hatch when I was finished.

After the police had taken my statement and politely acknowledged that such incidents rarely result in an arrest, I returned to the kitchen, poured myself some red wine, and drank it slowly. I might have killed the man if I hadn't seen the camera. He had taken a stupid risk. Was he trying to get to Miranda? What was he doing in my study? As I mulled over the incident, it seemed that I remembered something in his face just after he took my picture—an expression of excitement? No. I assigned it another word: glee. For an instant, Miranda's ex-lover, Eglantine's father, had looked gleeful. For him, I thought, photography is a form of thievery, a raid that acts as a stimulant. He was a man in the business of stealing appearances.

"IT SOUNDS LIKE something he'd do, and at the same time it doesn't," Miranda said. "He told me once that when he was in high school, he used to steal from stores, not because he wanted the things, but because it was an act of rebellion against consumer culture." She paused. "We argued about it. He called me a 'rigid moralistic prude.'" As she pronounced his condemnation, she smiled. "He didn't take anything from you, did he?"

"Nothing is missing, as far as I know." We were sitting in Miranda's front room. Eglantine was in the garden. I could hear her singing. "I think he was looking for you."

"You know what I think? He probably wanted to photograph the house, maybe get into our apartment and take pictures of me and Eggy asleep."

"Why?"

"Well, he likes to take pictures of people sleeping. He likes it because the subjects don't know, because they're vulnerable."

"But you're not afraid of him?"

"I don't think he'd hurt us, if that's what you mean." Miranda looked away for a moment. It was difficult to know what she felt or didn't feel for Lane. After a few seconds of silence, I asked to see some of her dream drawings.

Despite my earlier glimpse of Miranda's monster, I didn't know what to expect. She explained that for dreams she liked a form with framed boxes to tell the story. The first panel took up an entire page. I looked down at a large, meticulously rendered interior stairway, colored in cool blues. Its precision and detail made me think of the Superman comics I had hidden under my mattress as a boy. Miranda had used pen, colored pencils, and some watercolors. After a moment, I noticed that the perspective was slightly wrong, that is to say, it didn't follow the rules we have come to expect, and this slight alteration created the dream effect Miranda had mentioned at the dinner. Near the top was a narrow red door, its angle also tilted. The second drawing was of a large room with a lone piece of furniture: an iron bed with a tattered, striped mattress. High above it was a single window with four panes. In the next drawing, the bed was viewed from above, and a person had appeared in it, a frail old person whose body was covered by a sheet. I wasn't sure whether it was a man or a woman, but the pale figure's head was tiny and shriveled, rather like a shrunken head I had seen once, except that this one was the color of cream turning to butter—a whitish yellow. Under the sheet, one could see the outline of a tiny body curled up in the fetal position. In the final image, the sheet had been pulled away, and although the head remained, the exposed body now overwhelmed the narrow bed: the miniature head was attached to a robust female torso with long, athletic limbs, colored a deep brown. One of the feet was chained to the bedpost. The wizened pinhead on the voluptuous body was grotesque, and I made a sound of surprise.

"I know," Miranda said, "it's awful, and I think it was even worse in the dream. I was terrified. I drew a sketch of the head right away, but while I was working on the sequence, I suddenly understood where it came from. I've been reading a lot of Jamaican history." She pointed to the wrinkled skull, "This is like the little white colonial head that wanted to rule the huge black body of Jamaica. Look, one foot is chained, enslaved, the other is free, like the Maroons. It's as if my brain collapsed it all into a single horrible figure." She paused. "But I also think that the tiny old head and body in this part," Miranda traced the covered body with her finger, "must have come from my gran. She got so little when she was dying, Mum said it was like holding a child at the end. Her grandfather was a white man, so you see, it's all mixed up, and there's Indian blood in the family, too. Gran was many things. She went to Anglican schools, read English poets, and was big on propriety and manners. Her daughters and granddaughters were going to be perfect ladies. At the same time, she knew a lot about herbal cures and loved to tell stories about duppies."

"Duppies?"

"Ghosts, spirits."

"My grandmother used to hear my grandfather's ghost walking in and out of the house. She swore that his hat came and went with him."

I had hoped to see more dreams, but Eggy ran into us, and bouncing up and down in front of her mother, she said, "Please, Mommy, please, can we go to the park, please?"

The three of us walked in Prospect Park for about two hours, making a great loop through the meadow to the pond, and then we pushed into the woods on paths I had never taken before. Miranda and I walked. Eggy skipped, twirled, did lopsided cartwheels, and ran. After asking permission from the owners, she petted every dog we passed. She called to the ducks, complimented pedestrians on their clothes: "That's a lovely hat," "I like your dress," "Cute sneakers," and made it generally impossible for the three of us to pass any human being or animal unnoticed. As I watched the child in front of me, memories of the night before returned intermittently to my mind, but even when I wasn't actively recalling the man who had come through the roof, I understood that the encounter had left its trace in my body, an aftermath of anxiety that made me quicken to noises and sensitive to people near us. Several times, I turned my head to identify the source of footsteps. Although we said nothing, I felt that Miranda was skittish, too. When Eggy pursued a squirrel off the path and disappeared into the brush, Miranda called her back in a high-pitched tone I had never heard her use before. Eggy jumped out immediately. "Mommy," she said, looking up at Miranda with a puzzled face. "I'm here. I'm here. Don't worry." Miranda looked embarrassed. She bent over and smiled at her daughter. "I have to keep track of you, that's all, so don't disappear."

As we walked, Miranda told me her family had moved to New York after her uncle died. Her father and his younger brother had been in business together, and his death had been a terrible blow to her father, who had a sister in London, and another brother in Jamaica, but he had never been as close to them as to "Uncle Richard." When she said his name, Miranda lowered her voice and turned her face away from me. Her father had sold the business and started over in Brooklyn, where he had a number of connections in the Jamaican community. The family bought a large Victorian house in Ditmas Park, where her parents still lived. Miranda's paternal great-grandparents had both been active in the Pan-African movement and had known Marcus Garvey. It was obvious that Miranda was proud of them, especially her great-grandmother Henrietta Casaubon. "She was very light skinned, and in those days that was status. She was well educated and got a degree in history—very pretty, too," she said. "Then she met my great-grandfather, George, who was full of big ideas about black identity, and well, she became enlightened. I guess he ran after women, though, and the marriage wasn't all that happy. They lived in Harlem for a while but ended up back in Jamaica. My father told me that when they were in New York, Henrietta had a first cousin she couldn't visit because she was 'passing.'"

Eggy eventually grew tired, and I carried her several blocks on my shoulders as she gripped my chin with her hands and I held firmly onto her legs. After a while, she pressed her cheek against my head and began to sing in a small soft voice, "Oh, doctor Erik, he was a berik, deedle doo, bah, bah, loo, ferdle foo, ferdle foo, fer-dle foo." The ferdle foos then dropped off to a thin high hum with pauses in between.

Reluctant to let them go, I persuaded them to share some food with me. We ordered from a Thai restaurant, and I realized that I liked the way Miranda ate. As she chewed patiently, she would look up at me with those dramatic eyes of hers and listen so intently that I became conscious of every word I uttered. After we had settled Eggy in front of a video of *Singin' in the Rain*, she asked me about my work.

"Why did you quit your job at the hospital?"

"It was hard," I said. "Long hours. One crisis after another. The bureaucracy got worse, and the care got worse. The insurance business. They don't let people stay anymore. They throw them out too quickly. I also made less money than I do now." And, I thought to myself, *Sarah*.

I can't say this word to you. I can't say it because it's forbidden and it makes no sense. I've written the word on paper. I look down at the word. Sarah had written the pronoun I.

"Are you all right?" Miranda asked gently.

"Yes," I said.

"You probably think Jeff's as crazy as your patients, but I don't believe that. When he was sending the pictures, I was upset, but the fact is he was always working on some nutty project. He's got a million photographs plastered all over the walls. He'd wipe out a nose or an object and replace it with something else. He's followed lots of people around, taking their pictures and then manipulating the results. He'd say, 'I'm remaking the world.'" Miranda looked past me toward the kitchen.

I put my hand on hers. She glanced down at it and then tugged her fingers out from under mine. The song "Make 'Em Laugh" rang forth from the next room, and I wondered if Eggy had turned up the volume. Miranda looked at me and said, "I can't tell you how grateful I am for your kindness to me and Eglantine." I heard the return of the old formality in her voice and diction, and I looked away. "You've been wonderful." My whole body hardened as she continued, and although I listened to her, I felt a part of me escape and leave the two of us behind. I was waiting for the word I knew was coming, and it did. "Your friendship is important to me. I don't want to lose you as a friend, but things are very complicated for me now." Miranda spoke at some length, but I don't remember much of what she said after that because none of it mattered. I was being ordered into retreat, and as I sat there across from her, pretending to hear her words, I looked at the white boxes of half-eaten pork with basil and curried chicken and a lump of sticky rice left on Eggy's plate, which she had shaped into a ball, and was vaguely aware of the song reaching its crescendo: "Make 'em laugh, make 'em laugh, make 'em laugh!" The pain just beneath my ribs arrived, dull and familiar, and an archaic word came back to me, *dolor*, from the Latin. Dolorous, I thought, dolorous Dr. Davidsen. After the two of them had left me, and I threw away the boxes and was scraping the dishes, I remembered a story my father once told me about a relative of ours, a Sjur Davidsen, who left Bergen, Norway, in 1893. My father had some letters the man had written to my grandparents, but in 1910 he stopped writing. My father tracked down one of Sjur's nephews, wrote to him, and received a reply. In 1911, Sjur Davidsen had taken his own life in Minot,

North Dakota. "They said the reason was *kvinnesorg*," my father told me. Literally, the word means *woman-grief*.

I DROVE MY mother to the airport. For a good part of the trip, she talked lightly about her return to Minnesota, the small apartment that was waiting for her, and various friends she looked forward to seeing again. We were silent for some time after that. Then she asked me what I knew about Henry, and after I said "Next to nothing," she nodded thoughtfully.

"Miranda has beautiful manners," she said.

"Yes, she does."

"Refined."

"Yes," I said, looking at my mother and wondering where she was going. My mother's thoroughly bourgeois childhood in Norway had made her ever sensitive to the nuances of social comportment.

"It can be difficult," she said.

"Are you talking about the fact that Miranda is black?" I said.

My mother turned to me and smiled. "That," she said, "and the fact that she has a child from her first marriage and that from her I felt some . . ." She paused and picked her word. "Ambivalence."

She didn't need to say "toward you." I felt a pang of hurt pride mixed with irritation at my mother's overly delicate reference to race. I also noticed that I didn't correct her about the first *marriage*. We fell silent again.

The traffic was moving well, but then, not long before the exit to LaGuardia, the cars slowed and, as we inched along, she said, "You know it took me a whole year to get the visa I needed to travel to the United States so I could marry your father."

"I remember," I said.

"I hadn't seen Lars for a long time." My mother fingered the purse she held in her lap. "When I came down the gangplank, he was there waiting. He walked up to me, and I looked into his face, and it was as if I didn't really know him, as if he were a stranger to me. I can't tell you how disturbing it was, Erik. But then your father started talking to me and gesturing with his hands, and all of a sudden, he was the same, dear Lars again."

"How long did it last—the period of not recognizing him?"

"Well, I recognized him, of course, but it wasn't him somehow. I don't know. It was very brief, not even a minute, maybe just seconds, but I've never forgotten it."

When we parted outside the security check, my mother gave me a single strong hug and then looked me in the eyes. "Erik," she said in a low, tender voice, "I'd cast a spell on her if I could," and then she turned around, placed her purse and shoes on the conveyer belt, and waited for the uniformed woman to wave her through the arch.

DESPITE THE JOY of coming home, my father wrote, I lived through a summer of pervasive discontent. I was homesick at home. I missed army life, not only my circle of friends, but the camaraderie that only military service can give. I missed the rough-and-tumble character of our daily life, the boisterous and good-natured banter that went with it, a pattern of working hard and playing hard without mixing the two. I had come to like military order and regimentation as long as it was fair. I even liked army over-kill when it came to maintenance of quarters, gear, equipment, and weapons. I found civilian life, my own home included, to be slipshod, and at times, chaotic.

My father spent a good portion of the summer of 1946 chopping down trees. It began with a conversation between my grandfather and a neighbor. Old Larsen had said that a number of trees were dying on his property, and my father offered to buy some of those trees as standing timber. *We met the next morning and marked those that would be mine, magnificent oldsters that shot up forty feet before the branch. The oak trees came to four dollars each. Basswood, a soft wood, went for three. Cutting timber is not proper summer work. The woods are hot and humid with little movement of air and mosquitoes and gnats are ever about. My tools were a crosscut saw, an ax, a maul, and a set of iron wedges. Save for help from Father and Fredrik in felling the trees, I worked alone. I savored the solitude of this work and I had endless energy that demanded use. I recall the satisfaction of going to bed physically worn. A one-man crosscut saw will do that to you. Unlike the two-man saw, you have to provide both the push and the pull.*

I remember my father behind me, his hands over mine as we lifted the ax together and then brought it down squarely onto a log, which split along the grain into even halves. Later, I learned to chop wood alone under my father's watch. After a while, my arms would ache and my whole body would grow tired, but I never told him. And he was right: there was pleasure in hitting the mark just right and seeing the log fall open before you. I can see him now, smiling as the sweat pours down his face, his shirt rolled up above his elbows, his hands on his hips as he surveys the mounting woodpile. "Looking good, Erik, looking good."

Alone in the woods, the former sergeant thrust and heaved with his one-man cross-cut. He hacked and smote the bark of dying trees, his towering opponents in a game of emotional necessity. He had no idea what he was going to do with the lumber, but felling those oaks and basswood served a purpose beyond utility: work as exorcism. It was Uncle Fredrik who told me that he had no idea what my father had been through during the war until one night his brother rammed his fists through the ceiling tiles in his room while he was asleep. Fredrik didn't elaborate, but I suspect my father's devils were legion. Some had entered him in the Pacific, but there were others, too. After he had assured that half-assed military psychiatrist at Fort Snelling that he liked girls, he may have thought that he was leaving the old demons behind him forever. It may have been the place that brought them howling back, the sight of the tiny house and the sagging, empty barn "out home."

THE ACHE I'D felt during Miranda's speech didn't leave me. I understood that I had projected myself into a future that included her and Eggy, and without that imaginary time-yet-to-come, I was cast into the far bleaker mode of the loveless present. In the morning I woke to a cloud, and although it usually lifted when I was with my patients, I knew that I had entered a period of what in medical jargon is called anhedonia: joylessness. I was aware, too, that my response to Miranda's declaration couldn't be extricated from my father's death, a death I felt I had insufficiently mourned. My scrutiny of his memoir and my daily jottings about the man were clearly forms of grief, but there was something missing in me, too, and that absence had turned into agitation. My nights were bad. Like a man possessed, I listened to myriad voices clamoring for room inside my head, a fragmented inner speech accompanied by images, which inevitably became more disjointed as I entered the borderland between wakefulness and sleep. One night, I saw a figure like my mother's alone in the old house and then walking near the creek, her slender body striding ahead with determination, but then she slowed and began to weave on the path. *I'd cast a spell on her if I could.* How did she know? No one knows why we sleep or why we dream. *I know you will never say nothing about what happened. It can't matter now she's in heaven or to the ones on earth.* The words of Lisa's letter plagued me, as if I were somehow involved, responsible. Sometimes, as I felt myself finally drift toward sleep, I would hear my father cough, a sound as unmistakable as his voice, and it would jolt me back to consciousness. An ever-changing host of erotic phantasms kept me up as well, obedient bawds invented to relieve the sexual pressure I felt, tight as the straps on a straitjacket. But as my masturbatory lust soared, the figments would inevitably begin to resemble Miranda, and my imaginary copulations with her stand-in weren't gentle, but hard and angry, and afterward, bitterness and guilt would settle in my chest like a cold iron bar. And so, one anxious thought climbed onto the next. I worried about Lane and thought I heard his footsteps on the roof. I dreamed I found a camera near my bed, and when I opened its back, it leaked blood and mucus all over my hands as if it were an injured animal. I worried about my sister and the unknown woman in the park, and wondered about Henry. The man's eyes were hawklike. He was writing a book on Max. *I think it's about Dad.* Max's characters, Rodney Fallensworth, Dorothea Stone, Mrs. Hedgewater, and the clown, Green Man, fell under suspicion during my nighttime fits, as if they were fictional clues. I remembered the strange narrative of *A Man at Home* and wondered if Horace's lost family concealed its author's secret wish or dread. I saw Arkadi's fingers forming words in *Into the Blue* as if the signs were a hidden message. What had Inga been looking for when she watched the film? What did that redheaded journalist with her shameful grin think she knew? I saw Sarah crawl out her mother's window and watched her fall twelve stories as if I had been there to witness it. Then her mother, distraught and screaming in my office, "You were the one who released her! You killed her!" the stiffly coiffed hair motionless despite her hysterical gesturing. Ms. L.'s voice: a battering ram. My fear. Peter Fowler's voice, his hand on my back. "Carbamazepine, buddy, helps with the anger." High-handed, self-important pharmacology Fowler. "Gotta keep up, Davidsen. New stuff on BPD coming every day." My fist ramming his jaw. The man's head hitting a wall and the fantasy giving relief as bits and pieces of articles would run through my head: "affect dysregulation, identity disturbance." *Neutrality*, I thought. What does it mean? Another lie. Mr. T. channeling his revelations: "Derailed. I failed. She bailed. He's afraid. Can't make the grade." And Ms. L.: "How can you believe in this therapy crap? I mean, it's so stupid, sitting here watching you. You really think you're something, don't you?" I imagine her on the floor, my hands gripping her wrists. *I hate you.*

In short, my nights became wrestling matches with myself, and I felt the strong lure of pharmacological oblivion: zolpidem—to sleep fast. I had taken it on occasions when I traveled to Europe for conferences, and the drug not only eliminated the wait for sleep, it banished the experience of sleep: no dim waking in the middle of the night, no sense of rising up out of a dream, no shrouded awareness of my body in the bed. The pill's uncanny ability to shut me down for seven hours, a quality I had always mistrusted, now gleamed like a tiny, white promise of paradise.

"MOM'S NOT HOME," Sonia said over the telephone. "I'm really worried, Uncle Erik. It's not like her. It's nine o'clock. There was no note for me, no nothing. She's not answering her cell phone. I've been home since six, just waiting and calling."

"Are you sure she didn't mention a meeting or a dinner or something and you just forgot?"

"No!" I could hear Sonia breathing loudly. "Maybe she's hurt somewhere or got mugged. And then there's that woman."

"What woman?"

"That stupid journalist, Linda Somethingburger."

"The redhead?"

"Yes. She's been calling. The other day I overheard Mom say, 'I have nothing to say to you. I've told you that many times.' She sounded so rattled, and she looked so white afterward." Sonia paused. "That night, I heard Mom talking to someone else in her bedroom, a long talk. She kept her voice down, but I could hear she was upset, and she's been weird, distracted, writing like crazy, tiring herself out, and not really asking me about my work or anything. Something's going on, something bad." After another pause, Sonia said, "Uncle Erik, can you come over? You can go to your office from here, can't you? I'll make up the bed for you. I'm so scared something's happened. I'm going crazy."

I found Sonia in her pajamas walking back and forth in the large front room of the loft, which smelled of cigarette smoke and air freshener. The coffee table was littered with books, papers, orange peels, gum wrappers, and loose change. It wasn't lost on me that for the second time I found myself waiting for someone's mother to come home. I did my best to reassure Sonia, but I, too, was worried. Inga was responsible, never careless about time, and she was diligently protective of her daughter. It made no sense.

"Maybe she's with Henry," I said.

Sonia made a face.

"You don't like him?"

"He's okay. I already called, and she's not there."

Sonia left several messages for Inga. She turned on the television, and we absently watched as greatly magnified earwigs wandered across the screen and a male voice droned on about their marvels. Sonia was twisting her hair at an alarming rate, and after searching through hundreds of channels and finding nothing we considered even remotely entertaining, I asked her if she would consider reading her poem to me. At first she balked, saying she couldn't concentrate, that she was too nervous, but then she relented, and after explaining that she was still editing, that she wasn't sure of every stanza, a very important one hadn't been written yet, and that she had chosen a constrictive form in order to see if she could do it, she picked up a small sheaf of papers from the coffee table and began to read to me in a clear voice.

> Five years ago, I watched my father die.
> His vacant corpse had lost the man I knew,
> the man who used to sing a lullaby
> at night or tell me tales from Paradou,
> the little town where phantoms sob and sigh,
> their windy voices keening, calling to
> the ones they left behind. They frightened me,
> those spectral beings of eternity.
>
> Today, I'd like to face those ghosts again
> because I've understood the dead don't grieve,
> the living do. Dear God, change now to then,
> I pray. Dear God, grant me one reprieve.
> Return me to the long-lost regimen
> I loved. One bedtime kiss and I'd believe
> my father knows the truth: the part I played
> required a stoic mask. Beneath, I was afraid.

I cleared my throat. Genie and I had visited Max, Inga, and Sonia one summer in Le Paradou, a tiny town in Provence, not far from Les Baux, where they had rented a house. I remembered Max grinning in the candlelight that flickered on the table as we sat outside in the cool air. A cigarette between his teeth, smoke circling upward, he had raised his glass in a toast to the season, to the good life, to family.

Sonia looked up at me, "You don't hate it, do you?"

While I was shaking my head, she continued, "It's the same form as Byron's *Don Juan*. These octaves are usually comic, you see, but I wanted to see if they could be serious." She paused, and I thought of Mr. T.'s linguistic machinations and crazed rhymes. "There's supposed to be one about September eleventh next, but I haven't been able to write it. I've tried over and over again, but it's too hard. Maybe I'll just have a blank there—a nothing, a big empty spot with only the date." Sonia looked at me, her expression suddenly fierce. "Then there's these two."

> They say the young don't know mortality,
> but that's all wrong. I feel it in my bones,
> my brain, my eyes, my limbs, in all of me,
> in dreaded things as well, like telephones
> that ring with news of fresh calamity,
> in sounds I hear before I sleep, the moans
> of disembodied voices in my head,
> my own despairing echoes for the dead.
>
> Policemen came one day to search our roof,
> two long-faced men with gloves and plastic bags.
> They climbed the stairs in hope of finding proof
> that body parts still lay beneath the flags
> we flew before their meaning turned to spoof.
> I see him clearly still. He kneels and drags
> the tar, an officer whose empty eyes
> betray no hope, no sorrow, no surprise.

Just before she had pronounced the last word, we heard the sound of Inga's key turning in the lock. My sister came rushing into the room, and Sonia burst into tears. I hadn't seen Sonia cry since she was a little girl, and the sound made me temporarily speechless. Inga ran to her daughter, threw her arms around her, and began a vociferous apology as she held her daughter's dark head to her chest, but after only a few moments Sonia pushed her mother away and in an adamant voice said, "What's going on? What's going on? I want you to tell me. Now!"

Inga leaned back in the sofa between Sonia and me. Her forehead creased before she spoke, and her blue eyes looked mournful.

"It's about Dad isn't it? What does that Burger woman want?"

"Linda Fehlburger."

"Yes!" Sonia said. "What does she want?"

"She wants me to talk about my marriage to your father, and I don't want to do it, not to her. She's gone around trying to get to all our friends and half-friends. . . . She's been after them, as they say, 'for dirt.' She's relentless, but I think she's finally gotten the message." Inga looked down at the floor. "Don't worry, darling," she said. "You mustn't worry."

Sonia didn't press her mother further, which surprised me at first, but then I thought perhaps she didn't really want to know. It was safer that way.

Inga made cheese omelettes, and the three of us talked pleasantly about nothing much. I noticed that with the presence of her mother, Sonia's body had changed—the hair-twisting, hunched girl had reverted to her sweet but inscrutable old self. At about midnight, my niece excused herself. Before she left the room she put her long arms around my neck and kissed my cheek. "I love you, Uncle Erik," she said. "And thank you for coming."

This tribute, I'm glad to say, arrived like a welcome glint of sun through clouds in winter, and as I said my goodnight to Sonia, I felt a sudden warmth rise to my cheeks.

That was the night we talked, my sister and I, about what she had been hiding. She didn't blurt it out but flew in circles around the story at first, and I didn't push her. "Remember the scene in *Into the Blue*, when she wakes up and doesn't recognize him?"

"Of course," I said. "I watched it again a few weeks ago."

"It's a really terrible moment, isn't it?" Inga continued. "To be seen but not known. He's turned into a stranger again. And then there are those paintings she'd done of him that he finds in his room after he's searched high and low for her, and he takes them out behind the inn and burns them, an inflagration of himself. We know then that he's given up."

I nodded.

"This trouble," I said. "It's about the movie?"

"That's where I was tonight. I was visiting Edie Bly."

"The actress from *Into the Blue*?"

"Yes," Inga said. She turned to the window as if the actress could be found across the street.

"Something happened to us, Erik, to me and Max around the time of the movie, well, no, before it, actually. It was after Sadie died. Max didn't know his mother's death would hit him so hard. His panics started then. It was terrible until he got the medicine. He used to look at me in a certain way. I mean for years and years. His eyes were so alive and shining, and then they went dim." Inga bit her lip for a moment. "Well, one night we were fighting about something that I've completely forgotten, and he looked at me and said, 'Maybe it would be better if we lived apart for a while.'"

I looked at her. "But Max never left you, did he?"

Inga shook her head. "No, but when he spoke those words it was like losing my insides. Isn't that funny? I mean, it happens all the time, to everybody, but I realized then, at that moment, that we had different ideas about it all. For me, marriage was, is an absolute. Max had been married twice before. . . ."

"Yes, but not for long," I said.

"That's true. Nevertheless, those words hurt me so much." Inga pressed both her palms to her chest. "Even at the time, a part of me thought, 'Oh, God, this is so banal.'" She pronounced the last word dryly and with an ironic coldness I had rarely heard from her before. "The aging husband feeling his age gets tired of the all too familiar wife. . . ." Her voice trailed off.

"I told him I didn't want that. I said that marriage can be hard; it's always changing, but that I loved him terribly. He was kind then. God, he could be so kind, but I didn't want kindness. Once he started working on the movie, I hardly saw him anyway. He was on the set, went to rushes every night, came home after I was already asleep. He was happy though, keyed up, but happy. He loved the work." Inga took a breath. "But you see, the trouble between us was *my* fault." Her lips quivered for an instant. "I was difficult then, half mad, actually, when I think of it now. I'd finished my book. It was so hard to write, so painful, but I knew how good it was, how unusual. I also knew, or thought I knew, that it would be attacked, or worse, ignored, and I felt I couldn't bear it. I carped and moaned and complained about my fate as the forgotten, misunderstood woman intellectual. I suffered in advance what I feared would happen, and I made Max suffer."

"But your book did very well," I said.

"You should know, Mr. Psychoanalyst, that reality isn't the problem."

I smiled.

"It didn't help," Inga continued, "that by then whatever Max uttered—I mean, he could say, 'I had eggs for breakfast'—and it was as if God had spoken."

"He was attacked, too. All his life, Inga."

"I know," she said. "I'm not excusing myself. I began to understand how crazy I'd been, how difficult, vain, and blind. The irony was that I'd been writing about seeing, about how we perceive the world and that, as Kant said, we can't get to the thing in itself, ever, but it doesn't mean there isn't a world out there. The problem is that we're all blind, all dependent on preordained representations, on what we think we'll see. Most of the time, that's how it is. We don't experience the world. We experience our expectations of the world. That expecting is really, really complicated. My expectations became crazy. I was never taken as seriously as I wanted to be. I starting wishing I were a man. I wished I were ugly."

"Not really," I said.

"Half really. Because the world is prejudiced, I got angry. My perception of my very serious important self and the way I imagined others perceived me were out of wack."

"*Imagined* is the key word," I said.

Inga frowned. "I know. But Erik, there were people, both before and after Max died, who didn't recognize me without *him*, people I'd had conversations with, had cooked dinner for here at the house, people I *knew*, not dear friends but people who should have known me. He became the sole context for their perception of me. It wasn't Max's fault. He hated it. He felt sorry for me, and of course my pride was terribly wounded. When I first saw the movie, I thought the forgetting scene was written for me, but inverted. A woman forgets a man."

"You've forgotten people, Inga. In fact, I've seen people come up to you, and you don't remember them at all."

Inga wasn't listening. "Now I think that it was about something else, the scene."

"What?"

"It was about Edie."

I felt a clutch in my chest. "In what way?"

"He fell in love with her, Erik. He was the one who wanted to cast her. She hadn't been in much, you know, just a couple of obscure independent films, but he fought for her. I think he fell for her before he ever spoke to her. She was very young then, very pretty, and wild. I remember her dancing at the wrap party and thinking to myself that she had something savage in her, like an animal, not really cruel, but thoughtless, if you see what I mean. That's very desirable, isn't it? Men love that."

"I don't know," I said.

"Yes, you do. You married one of those girls."

I ignored the comment. "You're telling me they had an affair."

"Yes." Inga's face was rigid and her eyes cold.

"Did you know then?"

"No, but I was suspicious. I was jealous of her because I felt the tug in him. I'd never felt it before, not like that."

"Whatever happened between them, Max came back to you." I said these words in a low voice, and I'll never forget my sister's face as she listened to me. She was smiling—a taut, grim, callous smile. A piece of hair fell over her left brow and she wiped it away.

"That's what I always thought, Erik, that if there had been something between them, it didn't matter because he returned to me." Inga pressed her palms together as if she were measuring the length of her fingers. "But tonight she told me that *she* left him, that he wanted her desperately, but she threw him out, ended it. So, you see, I may have had Max by default." Inga was still smiling, and I found her brittle expression hard to look at.

"Inga," I said. "You know life isn't like that. You can't assume such things. Let's say Max had run off with her. Would their affair have lasted? For how long? He might have been back in your arms in a week."

"She has his letters, and she's going to sell them."

I groaned. "It was Edie you were talking to in the park when Burton saw you."

"To publish the letters, she needs my permission. Because Max is dead, I own their contents, but she owns the physical letters and can do whatever the hell she wants with them."

"Well, then, it's not a problem," I said.

"But the contents can be paraphrased, used. It's happened before."

My sister stood up and walked to the window. She had her back to me, but I could see in her shoulders and neck that she had braced herself, had tethered the emotion inside her as tightly as she could. She placed her long thin fingers on the window frame and said, "I feel I'm in the middle of a bad soap opera or some secondary plot in a late-eighteenth-century French novel. I'm continually aware of how unseemly it is, how smarmy. I mean it's one thing for this to happen, and it's another for it to be trumpeted all over the place, for people's inner lives to be bought and sold like a bag of cheap goods, and I have to play the dull, stupid part of the wronged wife." For several seconds she said nothing as she pressed both hands on the glass. "What's truly odd," she said to the darkened street, "is that I've suddenly discovered that I lived another life. Isn't that strange? I mean, now I have to rewrite my own story, redo it from the bottom up." After another long pause, my sister wheeled around to face me. She clenched both her fists and shook them at me, her face tense and livid. "I have to add at least *two* new characters." Inga kept her voice low, and I understood that she was being careful not to wake Sonia. She shook her fists at me again and then, in a single, distraught motion, gripped her head.

I stood up and walked toward her. When I reached for her hands to take them, she said in a quiet, shaking tone, "Don't, don't touch me. I'll break down."

"Inga," I said.

"There's more." Inga let her hands fall to her sides. Her eyes were blank, and her voice had a detached, unfamiliar quality. As she spoke, her face lost all its color and I saw her sway for an instant. "I've had the lights for a while. I'm dizzy. It's my damned head." She put one hand on her stomach.

After I guided Inga to the sofa, I found her pills, gave her a drink of water, and covered her with a blanket. She said, "She claims that Max is the father of her son."

I didn't respond for a few seconds. Another child, I thought, a son. "Do you think that's true?"

She shrugged her shoulders. We both knew that intense emotion could bring on her migraines, and once she was lying back with her head on a pillow, Inga relaxed into the relief that sometimes only illness can offer. She smiled at me. I've seen it countless times in my patients—that weak hospital smile. We talked on, our voices quiet and our words slow. Inga told me that Edie had been involved with someone else at the time she was seeing Max, so she had doubts about the story. When I asked why Edie had waited all these years to announce the identity of her son's father, Inga said, "She's divorced now. The man's out of her life, and I guess she started thinking about Max." My sister hadn't seen the letters in question. Edie had refused to give her copies, and she had been coy about what was in them. She had hinted, however, that they had some special meaning beyond the fact that Max had written them to her. I reasoned that although the Fehlburger woman might be snooping for a story, it was unlikely that her magazine would fork over the money to buy the letters. Max's papers were in the Berg Collection at the New York Public Library, and I knew that scholars needed permission to visit the archive. Would a private collector be interested in them? I didn't know enough about it. I understood that, for Inga, protecting Sonia was what mattered most. "I can't bear to see her hurt by this," she said.

At around one-thirty, I looked over at my sister under the blue blanket. She had her legs curled up near her chest, and her delicate face looked pale and exhausted. I told her she should go to sleep. She reached out to touch my hand and said, "Not yet, Erik. I want to talk to you a little more, but not about this business. Now that the house is gone, I've been thinking a lot about you and me when we were little. Do you remember how I used to make you play prince and princess?"

"Yes," I said, and began to smile. "I remember I drew the line with you when I hit six or seven. No more Snow White, no more Sleeping Beauty."

Inga smiled back at me. The faint violet-colored shadows under her eyes made them look deeper. "When you were really little, you used to like to be the princess. I'd dress you up like a girl and play the prince."

"I don't remember that."

"You liked to be dead and wake up. You could do it over and over again. Later, you would only play the prince. I loved lying there waiting for the kiss to wake me, pretending you weren't my little brother. I loved opening my eyes and sitting up. I loved miracles." She closed her eyes and then, while they were still closed, she said, "It was erotic. Being stirred to life." She took a breath. "It's been happening to me these days with Henry. I'd almost forgotten that there could be frenzy."

I didn't answer her. The word *frenzy* echoed in my mind for a few seconds and then Inga said, "Maggie Tupy."

"Little Maggie Tupy from down the road. I liked her."

"Do you remember the day we danced in our slips for you? Maggie and I wore them outside in the open air. It was exciting, so close to nakedness, and I felt that I had to pee, but I didn't really. I must have been nine. I remember running and twirling until my head felt all light and I had an ache in my side."

"I kissed her that day." I saw Maggie Tupy with her brown curls, snake grass rising on either side of her. All at once, I had a memory of her bare knees under the smudged white slip. They were stained green with grass, gray with earth, and red with new blood from the shallow abrasions that never healed because the tiny scabs were always reopened. Maggie was squinting at me through one eye, and she had screwed up her mouth so as not to burst out laughing, but I wanted to kiss those tense lips the color of raspberries, and I bent near her, pressing my mouth to hers quickly but emphatically. I had felt a great happiness. "Maggie Tupy," I said aloud.

Inga lay back and closed her eyes. "And then there was the day the birds really ate our breadcrumbs. Do you remember?"

I saw the uneven patches of sunlight on the ground, scattered by the foliage above us as we stood at the top of the steep embankment behind our house that led down to the creek. Then we heard the rush and saw the sudden rising of a flock of starlings in the trees over our heads, and the sound of the creek's moving water became distant as the noise of shuddering wings grew loud and we watched the birds dive for the bread we had left in a long trail below us.

My sister closed her eyes. "It was like magic, wasn't it? As if the story had come true, and the world really had been enchanted."

I took Inga's hand, squeezed it, and after a brief pause I said, "It was."

MY FATHER STARTED college at Martin Luther again, this time with money from the G.I. Bill. He was twenty-four years old. I imagine him sitting beside his friend Don at the choir concert. They are seated in a pew, because I'm guessing that the choir sang in the college chapel. *One of the numbers*, my father wrote, *"O Day Full of Grace," triggered in me a recall of events, pleasant ones at first that led step by step to the horror images of the unnecessary killing of the Japanese officer. To Don's alarm, I began to tremble. I lied and said it was a touch of malaria. This was my only daytime flashback, but I lived in fear that more might come.* I read these sentences to myself many times, trying to penetrate their meaning. "O Day Full of Grace" wasn't listed in the red Lutheran hymnal that found its way into my possession years ago, but I wondered if perhaps somewhere in the text or in the music there was a cue that set off a train of images my father couldn't stop.

Traumatic memory arrives like a blast in the brain.

"I thought we were going to die in the apartment," the young woman told me. "But a policeman found us. He got us out and we started running." She took a breath. "We could hardly see or breathe. It was dark and we walked in this dry choking rain. And then on the ground, I saw a person's hand. The blood was a strange color. I even thought that." She began to breathe harder. "I had to step over it. We were running. I thought we were going to die. But that's what happens to me, mostly at night. It's that feeling of blind running. I'm there again. I wake up with a shock, like I'm exploding, my heart beating. I can't breathe. It's not a dream." Her mouth contorted. "It's the truth." She closed her eyes and began to cry.

That day, we waited for the injured in emergency rooms all over the city, but they never arrived. They came to us later with their wounds of indelible memory, the images that were burned into them and then released again and again in a hormonal surge, the brain flood that accompanies a return to unbearable reality. *O Day Full of Grace.*

The choir sings. A young veteran sits in his pew and listens to the collective voice thanking a beneficent God. Perhaps he remembers a hymn he used to sing in church when he was a child with his father beside him. It is a warm memory. He recalls the low mumbling of prayers in Urland Church as the congregation beseeches the deity for forgiveness, and then there is another vision that imposes itself with brutal suddenness: a man is kneeling in the grass with his hands pressed together. He is praying for his life.

"SOMETIMES," MAGDA SAID, "an analyst can suffer too much with a patient or be so afraid that it strangles the treatment."

I looked at her small, old face, at her white hair neatly cropped to the chin, at her elegant embroidered jacket. With age Magda had become thinner, but her mild eyes and small mouth were exactly as they had always been. "There are obvious reasons to fear patients, patients who stalk you or threaten you and so on, all quite straightforward. I had a patient once who told me his sadistic fantasies in great detail. I was appalled, but not frightened until I began to feel his arousal. I found it intolerable. It took me some time to acknowlege material in myself I had kept safely buried."

"I've tried to do that," I said. "I'm aware that she's touched sadistic elements in me, but there's something hidden, something I can't get to." Inga's words came to me: *I had forgotten there could be frenzy.*

"Years ago, I treated a girl who was admitted to the clinic after she tried to set herself on fire. She was seventeen. Grew up in Dominica. She lived with her mother for a couple of years, and then she was bounced from one relative to another, none of whom kept her very long. When she was nine, a friend of her father's beat and molested her. The man went to prison, and she was shipped off to an aunt here in the city. It went well at first, and then there were scenes, accusations, and fights, physical fights. She ended up in foster care. I interviewed the foster mother. In the beginning, she said, Rosa had been a dream. That was the word the woman used, *dream*—helpful, sweet, affectionate. She wanted the woman to adopt her."

"And then she turned."

Magda nodded. "She fought, screamed, was out of control. She accused the foster father of sexual abuse. I believed her story at first, but then each time she told it, it changed. She didn't seem aware that she had given me other, quite different versions before."

"She was lying."

"Yes, she was lying, *and* she was delusional, genuinely paranoid. After a while, she began to refer to herself almost exclusively in the third person. Rosa wants this. Rosa believes that. He did this and that to Rosa. Rosa doesn't have anything to say."

"What did you make of it? A dissociative symptom?"

"Well, the girl had huge identity problems, but I understood that she had also regressed with me back to a little child who identifies herself in the third person."

"And Ms. L.?"

Magda shook her head. "It depends on what you can tolerate. You said your father has been dead for five months."

I nodded.

"I know how strongly you identify with your father."

I felt defensive. "You think that what's happening with Ms. L. has something to do with my father. How could it?" I spoke too loudly.

Magda's penetrating eyes suddenly reminded me of my mother's, and I wanted to retreat. I admitted this to her. She smiled. "Erik, we all go to pieces with our patients at one time or another. We all go to pieces now and then even without a patient to help us along. Your grief makes you more fragile. You know I've always thought of wholeness and integration as necessary myths. We're fragmented beings who cement ourselves together, but there are always cracks. Living with the cracks is part of being, well, reasonably healthy."

"Were you able to help Rosa?" I asked.

"In the short run. After she was discharged, she was in school and living with yet another family, but when she turned eighteen, she was out of foster care, not in touch with her family, and no one could tell me what had happened to her."

I thought about all the patients I hadn't been able to track down, the ones who just vanished. Then I looked at Magda's cane leaning against her desk and thought, I don't want her to die.

"And what about the patient who bored you to sleep?"

"Oh, Ms. W.," I said. "There have been developments there—good ones."

Magda said, "Hmm." The hum of empathy, I thought to myself.

When I left her office and walked out into the warm May air, I felt restored, despite the fact that I knew little more about my confounding case than when I had walked through her door. Central Park looked green, and for some reason I thought of Laura Capelli. I wondered if I still had her telephone number.

MIRANDA WAS LOCKING her door when Eglantine saw me. "Dr. Erik," she said in an accusatory voice, her hands on her hips, in imitation of a severe grown-up. "Where have you been?" I had expected this to happen, the inevitable chance meeting outside the house or on a nearby street. In fact, I was surprised it had taken so long. As I looked down at the child's upturned face, her brown hair looked soft, and I had a sudden urge to put my fingers on those curls and pat her head, but I resisted it.

Miranda walked toward us, carrying a large bag.

"I've been here," I told Eggy, avoiding Miranda's face. The child hadn't been up to see me either. I wondered if her mother had said no to the visits.

"We're going to the park to draw," Eggy said, as she stood on tiptoe and lifted one leg in front of her, balancing herself with both arms before she let the foot drop. "Want to come along? You can use our paper and crayons and pencils and charcoal and everything."

"I'm afraid I don't have time," I said, hearing the stiffness in my voice.

Miranda stepped toward me, and I looked down at her. Whether the discomfort I felt was revealed in my face, I don't know. Her eyes were calm, steady. "Are you sure you don't want to come?" she said, and then added, "It's a beautiful Sunday."

That afternoon has remained in my memory as a collection of fragments. Lying on my back on the plaid blanket studying the branches, the leaves, and the visible pieces of blue sky above me, an angle of vision I remembered from childhood. Miranda's bare brown legs on the blanket and her shoeless feet with red toenails. Eggy on my lap as she examined my ears, her face close to mine, "They're big. Did you know that? Very big." Miranda's improvised drawing of her daughter in an imaginary wide-brimmed hat and lacy dress. "No, Mommy, I want a long dress down to my ankles! Change it!" The sound of the eraser. Eggy humming. Miranda in sunglasses. The warmth of the sun on my back and a feeling that I could sleep. A red package of raisins in the grass inches from my nose. The clover. Eggy on her stomach, a thin stick in each hand, one slightly longer than the other. "I'm not going to listen to you just because you're big, you gooney prune!" The short stick leaps into the air. "Don't boss me!"

"You have to listen," the long stick utters in a deeper voice.

"No, I don't," sings the little stick. "I'm Power Girl!" Power Girl flies over my head. "I want Dr. Erik to come and see me in my theater class. It's Saturday. Right, Mom? Next time. *The Mitten*," Eggy chimed. "I'm the mitten!"

I felt hopeful. Although Miranda showed no signs of flirtation, gave me no hint that her feelings had changed toward me, I had spent two hours with her body only inches from mine. I had day-dreamed of reaching out and putting my hand on her thigh, of rolling over on that plaid blanket and taking her into my arms. That evening, after speaking to both Inga and my mother on the telephone, I read for a couple of hours in my study. Before I finally turned in, however, I found myself walking to the window. I have since wondered if I heard their low voices in some subliminal way or if I was drawn to look out, as I often am, and the sighting was pure chance, but, from the second-floor window, I saw Miranda and Lane together on the sidewalk in the light of the gas lamp. I saw him reach for her and pull her toward him. For a second or two, she resisted, and then her body gave way and she fell into him. I watched them kiss. I watched them walk toward the house and vanish behind the stoop. For a while, I waited there, hoping to see Lane reemerge, but he didn't appear.

As I lay in bed, I remembered the last couplet of a John Clare poem.

> *Even the dearest that I love the best,*
> *Are strange—nay, stranger than the rest.*

I repeated those lines to myself twice, and then I took the little white pill.

AS SOON AS I saw Burton at the table, I had the impression that something had changed about him. After I sat down, I tried to puzzle out what exactly had created this sense of newness. Was it his posture? Was he less moist? Was he dressing better? My old friend was slumped in his chair, and his broad face was shining with sweat. I noticed that he must have left his bulky undergarment behind, because his shirt was several shades darker under the arms. He had looped an ocher scarf around his neck, but this frayed article served as a mere wave in the direction of dandyism; his worn shirt and trousers were pure Salvation Army. When Burton called me, I had happily accepted the dinner invitation, knowing it would distract me from thoughts about *The Mitten*. I hadn't decided yet whether to attend the play, which had ballooned to dreadful proportions in my mind and come to signify the return of Lane, dubious father and suspicious lover, a man I had seen exactly twice, both times in the dark.

"As I mentioned on the telephone, we would like to recruit you," Burton said over his lasagna. "Well, *recruit*, that's rather too military. These days I avoid all reference to the martial, solicit, encourage your attendance, that is, at our monthly meetings. This meal, the official cause of our get-together, has the extra benefit of making the bill tax deductible, as it were. I use the plural, you understand, we being members of the Institute of Neuropsychoanalysis, the herald of a new day, a rapprochement between disciplines: brain and mind, the old quandary reexamined. First Saturday of every month. The sessions begin at ten sharp. Neuroscience lecture followed by a discussion. Luminaries have lectured, Damasio, LeDoux, Kandel, Panksepp, Solms. We're about twenty, sometimes thirty, I'd say, a contentious cabal of neuroscientists, analysts, psychiatrists, pharmacologists, neurologists, and a couple of AI and robotics fellows thrown in as well. I'm the only historian. Met a fellow there, David Pincus, doing brain research on empathy. Terribly, terribly interesting. Mirror neurons, you know." Burton took a deep breath and swiped his forehead with his handkerchief, a gesture that somehow resulted in the transfer of tomato sauce into the rather long hairs of his right eyebrow and left me in the awkward position of wondering whether I should point this out to him or not. His embarrassment would be extreme either way. While my gaze was fixed on the sauce, Burton gave me a not-so-brief elucidation of an example of the connections in question. Freud's 1895 idea of *Nachträglichkeit*, he said, was remarkably similar to the far more recent notion of *reconsolidation* in neuroscience. Our memories are forever being altered by the present—memory isn't stable, but mutable. When he paused, I told him as gently as I could that he had managed to get a small part of his dinner onto an eyebrow. Flushing deeply, he began to rub blindly but vigorously at the soiled hairs until I confirmed that the area was food-free. Then he went silent and eyed his plate. A couple of seconds passed before he lifted his chin, opened his mouth as if to speak, but no words came. After he had repeated this pantomime, I said, "Burton, what's on your mind?"

"I'm somewhat anxious about revealing this," he said. "It's in reference to Inga."

"Yes?" As I looked at Burton across the table, he suddenly reminded me of a walrus. It may have been the bags under his eyes, which accentuated his already forlorn expression, but the image led me to think idly of Lewis Carroll's Walrus and Carpenter as I waited for him to muster his courage to continue. "'The time has come,' the Walrus said, 'to talk of many things.'" Here we are, I thought, the squat, wet Walrus and the high and dry Carpenter, an absurd pair: cabbages and kings.

"I think I should warn you, well, alert you to the fact that there may be some unsavory, yes, unpalatable, even disreputable aspects to what I intend to divulge." Burton sighed, rubbed his streaming face all over, and plunged ahead. "It has to do with, revolves around, yes, that's better, around, around"—Burton's chin shook—"Henry Morris."

"Henry Morris, Inga's friend?"

He nodded, then gazed fixedly at the table. "I, uh, I've been keeping a watch on Inga."

"What?" I said loudly.

Burton waved his palms at me, a sign to keep my voice down. Then he muttered, "Been maintaining a degree of vigilance on her behalf."

"Inga asked you to be vigilant about something?"

"No," he said. "No, I wouldn't put it that way."

"What way would you put it?"

"After the, the incident in the park and the dinner party, so very pleasant, wasn't it? Well, I took it upon myself to, well, keep an eye on things."

I leaned forward. "*Things.* My God, Burton. You're not saying that you've been following Inga and Morris. What's gotten into you?"

I knew perfectly well what had gotten into Burton. Love. He confessed as much, employing every word but that one to make me understand that his spying was somehow made legitimate by the strength of his feeling for my sister. Besotted, Burton had given up whole days to trailing Inga and then Morris "for her protection."

"I believe," Burton said, "Morris is trafficking in private stories."

"What does that mean?"

"I saw him with the woman in the park," Burton said darkly. "The same person I saw with Inga. I overheard them talking about *letters.*"

Burton picked up his napkin instead of his handkerchief and began to dry his face with fierce strokes. "Her name is Edie Bly. She was in Max Blaustein's film. Pardon the expression, but I think those two are in cahoots."

"Didn't Morris recognize you? He was at the dinner, after all. How on earth did you get close enough to hear their conversation?"

Burton's forehead was dripping again. He used both his napkin and handkerchief to pat himself down, and then in a hoarse whisper croaked out a single emphatic word: "*Disguise.*"

It turned out that, even incognito, Burton hadn't been all that close to the two of them, who had met in a restaurant in the Village and had been talking together in low voices, but he believed that he had distinctly heard the word "letters" uttered by Morris a couple of times. At one point during the conversation, Edie Bly had begun to weep loudly and then at some later moment had mentioned her AA meetings and had brought up the name Joel. She had drunk three espressos during the talk and lit up a cigarette on the street as soon as they walked out the door.

I gave Burton the speech he was expecting: intrusions like his could lead to unhappiness for most of the people involved; amateur sleuthing might take him to places he didn't really want to go; and perhaps he, too, was "trafficking in private stories" by trailing people without their knowledge. Although he understood me perfectly and acknowledged as much, Burton had come to regard his surreptitious activities through the lens of chivalry. He was on a mission for his Lady. According to that code, it mattered little whether the Lady wanted him or not. He was acting in her name.

Since it was obvious that Burton hadn't spoken to Inga, I asked him what he expected me to do with this information, which was sketchy at best.

"Why," he said with surprising directness, "whatever you like. I trust you."

When our coffee arrived, Burton asked me how Miranda was and said that he had found her "lovely, interesting," and after several qualifications, arrived at the word "alluring."

"Me, too," I said to him. "But I'm afraid she has no romantic interest in me whatsoever."

Burton looked me in the eyes, reached across the small table, and clapped his damp hand on top of mine before he hastily withdrew it.

"IT'S A QUESTION of censorship," Ms. W. remarked in her brittle voice. "Maisie says anything that pops into her head, sometimes silly, stupid things, but I see that people listen to her. She smiles and nods and laughs all the time. I stop before I speak and deliberate, but I can tell people find me boring, even though what I'm saying is far more intelligent."

"Conversation isn't just words. It's often a way of playing freely with another person," I said. "You stop yourself before you can play."

Ms. W.'s hands were folded in her lap. She didn't speak for several seconds. "A barrier," she said in a soft voice. "A fence in front of the playground." She crossed her legs, and I felt a rush of sexual feeling I had never felt for her before. Ms. W. was in her fifties, rather heavy, and had never attracted me. What had happened?

"One you remember?" I said.

"I don't know. I've told you that I've forgotten so much— hardly anything is there, in childhood, I mean, that's particular." She looked tired all of a sudden.

"I think perhaps you were playing just now, with me. When you mentioned the fence, I felt alive with you, interested, personally involved."

Ms. W. blinked. A small smile lifted her mouth at its corners for an instant, then it vanished, and I thought she might be falling asleep. She closed her eyes. I watched her breathe. For some reason, I thought about my father in the yard, sawing boards. Then an image of a barbed-wire fence came to my mind.

When she opened her eyes, she said, "I'm exhausted."

"Sleep keeps you from me in the playground, which is frightening. I'm dangerous right now."

"I'm curious about what you say; it seems that there's something in it, and yet I get confused and then sleepy."

"Do you remember you told me that you didn't like your father to help you with your homework when you were in high school?"

"He would get too involved."

"You're using the word I used earlier, *involved*. Maybe today I'm taking the part of your father."

She squinted. "It's also that my mother didn't like it. She would always come into the room."

"She was anxious?"

I watched as Ms. W. pressed her fingers to her mouth.

"Both you and your mother felt uncomfortable about your father's involvement?"

"He stopped hugging me," she said, with her eyes closed, her voice cool. "He never hugged me after the seventh grade. He stopped."

"I think," I said, "that your father was protecting you." I paused, then added, "From his feelings. You were growing up. There was an attraction, and he put up a fence."

As she looked at me, I felt an incalculable sadness for all of us. Although her expression remained the same, I saw that her eyes were wet. Then the tears ran down her cheeks in two thin streams. She didn't hunch over or lift a hand to wipe the tears away. She remained perfectly still, as inert as a statue of the Virgin that suddenly begins to weep in the town square.

IN A LOW voice over the telephone, Inga said, "Burton was sure, sure it was Edie?"

"Yes. Do you understand what's going on?" I asked her.

"No," she said slowly. "Henry didn't mention seeing her for his book."

"How would he even know about the letters?"

"I told him," Inga said, her voice rising. "I *told* him. The question is why he didn't tell me he'd gone to see her."

"Maybe he went to her to try to protect you," I said, "to reason with her."

"He said the smart thing was to let it go, that it was possible there were no letters at all, since I'd never seen them. As for her son, he said, short of a DNA test, paternity couldn't be proved, and they would need Sonia for that. Literary scandals come and go. There's a brief moment of titillation, and then it's over. The work is what matters, except in cases of suicide young, then the suicide colors everything. . . ."

"It sounds rather callous to me," I said. "He's talking about your life, after all."

"It is," she said. "But detachment can be comforting." Inga fell silent.

"Are you okay?" I asked.

"No."

"I don't think you should jump to any conclusions, Inga."

"Erik?"

"Yes."

"I've been happy. I've felt young again after years of feeling old. You know that excitement you get, and it's hard to eat. You keep thinking about the person, lusting after him, hoping that he really likes you . . ."

"I know," I said.

"I'm afraid it's about Max."

"What do you mean?"

"Well, Henry really loves his work. It's terribly important to him. We have that in common, and it's been a pleasure talking to him about it."

"And?"

"What if being close to me is more about Max than it is about me? Sleeping with the widow, you see what I mean?"

I did, and the thought distressed me. "You'll have to talk to him."

"Yes," she said, and I heard a small gasp of anguish in her voice.

Before she hung up, she said, "It's strange, isn't it, that Burton just happened to see the two of them in that restaurant, but I guess those things happen."

"All the time," I said. "They happen all the time."

FOR A FEW years after the war, veterans inundated the campus of Martin Luther College. War-tough, hard-drinking, often scarred, and years older than the boys and girls who arrived straight from Midwestern farms and cities to embark on their educations, the ex-soldiers took the place by storm. I distinctly remember my father laughing as he told me a story about a night with the boys. A fellow vet, who later became a physics professor, rigged up a pulley system in the rafters of an attic that had been converted into a dormitory for the new breed of students. Bottle of whiskey in one hand, the future author of *Contemporary Debates in Science and Religion* sailed over his comrades' heads bellowing like Tarzan. The campus was dry. It's still dry, but my guess is that the administration feigned blindness when it came to the alcoholic high jinks of its returning heroes. Poker games proliferated, and no doubt more than a few townie broads were smuggled in for midnight trysts.

Throughout the memoir, my father refers to himself as "a plodder." *For me, clarity about things came only after much effort and even then I had little sense of arrival. I became a repository for facts, details, and trivia. I like to believe that slower learners like myself can make reliable teachers. We understand the ordeals of learning. My own struggles, the difficult moments I would rather have been spared, became useful to me later as a teacher and student advisor.* And yet, my father joined an informal seminar of five or six vets, who read everything from Augustine's *Confessions* to Mailer's *The Naked and the Dead*. He gained a reputation as a wit, was an excellent student, won prizes, was admitted to the honor society, and received a Fulbright grant after graduation. Plodding evokes a man trudging forward in heavy boots. Earthbound. There are weights in us that other people never see.

I saw Marit with increasing frequency, my father wrote. The year was 1950, and his Fulbright had taken him to Norway. *An incident stands out. On one of our dates, Marit wore a shaggy pink sweater that shed like a collie in spring. I must have held her close when we said goodnight, because on the following morning, I discovered that my jacket was all but pink from clinging fibers. During the half hour or so it took me to remove these strands, one by one, there welled up in me an overpowering feeling of tenderness, the kind that swallows you whole and turns you into mush. If I were told that I could only save one memory from my life and all others would have to go, I would choose this one, not so much out of romantic nostalgia, but because the event marked a seminal moment in my life. It pointed forward to our marriage, to the two children we would have together, to the home we founded, and to the joys and sorrows we later shared.*

I imagine my father in a small room, sitting on a chair or the edge of a bed with the jacket on his lap. As he takes the fibers of what was probably angora between his thumb and index finger and flicks them into a wastebasket or gathers them into a ball to discard later, he understands that he is in love. It doesn't happen while he is looking at the young woman or kissing her, or even as he lies on that same bed thinking about her after the evening is over. It happens the following morning when he discovers that her sweater has mingled with his coat. Together, the garments become the vehicle in a metaphor I suspect my father felt only subliminally. Hidden behind the "all but pink" overcoat is the promise of two passionate bodies, one inside the other. As an old man he will remember the intensity of his feeling and understand that a turn was made in that moment. I think there were many things my father regretted, rightly or wrongly, but not that half hour spent alone in his room in Oslo with a linty jacket.

BY THE TIME I arrived for Eggy's play, the folding chairs had all been filled and I stood at the back of the room near the door. Before *The Mitten*, I watched *The Maple Leaf*, a production that included six feminine cardboard leaves prancing about the room "fluttering" and "falling," and one badly confused male leaf who continually hissed into what would have been wings if they had been performing on a stage, "Do I do it now? Now?" When the cue came at last from a woman sitting off to the side (long gray hair, wire-rimmed glasses, forehead wrinkled into a permanent expression of concern), the hapless leaf thudded to the floor, his face awash with relief at having completed his theatrical mission. Eggy's play, following the logic of seasonal change, came next. A little blond girl, heavily overdressed for the early June day in a snowsuit, skipped across the stage waving two red mittens in her hands. Then she casually let one of them fall to the floor. I understood that the highly calculated gesture was meant to be an inadvertent one, because a moment later Eggy, in a large red-knit costume that covered her entirely—except for her ankles, her feet, and her intense little face sticking out of a hole—waddled in, placed her sneaker directly on the small mitten to hide it from view, and launched into her soliloquy. With one arm straight out to provide the necessary protuberance of a very large thumb, she faced her audience and began her speech. "Woe to the mitten," she exclaimed in a surprisingly commanding voice. "Woe to the mitten that has lost its mate." She paused and wailed, "Woe! Woe!" Eyes to the ceiling, arm cum thumb beating her breast, Eglantine bemoaned her sorry fate. Her tortured expression shifted to one of ineffable joy when Bundled Blonde reappeared, waving a small version of Eggy herself. Thunderous applause, considerable laughter, and a couple of whistles were then heard from the gathered audience of highly appreciative relatives and friends.

After the winter drama, I watched *The Tulip* and *The Sprinkler*, and located Miranda in the audience near the front. When I identified the back of her head, I felt a flash of excitement, followed instantly by agitation. Why had I come? When the leaves, water drops, tulips, mitten owner, and mitten had taken their final bows and the applause subsided, the room erupted into noisy and chaotic congratulations. Lilliputian thespians squealed, shouted, and ran. I watched Miranda embrace Eggy and was able to pick out the child's grandparents, a corpulent man with pale skin, a scattering of moles on his face, and the grandmother, as tall as her husband, but slender, darker-skinned, and dressed in an elegant tunic of some kind. Some of the others who hugged Eggy must have been Miranda's sisters and their husbands. A baby with wild hair, who I gathered belonged to the family, was happily using the chairs as props to cruise up and down a row. No Lane, however, and his absence made me momentarily glad. Eggy spotted me then. "I told Mom you'd come!"she called out, her mouth stretching into a wide smile. Introductions were made. I noticed that Miranda's father had a strong handshake and her mother's low voice was attractive. The three sisters were not as pretty as Miranda, to my mind, but all seemed affable. Although we had exchanged polite, easy kisses before, that afternoon I shook Miranda's hand good-bye. The presence of her family acted as a mysterious constriction. "You may be raising an actress," I said to her. With Miranda, I inevitably fell into banalities. The more I wished to charm, the more my wits failed me, and the more I regretted my dullness. She smiled graciously, however, and in a near whisper said, "*Ham* might be more accurate."

On the sidewalk, Eggy gave me a casual wave. Miranda smiled, nodded, and turned around. In the heat her skirt, made of some thin material, clung to her buttocks and was caught between her thighs. An instant later, I saw her snatch at the skirt with both hands, and my glimpse of a veiled paradise vanished. I watched as she went with the rest of the Casaubon clan to various vehicles parked somewhere in the neighborhood. They were off to a family dinner. Chilean sea bass had been mentioned, and a cricket game on cable television. As I watched them leave, I suffered a feeling of exile, and when I turned away, I realized I didn't want to go home, so I made my way to the park. As I walked, I remembered sitting on the bench game after game, remembered finally getting my chance, rushing onto the court and being so rattled I gave up the ball. I remembered my parents' sympathetic faces, the cold taunts of my teammates, the heat of humiliation. I thought of that asshole Kornblum's attack on my paper at the Brain and Mind Conference, his refusal to engage me, his patient, condescending tone as he pointed out my "errors." I remembered Genie telling me she couldn't stand the sight of my body anymore. "I'm fucking Allan. It's time you knew. Everyone else does." I walked fast and hard, first on the road and then on paths into the woods, my fury and bitterness rising with every step. It wasn't until I had walked for an hour that I thought of my father and his fugues. *I know how strongly you identify with your father.* My step slowed then. I changed direction. My anger turned into dull misery. When I returned to Garfield Place, I opened my notebook and began to write. I wrote for close to an hour, moving from subject to subject. The last thing I recorded was a memory I hadn't thought about for a long time.

I'm back on the farm and it's summer. Inga and I are in the crawl space above the garage. I don't think we'd ever been up there before, nor did we ever go again. Just that once. Light is coming from somewhere. A small window, its glass opaque with mire. We find an old trunk covered with a thick layer of dust the color of charcoal. I pull open the leather straps, then the lid. Inside is a brown jacket made of stiff, heavy cloth. It feels rough against my fingers. I lift it up and first see the stripes on the sleeve, then the medals pinned to its front. I know it's my father's uniform from the war, and I feel a quiver of pride. We climb down with the treasure and run past the grape arbor and the apple trees with the jacket between us, each holding the end of an empty sleeve as if it were a headless companion. We yell for our father. "Look what we've found! Look, Pappa, look!" And then our father is standing in front of us. I lift my eyes to his face and am startled to see that he's angry.

"Put it back," he barks at us. "Right now!"

"But the medals," I managed to say. "What about the medals?"

But there is no familiar softening in the face, no tender smile. This is another father. He repeats the order, and we walk back to the garage. *O Day Full of Grace.*

THAT WEDNESDAY WHEN I left the office, my head was full of patients. Ms. L. had been more talkative. "Some days, it's like I don't have any skin. I'm all raw and bleeding." This comment had helped me. I had talked to her about following a metaphor. No skin, no barrier, no protection. The borders are important. I mentioned the rag doll, too, as a good metaphor for her mother's neglect. "She couldn't recognize you as a whole separate person with needs and desires of your own, someone with a real inside." Ms. L. had wanted to hug me at the end of the session, but I said it wasn't a good idea, and after she had delivered a few barbs about the stupid rules of therapy, she aquiesced. I was thinking, too, of the eight-year-old boy I had interviewed that day. He had not spoken to any adults except his mother and father for two years. Although he did his homework, he never answered his teachers or any grown-up friends of the family. He didn't speak to me, either. He shook his head, nodded, grinned, or glowered, his mouth clamped tightly shut. When I asked him to draw a self-portrait, he etched a tiny figure in the corner of the page with a straight line for a mouth crossed by short ragged strokes of the crayon that reminded me of barbed wire. I was thinking about that mouth when I heard a voice behind me. "Hey, Dr. Davidsen."

I turned around and was startled to see Jeffrey Lane standing behind me on the sidewalk. A combination of surprise and alarm caused me to freeze for an instant in silence. Then, in a cold voice, I said, "We've met."

He smiled, and I noticed that he was handsome. His black hair had been cut so that it stuck out in little spikes, a sign of the af-fected nonchalance the fashionable have and probably always have had in one form or another. He had a narrow face and clear tanned skin, and his teeth as he smiled at me had a gleaming bleached quality that reminded me of people on television. His arms, ex-posed by his gray T-shirt, had seen many hours in a gym. Looking at him made me feel huge and puny at once. "Sorry about that," he said. "You left your fly open, so to speak. The temptation was too strong."

"Is there something you have to say?" I asked.

"Yes." He nodded. "There is. I want to invite you to my show. *Family* photographs. That's the theme. It should be interesting material for a shrink. DID. That's an acronym you throw around, isn't it? Dissociative identity disorder, used to be multiple personality. My pictures are DID. It's not for some time yet, but I wanted to make sure you put it down in your calendar, so you don't miss it. November eighth at the Minot Gallery on West Twenty-fifth Street."

I said nothing for a second and then, "It's June."

"I know, but guys like you are busy, right?"

I stared at him.

Lane tilted his head to one side. "I'm not kidding. I really want you to come. I apologize for scaring you that night. Really and truly, I didn't mean to. I thought I could get in and see her." He paused. "She's my kid." After another second, he reiterated, "She's *my* kid."

"There are other ways of seeing one's child besides breaking into people's houses in the middle of the night," I said. Every word I uttered sounded alien, as if someone else were speaking.

"Not then there wasn't." Lane seemed earnest now. He had completely dropped his bantering tone, and it threw me off guard. Before I knew it, he had grabbed my arm. "I want you to talk to Miranda," he said, gripping my shirtsleeve. "She admires you. She'll listen to you."

"Talk to her about what?" I asked, shaking my arm loose.

"About me, my rights. My life depends on it."

"I can recommend a family therapist. A mediator."

Lane groaned. "Come on," he said. "You don't have to play Mr. Expert here. I've seen you with her. I've photographed you, man. You're an open book." He stopped for a moment to collect his thoughts. "How do you think it feels to watch another man hanging out with my kid?" I noticed that Lane had rolled up onto his toes and then back onto his heels a couple of times as he spoke.

I felt my fist grip my briefcase more tightly. "That's for you to take up with her." An image of the two of them on the sidewalk pulsed through my head.

"You like black girls? Pretty exotic, huh, for a white-bread guy like you? You're not really her type, though, sorry to say, a little on the tame side." He drawled the word *tame* and rolled up on his toes again. "She's a real banshee in bed." He smiled. "And I say that as a one-eighth Native American."

My feeling of disgust during his first two sentences was followed by a burst of rage at the third, and before I knew it, I had lifted my right hand, briefcase and all, in a gesture of threat.

Lane laughed. I lowered my arm, my face hot. I turned and began to stride toward the subway thinking, I wish I had decked him. I wish I had decked him.

THE GROUND WAS frozen solid when my father died, so we waited to bury his ashes until my planned vacation in June, when I could stay for a while with my mother, Inga, and Sonia. All my patients had been notified well in advance. For a few of them, my absences were harrowing. As we drove south on 35W from the Minneapolis airport, I looked at the green fields on either side of me and thought, by August they'll be turning yellow. The sun will scorch this landscape of corn and alfalfa fields. It happens every year, and then I imagined the snow—the white world of my childhood winters. Sonia slept in the back seat. I could see her face in the rearview mirror, soft and childlike in her nap. Inga leaned back in the passenger's seat beside me, her eyes closed. She had learned to drive at the age of thirty-six but rarely took the wheel. Too nervous in traffic, she explained, and therefore too slow. I like driving. The vibration of the tires moving under me brought memories of early freedom, the days when, with a new license in my pocket, I'd take the back roads to nowhere, cruising aimlessly until I started worrying about the gas I was wasting. Some sadness accompanied this vague reminiscence. I wasn't recalling a particular drive but dozens of them from my adolescence, and I suppose the longing and pathos of that time mingled with the release and pleasure I had found in my junk Chevy, bought for two hundred dollars, which I had earned at the Red Owl carrying groceries one long, sweltering summer. Old places fire the internal weather of our pasts. The mild winds, aching calms, and hard storms of forgotten emotions return to us when we return to the spots where they happened.

As I drove, I realized that the countryside beyond the windshield belonged to my father more than to me. He never really left it, couldn't leave it. It wasn't my mother's landscape. She adopted a small part of what was there, the creek behind our house, the woods with its stones and moss and underbrush, and the bloodroot, bluebells, and violets that came up in the wet earth every spring. All this became intimate, but the fields with their endless rows that met the horizon under an immense sky held no real meaning for her. How does one love so much blankness?

I'm not sure why I remembered the story at that moment. It might have been an awareness of my mother's estrangement when she left the ship and for a few moments looked at a person she didn't know, but the old man came to mind. I was sitting on the floor not far from the wood stove, looking up at his brown, wrinkled face with its prominent white stubble from cheek to chin. He was telling a story slowly in a telegraphic style, not to me but to the adults who were sitting in the room. I've lost a clear picture of who was there. "Couldn't take no more was what they said. Went out of her mind two days after the funeral. Didn't believe Hans was Hans."

"What are you thinking about, Erik?" My sister's voice broke this reverie.

"A story about a woman out here in the country, the grandmother or great-aunt of one of the neighbors. I think it was Hiram

Flekkestad who told it that day. I couldn't have been more than ten, but I've thought about it for years. When I asked Grandma about it, she explained that the woman broke down after she buried her third baby. She thought her husband wasn't her husband, that he looked exactly like him but wasn't him, that she was living with an imposter. In medical school, I discovered that it had a name—Capgras's syndrome."

Inga shook her head. "I never knew such a thing existed." She took a breath. "You'd think I'd remember that story, but I don't."

"It's probably a disconnection between the neural circuits for face recognition and the ones for emotion, so people recognize family members but don't have the feeling about them they used to. They can't make sense of what's missing and explain it by saying the people are fakes."

My sister squinted as she looked straight ahead. "If I didn't feel what I feel when I saw you, you'd be someone else. It would be horrible. It would mean that I'd lost the memory of loving you."

"That's it exactly," I said, and then, as we turned off the highway and took the road into town, Inga looked to her right through the window and said, "It's all so familiar, it's strange."

THE ANDREWS HOUSE had once been a hotel for men only. Its residents had remained largely unseen by the general population, but when they did appear on Division Street during my boyhood, they had seemed oddly interchangeable: unshaven, shuffling old geezers with stained pants and farmer hats that hid their vacant eyes. The building had since been renovated in a style that Inga called "Midwestern Tchotchke," a décor that included silk flowers in crockery, embroidered pillows, liberal use of doilies, and paintings of wide-eyed children in nineteenth-century garb hugging dogs. As I sat down on the canopy bed in my room and stared at the flowered bedspread, I felt a sudden wave of dizziness. I lowered my head and waited for it to pass.

"Oh my God, Uncle Erik!" Sonia was standing in the door. She threw her head back and laughed, her eyes bright with hilarity. "You think you're going to fit in that bed?"

Inga appeared beside her, glanced at the bed, and frowned. "Poor Erik, your feet will stick out."

Buoyed by sleep, Sonia danced across the room. She rolled her hips and waved her hands above her head, gestures that reminded me of a dancer in old Hollywood's faux version of the exotic. As I watched her, still recovering from my wooziness, Sonia laughed again, stopped in front of the small window, and, with her nose against the pane, peered down on Division Street. "You know, I can't believe you actually grew up here," she said in an awed voice. Then she turned around to face us. "I mean, what did you *do*?"

That was how our two weeks in Minnesota began, but my thoughts were back in New York. I had told Miranda about Lane's appearance outside the hospital and that he had wanted me to intervene on Eggy's behalf. With some awkwardness, I also managed to blurt out that I had found his manner "alienating." Alienating? It had been despicable. But I knew that under my inhibition was a reluctance even to paraphrase his racial comments. Lane seemed to believe that by citing his fraction of nonwhite blood, he gained some right to speak that I didn't have. He had also borrowed a racist notion to humiliate me, namely that "people of color" were sexually more potent than white-bread types like me, and I had risen to the bait. I remembered a story Magda once told me about Horace Cayton, a black sociologist, who had been in analysis with Helen V. McLean in Chicago. He had chosen McLean because she was a woman and because she had a withered arm, qualities that would help her understand his "handicap." After five years of analysis, Cayton, who had struggled with the idea of race as a rationalization or excuse for personal inadequacy, came to feel instead that it had penetrated his very core. Pernicious ideas can become us. As I thought it over, I began to feel that I should have told Miranda everything Lane had said, that my withholding wasn't only about protecting her but about my own cowardice, a quality that ironically supported Lane's accusation that I was too "tame" for her.

Some days after *The Mitten*, but before I spoke to Miranda, Eggy had been reunited with her father. Miranda said that at first her daughter had whispered, "That's not him," and fell silent. After he left, however, she had leapt around the room beating the air with her jump rope like an avenging Fury and had refused to go to bed. Eggy had no doubt expected someone else, the flying paternal creature of her drawing or the person stuck in a box, but not the man who came to the apartment. Miranda told me that Eggy had bad dreams, and more nights than not she would come crawling into her mother's bed. "Maybe you could talk to her," she had said, "as a doctor." A dry feeling had come over me then—a sense of remoteness and renewed melancholy. "I can't do that, but I can recommend someone I know." Miranda's inner life was far more tumultuous than I had imagined, and the morass of emotions she obviously felt for Lane had leaked into Eggy, who had to struggle with the belated appearance of a real, not imaginary father. And yet, I didn't want to be their psychiatrist in residence. Twelve hundred miles from New York City, I continued to dream of Miranda. I imagined her mouth opening to mine, saw her naked body lying on my bed, and made furious love to her phantom double every night. The real Miranda was someone else. Before we said goodbye, I wrote down the names of two colleagues, both of whom worked in family therapy. As I handed the paper to her, I knew that I might as well have put on my white coat. She took the card between her long fingers and, without saying a word, looked me in the eyes. I saw more pain in her face than I had ever seen before.

"I KNEW," MY mother said, "because I heard the nurses talking in the hallway outside my room. I heard them say, 'The foreign girl's baby is in trouble.'"

"They called you the *foreign* girl?" Sonia said. "I thought this town was full of Norwegians."

"Not real Norwegians," I said. "They don't speak the language anymore. They're not foreigners."

"Still," Sonia insisted. "You'd think they could have called her the Norwegian girl. Can you imagine anybody in New York saying something like that?"

"In New York City," I said, "almost half the population was born in another country. You'd have to call every other person a foreigner."

"I thought I was going to lose you," my mother said to Inga. After a moment of silence, she continued, "Lars just shut off while we waited to find out if you would live or die."

My mother's idioms sometimes wandered. Did we say *shut off* in English?

"He couldn't really do much for me, or even talk about it. It was like he disappeared." I watched my mother's neck move slightly as she swallowed.

The story of Inga's birth and near demise had come up around ten o'clock that first evening as we sat in my mother's apartment and talked. Not long before we left for the hotel, Inga brought up Lisa and the note. She did it casually, as if she hadn't been keeping it to herself for months. She told my mother that through Rosalie she had discovered that Walter Odland had moved to a nursing home and that we planned to talk to him there. Rosalie Geister was one of Inga's oldest friends. Her family had run the funeral home in town for three generations, and she was now director of the business. Her mother came from Blue Wing, and she had promised to help look into the story of Lisa.

My mother shook her head. "I don't know anything about it. There were several suicides out there. Maybe that's what this girl wanted to hide. The truth is they talked a lot about this person and that one, as if I should know which neighbor was which, but mostly I didn't. Sometimes their words blew right through my ears. They were very good to me, your grandmother and grandfather, but it was a closed circle. Lars was different when he was with his family. It was as if he went back in time, the way he talked. Even his manners changed."

"When you met, Mamma," Inga said, "did Pappa tell you about his family and the lost farm, about the Depression, their poverty?"

Even before my mother spoke, I knew the answer by looking at her face. The handsome, articulate young American Marit Nodeland met at the University of Oslo after the war hadn't told her much about the farm in Goodhue County, Minnesota, or much about his childhood, and what he had told her didn't emphasize its sorrows.

After we said good night to my mother, we walked down the silent corridor of the retirement center. A lone woman with a walker moved steadily toward us. When we passed, she smiled and nodded. "Davidsen children, aren't you?" We agreed that we were, and then I suddenly remembered my father sitting on the edge of my bed, his fingers gently pressed against my forehead and the lilt in his softly accented voice, "Morning, my boy. It's morning."

AS A WARM wind blew through the window of Inga's fussy but comfortable room in the Andrews House, she told me the story of

Edie Bly. After *Into the Blue*, the film roles Edie had hoped for didn't materialize, but she was still young and promising and had whirled around the city's nightspots in a toxic haze of legal and illegal drugs, juggling lovers, losing friends, and making hundreds of acquaintances. Edie told Inga that she had been a "little fool," but at the time she had loved her power, loved men's eyes on her, loved the kick of it all. This was when she "carried on" with Max, meeting him on the fly for sex in hallways, in elevators, on rooftops, but their affair hadn't been without its troubles. Max had put up with a lot, Edie said. She ditched him at the last minute, called him for money at his studio, and told him endless sob stories to excuse her drinking and drugging. My brother-in-law had scolded her about her habits, which shows that there are degrees in all things. After a year, fed up and bored with her aging lover, Edie cut their tie and moved in with a jazz guitarist in his late twenties. Her personal revolution arrived the day she woke up on the floor outside his apartment lying in her own vomit and later that week discovered she was two months pregnant. With help from "Mr. Jazz" and her parents in Cleveland, she had gone off to High Watch Farm for her twelve steps, where she found, not God exactly, but some version thereof, a miasmic "higher purpose." Imbued with new spiritual courage, she had allowed the baby to grow inside her until he emerged seven months later as a person named Joel.

When I asked Inga how Edie could be sure Max was the father, she said, "She insists that the dates are right, that the month it happened there was only one man in her life, Max." When I said, "What about Mr. Jazz?" Inga replied, "Edie says they weren't lovers until later." I told her that it seemed unlikely. Ms. Bly probably had found a story to sell, perhaps even to herself, one which had definite financial advantages.

"The funny thing is," Inga said, "I kind of like her, even though she's shaky. Makes me feel like a goddamned rock, which is something new. She touts that half-baked, naïve, shiny American brand of mysticism, you know, Far East via California and Hallmark. Max hated that stuff. She told me she tried to read *one* of Max's books, but it confused her. Don't you find that odd? She has a love affair with this man who she claims is the father of her son and then doesn't even read his books? She's still very pretty, but kind of worn looking. And yet, she has something in her, some light, some charm. She works in a real estate office and goes to AA meetings every day. I knew that I had to find out about her, that I had to keep seeing her for my own sake, to try and understand it, and in a way, it's worked. In the last month, I've lost my rage. There's too much pathos in her, and to be frank, she's too ordinary. I can't imagine Max wanting that for very long. On the other hand, it's worse now, too, feeling sympathy for her and for Max. I keep remembering those months when he would leave for *appointments*. Of course it was Edie. The times when he came home late and would just roll into bed and fall asleep or sit up with a whiskey, his eyes all shrouded. I'd sometimes ask him what was wrong, and he wouldn't say. I keep thinking of one night when I heard him come home, then found him on the sofa with a drink. I just put my hand on his shoulder and said, 'Tell me, darling, tell me.' He grabbed my hand and squeezed it, then shook his head, and for a second I saw his eyes fill with tears." Inga put the back of her hand to her mouth and pressed it against her lips. "Anyway," she continued, "sitting there in her little apartment in Queens, I had the strangest sense of unreality. I kept thinking that the story was so curious, so immaterial. A part of me doesn't really believe that Max loved her. The other part knows he did and feels sick—a mucky combination of shame and hurt. And then there's Joel."

"Does he . . ."

"He could be Max's, but there's no glaring resemblance. I

found myself studying the poor kid for signs. But if he really is Max's . . ."

"What's he like?"

"A little shy and remote."

"How old?"

"Nine."

"And the letters?"

"I've offered to buy them."

"So they exist."

"She showed them to me—or rather, the envelopes. It's Max's writing. There are seven of them, and even though she was straight with me and hard on herself when she talked about the affair, there's something she isn't telling me. I can feel it."

"How?"

"She's stepping around something, but I don't know what it is."

"Do you think it's in the letters?"

"I don't know."

"What would you do with the letters if you had them?"

"When I was really angry, I was going to burn them, but if she lets me have them, I'll wait until we're all dead, then they can go with his papers. I'm afraid to read them."

"It would be hard not to," I said. "And Henry?" I added gently.

"He wanted to know if there was anything in the letters that would contribute to his book and decided to ask her directly. He didn't really expect her to tell him but thought it was worth a try. He kept it from me so I wouldn't be hurt. He knew it was a sensitive subject. While Henry was explaining his reasons for seeing Edie, I believed him. Afterward, though, I began to have doubts." Inga closed her eyes. "The explanation makes sense. I just think it may be more complicated. . . ." Opening her eyes, she said, "You know, he never refers to his ex-wife by her name."

"What does he call her?"

"The Ogress, the Harpy, the Succubus."

"Pretty hostile."

Inga nodded and adjusted her position on the bed. I felt light-headed again and leaned back in my chair. From outside, we heard a train whistle and the rumble of wheels. *The Great Northern.* I remembered the words inscribed on the freight cars as they rumbled through town. From her expression, I could tell that Inga was listening, too. "I miss my father," Inga said. "I miss Pappa."

"Tomorrow," I said, "we're going to bury him. We're going to bury his ashes."

THAT NIGHT, I woke with a fever and the dim sensation that I had been working to pry open a huge metal box with my fingernails, a troubling dream-remnant that infected the unfamiliar, darkened room. A couple of seconds lapsed before I understood where I was. Then I hauled my aching body to the bathroom, downed a couple of Tylenol, and gulped lukewarm water from the tap. For a while I shivered in the too-short bed, and then, somewhere between full wakefulness and sleep, I listened to my own internal voice as if it didn't quite belong to me anymore and watched the metamorphosis of colors and forms in that strange theater behind my closed eyelids. The hallucinatory content of the next hour was probably caused by a combination of the virus or infection inside me and the fact that I had been rereading parts of my father's memoir before going to bed. I dozed, then woke, then, nearly asleep again, I saw an amputee clomping down a long corridor on his stumps. The image forced me awake and I sat up in bed, my heart beating, the dwarfed figure burning in my mind. As my fear subsided, I understood that I had seen some half-conscious version of my grandfather's brother, David, the family's oldest son, born after Ingeborg, the dead baby girl my grandfather said had been buried in a cigar box.

After leaving the farm in 1917, David wandered west and made his way to Washington State, where he somehow managed to fall under a railroad car and sever his legs. Nobody knew how the accident had happened. He wrote asking for money, and my grandmother sent her inheritance, or part of it. Twelve hundred dollars? Yes, it was at least that, a loan to buy prosthetic limbs. It was never repaid. The rest of her money disappeared in the thirties when the bank went under. I closed my eyes and felt my thoughts move elsewhere. A memory from years before: my patient Mr. J., rolling up his trouser leg to show me the prosthesis. "What woman could take this?" I thought about carrying Dum's leg to the sink, about limbs discarded in hospitals, about field hospitals. In Iraq now, I thought. The name Job came to mind. "He was Job at the end," my mother had said, "so many things had gone wrong with him." The image of my father at his eightieth birthday party, the man in his wheelchair, attached to a traveling oxygen tank, his bad leg stiffly stretched in front of him, hearing aids in place, his reconstructed nose wrinkling under his glasses as he smiled, surveying his audience before he began to speak. "I read a small ad in the newspaper not so long ago," he said, "that went like this: 'Lost cat. Brown and white, thinning fur, torn left ear, blind in one eye, missing tail, limps on front right foreleg,'" pause, "'answers to the name of Lucky.'" They laugh in the large room, the April light brilliant in the windows. My father goes on with the speech.

David returned to the farm in 1922 with artificial legs, a cane, four inches missing from his former self. I saw the house, the fields. *Forsaken.* The word arrived as if by its own volition. Then *tuberculosis.* I saw the small one-room shanty David built for his dying brother, Olaf, to isolate the contagion. Later, they would add the little structure to the house as a summer kitchen. When I closed my eyes, I saw blood on a towel, not brown and dried but a brilliant red. I shifted under the covers, turned the hot pillow, and wondered if I should get a cold cloth for my head, but the light shining through the door from the bathroom, only steps away, now seemed distant. Too far. David had spent 1926 in the Mineral Springs Sanitarium. Had I ever seen it? A building came to mind. No, I was inventing it. Then David disappeared, left for reasons unknown. I'm so tired, I thought, and began to lose track of the story. I remembered the sound of my father's footsteps, unlike anyone else's; strange that we recognize the rhythm of a person's walk. The noise of the door as it shuts. "You cannot take the path until you become the path itself." My father had jotted this quotation from the Buddha in a notebook. In the morning, Lars had not come back. I saw my mother getting into the car to look for her husband. "Dear Lars. *Kjaere Lars.*" *I'm bruised*, the internal narrator was saying, and I steered myself back to David. There had been a cousin, Andrew Bakkethun, who bumped into David in 1934 in Minneapolis and they spent the evening together. The next day, Andrew had offered to drive David "down home" for a visit, but he said no. Andrew had then carried the news to my grandfather. My father was twelve years old and had no memory of his father's brother. I imagine them in summer, in the little kitchen, seated at the table with the oilcloth over it. Flypaper hangs from the ceiling with tiny black corpses trapped in the yellow glue. It fascinated me, that curling paper. My grandfather listens to Andrew, a vague figure in my fantasy who wears a hat with a brim. The boy Lars is there, too, listening to everything, and he watches his father excuse himself, stand up, walk out of the room into the little addition, and push open the flimsy screen door that bangs shut behind him. *He found some chores that needed to be done in the barn*, my father wrote, *where I suspect he gave private expression to the grief he felt.* We do not cry where others can see us.

In January 1936, an article appeared in a Minneapolis newspaper about the death of a person known as "Dave the Pencil Man."

The family wasn't certain that the Pencil Man was their David, but my grandfather borrowed money to make the trip to Minneapolis. *January 28, 1937. Today is a year ago since Dad was up in the cities to identify uncle David after hearing he was dead.* As I recalled my father's entry in his diary, I began to sweat, and the sheets turned clammy. I lay still for some time, then, feeling more awake, I turned on the small porcelain lamp beside the bed where the memoir lay on the table. *He no longer had his artificial limbs. Instead, he wore a form of elongated shoes. They were custom made, bulky and cumbersome, but sturdy enough to last a lifetime. By inserting his stumps into these, he actually walked on his knees, perhaps with reasonable comfort because they were warmly lined and well padded. He made a living selling pencils in the Minneapolis business district, on the street, and in the lobbies of office buildings. He had a room in a working-man's hotel.*

Dave the Pencil Man Perishes from Cold

For years he has been known simply as "Dave the Pencil Man," the crippled yet cheerful figure who struggled along the sidewalk daily on Washington Avenue. Dave's legs were severed at the knees. They knew how old Dave was when he sang out to a group of his friends, "I'm just eight years older than England's new King Edward." That made him forty-nine. That was just about all the information Morgue Keeper John Anderson had Friday when he set about locating Dave's relatives. Thursday afternoon Dave struggled through the door of the Park Hotel, 24 Washington Avenue South, numbed by cold. He died there. Hotel employees knew him as David Olafsen. There was one penny in his pockets, the sum total of his earthly goods, aside from the few pencils yet unsold.

I read the little article a couple of times, as if I could learn something. The reporter had managed to suffuse my great-uncle with a Dickensian aura, the grotesque but good-natured cripple who hobbles in the street and repeats his signature phrase. And although the writer's confusion about the cause of death was probably an honest mistake, his choice of freezing must have summoned in his readers the heartrending conclusion of Andersen's "The Little Match Girl." David died of heart failure. After washing my face and changing into a dry T-shirt, I scribbled some further notes, and then it came to me: another entry my fifteen-year-old father had made in his diary in 1937: *June third. I plowed and dragged today. King Edward and Mrs. Wallis Simpson.* All inner worlds have their codes. My father hadn't suddenly developed an interest in the doings of English royalty. The distant monarch, who had given up his throne, was bound in a boy's mind to another equally invisible, but far more important figure, one who happened to share a birthday with the king: his vanished uncle, cut off at the knees, the man who dragged himself forward in his specially made shoes on Washington Avenue in Minneapolis as he hawked his pencils to the businessmen who bent over to hand him their pennies, the man who had caused his beloved father to grieve alone that day in the barn.

WE WERE THE only people in the small graveyard beside Urland Church. The weather was cooler than the day before, and a wind ruffled my sister's black skirt as she stood and looked out in the direction of the farm. My mother had brought ivy geraniums to plant after the grave was filled, and she squatted beside them to remove a few brown leaves. Sonia wandered past the stones, reading the names, and Uncle Fredrik stood in his dark suit with his hands in his trouser pockets, looking at that moment as if he were a man in a photograph. Tante Lotte sat in her wheelchair beside him, hunched over in her seat. Her narrow, flaccid face, surrounded by fluffs of white hair, had the confused look that had become familiar to me. The minister and Rosalie, the two officials of our party, hadn't yet arrived. Behind the small figures of my family in their sober attire was the broad vista of corn and soybean fields, the naked strip of road that ran to the horizon, and the woods to my right. No visible water. It was the emptiness that struck me then, and the realization that physically nothing had changed since I was a boy. There were no additional buildings or developments; the traffic was as thin as ever. Two or three cars passed while we waited. The white church with its classic steeple had gained a rather peculiar front entrance, but that was all. In winter, when there was no foliage to obscure it, I would have seen my inheritance: a white farmhouse on twenty acres of land.

After Pastor Lund arrived with Rosalie and the small box that held my father's ashes, we gathered near the deep square hole that had been dug in advance. Lund was a plump man with a bald pate and a vaguely suspicious manner. As he read, he looked over the top of his hymnal at Inga and me a couple of times, as if he were expecting us to object. The pastor had wanted my father's soul. I knew that. He had come to his sickbed with shared immigrant stories, Lutheran dogma, and Holy Communion, no doubt aware that however interested my father was in points of theology, his beliefs ran mostly in a secular direction. There was no fanaticism or intolerance in Lund. Like a long line of Lutheran ministers I had known before him, he was well-meaning if somewhat narrow in his views and comfortable in his faith without being smug. At the same time, it had always impressed me that in the hands of men like Lund, the strange, bloody, and wondrous Christian story inevitably turned rather drab.

When it was time to lower the box into the ground, we realized that we had no means of doing this, no rope or pulley or other contraption. We began to discuss the possibilities. The interruption in the ceremony disturbed Tante Lotte. Dumb since her arrival, she began to ask in a loud voice, croaking with anxiety, "Did you say ashes? But who is it?" When she was told, she shrieked,

"Rubbish! My brother Lars? He's overseas. We had a letter last week." Then her face wrinkled as if she were searching for some lost word; her head dropped forward, and she began to play with the buttons on the front of her cotton dress. It was decided that I, as the tallest member of the family, take the job. I lay on the grass, grabbed the box firmly in my hands while Inga and Sonia held on to my legs, and reached into the hole. The full length of my arms and a good part of my upper body descended into the grave. I remember the sight of my hands clutching the smooth mahogany box, the odor of the dirt, and the pale roots that protruded from the earth walls on either side of me. I let the object fall the final inch. This was my father, I said to myself in awe, my father. And then, still in the hole, I felt afraid.

Except for the rustling branches in the trees to the left of us, there was no noise. Then came the dull sound of dirt hitting the box.

"Forasmuch as it has pleased Almighty God of his great mercy, to take unto himself the soul of our brother; we therefore commit his body to the ground; earth to earth, ashes to ashes, dust to dust."

I've retained a few more images from the day, sun-baked visual fragments of the family: the small clods of dirt on my suit jacket, Inga's swimming blue eyes as she knelt by the grave, the knot in her hair undone by the wind. Sonia's clenched fists as she walked to the car. The silent Fredrik pushing his sister in her chair over the uneven ground as her head bobbed. My slender mother in her brimmed hat kneeling beside the open grave, her hands patting around the geranium roots. The vast indifference of a cloudless sky.

"IT WAS HARD for him that you grew up," my mother said. "When you left home, it was more difficult for him than for me."

We were paging through family albums when she spoke, examining the photographs of my young father and mother. Sonia, bored by our old stories, was enlivened by the snapshots of her baby self and her parents. I watched her trace an image of her father with her index finger as she sat with the book open on her lap. There were pictures of Genie, too, smiling and pretty, the lost family member. The sight of her now seemed unreal. I was married to her, I thought. We were *married*. And as the four of us dredged up old stories, both pedestrian and mythical, I found myself thinking about what Miranda had said, that in our dreams we live a "parallel existence." There had been nothing particularly unusual about this comment, and yet during my trip to Minnesota I was plagued by the thought that I was in a dream, wading forward through heavy air in a distorted landscape. I had a briefcase full of papers on affect and the brain but was unable to read them. My life had suddenly slowed down. Without patients and the constant pressures of a daily routine, I realized that my perception of time had been skewed. Despite the new "developments" on the outskirts of town, filled with towering houses that sat on tiny, nearly naked lots, and the arrival of Mexican workers, which had significantly broadened the selection in the local supermarkets, Blooming Field didn't look much different and remained a catalyst for memories, some explicit, others dim, but these too felt dreamlike and unreliable. The fever that had come and gone in a single night seemed to have left a residue in my head, a vague throb that made me sleepy, and I often found myself dozing. In this curious state, I welcomed the outing to Walter Odland in Blue Wing, whatever might come of it.

My mother's indifference about Lisa and her mysterious letter did not surprise me. My father's early life had overwhelmed him. By becoming a historian of his own immigrant past, he had found a way to return home again and again. Like countless neurologists, psychiatrists, and analysts I know who suffer from the very ailments they hope to cure in others, my father had relieved the raw sore inside him through the work he had chosen. He had archived innumerable diaries, letters, newspaper articles, books, recipes, drawings, note-books, and photographs of a dying world. He had analyzed the orga-nization of parishes, country schools and higher education, immigrant novels, stories, and plays, and the ongoing language de-bates that riddled those communities. His was an illness that besets the intellectual: the indefatigable will to mastery. Chronic and in-curable, it afflicts those who lust after a world that makes sense. My mother had been a champion of my father's work, but the injury that generated it had given her pain, too, not because she had been al-lowed to see it or dress the wound, but because he had kept it care-fully hidden. I knew my mother would listen to the story of Lisa, if we were able to uncover it, but she did not *have* to pursue it. "There are so many things," she said, "that we'll never know."

ROSALIE DROVE. THE navy blue suit and sturdy shoes she had worn to the burial had been replaced by what Midwesterners call slacks, no-iron trousers fashioned from some synthetic material, and a T-shirt embellished with a large mosquito, under which was writ-ten "The Minnesota State Bird." Despite the fact that she wasn't unattractive—short, curly brown hair, a round pleasant face that suited her round pleasant body—Rosalie had little use for the trap-pings of vanity. She was an unperfumed, unmade-up, thoroughly unadorned woman whose vision of the world was aided by a large pair of brown glasses that magnified her eyes. It seemed to me that I had always known Rosalie, and that despite getting older, she had remained remarkably unchanged over the years. The Geisters of the Geister Funeral Home were a prominent family with seven chil-dren, including a pair of twins, and I had sometimes wondered if the Geister fecundity hadn't been a logical response to the lugubrious nature of the family business. Rosalie and Inga had been inseparable in junior high and high school and had remained close friends.

As she drove (very fast, I noticed), she steered with one hand and waved with the other for emphasis. "I don't know if the old guy is compos mentis. The lady from the nursing home would only say he *welcomes* visitors. 'With a few exceptions, all our residents welcome visitors.'" Rosalie imitated the woman's cloying tone. "Worked in a hardware store for years, according to Mom, who has access to a bubbling brook of Blue Wing gossip, rivaled only by the rushing torrents of Blooming Field. Bless her heart. A couple of days with her nose to the ground and good old Mom sniffed out a trail of scandal a mile wide."

Rosalie did not hesitate, I noticed, to shift her metaphors abruptly from bodies of water to dry land.

Sonia removed her earphones. "You're kidding."

"Rosalie is always kidding," Inga said.

"Not entirely," she said to Inga. "Your Lisa Odland, after some years of not-being-in-town no-one-knows-where, became Mrs. Kavacek. Mom's seven years younger, so they weren't school chums. *Mr.* Kavacek died young. They had one child, a girl of some ill repute, according to Mom, but that could mean just about anything, as we well know." Rosalie winked theatrically at Inga. "From a penchant for miniskirts or a butt with a little extra wiggle in it to a full-blown felony. In all events, Dubious Daughter skedaddled years ago, and after that, Mrs. Kavacek, a.k.a. Lisa Odland, became a shut-in, doesn't set one little piggy out of her house. Doesn't attend *church*. Doesn't have the pastor *in*. No manure richer for the rumor garden than that. You know, 'What's the old bag doing in there?'" Rosalie hummed a dirge.

"She's still alive," Inga said.

"Yup, it seems so, but I think we better pay a call on Grandpa Walt first. She won't see *any*body."

Sonia's eyes were wide. "She's probably got agoraphobia or something, but how does she eat?"

"Well, she found herself a companion, a niece on her husband's side, Lorelei, a strange bird apparently, with a bum leg, who comes and goes, does the shopping and errands, and makes some money sewing for people."

"I think the word *scandal* might be an overstatement," I said to Rosalie.

She grinned at me in the rearview mirror. "Don't rush me. There's more. The two ladies, it seems, are manufacturing some item in the house. Packages come and go. Deliverymen drop off. Others pick up, but nobody knows what's in those boxes."

Inga turned to Rosalie, opened her mouth, but said nothing.

"There's been trouble with kids on the property. The tried and true I-dare-you-to-go-look-in-Old-Lady-Kavacek's-window routine. One boy fell out of a tree trying to get a glimpse inside."

"Nothing changes," Inga said.

"Nope," Rosalie said merrily. "Remember snooping on Alvin Schadow while he practiced the waltz to those dance tapes, that poor cushion clasped tightly to his chest? Oh my God, it was hilarious."

"I didn't look," Inga said. "I thought it was awful."

"Oh, Mom," Sonia groaned.

"She *did* look," Rosalie said, "But she didn't laugh. That tender heart of hers was squeezed all out of shape."

"Well, poor Mr. Schadow," Inga said. "I might have to take to cushions sometime soon, so I don't think we should be too high and mighty."

Sonia gave her mother a troubled glance, replaced her earphones, lay back in her seat, and closed her eyes.

WHEN WE ENTERED the room, Walter Odland was sitting in a chair in the narrow room, half of which belonged to another man, a wizened person with a long nose in striped pajamas, who lay on his back in a dead sleep, mouth open, a tray with a half-eaten meal on a small mobile table beside him. Odland had the sunken posture of the very old. His watery eyes had receded into his head, and his narrow lips were flanked by two flabby, mottled jowls, above which was a round and fleshy nose. Despite the fact that we had been told he suffered from some dementia, he appeared alert. When we told him that we had a few questions about our father, he nodded, but the name Davidsen didn't do much for him. When we mentioned Bakkethun, however, it caused a tremor of recognition, and his sister's name coupled with some inquiries about his parents' marriage produced an outburst.

"Ah, well," Odland said, "was a mistake, as I see it, nah, it was a downright lie, don't you know it. Was for her protection, I s'pose, but she had the scar right there on her neck. Said it was from a candle or some such nonsense. Didn't know myself until years later, you understand. Went to her with it. Blamed me, too. We was never close."

Inga leaned near him and touched his arm gently. "What did you tell her?"

Odland turned to Inga as if he were seeing her for the first time. "Why, you're a looker, aren't you?" he said. "Handsome woman."

"Thank you," Inga said. "What did you tell her?"

"About the fire."

"What fire?" Rosalie asked.

"In Zumbrota."

I was standing in the small room and leaned over to speak to the man directly. "You and Lisa didn't have the same mother, did you?" I said.

His face changed, and the man avoided looking at me directly. "Weren't right to neither of us." His chin began to bob up and down as he looked out at the room, and then he shook his head. "Where am I?"

"The Blue Wing Care Facility," Rosalie said.

"I forget," he said simply, and I noticed then that his eyes were a flecked olive green.

"Mr. Odland," I continued, "what happened in the fire?"

"They died."

Inga reached over again and placed her hand gently on his arm. "Who died?" she asked.

Odland was agitated now, and a feeling of guilt washed over me. We had stirred up old family troubles, and he was shaking his head emphatically. "Weren't right not to say." I turned to Inga, shook my head at her, and mouthed the words "No more." She nodded.

Rosalie, who had taken in my noiseless message, promptly took both of Odland's hands in hers and, maintaining a firm grip, looked into his eyes and said slowly, "Mr. Odland, you've done us a service, and we thank you. We're grateful."

"You're the other one," he said.

"Yes, I'm the other one. I'm telling you thank you."

"You bet," he said, brightening. "Okay. Thank you."

A loud, high-pitched wheeze was heard from the little sleeper, and a nurse entered the room. She peered at the unconscious person and then turned to us. "So nice to see you have company," she said to Odland.

The man grinned and pointed to Sonia. "Come here, young lady," he said.

Sonia obediently approached him, and he reached his hands toward her, his face wrinkling into a smile. Then he patted his fallen cheek. "A smooch," he said, "Right here."

"Now, Mr. Odland," the nurse said.

Sonia reddened, and I saw the conflict in her face, but she bent over, just as the nurse was closing in on him, and gave the old man a quick peck.

Odland chuckled happily, then came out with a surprisingly robust wolf whistle.

Before we left, the woman turned to us and said, "I hope you come back. He doesn't have many visitors, and it does him good."

SONIA KNOCKED ON my door around midnight. My niece looked grave when she entered the room barefoot, dressed in an enormous blue T-shirt that reached her thighs and a ragged pair of pajama bottoms. "I'm glad you're up," she said. After sitting down on the puffy chair near the window, she looked straight into my eyes. "I know about Dad and Edie Bly."

"Your mother told you?"

"I had a feeling she knew when she kept looking at the film, but in case she didn't, *I* wasn't going to tell her."

"How do you know?"

Sonia looked as if she was going to cry for a second, but she paused and took a breath. "I saw them together. It was in the third grade. On Varick Street."

"That was a long time ago."

She nodded. "I was nine. Mom let me go around the block sometimes to visit Dad at his studio. She was always really nervous, but I begged and begged and we made a plan about it. He would call her as soon as I arrived. It was only two blocks. That day, we didn't call him first. She said I could surprise him. I skipped over there, and at the end of the block, I saw him coming out the door. With *her*. He had his hands on her."

"What did you do?"

Sonia stared straight ahead, but her eyes didn't meet mine. "I ran home. I told Mom he must have gone out. It felt like the air had been kicked out of me."

"And you never said anything to anyone?"

She shook her head, her eyes shiny. "The thing is, I was so angry at Dad, and then I kept thinking they'd get divorced, like all the other kids' parents. I'd hear them fighting. I used to sing when I heard them. I'd sing at the top of my voice; then they'd get embarrassed and quiet down." Sonia's face was hard. "But it didn't happen, the divorce, I mean, and I started to feel like what I saw wasn't real—that maybe she hadn't really been there. It started feeling like a movie or something, and Dad was his old self, just the same. Then he got sick." Sonia folded her arms and let her head drop as she spoke to her feet. "I would watch Mom beside him in the hospital, talking to him, reading him stories, and kissing his hands . . ."

"You were still angry with your father?"

Sonia lifted her head. "No. Maybe. I don't know. It was something else, like I couldn't *do* anything, and I can't take it back now. I wasn't good to him. I was stupid. I didn't even *talk*. The smell in the hospital, the nurses, those blue plastic bedpans, the tubes, I don't know, I, I . . ." She stopped, then said, "When he got really bad, he didn't even look like my father anymore."

"Before he died, he said to me that you and your mother were his soul. Those were his words: *They're my soul. Take care of them.*"

"I wonder what Edie Bly was, then," she said.

I shook my head. "I don't know, Sonia."

"Everybody's supposed to be cool about this stuff. Sally Reiser's got a stepmother five years older than she is. Ari's father is on his fourth wife, and his mother's on her third husband. But we were different. We weren't like that," she said, shaking her head. "I always thought we were different."

The two of us sat in silence for some time. I planned several sentences about adults and their foibles, the passionate forays of older men that could dry up rather quickly, different kinds of love, and so on, and then didn't say any of them.

"You should talk to your mother."

"You can't tell her I know," she said forcefully.

"I won't. You should tell her. It will come as a relief to both of you."

Sonia looked down at her knees. I saw her chin wobble, and her mouth contorted as she tried to control it.

I stood up from the bed, walked over to her, and put my hand on her shoulder. She reached for my hand and held it. "My poor girl," I said.

She raised her head and, although her eyes were wet, she didn't cry. "You sounded just like Pappa when you said that, *just* like him."

AS I SAT in the small chair in the Andrews House the next day and made notes on my telephone conversation with Ms. L., I thought about what we called her "voids," the hours she spent in limbo with her fantasies. "I thought about you leaning over me and touching me down there and then I was afraid I would piss, so I started slapping you hard." I wrote down Bion's word "container," the analyst as a vessel, a place to put your mess. Me, the urinal. I missed work. Work was my skeleton, my musculature. Without it, I felt like a jellyfish. The forms of things—the outlines. We can't live without them. "Don't touch my nose, you shit!" one of the inpatients had screamed at me after I had briefly scratched my own during the interview. I was a young psychiatric resident then, and his words passed through me with a jolt. After that, I learned how precarious it all is—where we begin and end, our bodies, our words, inside and outside. Psychotic patients are often cosmologists, obsessed with the mysterious structures of the invisible, with God and Satan, the stars, a fourth dimension, what lies beneath or beyond. They're looking for the bones of the world. Sometimes the hospital can build a temporary shelter of dull routine—meds and lunch and arts-and-crafts and movement class and visits from the social worker and the doctor—but then the world beckons. The patient walks into the open air, and the fragile ones go to pieces again.

My father worked hard to order his world: early rising, long hours, proofreading backward, scrupulous notes, detailed maps, straight rows of corn, potatoes, beans, lettuce, and radishes. But when accident intervened—car trouble, a child's bump or wound, a wrong turn, bad weather—he suffered inordinately. I remembered his face tightening, the catch of anguish in his voice, his fists clenched as he shook his head. Feeling travels. My mother's voice: "Don't be upset, Lars." My sister's stricken face in the backseat. I would shrink into myself. Sonia sang. I counted. It was never the event, so unimportant really, or what my father did or even said. His eruptions were controlled. It was the volcanic emotion we felt inside him.

That night I dreamed that I was back on the units in the hospital and had just locked the glass door to the North ward when an intern tapped me on the shoulder and handed me a chest X-ray. I looked at the picture. The heart was so enormous, it filled the entire chest cavity. A radiologist suddenly appeared beside me, and I noticed that his coat was dirty, dripping with some vile yellow liquid. He leaned toward me and I pulled away, trying to avoid the filth on his coat. He whispered in my ear, "Atrioseptal defect." I asked him what he was doing in psychiatry. Then, for some reason, I understood that the X-ray was of *my* heart, that the congenital lesion belonged to me. I grabbed a stethoscope from my pocket and began to auscultate my own chest. I heard the loud whoosh of the murmur, and then through the glass I saw my father lying in a hospital bed in the middle of the broad hallway in South. He shouldn't be there. *He's in the wrong unit.* I took out my key to unlock the door but found fifty keys of various sizes on the chain instead of one. I began to try one key after another, but they wouldn't turn the lock. All at once, I couldn't breathe, and then, in a panic, I started screaming for help. My father lay motionless, his mouth open. The radiologist was still there, but he had another face. He whispered to me, "Psychotic disorder following pulmonary hypertension." With that nonsense in my ears, I woke up. As I wrote about the dream the next day, my first notation was "Physician, heal thyself." But then I understood that the "hole" in my heart had also been a reference to the hole in my father's chest when the doctor in Emergency reinflated his collapsed lung, and that I had desperately tried to open the door to him with "unknown keys."

INGA AND ROSALIE found an article about the fire in *The Zumbrota Reporter.* On May 14, 1920, a "tragic" fire had taken the lives of Sylvia Odland and her infant son, James. The two-year-old Lisa Odland had suffered burns but was rescued by a fireman who had pulled her out of the house through the front door. Lisa's parents were divorced, and the article mentioned that the child would go to live with her father and his second wife. They never told her about the deaths. Walter Odland had spoken the truth. "It wasn't right." The implicit memory of the fire, one she never consciously retrieved, must nevertheless have primed her emotional responses. The loss of her mother was never acknowledged, never openly mourned. She had been offered a replacement. Years later, her brother had come to her with the news. Now she was a shut-in.

But as Inga pointed out, the story of the fire had nothing to do with the mystery of the note or our father.

"I FEEL LARS," my mother said. "And my mother. They're both here with me in this place. I never feel them in New York."

Sonia looked at my mother with a puzzled expression. "Like ghosts?"

"No. Presences. It isn't frightening."

"I hear Max," Inga said simply.

"Really?" Sonia said.

Inga nodded. "I hear him saying my name, not often, but every once in a while. Pappa once told me he heard his father. He heard his father calling him."

My mother was sitting on the sofa, hugging her knees to her chest. From my place in the chair across from her, I watched her turn her head toward the window, and in that instant I saw her as if she were a person I didn't know. Her small head and the delicate features of her profile were illuminated for a moment in the shaft of sunlight that came through the window. I saw the deep wrinkles around her mouth and across her forehead and the intense blue iris in her visible eye. Her white hair was brushed back from her face. "Lotte once told me the story of the day your grandmother lost her savings. Ivar came home, delivered the bad news about the bank, and then he quoted a psalm: 'The people asked and he brought quails and satisfied them with the bread of heaven.' Hildy grabbed a plate off the table and smashed it on the floor."

"Pappa never told you about it?" Inga said.

"No. I wish he could have told me more, but he couldn't. I once said to him, 'It must have been hard growing up with so much animosity between your parents.'"

"What did he say?" I asked.

"He wouldn't hear of it." The sun must have been obscured by a cloud, because the room darkened suddenly.

I made an effort to think back, to remember something, a clue from my childhood. I had loved my grandmother, loved her arms with their hanging flesh and her long white hair that she always put up with wide hairpins she kept in a little bowl on her dresser. I had loved her laugh, her stories about her girlhood, and I had loved when she put on her straw hat with flowers on it before she took us out for a drive. She had never been able to pronounce the "th" sound in English. It was just a plain "t." I thought of my father's paternal grandfather lowering the trunk he would take to America down the mountain at Voss by rope and pulley, and the dugout where he first lived, a hole in the earth covered with grass, and then the log house that burned after his wife died. *In the fall of 1924, a faulty stove or chimney set his house on fire. The details are not clear. Two neighbors, Hiram Pedersen and Knut Hougo, fortunately drove by and saw the fire. They found Olaf trapped behind a table that he was trying to push out a door. By this time he was badly burned, especially his hands and portions of his face. He was in bed the last time I saw him, unable to speak. He put his scarred hand on my head as if to bless me. He did the same for my sister, Lotte.*

"I don't blame her for throwing the plate," Sonia said. "God didn't feed them, did he? They lost everything."

My mother shook her head. "They were so different, those two. Hildy could be irrational, but she had spirit. When Ivar was dying, when he was in a coma, he seemed to come up out of it every once in a while and see us. He couldn't speak, and the look in his eyes was terrible, so hurt, as if he just wanted it to end."

Not one of us spoke for at least a minute, and then my mother turned to Sonia and continued. "My father got sick during the war. It was his heart. He'd been so athletic, you see. He could run like a goat up the mountain. He never lost his footing, but then . . ."

My mother put her hand to her chest. "He found it hard to catch his breath, and I'd hear him breathing too fast, and I remember thinking, he can't die. Pappa can't really die."

"Like Dad," Sonia whispered. "That's what I kept saying about Dad."

My mother pulled Sonia into her and stroked her hair. Inga watched the two of them, her face stretched with emotion.

My mother didn't stop. Her steady voice carried the cadence and lilt of the language that lay beneath the one she was using, and I think as she talked to us, she was talking to herself as well. "In those days, when someone died, the body was dressed and laid out for viewing. People came to say good-bye. It was a ritual, of course. I remember looking at my father lying there, without himself. My dead father was a stranger." She paused. "There was no embalming or gruesome American thing like that, you understand. After you died, you were wrapped in a white shroud and put in a simple wooden coffin and buried." My mother took a breath. "As I looked at the body, my mother said, *Kyss Pappa*. Kiss Pappa," my mother translated for Sonia.

"I know *that*, Mormor," she said.

"I didn't want to," my mother said. Her face stiffened.

Sonia, who had been listening with her head against her grandmother's chest, looked up.

"Mamma said it again, *Kyss Pappa*." My mother turned her eyes away, and she gazed at the candlestick sitting on the table in front of her. "I didn't want to, but I did it." She looked down at Sonia and said, "My mother was wonderful. I loved her very much, you know, but she shouldn't have said that."

The enduring light of the June day had vanished as we talked, and I realized suddenly that we were sitting in a darkened room. Not one of us moved to turn on a lamp, however. Sonia moved away from her grandmother's embrace, and I noticed how erect my mother's posture was as she sat perfectly still on the sofa, her shadowed face taut with memory.

Marit, Marit, Marit, Marit. As I closed my eyes that night, my father's incantation came unbidden to my mind, the strange involuntary repetition of a woman's name. Lifeline: *Marit, Marit, Marit.*

> Tanya Bluestone wanders here.
> Nobody's muse, she howls
> Mute—dreams awake in fear.
> Locked throat and streaming bowels,
> A twin ablaze inside of me.
> The burn recast in memory.
> > Sonia Blaustein
> > P.S. I told Mom.

I found Sonia's poem and postscript under my door when I got out of bed. I read it several times, then folded the paper carefully and put it inside my journal. For a while I stood at the window and looked down onto Division Street, still empty at seven in the morning. I remembered the smoke rising in the sky, the dry choking rain of paper, a haze in the Brooklyn sky, and the hush that fell over the neighborhood. On Seventh Avenue, the pedestrians that day reminded me of sleepwalkers, mechanical, alien drifters, their faces covered with handkerchiefs and surgical masks.

IT WAS ROSALIE, with some help from her dauntless mother, who arranged the meeting at the Ideal Café in Blooming Field. Lorelei Kavacek had business to take care of in town and had granted us an interview. Despite the fact that the woman was a cipher to me, I had conjured for her a vague persona based on the scanty information we had gleaned. Lorelei lived with a reclusive woman connected to my father and the community where he'd grown up. She was lame and, at least by association, secretive. These fragments must have pulled me back to the old people I had met as a child and to the stories I had heard about them. I remembered seeing the ancient Bondestad sisters as they walked arm in arm on the dirt road in their long black dresses. When their father died in 1920, they donned their mourning clothes and never took them off. They had cooked, plowed, and harvested in black. I think I mingled those sisters with Norbert Engel, the local hermit, of whom I retain a single memory: a wiry little man sits on a stump under the trees—wrinkled brown face, a few brown teeth, wearing clothes, if not brown, then drab. He rolls a cigarette between yellow fingers, and their deft motion amazes me. The name Lorelei had no doubt added an aura of legend to the Gothic image that hovered dimly in my awareness: an aged, sun-baked rail of a woman, dragging a dead leg behind her, dressed in garments that resembled the Bondestad weeds. I wasn't aware of this fantasy, however, until Lorelei Kavacek thoroughly dispelled it when she walked through the door.

She limped, but had clearly mastered her gait to minimize the appearance of a handicap. The rest of her resembled nothing so much as a respectable Minnesota woman of the old style. She was full-bodied, but not fat. She wore a short-sleeved cotton blouse of a pastel plaid, a navy blue skirt well below her knees, stockings, and solid shoes. I guessed her age at around sixty, but she could have been older or younger. After she sat down at the table, she smoothed her skirt and placed her purse, a stiff rectangular affair with a large clasp, in her lap. When we introduced ourselves, she looked at each of us for a moment with her large, slightly protruding eyes. I decided that she had never been pretty, but despite her drooping cheeks and neck, she had even white skin that looked as if the sun had never touched it. We ordered coffee, and she said in a voice rich with long Minnesota vowels. "My aunt remembers yer dad, but she said she never saw him since before the war, read some articles on him in the papers though."

While Inga talked about the letter and its contents, I continued to look at Lorelei, and despite the fact that she was nothing like the half-conscious image I had seen in my mind, her presence evoked a feeling of my childhood. At first I couldn't understand what it was, but after a few seconds I realized that she smelled of a cologne I couldn't name, but which had wafted about in the basement of St. John's Lutheran Church "many a Sunday." The expression appeared to me in the moment, no doubt an effect of the memory, which in the same instant brought with it a feeling close to affection. "She don't see anybody, you know," Lorelei Kavacek said to me. "Never."

Inga leaned forward. "We know about the fire and Mrs. Kavacek's mother. We spoke to Mr. Odland a few days ago." My sister gave the name its Norwegian inflection, with a long "O." "It must have been hard for her to find out so many years later."

"Around here we say *Odd*-land."

Inga blushed. "Of course," she said.

The woman's face changed, and her big pale eyes looked suddenly rheumy. "As for the other—a bad business. Like being the wrong person all yer life long. She says she always had a feeling about it, though, like she was missing her liver or some such organ in her." After a pause, she sighed and looked at Rosalie. "Let me see, I've been living with my aunt Lisa going on thirty years now. Not long before I moved in with her, Walter found the divorce papers and put two and two together."

"Why won't she see anyone?" Inga asked.

Lorelei shook her head, but she avoided Inga's eyes, and I noticed that she held her purse with two hands as if to steady herself.

"One day she just stopped leavin' the house. She won't say, but she's got fears. I tried to get her to talk to Pastor Wee, but she'd have nothing of it." The woman looked at the white coffee mug. "It's upset her, this business about yer dad. Those were hard times. She's an old woman, and she's got a right to fix her life how she wants it. We've got things pretty well arranged now, and our little business has been good for her."

"What business is that?" I asked.

"Toys," she said matter-of-factly. "Not just any toys. We've sent some to New York City." She eyed Inga suspiciously. "That's where *you're* from, isn't it?" she said curtly.

"Erik and I live there now," Inga said. "We're *from* here."

Lorelei raised her eyebrows in an expression that could have signified disapproval, disbelief, or irritation. She gave Inga a hard look, sniffed, but said nothing, "Aunt Lisa's been doin' it all along, but it was my idea to sell them. I had a sewing shop for twenty years with Doris Goodly, couldn't keep it going after Doris died, but I have a knack for it and the energy to do it. It's given my aunt some pride." The woman straightened herself, as if the business had added something to her as well.

"You manufacture toys in your house?" I asked.

"All handmade. We're not getting rich off it, heaven knows, but it's keeping us fed and clothed. I sent off a pair to Berlin, Germany, well, let me see, it was two weeks back."

"A pair?" Inga said. My sister leaned forward, put her elbows on the table, and cupped her chin in her hands.

"A mother and her boy," Lorelei said.

"Dolls." Inga breathed the word happily. "You make dolls."

"Figures of all kinds," the woman answered.

"Can we see them?" Inga asked.

"Wouldn't hurt, I don't suppose. I'll speak to Aunt Lisa. Some of them are off limits—legacy items. Nobody sees them but us."

"Legacy items," Inga repeated, her eyes wide. "What does that mean?"

In answer, Lorelei patted her purse. "Private collection."

Inga reached out and very gently touched Lorelei's plump white arm with her three middle fingers. I had seen her make the gesture hundreds of times. I sometimes wondered whether she knew she was doing it; it confirmed for her, I think, that she really was having a dialogue, really engaging with someone else. I half expected her interlocutor to flinch, but she didn't. "You know, don't you?" Inga said. "You know what happened with Lisa and our father."

Lorelei Kavacek's face turned masklike, and she squeezed her purse more tightly. "I wouldn't be free to say," she said, "wouldn't be free to say one way or the other."

Not much of consequence happened after that. We agreed that we would call Lorelei to see if it was possible to look at the toys. We watched her walk toward her car. She opened the front door, sliding sideways, and pushed herself backward before manipulating her bad leg into driving position. After her car pulled away, I saw that the weather had changed. The sky had turned a twilight hue, and the spindly tree outside the window bent in a strong new wind. It's going to rain, I thought, a real June storm. A few minutes later, when we left the Ideal Café, the sky opened, and the rain came down in dense soaking sheets. My last memory of that coffee date with Lorelei Kavacek is not of her, but of my sister and Rosalie running across the street together, hand in hand, their faces turned upward as they shrieked and laughed like a pair of schoolgirls.

"DID YOU SEE the look Lorelei gave me?" Inga asked that evening as the rain fell outside my mother's window. It seemed that a door to an entire world of provincial cruelty had been opened by that single glance. Inga remembered her sixth-grade nemesis, Carla Screttleberg, and the other mean girls who had called her "weird," "fake," and "snob." She remembered the teacher who had declared her "uppity" in high school for writing a paper on Merleau-Ponty, and the cold stares from fellow students at Martin Luther College. The irony was that, if anything, Inga suffered from a lack of protective artifice and a surfeit of sincerity and passion, a quality of too-muchness that intimidated some people and made others hostile. Beneath Lorelei's look, which I had read as insecurity and Inga as contempt, lay a tangle of class relations, prairie egalitarianism, and just plain human nature. As I looked at my sister across the table, I noticed that she was wearing a white sleeveless shirt and narrow dark blue pants, which, despite their innocuous simplicity, had an expensive shine, a quality in clothing that has always mystified me but that is nevertheless immediately apparent. Lorelei was probably only ten years older than my sister, but in appearance the gulf between them was immense, and I understood that just by being herself, Inga could be taken as an affront. Inga, on the other hand, who felt her age and loneliness intensely, could hardly be expected to have sympathy for the prejudices against her.

"Our own father used to talk about city slickers," I said, smiling at my sister. "But every perceived difference, no matter how slight, can become an argument for Otherness—money, education, skin color, religion, political party, hairstyle, anything. Enemies are enlivening. Evil-doers, jihadists, barbarians. Hatred is exciting and contagious and conveniently eliminates all ambiguity. You just spew your own garbage onto someone else."

"After the war," my mother said, "they ostracized the children of German soldiers and Norwegian women. *Tyskeunger*. German brats. As if those children were guilty of anything."

"Injustice eats your soul," Inga said. "I've been thinking about the fact that Pappa didn't write about the hoof-and-mouth disaster in his memoir. He left it out."

"What was that?" Sonia said.

"A government inspector came to the farm. I don't know what year it was. He claimed the animals had hoof-and-mouth disease and had to be destroyed." I said. "There was nothing they could do. He had the power, and the animals were killed. It turned out the man was wrong. The animals were slaughtered for nothing."

Sonia spoke slowly. "So Pappa must have *seen* them dead."

I imagined their immense carcasses, the cows and the horses, then the empty barn, the eyesore.

"Some memories hurt too much," Inga said.

"When he left, where did he go?" I asked my mother. "Where did you find him the time he stayed out all night?"

My mother looked at me sharply. "I didn't know you knew. I didn't want to worry you, and your father always left for work so early in the morning. I thought you didn't know."

"The time I'm thinking about, I heard him leave," Inga said. "I stayed awake waiting for him to come home."

"In the morning," my mother said, "I started looking for him, first at his office, then in the library. He had no classes that day. I was standing in the stacks trying to think of where he might have gone, and then it came to me. It was a few months after your grandfather died, and your grandmother had started leaving the farm in the cold months, so nobody was living there. It was late October, I think."

"And Pappa was there?" Sonia said. "At the farm?"

"I found him asleep upstairs in his father's bed."

"Seventeen miles," Inga said. "He must have walked all night."

"What did he say?" I asked.

"Nothing," my mother said. "He seemed disoriented after I

woke him, but when I started saying how worried and upset I had been, he didn't answer, or rather he acted as if nothing out of the ordinary had happened."

He went home. Nobody was there, but he went home. It wasn't that he loved it there, but something about the place drew him toward it.

"When Hildy was very old," my mother continued, "years after Ivar was dead and not long before she died herself, I was sitting near her bed, and we were talking. All at once, she burst out in a loud voice, 'I should have been nicer to Ivar. I should have been nicer to Ivar.'"

Sonia's face fell. I saw her mouth and chin tremble. In the same instant, my mother turned her head to look at her granddaughter. Inga, her eyes on Sonia, hesitated, then placed her fingers on her daughter's plate, not on her arm or hand. "I have to go to the bathroom," Sonia said, then stood up and left the table.

Language is often flimsy, I thought, a thin drool of received knowledge empty of any real meaning, but when we are heavy with emotion, it can be excruciating to speak. We don't want to let the words out, because then they will also belong to other people, and that is a danger we can't risk.

TO INGA'S GREAT disappointment, we weren't allowed to visit the Kavacek house or see "Aunt Lisa," but Lorelei agreed to bring some toys to Rosalie's, where we would all be permitted to view them. We didn't learn until we arrived, however, that Rosalie had lured the dollmaker by telling her that we were "loaded" and that she might make a sale. The last afternoon of our visit, Sonia, Inga, my mother, and I drove to the large white house on the east side of town where Rosalie, her veterinarian husband, Larry, and her three sons, Derek, Peter, and Michael, nicknamed Rusty, had lived for years.

We settled into the commodious living room, which appeared to double as a repository for sports equipment, numerous sweatshirts, several pairs of large sneakers, a month's supply of newspapers and a year's worth of magazines, as well as several objects usually found in a kitchen: a frying pan, measuring cups, and three or four spice jars, one of which had spilled its dead green leaves onto the coffee table near a bowl that contained a repugnant-looking brown liquid.

With a glance at the table, Rosalie raised her hands palms outward and exclaimed in mock horror, "Good Lord, Rusty's science project seems to be multiplying." Then, in a deep voice, she bellowed, "Rusty!"

When Rusty failed to appear, she howled again. While Sonia and Inga looked deeply amused, my mother, true to her upbringing, carefully removed three dirty sweat socks from the chair Rosalie had offered her, laid them on the table, sat down in her seat, and folded her hands in her lap.

When the young scientist entered the room, he was dressed in wide shorts and a T-shirt with a skull on it. The symbol of death was not at all in keeping with his soft, sheepish, well-formed face and athletic body. The boy, who looked to be around thirteen or fourteen, glanced a couple of times at the lovely Sonia as he cleared away the remnants of his experimentation, muttering, "I didn't know *people* were coming."

When the doorbell rang, Rosalie snatched up several garments that were lying on the remaining unoccupied chair, rushed to a closet, threw them into it, and, with a wink at us, waltzed off to open the door.

Lorelei appeared, looking very much as she had the first time, except now she was a bit more dressed up, wearing a neat, starched blouse the color of honey and a green skirt. She placed three shoebox-sized containers on the table, and one by one proceeded to open them.

The first figure to emerge was about six inches tall, a girl doll with long braids made from shiny brown thread, wearing a blue dress with a full skirt. As far as I could tell, it had been constructed entirely from cloth, but there must have been a wire interior that allowed the toy to hold its shape. I'd never given much thought to dolls, but seeing this one made me aware that most of them exaggerate one feature or another—large heads and eyes, for example, or bodies that are too short or too long. This figure's proportions looked accurate. The detail, not only in the clothes, but in the tiny embroidered face, was so fine that my mother let out a gasp when it was put down in front of us. The doll had a cast on its leg, and a moment later Lorelei retrieved two wooden crutches from the box and tucked them under the doll's arms.

"Ruth. She fell down the stairs *at home*." She mumbled this comment darkly, as if to herself.

No one answered her. The more I looked at the figure, the more I saw. She appeared to have a scab on her left knee which, when examined closely, turned out to be embroidery, but there were some painted details, too—the flush of her cheeks, tiny freckles, a blue bruise on her elbow, and tiny fingernails. It wasn't that the doll looked like a miniature person but rather that the multiple gestures toward realism had an uncanny effect. It was as if the toy belonged to a universe with laws and logic similar to our own. She was a mortal toy who came from a world where children fell, broke bones, wore casts, and needed crutches.

After that, Lorelei took out an old-woman doll in a long flannel gown, which she placed on a narrow bed. The fabric of the face had been folded and sewn to mimic networks of wrinkles, and its thread hair was short, white, and ragged. I also noticed the shape of the doll's body under the nightclothes—its fallen breasts, distended belly, and long, thin legs. Lorelei covered the figure with a quilt and turned its head to one side.

"Look at the veins on her hands and wrists," Sonia said. She had left her chair and was kneeling on the floor beside the coffee table. Rusty hovered over her, his face a mixture of distaste and awe. "It's sad," Sonia said. "Poor thing."

"Milly," Lorelei said, "on the day she died."

I began to feel that I had been mistaken about Lorelei Kavacek. The steady, pragmatic matron with her brown shoes and support hose had a story for every toy. The whole venture was steeped in eccentricity, at the very least, and I wondered what the two women were living through with these figures. I recalled a patient who had told me that when he watched movies, he "went into them, really in. I'm there. I'm them."

The third figure was a middle-aged man in overalls and work boots. Lorelei put him in a stuffed chair, where he sat, hunched over with one hand on his forehead, the other in his lap, which loosely held a tiny piece of paper. By far the most disturbing doll of the three, this one had closed eyes and a mouth contorted into an expression of grief. My mother, who was standing over the table, leaned down and asked Lorelei whether she could touch him.

Lorelei nodded, and my mother briefly put her index finger on the doll's flannel shirt, then withdrew it. "Who is he?" she asked.

Rosalie was only inches away from the small letter. "We regret to inform you," she said. "It's a war story."

"Arlen," Lorelei said. "It's right after he got the news about his boy, Frank."

"What comes first," I asked, "the story or the doll?"

"Why, the story, of course. Couldn't make 'em without knowing who they are and what's happened to them."

"They must be very expensive," Inga said. I thought her face looked a little wan, and her voice had a breathless quality. "How long does it take you to do them?"

"Months. We've got Buster who does the furniture for us—to order. He lives here in Blooming Field."

"And the price?" Inga said.

"Depends. They start at around five hundred."

"I can imagine," Inga said. She looked down at the old-woman doll and, in a gesture jarringly similar to my mother's only seconds before, touched its sleeve. "Thank you so much," she said. "I'll have to think about it."

"There are more," Lorelei said. "I could send photos."

"Yes," Inga said, looking rather stunned. "Yes, I'll give you my address."

After Lorelei had written down Inga's information, she carefully packed the figures into their boxes. Then, without ceremony of any kind, she nodded at us and said, as she had once before, "Best be going." We watched her walk to the door. She limped, but with a decided air of triumph in her step.

Once we heard her car engine turn over, Sonia said, "Were they really as strange as I thought?"

"Yes," my mother said, "they were."

"You aren't actually thinking of buying one of those dolls, are you?" Rosalie was speaking to Inga.

My sister didn't hear her. She was in one of her "departed moods," as I used to call them when we were children. Her eyes were focused, but not on anything in the room. She was deeply concentrated on some internal thought. When the question was repeated more loudly, Inga looked at her friend and said, "Yes, I think I am. I think I want one of those damaged little people for myself."

"WE FOUND THE wrong story," Inga said to me on the plane back to New York. "We were looking for one story and ran into another."

"The fire, the deaths, the hiding, and the lies."

"I'm sure they felt they were protecting her."

"No doubt," I said, "but that kind of protection never works. Lisa always felt something was wrong."

"Lorelei knows," Inga said. "I'm sure of it, but I doubt she'll ever tell us. Did you see her face when she wrapped up those little people? It was as if she were saying, 'I've got these uppity folks from New York just where I want them.'"

"The dolls were testimonies of some sort."

Inga nodded. "Telling but not telling. If we knew what happened between Pappa and Lisa, if we knew who died and how, we might understand him better. Secrets can define people." She glanced at Sonia who was fast asleep in the window seat across from us. "Every day, I think about the fact that she knew about *them* and didn't say anything. It's like a knife in me. And still, when we talked, I couldn't bring myself to mention Joel to her." She lowered her voice to a whisper. "What if she has a brother? I've been thinking about it. Wouldn't it be terribly wrong to keep siblings apart? And yet, what are they to each other, really? I mean, what does biology mean in a case like this?"

"It has a strong hold on people," I said. "Think of all the adopted children who go looking for their 'real' parents."

"DNA would tell for sure whether there's a genetic connection?"

"Yes."

"That seems a little brutal, too. We'll be kind to you if your genes show you're related to us, and if you're not, we'll ignore you." Inga fingered the book on her lap. I noticed that it was about Hegel and looked down at a drawing of the philosopher's face on the cover.

"He had an illegitimate son." She tapped the book. "Ludwig. Hegel and his wife took him in for a while, but it didn't go well."

Inga sounded tired. She turned to the window as if to tell me she didn't want to talk anymore.

"You have to tell her," I said.

"I know," she answered. "I will."

So many things to hide, I thought, and then I remembered sitting across from P. in the North ward, listening to her small, earnest voice. *I don't remember when I started hurting myself. I wish I did.*

"What are you thinking about?"

"A girl I treated at Payne Whitney."

"It must be a relief not to be there anymore. It wore you out."

"I miss it."

"Really?"

"I miss the patients. It's hard to describe, but when people are in desperate need, something falls away. The posing that's part of the ordinary world vanishes, that How-are-you?-I'm-fine falseness." I paused. "The patients might be raving or mute or even violent, but there's an existential urgency to them that's invigorating. You feel close to the raw truth of what human beings are."

"No hypocrisy, as Pappa would have said."

"That's right, no hypocrisy. But I have to admit that I don't miss the paperwork or the commands that came down from on high. I ran into an old colleague about a month ago, Nancy Lomax. She's still working on the units. She told me that patients are now officially referred to as *customers.*"

"That's revolting."

"That's America."

WHEN I ARRIVED home, the house felt empty. I heard no noises from downstairs, and I wondered if my two tenants had also taken a vacation. *Woe to the mitten!* I thought, and reentered my solitary existence. Although I heard them return late Sunday, I didn't see Miranda and Eggy until the following Saturday. I had turned up Garfield from Eighth Avenue and spotted them with Lane near the park. He was crouched with his camera poised while Miranda made a defensive gesture with her hands and Eggy hid her face in her mother's dress. Seconds later, Lane lowered the camera, and the three of them assumed different and more relaxed positions, but it was the first image that stayed with me—Miranda with her palms turned outward in front of her face, Eggy's clinging form, and the intense, almost explosive energy of Lane's body as he took his shots. It may have been that I wanted to focus on those seconds of discord, that they reassured me. Whatever the reason, that view of them in the sunshine has fixed itself in my memory and hardened over time until it is now as static and isolated as a color photograph in a family album.

ON SUNDAY IN the late afternoon, I was reading an article Burton had sent me a few days earlier when the doorbell rang. Through the glass door, I saw Eggy standing on the steps, a stuffed backpack lying at her feet. She was wearing a baseball cap, a fluffy pink skirt that looked too large for her, and black rubber boots. When I opened the door, she looked up at me, her eyes tragic. She didn't answer my greeting, but when I invited her in I noticed that she turned her head to look behind her. I said nothing, but I suspected that Miranda knew her girl had come to my door.

Eggy dragged the stuffed backpack into the hallway, dropped it there, removed her cap, and walked slowly into the living room with her hand on her heart. She took several loud breaths before she sat down and leaned her head against the pillows, her eyelids fluttering feebly.

"I see you're not feeling well," I said.

Eggy placed the back of her hand on her forehead and blew a long stream of air out of her mouth. I thought of *The Mitten*. I also suddenly remembered faking a limp after a fall in the third grade. I had kept it up for hours.

"My chest hurts inside, and my eyes aren't working too well."

"I'm sorry to hear that."

"Yes," Eggy said, glancing at the hallway before she continued. "I might need pills like Granddad. He has blood pressure, you know."

"That doesn't happen to children very often."

She looked thoughtful for a few seconds and then spoke in a low voice, "My other grandma and grandpa were killed by a car crash." With this statement her expression changed, and her distress looked genuine. Eglantine leaned forward, her eyes on mine. "They died instantly." This must have been a quote. Had her father told her that, her mother?

"It must be scary to think about that."

"It is." She seemed to be searching for more to say. "I might go live with my daddy."

"You're leaving your mother?"

Eggy's booted feet dangled several inches above the floor, and she started to swing them back and forth nervously. "He lets me do stuff. He's going to take me to Six Flags." Despite the optimism of this sentence, Eggy looked miserable.

"That sounds nice," I said, "but you don't look too happy about it. You look sad."

Eggy turned to the window. Her face lit up, and a second later I heard the doorbell. I answered it, ushered Miranda into the living room, and we both looked over at Eggy, who was now collapsed on the sofa, her hand on her chest again, blinking furiously.

"Eglantine is suffering from some physical symptoms," I said to Miranda.

Miranda stopped a few feet from her daughter and folded her arms. "Yes, she's been spending a lot of time with the nurse at day camp, haven't you, Eggy? Her heart, her eyes, her stomach, her head, her arms, her legs, all going bad."

Miranda smiled at me for an instant and then turned to Eggy, who was breathing loudly and had begun to moan. Miranda walked over to the sofa, and after adjusting Eggy's legs, moved in beside her. She picked up one of her daughter's arms and began to stroke it. "Does this help?" she asked.

Eglantine nodded.

She put her lips to her daughter's forehead and began to kiss it. Then she kissed her nose and her cheeks and her chin. "How about this?"

Eggy closed her eyes. Her mother continued to kiss her arms and hands and the naked spot between her T-shirt and the skirt.

"Is this good?" Miranda murmured.

I watched Eggy's arms enfold her mother. "You're not fed up with me, Mommy, are you?" She pronounced the words *fed up* very carefully, as if they were foreign.

Miranda leaned back a few inches and looked at Eglantine. "What?"

"Fed up, you said you were fed up."

"When?"

"When you were drawing. I heard you."

"I'm not fed up with you. I could never get enough of you, Eggy Weggy. What are you talking about?"

I sat down in a chair and looked over at them. Eglantine's eyes were huge as she examined her mother's face. "I thought you were fed up because I'm so . . ." Eglantine took in a breath and let it out. "Difficult."

"You, difficult?" Miranda's face broke into a smile, and she laughed. "What a thought."

Her daughter smiled back at her, then buried her head in her mother's neck and began to kiss Miranda passionately. "Mommy," she said, "Oh, my own mommy."

"Should we go home now?" Miranda said. "I'm sure Erik has other things to do."

"Carry me," Eggy said. "Please carry me down. I want to be carried."

"You're big, Eggy," Miranda said.

And so we carried the small malingerer together. Miranda grabbed the child under her arms, and I took her legs. We hauled her down the stairs, swung her back and forth in the hallway, and ran with her into the front room of the apartment. Eggy laughed the whole way. I left the two of them entwined on the blue sofa. When I closed the door, I heard Miranda singing a sweet tune I'd never heard before. She had a thin voice, higher than I would have expected, and she carried every note.

THAT SAME EVENING, I called Laura Capelli. The little scene that had taken place in my living room between Eggy and Miranda was no doubt behind my sudden decision to take out another woman. During the afternoon, I had seen a different Miranda. With her daughter, she had been tender, open, affectionate, and full of humor. Her instincts with Eggy had been unerring, and I realized that those same instincts made her guarded and remote with me. Laura lived only seven blocks away, and when I asked her if she would have dinner with me in the neighborhood, she said, "Sure, why not?" In spite of her equivocal answer, the tone of her voice was warm, and on Friday, the day of our rendezvous, I found myself looking forward to seeing her.

When she entered the restaurant, I was already sitting at the table, and the first thing I noticed was that she was wearing a low-cut blouse that showed a lot of cleavage, which meant that during the dinner I would have to keep my eyes from wandering down to her breasts. It also occurred to me that, because she was a psychotherapist, she wouldn't be oblivious to the meaning of clothes, and yet I'd often been surprised by the obtuseness of my colleagues when it came to their own actions, so I told myself to avoid jumping to conclusions.

Laura Capelli talked, laughed, and ate with zeal. She had olive skin and nearly black hair that curled around her face. Her breasts were large, round, and distracting. She had a busy practice, an ex-husband, and a thirteen-year-old son, who had become obsessed with his hair. He spent an hour in the bathroom every morning with gels and brushes getting it just right, but when his mother remarked on his labored do, he had looked right through her. "My hair?" After Laura had polished off a crème brûlée and commented on what she thought was a skimpy appetite for a man of my size, we found ourselves on the street, and I said I would walk her home.

When I leaned over to kiss her on the sidewalk, she grabbed me around the waist with both arms in a bear hug, and there was no stopping us after that. She led me quietly into the house, past her son's bedroom with a finger to her lips, up a flight of stairs, and into her room, where we threw ourselves onto the bed and began tugging at buttons and zippers, which, after a short struggle, gave way. We found each other's mouths and tongues and rolled over and under and into each other. Her skin smelled like powder and vanilla and tasted a little salty, and it had been so long that I had to hold back, did hold back until I knew she was coming. She was sitting on top of me, and by then our rhythm had become even and slow, and she threw her head back and closed her eyes and gasped as if she were stifling a scream. Within seconds, I had let myself go, and we were lying beside each other on the blue and white sheets. And then Laura sat up and burst out laughing. I sat beside her on the bed as she tried to muffle the escaping giggles, which had a distinctly hysterical tone. "Good God, Erik, good God," she whispered, as she covered her mouth. We lay beside each other for about an hour after that, talking in low voices, but I sensed she was nervous that her son might wake up, and I made my exit, tiptoeing past Alex's room, down the stairs, and out onto St. John's Place.

I found myself on Seventh Avenue around two in the morning. The night air was cooler than I had expected, and small groups of teenagers were still out, inebriated, jostling elbows and arms, hanging heavily on one another, laughing dramatically for the benefit of the others. The effects of the wine I had drunk earlier had long worn off. Agitated by my adventure, I felt sleep was impossible, and so, when I arrived at Garfield, I didn't turn but moved on past the closed shops, keeping up a good pace as I walked by lone pedestrians with dogs, a few lovers holding each other as they journeyed back to a bed somewhere, and I didn't stop until I reached Twentieth Street, where Green-Wood Cemetery lay stretched before me, its gravestones and monuments pale in the dim light of the street lamps. Laura's breasts returned to me, white beneath her suntanned chest. I remembered her pale ass in the air and her muffled cries with an erotic shudder, but the memory of her body already felt a little alien, recent visions in retreat.

When I turned around, I walked to Eighth Avenue and then along the park as images appeared one by one, some invented from the stories of others, some vague compilations of repeated moments, others temporarily intense and clear, but they arrived and fell away as my feet hit the sidewalk, a reverie with a rhythm. I watched my grandmother move heavily onto the stone step outside the kitchen, carrying two pails, the hem of her cotton dress lifted in a breeze. I saw my grandfather grip a bag of candy in his stub fingers and tear it open with the good ones, shaking out a hard ribbon of green and white into my waiting hand. I saw the stick-thin

Max, saw his hand, incongruously large and brown, engulf my sister's slender white fingers: "I want you to find someone else, to
marry again. You're still my young wife, and now you're my young
widow. Be a merry widow, a dancing widow. I don't want you to be
alone." I imagined my mother leaning over to kiss the cheek of her
dead father, and then Lorelei's old-woman doll on her deathbed. I
saw Edie Bly as Lili Drake walk with a heavy suitcase down an al-
ley in the unnamed city, saw the innkeeper step out of a door and
speak to her urgently in sign language. She answered in kind, her
fingers moving rapidly. I remembered the piece by Shostakovich
in the background, saw my father in his bed at the nursing home
and heard the noise of his cough as he tried to hack up the thick
phlegm from his ruined lungs, his expression closed and internal,
muttering, "I used to be able to get it up." I saw my mother button
his pajamas and straighten the collar, watched her move past me to
retrieve his toothbrush and a plastic basin and then help him brush
his teeth. I said goodnight to my father and hugged him. Afterward, he smiled at me, his eyes rueful. "These days," he said, "I
must work hard to avoid sentimentality." I stood in the hallway
and listened to my mother's voice. "Can you sleep now, Lars? Do
you need anything else?"

When I turned down Garfield and neared my house, I noticed
that a single light was on in the downstairs apartment. The shades
were drawn, but all three windows were open behind the iron
grilles that protected them. I glanced at my watch. It was three-
ten, and as I turned to go up the stoop, I saw a heap of papers on
the top step. Even before I bent over to pick them up, I knew.

There must have been a hundred pictures, most of them cheaply
printed on ordinary typing paper—a glut of photographs of Eggy
and Miranda and self-portraits of Lane with his camera. There
were other people I didn't recognize, and then several pictures
of me, walking into my office, having lunch on East Forty-third

Street with a book, striding toward the subway, picking up the *Times* on my doorstep in the morning, and one, shot through the front window of the house, in which I sat with my cup of coffee, looking out. I shuffled through them, quickly casting them aside until, near the bottom, I found an image of Miranda, naked and asleep in a bed, probably Lane's. She was lying on her side, her face partly hidden by the pillow. The paper had been crumpled. As soon as I was inside the house I put it on the table and, not without a sense of guilt, carefully flattened it out. As I looked at the curve of Miranda's narrow hip, her breast covered by one arm, I felt a sudden rush of anxiety, walked to my window, and closed the shutters.

Thirty seconds later, the telephone rang. "You got the photos?" It was Lane's voice, but he seemed to have made an attempt to disguise it. It sounded higher than I remembered.

"What's all this about?" I said. "I honestly don't understand."

Lane was silent. I suspected that he had not been prepared for my honesty. Then he said the last thing I had anticipated. "I need a shrink."

I laughed.

Then he hung up.

Again and again, I heard that laugh in my ears. I held it up for inspection, turned it inside out, and reflected on that single spontaneous guffaw until it had been broken down into a thousand pieces of probably useless analysis. A summary of the tortuous route of my thinking would go something like this: It could have been that Lane was in bad shape and truly wanted help, in which case, my laughter was a gross violation of professional standards; or he may have expected the laugh, and had hung up on me to create exactly the tormented quandary that followed; or he may have occupied some position in between and had acted without a fully conscious motive. He could have felt that hanging up at that moment was more aggressive than talking and, hoping to disorient me, he responded to that urge—*or* my laugh had wounded his pride, and not knowing what else to do and feeling momentarily that I had the upper hand, he had cut off the conversation. Before I went to bed, I thought of a bit of Russian folk wisdom a history professor had once told me: If you ever run into the Devil, the only way to get rid of him is to laugh in his face.

WEDNESDAY NIGHT, BURTON gave his report over Chinese food, tapping his chopsticks from time to time on the table to punctuate his commentary, which I took as a sign of increased excitement in his unofficial position as Inga's gumshoe. Despite my grave doubts about my friend's activities, I found my affection for Burton growing.

"I didn't actually enter the establishment, you understand, but remained poised without. My persona—the one I don for the job—would not allow it, as it were. The joint is too fashionable. Espresso goes for three dollars, out of my price range."

"Burton," I nudged, "what happened?"

"Yes, of course. Ms. Bly works in Tribeca now, not Queens. She's changed her job, you see—Tribeca Realtors, higher wages, fancy properties. She throws down her cigarette, walks into Balthazar. I note that she is expectant, decided. My reading of bodies, if I do say so myself, has become expert. You know the Libet research, of course, that the somatic intention precedes the conscious thought? A third of a second!" After my nod, Burton made another dash toward the point. "Fehlburger is lying in wait." Burton snapped his chopsticks, then wiped his forehead. "As they sit in the café, both of them are fortunately visible—well, not entirely. Their legs are obscured beneath the table, but the all-important facial areas, the sites of crucial interaction, entirely exposed. I noted tension between the parties, not hostility, no, that would be too strong, a strain in both necks and across the eyes. Words are exchanged." Burton paused. "Only one of which I was able to ascertain." The chopsticks hit the table. "Lip-reading has become essential, Erik. I consider myself in training, improving with each hour on the job."

"The word?"

"*Copies*," Burton said triumphantly.

"Of letters, I assume."

"That I would also assume, but no packages of any kind were passed between them." Burton began to dry himself vigorously with the familiar handkerchief, but his shoulders slumped. "It's unlikely that you're aware of the various materials to be found online about your sister. I confess to having kept abreast of the articles, interviews, and notices over the years. I had imagined that in this specific case, the target was Max Blaustein, muddying his reputation, but it has come to my attention that this Fehlburger personage, curious name, *Fehl* is *fault* or *blemish* in German, as you are no doubt aware. I seem to remember you studied German. In all events, this Fehlburger is intent on injuring, not the reputation of your deceased brother-in-law, but that of your sister, for whom she has particular venom, the cause of which I have not been able to uncover. There exist, however, online, several startlingly cruel and gratuitous attacks on your sister and her work written under several names, three of which I have been able to connect to this single woman."

"Good grief," I said.

Burton's face was streaming, and his expression turned grave. "She's freelance, you understand, not connected to any particular paper or magazine. It's been some time since you and I spoke, hence the plethora of news on this front, much of it available at the touch of a few keys. There is an entry on the Web site of Nebraska University Press about Henry Morris's forthcoming book, which is referred to *as*"—Burton dropped his voice to a whisper—"'a critical *biography*.' It seems, too, and I have tracked this, made the appropriate inquiries, that Ms. Bly is not alone. It seems that he has, that the man has, well, systematically, and one might say, voraciously, I would say it, yes, I would say it, visited the women in Blaustein's life, procuring their confidences and, in some cases, favors. I use the word in its illicit sense, and add, with all delicacy and respect, that I feel for your sister in this regard. Indeed, my heart goes out to her." Burton lowered his eyes onto the General Tso's chicken that sat in front of him.

"But can you be sure of this, Burton? I mean, you haven't been peering into bedrooms, have you?"

Burton's face turned a deep red. "Nothing so unseemly. No, I confess I have inferred the behavior, not actually witnessed it. Comings and goings. Entrances and exits. And my own reading, interpretation, even divination of character. The man in question has predilections, appetites, if you will, that augur poorly. I see black storm clouds, turbulent weather in the future."

Although I shared some of Burton's doubts, I couldn't be sure he was right about Henry Morris, whom he regarded as a rival. What I did understand was that my sister, or at least the idea of my sister, had become enmeshed in the personal dramas of at least three people: the vengeful, narcissistic projections of Fehlburger, the literary fantasies of Morris, and the more benign, but equally passionate obsession of my friend Burton which had, I felt, begun to take on quixotic proportions.

MS. L. BEGAN the session that Wednesday with a barrage of complaints about her stepmother and her pregnant stepsister. I knew the unborn child was important, but it was hard to find a way in with Ms. L. She called me a "smug asshole analyst who couldn't help a fly," an odd twist on the idiom "wouldn't *hurt* a fly," no doubt an expression of her frustration with what she referred to as my "impotence." She called me a "confused, lying S.O.B. who didn't know the truth when he heard it." She had been abused, thrown against the wall. She *remembered*.

I said she seemed to want rage from me. She pushed and tested me all the time. But there were rules that governed our exchange, her behavior and mine, and she was breaking them. "If you think I can't help you, why do you come?" I knew there was a remote quality to my words, knew that I was backing away from her, and yet I hoped to introduce some ambiguity into her perceptions.

Ms. L. looked up at me. "I don't know."

"Is it possible that some part of you still believes we can make progress?"

She was silent. Her eyes were blank and cold.

I tried again. "Remember when we talked about your voids? You said you hate being so passive, so unproductive. When you attack me over and over, you encourage passivity in me because I don't know where to turn or what to say. You create in me the very thing you hate in yourself."

Ms. L.'s head wobbled and she closed her eyes. "I don't feel well," she said. Then she stood up fast, looked around, and holding her stomach, she leaned over my wastebasket and threw up.

I brought her some Kleenex for her mouth, told her I'd be right back, carried the container to the bathroom, emptied it into the toilet, and watched the drab-colored, lumpy vomit disappear with the flush. I poured some water and cleanser into the basket, left it behind me, and returned quickly to my office.

"How are you?" I said. "How are you feeling?"

"What did you do with it?" she asked. Her face was pale.

"I took care of it. It's all right."

"You cleaned it?" she said in a low voice.

"Rinsed it out."

"You cleaned up my puke? Why didn't you get somebody else to do it?"

"It wasn't necessary."

"You're disgusting," she said sternly. "Look at you." It wasn't her voice; I knew I was hearing someone else, and I jumped in.

"Are you saying that to me?" I asked her. I could hear the pity in my voice, almost a sob. "You sound like a grown-up reprimanding a child."

A look of confusion came over her face. She shook her head. "I'm lost," she said. "I'm cold. I'm all alone."

THAT EVENING, THE anxiety hit. I found myself breathing rapidly, the pressure in my lungs was fierce, and I was overcome by a restlessness so intense that I began to pace around the house, from one floor to the other. I picked up the most recent issue of the *Journal of Consciousness Studies* and immediately knew I couldn't read it. I thought of my mother and her unread books, tried breathing exercises in a chair, but the sirens inside me continued to scream. I had seen this in some of my depressed patients. I recognized it, for Christ's sake. Mood disorder. How sanguine the diagnosis seems from afar. "It's a fine line," Magda had told me, "between empathy and distance. Too close, and you can be of no help. Without compassion, there's no alliance between you and the patient." I was racing. And then, *This is why he walked*. The sentence made me shake more. My father tried to walk it away—the speeding internal engine that wouldn't turn off.

When the doorbell rang, I had poured myself a Scotch hoping it would quiet the roar within me. I could have used a milligram of lorazepam. I left my drink on the counter, walked down the hall, and through the glass saw Jeffrey Lane. His arrival created more chaos inside me. Could I turn around and let him stand there until he left? I opened the door. He said he just wanted a few minutes of my time; it wouldn't take long. I let him into the hallway but didn't shut the door behind him. The man looked disheveled, and he was hunched over with one hand on his stomach. I noticed the heavy black bag slung over his shoulder and guessed it was camera equipment.

"I need help," he said. "I can't go on."

"Are you injured?" I asked, nodding at his stomach.

"Not physically," he said.

"I can recommend someone you can talk to." My tone was robotic, and my breath came in small puffs. I felt desperate to get rid of him.

"It's Miranda," he said.

"What's happened to her? Is she all right?"

"She's all right." He took a step toward me. "I'm the one who's in trouble."

"In what way?"

"I'm planning my funeral," he said. Then he looked up at me and smiled.

The smile was unintelligible, but my irritation with him seemed to direct my disquiet, which until then had been aimless, and this was oddly helpful. I breathed more easily. "What does that have to do with Miranda?" I asked.

"She'll be sorry." He closed his eyes.

"Listen," I said, my voice rising, "I'm not your physician. I don't like being harassed by you, and I don't like being photographed without my permission, but if you need help, go to the emergency room at Methodist Hospital and tell them."

Lane turned his back to me and faced himself in the wide hallway mirror. "I look like shit," he said. "My parents are dead. They never wanted me anyway. My girlfriend is sick of me. My daughter is a stranger." He eyed my reflection. "'Dr. Erik doesn't take pictures. He likes to talk.' That's what she said. But I need the photos, you see, it's not like I can help it. It's documentation, man, it's my whole splendid mess on film. Digital magic. Jeff's life. Warty, sad, but there it is. *Moi.* Giving that up would be impossible. The world's going virtual anyway; there's no reality left. Simulacra, baby."

I looked at his spiky hair. For some reason those small tufts of vanity were intolerable to me, and I had a brief fantasy of pulling them out by the roots. "I think you should leave now," I said, my voice shaking.

"You must have had your share of troubles, man," he continued, as if I had said nothing. "You're divorced, right? Must have fucked up with her." He continued to speak to himself in the mirror in a low, thoughtful tone. "Must be hard dealing with crazy people all the time." He paused and leaned toward his own face, then in a coy voice said, "Must *lose* some along the way."

I flinched and saw his eyes move to my reflection. My heart beat faster. I hated the man. I seized him by both shoulders from behind, pulled him backward and then shoved him into the mirror. His neck lolled backward for an instant and then his head hit the glass. It made a dull noise. Still gripping him, I was flooded by a sensation of joyous release and was about to do it again. Instead, I dropped my hands. He grabbed his forehead, turned around, took a few unstable steps, and slumped to the floor. The thought that I had killed him came instantly, and then the word *no* escaped my lips, a barely articulated word, more like an animal cry than a human voice. I bent over him. But Lane wasn't dead. He lay on the floor with his eyes open and a horrible smile wet with saliva on his lips. "Big man," he said.

"Are you okay?" I don't know what came over me, I thought, but I rejected the stupid incantation. I hadn't been in a fight since grade school.

He sat up. I put my hand to his forehead to examine it. There was no visible wound. "If you get a headache or feel any dizziness in the next forty-eight hours, go straight to the hospital."

"You just told me to go there for my *suicidal ideation*, didn't you?"

I noticed that he was using the jargon of my profession again, but I ignored it. "How do you feel?" I asked.

"I'm okay," he said. "I fell down just to scare you."

Rather than angering me, these words brought a feeling of relief and happiness. I helped him up, brought him to a chair, and offered him a Scotch, which he accepted. When he had the drink, he looked at me and said, "It's not what you think. I'm an explorer taking trips into the wilderness, documenting what he finds, and then remaking the trip when it's over." He waved his right hand. "Every biography, every autobiography is make-believe, right? I'm creating several in real time, but it's all staged, if you see what I mean. *I'm* staging it. You're one of the players. So is Miranda."

"And Eglantine?" I asked.

He nodded, but his face grew sober. "I wouldn't hurt her for anything. I love the kid."

He wouldn't hurt us, if that's what you mean. I remembered Miranda's words. Then thought, I hurt him. "Why the photos? Why tell me you're planning your funeral? You goad me and insinuate . . ." I didn't finish the sentence. It was Sarah, I thought, a hidden reference to Sarah that had made me push him. He knew about it. Somehow he knew about it. "Why are you doing all this?"

He lifted his eyes to mine and said, "I'm trying on my various personas for the work. It can't be simple, and it has to be dangerous. I have to go as far as I can."

Lane left soon after that comment. We shook hands, but I had no idea what the gesture meant, and when I had released him, I felt tainted and had a vague sense that I had been manipulated once again. I've had patients who leap from planes, deep-sea dive, bungee jump—high-risk sports that bring with them a feeling of being more alive. And then there are those who cut themselves repeatedly to feel a rush of realness, but exactly what Lane wanted remained nebulous. For a moment the violence had elated me, but within seconds that wild energy had been lulled into guilt. It would have been different if he had fought back. But coming at a man from behind? It was shameful, infantile, the act of a little boy on the playground who suddenly pushes a jeering playmate. As I sat in my armchair, I remembered a passage in one of Rilke's letters to the young poet: "For if we think of this existence of the individual as a larger or smaller room, it appears that most people learn to know only a corner of their room, a place by the window, a strip of floor on which they walk up and down."

"YOU PUSHED HIM?" Miranda said. "Is he all right?"

I don't know what came over me. "I lost my temper," I said aloud. "The photos, the phone call, his tone of voice. I had to tell you before he did. It was stupid, and yes, he seemed fine when he left."

Miranda shook her head. "I think he was hoping you'd admit him to the hospital, so he could see what it's like."

I was sitting beside Miranda on her blue sofa. She leaned back on a cushion, her gleaming brown legs propped on the coffee table in front of us. She was dressed in shorts and a T-shirt for the sweltering July night, and I had to work to keep my eyes off her calves and ankles. An air conditioner rattled from the back room, and a fan above us kept the temperature bearable, but the air was still humid, and my arms and chest felt clammy.

"He has a Web site, you know, very elaborate, with images and texts, some film sequences. He gets lots of hits, apparently, and he's advertising his show in November with the idea that it's going to contain some big revelation. He sends out mass e-mails about himself, updates on 'Jeff's Lives,' but with all kinds of quotations and abstruse commentary about simulacra and superconductivity and the psychotic sublime. He likes to say he's a post-Nietzschean." Miranda smiled to herself. "Remember when he blanked out my eyes in the picture? He told me he was *simulating* a stalker as a game with himself."

"Simulating a stalker?"

She shook her head. "He's investigating insanity because he thinks psychiatry is a mechanism of control, that madness is a form of creative being that's squashed in hospitals and clinics. He says the whole discipline's a fraud."

"Nothing new there," I said.

"He keeps quoting someone."

"Thomas Szasz?"

"That's it. Anyway, I think he wants you in the project because of what you *do*." Miranda looked down. "I'm sorry he's annoying you. He isn't that way with me, but since I've been seeing him again, I've remembered everything that bothered me almost from the start: his ambition, his flights into nutty philosophy, his immaturity." Miranda sighed. "The irony is that all those flaws are also his strengths, his charm. But I can tell you this: He's much too involved with his show to do away with himself any time soon."

I remembered Lane speaking to my mirror, recalled his bright eyes and my charged body as I looked at him. "Well," I said, "I guess a simulated suicide would, by definition, be ineffective, so that's one good thing."

Miranda smiled. "I found out that he never knew his black/Cherokee grandmother. His mother cut off relations with her when she left home at seventeen. He never had anything to do with that woman who's so important to his idea of himself. It's kind of sad."

"So," I said. "Your relationship to him now is . . ."

"I don't know what it is. He's Eggy's father, no way around that. He's started to help financially with her, which takes a burden off me. I told him I want a pause between us. He can still see Eggy. He's on the rise, I think, and that's good for him. There have been some articles on his work. Writer/visual artist/performance artist, the all-in-one. I noticed they all say he's twenty-five, which isn't true, so he must be fibbing about his age to make himself more desirable. If he's crazy, he's crazy in an ambitious, clever way." She paused. "And his work is good, Erik. It really is."

I looked at her. "What about your work?'

"I'm drawing."

"Dreams?"

Miranda looked suddenly remote. "In a way, yes."

"What way?"

I watched her hesitate, but then, she said. "I dreamed that I was pregnant again, but the child wasn't growing right inside me; it was a tiny girl shriveling up, and it was my fault because I kept forgetting about her, not doing the right things, and not wanting her enough. And then a woman was there, standing in front of me. A really tall dark-skinned woman. She said, 'We'll have to clean the knife.'"

"Can I see the picture?"

"When I'm finished. It looks like the dream drawings are going to be a book. A friend of mine showed a couple of them to somebody at Luce, the place that publishes artist's books, and they're interested."

"That's great," I said.

Miranda narrowed her eyes. She didn't respond to my congratulations. Instead, she said, "When I got pregnant, Mum cried. You can't know, but she doesn't cry, and looking at her face shocked me. It was awful, like seeing another person. She wanted me to marry right, not be a single mother." Miranda took a breath and looked away.

"Well, it's harder," I said.

"Yes," she said. Her white front teeth appeared for an instant over her soft bottom lip. "But you don't come second to a husband."

When she spoke, I felt as if a breeze were passing through me.

"And I can draw into the night when I have the stamina."

"Where's Eggy?"

"Sarah Bernhardt is with my parents tonight." Miranda smiled to herself and shook her head. "Anyway, the dream came from a story my grandmother told me."

Miranda seemed eager to talk. I wondered if my confession about Lane had made it easier for her. "When Mum was pregnant with my sister Alice, I went to stay with Gran. I loved that house. It's gone now, sold. One night, I remember, I was supposed to be asleep, but I couldn't, and I saw that Gran had her light on, and I went in to her. I expected her to send me back to bed, but she didn't. She was reading a book, and instead of yelling at me, she patted the bed beside her, and I climbed in. She smelled of camphor; my grandmother used it for her aches. That was when she told me about Cut Hill. It was a Maroon story, and I don't know how she heard it because the Maroons are very secretive about their knowledge. It was from the wars in the early 1700s. An English soldier chased down a Maroon woman who was very pregnant, with a big belly, and he tied her to a tree and was about to slice her open with his sword, but before he did it, he spoke to the baby inside her and asked, 'Are you a man or a woman?' The baby said, 'Me a man.' And as soon as the child spoke, the sword in the soldier's hand mashed up, and the Englishman fell down dead."

Miranda stared at her hands. "It made a deep impression on me, the baby speaking from inside his mother and the magic that protected her and the fact that Gran told it with such reverence, and of course, Mum was very close to giving birth. I was talking to Alice about it last week, and that same night I had the dream."

The story made us silent, and had I dared, I would have touched her then, put my hands on her and pulled her into me, but I was afraid of being rebuffed and losing the comfort between us.

"I'll be in Jamaica with Eggy for two weeks. My parents are going, too. I have my vacation."

That was when I offered to check on the apartment, water her plants, and take in her mail while she was away. She accepted, saying it would free her sisters from those duties. She looked at her watch, and taking the hint, I stood up. As I walked into the dark hallway, I saw something shining as it caught the light from the next room. When Miranda switched on a lamp, I identified the object. Lying on the low bench near the door was a small pair of wire wings embellished with silver glitter. They were crumpled, and there were rust-colored stains on the white fabric.

"I guess Eggy's been doing a lot of flying," I said.

Miranda smiled broadly, and the shrewd look I had come to recognize appeared in her eyes. I held out my hand to say goodnight, but she reached up for my face, pulled it toward her, and gave me two kisses on my cheeks. They were the usual chaste, friendly kisses, but that didn't prevent me from feeling her lips burn on my skin long after she had withdrawn from me and I was sitting upstairs in my study recording the dream and the story of Cut Hill.

THE DAY AFTER Miranda left for Jamaica, I had dinner with my sister on White Street, and she told me she had stopped *seeing* Henry Morris. Miranda had used the same word about Lane: She had been *seeing* him again. "Seeing" had become the euphemism of choice for relations between people that included copulation. I hadn't told Inga about Burton's suspicions. They had struck me as rather flimsy. *Comings and goings. Entrances and exits. Divinations.* Inga's story was different from Burton's, but there were similarities nevertheless. Inga knew that Henry had spoken not only to Edie and to Max's ex-wives but also to the "Burger woman." The journalist believed that Max's letters held some ugly secret above and beyond the fact that Joel might be Max's son, but she refused to say what she imagined that hidden information could be. Henry had found her "peculiar, obsessional, and maybe out of her mind." It wasn't the journalist who had come between Inga and Henry, it was Max.

"It's not that I felt he was dishonest," my sister said. "He didn't lie. The attraction between us was real. He told me I was beautiful, and he meant it. Old lady that I am." She shook her head, her face both sad and ironic. "But you see, he quoted Max a lot. We'd be having dinner and out would come a whole paragraph from *Derelict John* or *Mourning Clothes*. Of course, that's what he does day in and day out. He's on sabbatical, and he's writing his book. Still, it began to unnerve me. I tried to talk to him about it. He was sympathetic, but you know, I don't think he could help himself. He met Max only once, and so Max wasn't a person for him. He was a literary saint. Then four nights ago, we were in his apartment and we made love. It was a kind of drowning. I can only tell you, Erik. You're the only one. I can't even tell Leo, dear Leo who's half in love with me, I think, just half, but anyway, Henry was ferocious and strong. I felt all lit up. I was dizzy afterward. Then, as we were lying there, he said, 'In her he recovered the country he had lost. When he entered her body he was no longer in exile.'"

I looked at Inga.

"I recognized it right away. It's from *Living Mirror*, the first novel Max wrote after he met me. For a little while I just lay there stunned. But then I felt smothered. It was as if I had no value for myself. I got up and walked out. I spoke to him on the phone that afternoon. He said he hadn't meant to hurt me, but it's too late. I feel as if I've debased myself."

"That's entirely the wrong word."

"I don't know. What kind of a woman sleeps with her dead husband's biographer?"

The question was so odd, I didn't know how to respond. Then I said all kinds of women might sleep with their dead husband's biographer.

Inga grimaced. "Yesterday, when I went to read to Leo, I let him touch me."

"You did?"

"Yes, with my clothes on, but he ran his hands over my whole body."

"And it was nice, not awkward?"

My sister nodded. She looked up at me with that peculiar shining expression she used to have when we were children. "I can't live without intimacy," she said. "I can't do that anymore."

DURING THE TWO weeks while Miranda was gone, I took in her mail and mine, noting that there were no envelopes from Lane addressed to either of us. I let myself in downstairs to water the three plants in the front room and found myself slightly awed by my presence in the vacant apartment. I was alone with her things, and this felt mysterious in itself. Miranda had left the place spotless, but on a table in the front room seven drawings had been laid out, and I lingered over them every evening. The first three were of the woman in Miranda's dream, rendered several times in black ink on each page. The lines of the looming figure were swift and forceful, and I could see that she was trying to get it right. Each line had to do a lot of work. The woman appeared to be immensely tall, thin, but with powerful arm and leg muscles. A giantess. She wore a loose dress and held a raised knife in her right hand. *We'll have to clean the knife*. There were two drawings of a fetus: the first a shrunken little body in a sac and the second a hearty, much fatter creature with an open mouth. The enchanted manchild. The last two were unfinished—ink sketches of the same image. A man wearing a hat lay on top of a woman in a long white dress. He had pinned her to the ground by her wrists. There was an air of violence in the picture, which may have been created by the simple fact that the man was white and the woman black, a contrast that summoned the brutal story of white masters raping slave women. Although his face was invisible, hers was turned outward toward the viewer. She had the expression of a dead person—a blank. In the second version of the drawing, the color difference between the figures wasn't so pronounced. A gray wash had been applied to both their arms and faces, and they looked as if their bodies weren't discrete, but turning to liquid. They seemed to be lying in a shallow pool of filmy water. After three or four days, I found that the first thing I did after my brief chores was to lean over this second version of the sketch, stare at it for a while, and then go back upstairs.

Two nights before Miranda and Eggy returned, I carried their mail downstairs and went to look at the drawing. Examining it again, I asked myself what I was looking at. *What is it?* Was she dead? I leaned close to the fine lines of the woman's face, her long arms, the shoulders of the man, the brim of his hat. I closed my eyes to meditate on the two people, and for a fraction of a second, in this fleeting, blind afterimage, I saw the woman's wrists jerk upward. When I opened my eyes, I had the bleak thought that perception itself is a form of hallucination.

The last night, I walked down the stairs with four pieces of mail and laid them carefully on the pile in the hallway. I avoided the drawing but didn't leave the apartment. Instead, I walked through the living room and the galley kitchen, then into the hall, and opened the door to what I guessed was Miranda's room—the larger of the two bedrooms. For some time, I stood on the threshold and looked at the bed with its beige cover; the night table piled with books; the dresser, its surface ornamented with two bowls and a vase; the oval mirror that hung above it, and two large, framed black-and-white photographs of Eglantine, one as a sleeping infant, curled up among rumpled sheets like snowdrifts in light and shadow, and another, more recent one of the child I knew. She was wearing a tutu and a crown but was posing like a body builder, showing her biceps to the camera, a ferocious look on her face. I believe I told myself that I wanted to look more closely at the images, but this was an excuse to cross the threshold, which I did. My breath quickened as I examined Miranda's books. She had a book of Diane Arbus photos, a volume called *Caribbean Autobiography: Cultural Identity and Self-Representation*, three books on the Maroons, and five novels beside the bed. I picked up one called *Delusion*. It had a scarlet cover, bold lettering, and a white rectangle that contained a scribbled line drawing of a face. I guessed it was Miranda's design, and when I opened the book to check, I discovered I was right. The other four covers were also hers, and like the first, their designs were simple but arresting, with strong colors. There were no curls or frills, no slanted letters or extra ornament. The aesthetic was tough, masculine, restrained. I returned each book carefully to its original place in the pile, touched the cover of her bed very carefully, and then stood over her dresser for several minutes, listening to the sound of my own breathing. The urge to open it was overpowering. I wanted to see her clothes, her stockings and her underwear. If I hadn't looked up and seen my hungry expression in the mirror, I would have done it. The man I saw had a haunted, wild look. I backed away from him and fled upstairs.

My solitude had gradually begun to alter me, to turn me into a man I had not expected, a person far more peculiar than I had ever imagined, a man who hovered in a woman's room, breathing loudly, with his fingers near, but not touching the pulls on her drawer. I've often thought that none of us is what we imagine, that each of us normalizes the terrible strangeness of inner life with a variety of convenient fictions. I didn't mean to lie to myself, but I understood that beneath the self I had believed in was another person who wandered in that parallel world Miranda had spoken about—down streets and past houses with another architecture altogether.

MY ANXIETY CONTINUED. The worst bouts were at night, when I would often wake with a pounding heart after terrifying dreams, but during the day and with my patients I seemed able to keep it in check. I made a point of calling Laura, and during the sultry month of August we saw each other at least twice a week, always on days her son spent with her ex-husband. When she confessed to me in the middle of the month over a plate of gnocchi that she wasn't ready for "a serious relationship," I told her plainly that I liked her company but wasn't advertising myself for the role of second husband. I was happy to be, I said, a transitional object of sorts, one that might ease the way toward future connubial bliss. Like a ragged blanket or bear, I would serve happily until outgrown. Laura laughed, shook her head, and said, "What you really mean is that you don't mind having a fuck buddy." I agreed somewhat sheepishly. Released from worries about the nature of our rapport, we were able to devour each other guilt-free, or so I imagined. By the end of the summer, Laura Capelli had crept under my skin. I found myself thinking about the dark hair that curled at the back of her neck, her skin with its hint of green, her booming laugh, her breasts, her mother's involved recipes for tripe and veal, which she liked to dictate to me in bed, her spot-on imitations of Morton Solomon, an octogenarian analyst we both knew, a man whose slow, sing-song voice, with its unmistakable German accent, droned on and on at countless conferences and meetings as he patiently, painstakingly explicated some point in Freud (splitting of the ego, *Ichspaltung*, was one of his favorites), her tendency to raise her index finger and shake it at me when she was excited, and the little yelps she let out during her orgasms.

My downstairs neighbors returned, but I hardly saw them. August was a slow month in publishing, Miranda told me when I met her outside one morning on my way to work. She and Eglantine would be spending time in Massachusetts with "friends"—long weekends mostly. Inga and Sonia left the city, too, for excursions to the Hamptons and Connecticut. I stayed in Brooklyn, rode the subway, inhaling its odors of urine, sweat, and unwashed flesh, and tilted internally toward self-pity.

AFTER MOVING HER things into a dormitory room at Columbia, Sonia returned on the evening of September tenth and spent the night at her mother's. According to Inga, the two of them had a pleasant evening, and Sonia seemed to sleep well. The next morning, she woke up, walked into the kitchen, and rather than go to the refrigerator for her habitual orange juice, she went to the window. Inga was reading the newspaper and drinking her coffee. After freezing in front of the pane, Sonia put her hands on either side of her face and shouted, "I don't want this world! I don't want it!" Then she sank to her knees and began to sob uncontrollably. Inga tried to hold Sonia. At first she flailed and fought, but after a while Inga took Sonia into her arms and began to rock her. Sonia wept, and her mother rocked through the morning and into the afternoon. Then the girl began to talk. She talked, broke down, talked more, and broke down again.

The second anniversary opened an internal crack in Sonia, a fissure through which she released the explosive feeling that had horrified her for two years. The conflagration that had burned so many, that had pushed people into the open air, onto the ledges from which they jumped, some of them on fire, had left its unspeakable images inside my niece. Inga told me that during those hours she never let go of her daughter. Even when she had made them each a sandwich, she took Sonia to the kitchen with her and fastened her child's arms around her waist while she cut and buttered the bread. Sonia didn't want a world in which buildings fell down and wars were fought for no reason. She didn't want a brother, either, she told her mother, or that stupid former actress Edie Bly in her life. She hated them, and she wanted her father back. She wanted to tell him she was sorry.

After I had seen my last patient, I listened to Inga's phone message and made my way to White Street. By the time I arrived, both mother and daughter were calm, the calm of exhaustion. I noticed that they both moved a little slowly and stiffly, as if their joints ached. Sonia raised her swollen face and looked at me as I put my hand on her shoulder, and then she lifted her arms and placed them around my waist. There wasn't much to say by then. Sonia's memories wouldn't leave her; atrocities would continue to happen in the world every day; Max would not be resurrected; and the boy who might be her brother would not conveniently disappear. If anything had changed, it was that Sonia knew she could survive the power of her own emotion. And so could her mother.

It wasn't until I was leaving that I saw the doll. It sat alone among Inga's books. "You actually did it," I said. "You bought one of those toys from Lorelei."

Inga nodded. "I almost bought a widow, but it seemed too, well, masochistic, so I got this little guy."

I leaned forward to look more closely at the boy doll, dressed up in a dark suit and sitting on a wooden chair. His blond head drooped forward, and his small embroidered face seemed pensive.

We stood for a moment looking at the figure, and then Inga said, "She said his father was struck by lightning. It's before the funeral."

"Why on earth would you want something like that?" I asked.

Inga patted my face three times very slowly. Her eyes looked hollow. "Don't worry about it," she said in a tired voice. "I'm no crazier than I've ever been."

THAT NIGHT I dreamed I was on the farm, standing near the grape arbor to the left of the outhouse, looking toward the broad rolling fields ahead of me. The dream was colorless. I saw everything in shades of gray. My father was there beside me, but I had no clear image of him, except that he was erect and still young. Although his figure was obscure, I felt him, knew that he stood several feet away from me and was also looking west. Then, as we watched, an explosion burst on the distant horizon and sent a great ragged ball of smoke into the sky. Then there was another, and then another—three huge blasts that filled the sky. From behind us, a voice I recognized as my grandfather's said, "Queak." All at once, we were blown backward by some unaccountable force, and my father and I landed inside the house in a cramped enclosure that resembled a cellar or an attic, its beams just above our heads. The room began to rock back and forth violently, and my unseen grandfather spoke again. I knew he was there, but I didn't turn my head. This time, I heard him pronounce the word "Quake," followed by "Earthquake." As I woke, the walls had begun to splinter and break apart.

Dream economies are frugal. The smoking sky on September eleventh, the television images from Iraq, the bombs that burst on the beach where my father had dug himself a trench in February 1945 burned in unison on the familiar ground of rural Minnesota. Three detonations. Three men of three generations together in a house that was going to pieces, a house I had inherited, a house that shuddered and shook like my sobbing niece and my own besieged body, inner cataclysms I associated with two men who were no longer alive. My grandfather shouts in his sleep. My father shoves his fist through the ceiling. I quake.

ON OCTOBER NINTH, Burton called me, and in an unsteady voice explained that he had not been in touch because a week and a half earlier his mother had died. If she had lived another month, he said, she would have been ninety years old. I knew only the bare outlines of his family story. Burton's parents were German Jews who made their way to New York in the late thirties. His mother had been a teacher, I recalled, and his father had held a position in the New York Society for Ethical Culture. My friend had once called himself "a late surprise." His mother had been over forty when her only child was born. After his father's death in 1995, Burton had moved into his mother's apartment in Riverdale, an arrangement that had spared the son from abject poverty and had allowed the increasingly frail Mrs. B. to stay at home.

When we met a week later, I noticed immediately that my friend looked drier. He was still shiny, but not dripping. I didn't remark on it, but Burton volunteered that his hyperhidrosis had taken a turn for the better.

"I feel some trepidation," he said, "no more than that. I feel acutely uncomfortable mentioning my altered somatic condition to a psychoanalyst, knowing full well that perspiration, or rather the precipitous decline of the same at this point in my life, that is, after my mother's demise, could be construed as . . ." Burton paused and wiped his forehead, more out of habit, I suspected, than need. He settled on a word. "Symptomatic."

"Burton," I said, "grief has many effects on people. I wouldn't overinterpret what appears to be a good thing."

His cheeks flushed as he studied the tablecloth. "The last month," he said, "she didn't know me."

"That's hard."

He nodded. "Stroke. Hemorrhagic. She changed personality." He frowned. "Got sweeter. The laughter distressed me— inappropriate mirth, chuckling, giggling, smiling all the time, that sort of thing. Preferable to anger. That must be acknowledged. Read about a patient who started biting after a stroke. Very hard on the family. Broke the skin." Burton looked up at me. "It hardly needs to be said, and yet I shall say it. As she declined, she disappeared. I missed the woman, despite her many, her many ambiguities. Yes," he said, "I longed for the difficult, perplexed, tormented, acerbic woman of . . ." He hesitated, searching for the words. "Of, of yore," he said finally.

We were the last customers to leave the restaurant that night. I could feel the waiters grow restless as Burton told the story of his mother's death and what he referred to as his "revised circumstances." The apartment now belonged to him, and his inheritance, although not lavish, would "unpinch" him for a good many years to come. "It might even," he told me with a thoughtful, cryptic smile, "do a little good in the world for a person of quality."

Before we parted on the sidewalk to hail cabs traveling in opposite directions, Burton gripped my hand, pumped it, and said, "To articulate the value, to me, of our renewed friendship, one that had been in hiatus, interrupted, as it were, for many years, is quite impossible. My gratitude is all the more replete now as I wrestle, metaphorically of course, with the Beast Melancholia."

As I sped down the FDR Drive, I looked out the window at the immense Pepsi-Cola sign suspended in blackness on the other side of the East River, and I found it beautiful. At that moment, the glowing emblem of a slightly older form of American capitalism was suffused with a feeling of loss, as if the sign reflected a collective wish that had now vanished. It was foolish to feel any emotion in response to an advertisement for soda pop, but when its image had dimmed, I thought to myself, They're all dying now, our fathers and our mothers—the immigrants and the exiles, the soldiers and the refugees, the boys and the girls—of "yore."

ON OCTOBER SECOND, Ms. L. announced with a smile that she was "finished" with me. She had consulted a crystal healer and had joined a self-help group for "survivors of abuse," people who "understood" her. Some of them had perfect memories from when they were one and two years old. It wasn't the first time she had latched onto the clichés of popular culture, but that day I realized that the primitive distinctions trumpeted in the press and on the Internet fed her split world. As she spoke to me, I heard in her voice the remote quality of ready-made diction, the language of propaganda, demagogues, and newsmen on television. She wasn't there with me. I told her this and asked whether she had thought through her decision. She screamed "Yes," stood up from her chair, spat in my face, and rushed through the door, not forgetting to slam it.

I wiped the saliva off my face with a Kleenex and sat motionless in my chair until the session ended. I knew she wouldn't return. After all, I was only the last in a long line of doctors and therapists she had abandoned in a rage: Leave them before they leave you. What I mourned as I sat there were the moments of opening, her wrenching movements toward another way of being. However deluded she may have been, Ms. L. was a forgotten child from the beginning. Her scars may not have been physical, as she wished them to be, but they cut to her core. The ostensible crisis had hinged at least in part on memory, fragile and opaque as it is. Literal physical torture at the hands of her mother would have justified her pain, preserved her identity in that immutable category "the abused child." The thought alone had brought her consolation. It conformed perfectly to her inner reality, a structure so rigid and frail that spontaneous combustion was always imminent. All this I knew, but there was another strain between us—fear, my fear. Acutely sensitive, Ms. L. had picked up the odor of something I myself didn't understand.

ON SATURDAY EVENING of the following week, I walked home from Laura's around midnight. I paused at the bottom of the stairs to dig my keys from my pocket, heard urgent whispering, the sound of the door to the garden apartment closing, and before I could register what was happening, I found myself face to face with Jeffrey Lane. He looked me in the eyes and said, "Hey, how are you, man?"

I nodded at him. "I'm all right. How are you?"

"All right," he said.

I looked down at my keys.

"Well," he said. "See ya later." He moved past me, and once he was on the sidewalk, he broke into a run. I watched him. Exactly why I can't say, but I didn't move until I had seen his figure disappear. If I hadn't waited, I wouldn't have heard Miranda crying. The shades were drawn, but the window was open a crack and, as I took the steps like a man with lead shoes, her low sobs accompanied me.

After I had let myself in, I sat in my green chair, where I usually did my reading, and for the first time in a long time I had no thoughts of any kind. For an hour or so, I listened to the noises of the night—traffic, muffled voices from someone's television, distant music, and people laughing down the block. But I didn't hear Miranda. Perhaps she had dried her tears and gone to bed.

INGA'S CALL CAME after a long day. I had interviewed two patients who had been referred to me, and that afternoon Mr. R. had told me his wife was leaving him. Mrs. R. didn't want the altered Mr. R., the man who had told me that the world had taken on a strange new brightness. He laughed more, hurt more, and saw more. He also wanted more sex, a development that the object of his revived libido resisted. "She liked me better as a stiff." I was reading my notes from the session when the phone rang, and I heard Inga's passionate, cracking voice.

"Lorelei called. Lisa wants to see us. She's going to tell us the story. I just know it. We can go this weekend. She's sick. She may be dying, but she refuses to go to the hospital."

Her excitement annoyed me. "I have a conference," I said.

"You're giving a paper?"

"No."

"Then you don't have to go."

"Inga," I said. "*You* go, and tell me what happens."

"It's you she wants to see. She won't see me without you."

"What?"

"You're the son, the man, the heir. I'm sure that's it. The daughter doesn't count."

I didn't answer her.

"Are you all right, Erik?" Inga asked. Her voice was softer.

I could feel my lungs tighten and the tension inside me grow. "Yes," I said.

"It's too bad Mamma's in Norway now, but we could fly in on Friday night, stay at Andrews House, see Lisa on Saturday, and be back on Sunday night."

"Inga, don't you have enough to worry about? Do you really want to risk a wild-goose chase?"

"It's about our father. Don't you see?"

"I see," I said.

"You're afraid, aren't you?"

"I'm busy."

"You'll regret it. You regretted that you weren't there when Pappa died. You felt bad. You said so. It wasn't your fault. You'd just been there for over a week. I know you couldn't leave your patients. You have to plan way in advance. I know that, but still, you couldn't be there. You didn't see him die. Now you have a chance to know something about his life—a missing piece."

I told her I would think about it, said good-bye, and hung up the phone. As I sat in the kitchen staring through the glass doors into the garden, I remembered an afternoon alone with my father in his room at the nursing home. He was sitting across from me in his wheelchair with his back to the door. After looking over the medication list, I asked him if he had any pain. "Discomfort," he said, smiling for an instant. "My damned nostrils from the oxygen tubes, some itching here and there, but no pain." I saw a nurse enter the room as my father cocked his head slightly at the sound of her steps.

"Friend or foe?" he roared, his voice resonant with mock-heroic thunder.

The pretty young woman leaned over him, her face only inches from his. She patted his shoulder, grinning affectionately, and said, "You decide."

An unlikely combination of the stoic and the humorist, my father had been a favorite with the nurses, orderlies, and general staff. And his power to charm them had worked like an elixir on his mood. He had found his hospital smile. He knew that he was dying, that he would never go home, that he would never see more than what he could see from the narrow window in his room or a chair in the cafeteria with its fluorescent lights that illuminated his fellow geriatric patients, some of whom sat slumped over in their chairs, their blind eyes funnels to nowhere. Others were ambulatory but demented. I remembered the old woman who dropped her fork at lunch mid-bite, stood up, and emitted small high shrieks of distress that alternated with the words, "Help me! Help me!" One of my father's table partners, Homer Petersen, had retained his mind but steadily dribbled food onto the bib he wore to protect his shirt, turning the textured white paper into a multicolored abstraction at every meal. Homer's twin brother, Milton, a stony man of grunts and nods, was also a regular presence at the table. Neither brother had been blessed with a gift for conversation. "*Homer* and *Milton*," my father said, shaking his head. "I'm afraid the great hopes their parents had for them have been sorely disappointed." But despite his fellow inmates, a number of them on the brink of "sans everything," my father maintained a buoyant dignity. He withdrew from me only once, during a lapse in our conversation. I had seen him retreat into a thought or memory many times. When I was a boy, I had been able to call him back. He would look a little surprised, his eyes would regain their focus, and then he would smile at me and launch into a discussion of weather patterns or an Icelandic saga or the life of an average mole. As I grew older, it became more difficult to pull him from those depths. I seemed to have lost the trick. Sometimes his eyes avoided mine, and sometimes I avoided his. That day, as he receded further from me, I asked him if it wasn't time to turn on the game. He watched no movies at the end of his life and read little fiction, but his passion for football never diminished. The Vikings lost that afternoon, if I remember correctly. The score was 24 to 17. I called Inga and told her I would make the trip.

WHILE TRAVELING, I found out from Inga that she had visited Edie and Joel again. Edie still had the letters, and she still refused to tell my sister what was in them, but she swore she had not shown their contents to the Burger woman or to anyone else. She wasn't ready to sell them to Inga. "I think she doesn't want me to have them, because then I'd have control of all of Max's papers and she resents the idea. Still, the better my relations with her are, the better it will be for all of us, Sonia especially, although she doesn't want anything to do with them, and she still refuses to have a DNA test." Inga also told me about Henry. He had sent her the final draft of *Max Blaustein: Labyrinthine Lives.*

"It's strange to read the biography of someone you loved. It's Max, and it's not Max. It's Henry's Max. There's nothing sensational or leering about it, and he spends a lot of time on the work. I skipped over much of it. I mean, I know he had all those women, that his first marriages were hard, and I know about Edie now. Henry says Max had an obsession with her, that she was an addict and that Max found desperate people fascinating. That's certainly true. But you know, he argues that Lavinia in *The Coffin Papers* is based on me."

I remembered the story. An old man, a famous composer, marries a much younger woman, a dancer, who was forced to stop after she broke her foot. They live happily together for ten years. Then he begins to suffer from physical problems—poor eyesight and gout among them—and his wife becomes his nurse. He decides it's time to write his memoirs and begins the project. Every morning, for three or four hours, he scribbles his life story by hand into a notebook. Every afternoon, his wife types the manuscript. In the beginning, she records exactly what appears on the page, but as she continues working, she finds herself immersed in the project and begins to make changes in the text. She improves a sentence here and there, and then slowly, imperceptibly, she finds that she's rewriting her husband's life, making it more vivid, more "true." Although he can write, he can't read her pages. The old man dies shortly after he finishes the book. Lavinia places the handwritten notebook beside her husband in his coffin and sends her manuscript to the waiting publisher.

"The implication is," Inga said, "that I'm an ambitious widow carefully guarding the Blaustein legacy."

"Does he say that?"

"I said *implication*."

"Inga, Max worried about being a burden to you as he got older, and that story may have been a subliminal way of recognizing both your work and the fact that you would go on without him. Lavinia is an ambiguous character. The old man's story is dull, as I recall, and self-aggrandizing, and she reinvents it to save him. And then there's Henry. He worships Max Blaustein the writer. As Max's biographer, he may have displaced some of his own worries onto you. He's the one writing a life, not you."

Inga turned to me. "Yes," she said. "He's more like Lavinia than I am. That could be why he spends so much time on that late story."

"And I'm sure he has no idea that's what he's doing."

The conversation took place at LaGuardia Airport as we waited to board our plane. Inga folded her arms across her chest and hugged herself. Tears came to her eyes, and I was afraid they would fall in public.

"Why are you upset?" I asked in a low voice.

She sniffed. "Maybe it's true that I'm trying to control the story of Max's life. Maybe that's wrong. Maybe Edie should sell the letters and let it all go public, whatever it is, and I'll keep a stiff upper lip. It's just that I don't want Sonia to be hurt more than she is already." I looked down at my sister's thin hand as it gripped the seat of the plastic chair. I noticed the blue lines of some protruding veins and a couple of brown age spots on her white skin. It must have been the position of her hands that brought it back to me. I remembered her sitting beside me in the church pew, her hands holding the seat, her eyes raised to the stained glass of the sanctuary window. As a girl, Inga had loved the benediction. She had waited for it every Sunday, had lifted her chin up and closed her eyes when the pastor made the sign of the cross and blessed the congregation. I had found her posture embarrassing, and when I elbowed her once and asked her why she did that every week, she said, "I like to hear the words about God's face. I want to feel the light."

The Lord bless thee and keep thee.
The Lord make his face shine upon thee, and be gracious
    unto thee.
The Lord lift up his countenance upon thee, and give thee
    peace:
In the Name of the Father, the Son, and of the Holy Ghost.

THE SMALL GRAY house, with its sagging screen porch, was on a corner, its lawn clearly demarcated because on either side of it the neighbors had neatly raked their leaves. We opened the flimsy porch door, passed a ripped lawn chair and an aging plastic gnome, and rang the bell. As Inga stood in front of me, I noticed she was trembling. I knew she couldn't control it, but I felt a wave of annoyance anyway. When Lorelei opened the door, her soft moon face was grave, and her eyes narrow and focused. The "Come in" she uttered rang with both ceremony and self-importance. Without another word, she pointed to a sofa covered with a plaid blanket in the small front room and disappeared through an inner door. Inga and I sat down. Lorelei was on her own turf now, however humble, and this had created a subtle but noticeable change in her demeanor. The woman had an officious streak, a quality that inevitably contains a hint of sadism. While we waited, I looked at the small plaster sculpture of praying hands that stood on the table in front of us, and I realized I hated that ubiquitous ornament of rural America. It evoked a glutinous piety I detested, not to speak of the fact that it always made me think of amputations.

"It's as if we were about to have an audience with the Queen," I said to Inga.

"You're in a savage mood," she answered in a whisper. "What's the matter with you?"

As I searched for a cause, I found only an amorphous blur, a vague consciousness that my sister and two spinster doll-makers had lured me into this misadventure, and I resented it, but I also had an uncomfortable feeling of reenactment. It wasn't déjà vu, that curious sensation of having lived through an identical event. Rather, it was a form of parallelism. The word "revenant" appeared in my mind. Somewhere there was the faint smell of mildew. As I pondered the odor as a possible trigger for the experience of repetition, I felt Inga clutch my hand suddenly, and I looked up.

Lorelei was standing stiffly in front of the opened door. "Aunt Lisa is ready for you," she said. "You will not be allowed to see the other legacy items."

As my sister nodded, I quelled another fit of irritation at the woman's pomposity. Lorelei let us pass in front of her as she held the door open with her back.

In front of us in a double bed lay Lisa Kovacek, née Odland. Only her small head and arms were visible. The rest of her was hidden under the sheets and several heavy blankets. I noticed that another sheet had been draped over some large rectangular object to the left of the bed. Aunt Lisa did not look friendly. Her lipless mouth had a tight, hard expression, and a thick pair of wire glasses covered her sunken eyes, making them illegible. Baggy skin hung from her chin and arms, which made me suspect that her illness, whatever it was, had precipitated sudden weight loss. What little remained of her hair was white and had been curled tightly into coils, which lent the top of her head an air of surprise that didn't at all match the face beneath it. She moved her head toward me and, without lifting her arm or hand, motioned with her fingers for me to come closer. I felt Inga approach behind me. Lisa gestured again for me to sit in a chair beside the bed, which I did. She turned her face toward me, and I examined the deep crosshatched wrinkles of her sagging cheeks, her hugely magnified eyes, opaque with cataracts, and the long keloids that marred her neck. Those untreated eyes coupled with the scars made me remember the child in a burning house and brought a moment of genuine sympathy. When she groped toward me with her right hand, I put my hand near hers. She circled my wrist with her fingers, and I noticed both that her grip was strong and that she did not have a fever.

"Lars," she said in an emphatic voice.

"I'm his son, Erik."

"I know that," she said sharply. "You think I'm soft in the head?"

"Not at all," I said, and smiled. My response was automatic. I adopted the calm voice of the friendly physician I had used thousands of times before, but it seemed to please her.

"Yer dad was handsome," she said in a clear voice.

Lisa tightened her fingers as she spoke, and then Inga put her hand on my shoulder. I guessed it was to steady herself. Neither my sister nor I answered this statement. When I glanced at Lorelei, who continued to stand against the opened door, she appeared to have gone rigid with concentration.

Lisa turned her face toward the ceiling. "Never said one word to nobody."

At exactly that moment, I recognized that my irritability had taken the place of dread. I knew the old lady was going to confess, and the story she would tell might change how I felt about my father. As I looked at her in anticipation, I realized all at once that she was enjoying the scene, that it was a production. She had planned it, hairdo and all; perhaps even her sickbed was a charade. For a dying woman, she struck me as unusually robust. I watched as Lisa nodded to Lorelei, who walked across the room and lifted the sheet to reveal what I had expected: more dolls.

With Lisa's fingers still around my wrist, I shifted my position in the chair to get a clear view, and Inga moved away from me to crouch down and examine what had been exposed. On a low table there were three dioramas. That was the only word that came to mind—three wooden boxes about three feet by four feet with the familiar small figures inside them. I saw immediately that the scenes all took place at night outside. Fields, sky, stars, and a small white house had been painted onto the back of the box. The floor was covered with dirt, which I could smell from where I sat. In the first, a blond female doll was squatting on the ground in a blue dress. The doll's mouth had been stitched with red thread in imitation of a full-throated scream. After patting Lisa's hand, I gently removed her fingers from my arm and leaned forward. A dark string that came from between the doll's legs was attached to a tiny gray figure, a skinny infant that had been painted with red blotches.

In the next box, I saw the tall, thin figure of a boy in overalls. His hair was dark and curly, and he was bent over the girl in the dirt, a small knife in his hand. He was about to cut the umbilical cord. In the last box, with no house, only trees and fields in the background, the male figure wielded a spade, his foot pressing it into the dirt. The girl lay curled up on the ground, hugging her knees. The tiny figure beside her was wrapped in gray cloth.

"That's Lisa and Lars," she said. "That's the story."

"The baby?" Inga asked in a small voice.

"Was stillborn," Lisa said to the ceiling. "Dead."

"The baby was our father's?" Inga said, her voice rising.

Lisa jerked her head toward Inga. "No, was Bernt Lubke's."

"Who was Bernt Lubke?" I asked.

"Nobody," she said bitterly. "Wasn't connected to yer family. Blue Wing trash. Lars kept his promise to me."

Inga walked toward the bed. "Where did you go after that? Why were you out in the field to begin with?" She paused. "Wasn't it obvious that you were pregnant? How could you have hidden it?"

"Wasn't obvious," she snapped. "And it's not part of it. None of yer business." Her voice took on a hysterical squawk.

Lorelei stepped away from the door, her eyes alive with emotion: a mixture of satisfaction and cruelty, I thought.

I turned toward the woman in the bed and put my hand on her arm. "I'm sorry," I said.

She didn't turn her head but kept on staring at the ceiling. "Don't matter. Didn't want it. That's the truth." She paused. "Yer dad heard me, was what it was. He heard me and come running. That's a fact. I wouldn't let him get his mother. I made him swear. The labor pains was bad, real bad, but after it was over, it wasn't me no more. I was looking on. Saw the blood, the little thing, saw it all from afar. Just like when it was made. Was just like I had nothin' to do with it."

Inga moved to the end of the bed. "Why did you go to Obert's to talk to our father?"

Lisa closed her eyes. "He lent me three dollars that day. Never paid him back. He was handsome, yer dad, and a gentleman." She lifted her glasses and rubbed her right eye. "I was afraid they'd think I kilt it, you know. Lars told me it was a girl. He put it in the ground."

Nobody said a word. I imagined my father kneeling over the hole he had dug, burying the dead newborn. I found myself wondering about the unmarked grave, where it was on the property. The landscape I saw in my mind was gray.

For the first time, Lisa pointed to Inga. "You have Les Rostrum, don't you?"

Inga nodded. She wasn't shaking anymore. "The boy at the funeral."

"He was a bad boy," she said brusquely. She made a clicking sound with her tongue, took a breath, and kept talking. "Was way back I found I could do it—make them people. Was before Walter came and told me about the fire. I made up the legacy—going to Lorelei when I'm dead. I started making her—the burnt Lisa—and them others. Can't remember the fire. Just have this." The woman's hand wandered to her neck. "Don't even know how it happened." She solemnly folded her hands across her chest as if she were arranging her final position, closed her eyes, then opened them. "Found my mother and my little brother's graves growed over. We cleaned 'em up real nice, didn't we, Lorelei?"

"Yes, we did." Lorelei's voice was crisp. "We sure did." She walked forward and adjusted the pillow beneath Lisa's curls, a gratuitous gesture that must have given her a chance to move. "You're tired," she said. The old woman smiled faintly. Lorelei smoothed the blankets and then, with an abrupt, violent gesture, lifted up the mattress and thrust the sheets and blankets under it, after which she leaned over her aunt and said, "Tight enough?"

Lisa closed her eyes and smiled again.

Lorelei turned to us. "My aunt will sleep now," she said, her eyes on the door.

Lorelei followed us out, her stiff leg moving briskly. Before leaving, my sister lingered for a moment on the porch. "Where's the burnt Lisa?" she asked Lorelei.

"In another place. Can't see her, just the ones with yer dad."

"She must have done those figures some time ago," I said, "before her cataracts made it impossible."

Lorelei looked for an instant as if she had been hit. Then she said, "Yes, I've taken over the work now, but Aunt Lisa has ideas, you know. Direction."

There was no handshake, not even a goodbye that I remember. Inga and I wandered out onto the porch and waded through the brown leaves toward our white rented car. It looked forlorn to me, parked alone on that unprepossessing street in the heart of Blue Wing.

Inga and I didn't speak for several minutes. I watched the black road under the moving car, the long lines of telephone wires ahead, noted the red and yellow that remained on some of the clusters of trees here and there, which broke the flat landscape, and felt the cold air rush past my ear from the open window.

I broke the silence. "I treated a patient once who hadn't spoken to anyone for four years when he was admitted to the hospital. He had threatened his stepmother with a shovel in the family garage. She and his father brought him in. For the first few months, he answered me only with a nod or a shake of his head. Because he was so silent, I would sometimes read something to him, usually a poem. He was completely inert, but I sensed he liked it. His story was very sketchy. According to the father, his mother had died when Mr. B. was seven of 'a bad heart.' Everything was fine, he said, and then one day, his son stopped talking. When I brought up the incident in the garage, Mr. B. didn't respond. I'd been treating him for weeks when I asked again. He took a piece of paper and a pen off my desk and wrote, 'It wasn't me.' "

Inga didn't say anything for a few seconds. She nodded. "It sounds as if Lisa left herself after the birth, floated out of her body. She didn't feel anything." Inga turned to look out the window. "It was a secret, all right, kept for years and years, but it doesn't *explain* much about Pappa, does it?" she said finally.

"Except that he kept his word."

"And we knew that already," Inga said.

"Yes," I said. "We knew that already."

I COULDN'T SLEEP that night. Battered by confused, restless thoughts, I lay under the flowered quilt in the Andrews House for a couple of hours before I dressed and walked down the stairs, through the dim lobby, and out onto Division Street. Then I drove to the farm. I was lucky there was a moon that night, or I would have been forced to leave the headlights on. As I turned into the driveway, I wondered what I was looking for. There's nothing to be found out here, I thought, except perhaps an idea. The house was locked. It had been robbed long ago of the homely objects that over time had gained value as "antiques" or "semi-antiques." Vandals had done their business, too, gone at the few pieces of furniture with an ax. My grandmother was still alive then, living in St. Paul with my uncle, and I had seen her fury mingle with tears when she heard what they had done. For as long as he was able, my father had come to mow the lawn and paint the vacant house when the white enamel blistered and the gray wood began to show through. He had replaced the cracked windows and razed a storage shed that was going to pieces. He had enlisted my uncle in the chores, but maintaining the place was my father's obsession, and no one questioned it. Now I pay the meager taxes and the bills for minimal upkeep. I do it because my father would have wanted me to do it. No doubt he had wished for more, had hoped the carpentry skills he taught me would be given over to the farmstead. As I sat on the door to the root cellar, I turned my eyes to the pump's silhouette and beyond it to the field and the outline of the church against the sky, and I thought of the unmarked grave, the nameless infant, and the strange soft dolls. Birth, however, can't be conveyed through the inanimate—the feel of the wet, dark head, resistant under your fingers as you guide it out of a woman's gaping vagina until the infant's jaw is suddenly released, then the gush of blood and amniotic fluid as the small writhing body slips into your arms, its tiny chest cavity heaving as it fights for its first breaths, the strange hoarse cry, the clamp and the cut, then the tug at the umbilical cord to release the placenta, which slides out from between the mother's swollen labia in a gelatinous heap. He must have known all about it, I thought, from the farm animals, must have seen instantly that the small body he held in his arms was a corpse, must have dug the birth waste into the ground and then wrapped the motionless infant in his handkerchief. The two of them must have walked before they buried the child in a location close to the woods, where the mound of dirt wouldn't be plowed and tilled. By her own admission, Lisa had felt little or nothing. She must have hobbled beside him in a stupor until she thought to swear him to secrecy, and unless my father or Lisa was carrying a Bible, which I doubted, the oath was taken in the book's name. *It can't matter now she's in heaven or to the ones here on earth. I believe in your promise.* The rest of the story belonged to the inscrutable "legacy," the same word Inga had used for Max's "remains"—his art. Miranda's tale of Cut Hill came back to me then. The story collapses time. "Me a man." The fetus redeems his mother's life. Omen becomes legend: The Maroon warriors will beat back the British slavers and force them into a treaty, and this triumph will mark generation after generation. *We'll have to clean the knife.* Lisa Odland waited a lifetime to return to infancy, and now Lorelei played the role of revenant, the dead mother returned to swaddle her child. *Tight enough?* The air was cold. I felt a wind come up from the west, and I lifted my collar. Mr. B.'s mother had opened her veins in the bath. Her husband discovered her body when the bloody water leaked from under the door. After turning off the tap, his father had found his son downstairs in the kitchen and announced tersely, "Your mother is dead." Then he shut the boy in his room, where he sat for hours. The adults lied to him about his mother's death, although "heart" problems had served as an efficient metaphor for what had ailed Mr. B.'s mother. So many mutes. It happens that we all need to hold ourselves together, to shore up the walls of our houses, to patch and to paint, to erect a silent fortress where no one leaves and no one enters. I remembered Sonia's swollen eyes. *I don't want this world.* When it became too cold to sit still, I stood up and walked around the property. After that, I moved into the car to protect myself from the wind. I don't know how long I sat there, but I had the feeling I was waiting for something—a thought.

And then I was walking into the house. The screen door opened easily, and I stepped into the summer kitchen. A beam had fallen to the floor. The walls were peeling badly, and I noticed an old sawhorse in front of the great black stove. As I turned slowly to my right, I saw my father, not my old father but my young father, sitting in a chair beside the water bowl. He was wearing the black glasses I remembered from my childhood, and I drew closer to him. "Pappa?" He began to speak to me about footnotes, but I found it difficult to follow what he said, and his voice sounded distant, as if he were in another room, despite the fact that his unlined face was close to mine and appeared oddly magnified. There was no oxygen tank near him, no scar on his nose from the cancer, no hearing aids in his ears. His left leg wasn't stiff. He aged as I stood in front of him. My old father replaced the young man. The glasses he was wearing changed to the wire ones I had last seen him in, his face deeply wrinkled. I could see the purplish tint on the right side of his nose where the surgeons had grafted skin from his head to repair the damage made after they cut out the malignancy. He smiled.

"Father," I said to him. "Aren't you dead?"

"Yes," he said, leaning forward and reaching out for me, taking my hands in his and squeezing them. I felt the long bones of his fingers, his firm grip, and an intense aching happiness. His eyes were lit with the old affection, and he said to me, "Erik, this is how we can be together now." I was nodding hard. His warm hands did not let me go. And then he said solemnly, "But never on Fridays."

Through the windshield, I saw the first streaks of dawn on the horizon and noted the time on the dashboard. Sleep had come and gone without my knowing it. Startled by the lost hours, I turned the key in the ignition, backed out of the driveway, and headed toward Blooming Field. My father's ghost had been so vivid, I continued to feel its breathing presence, and as I drove, I was glad for the silent road and the minutes that allowed me to recover. When I passed the familiar sign that said "Blooming Field, Home of Cows, Colleges, and Contentment," the phantom's last words came back to me. They struck me as comic now that I was awake, and I had the thought that the distance needed for humor is always missing from dreams. Then I remembered Good Friday. The Christian story of death, burial, and resurrection lay hidden inside that peculiar sentence. That was the day my father could not visit me. He had come instead during the early hours of a Sunday. How strange the mind is, I thought, as I looked at the low-lying clouds in pink and blue that colored the sunrise above the squat, still-sleeping town.

AS WE DROVE to the airport, Inga said slowly, "Maybe you've kept a secret in your heart that you felt in all its joy or pain was too precious to share with someone else."

"What are you saying?"

"I'm quoting Kierkegaard, the preface to *Either/Or*. He's making a philosophical point about the internal and the external. He says that he's always had doubts that the two are the same. He's certainly right about that. Then, after making us think about *not* speaking, he begins the second paragraph by saying that *gradually* the sense of hearing has come to be his favorite sense. Just as the voice best reveals human inwardness, the ear detects it. He writes about the confessional, which separates the speaker and the listener with a screen. When you can't see a person's face, he says, there's no dissonance between vision and hearing; the listener makes an imaginary picture of the speaker; which is, of course, what we do when we read, but he doesn't *say* that. And then, without warning, he launches into a story. It begins when he sees a fine piece of furniture in a store window, a secretary. He finds himself passing the shop often, gazing at the handsome object. After a while, he breaks down and buys it. He's very happy with the thing, time passes, and then the morning he's supposed to leave for the countryside, he oversleeps. When he wakes up, he jumps out of bed, hurries around, and realizes that he needs to take a bit more money with him, so he goes to his cash drawer in the secretary, but he can't open it. The driver's waiting outside, and in his frustration and anger, he bangs his beloved secretary with a hatchet. That's when a hidden drawer pops open, complete with a pigeonhole stuffed with papers that turn out to be two manuscripts written by two men. You remember?"

"Vaguely," I said. Actually, I remembered nothing, although it seemed to me that I had once read at least a part of the book.

"Well, it's all made up, of course. The preface is written under a pseudonym, a fictional editor named Victor Eremita, a *screen* between the writer and the reader."

"Are you telling me this for some reason?"

"Bear with me," she said curtly. "I've always felt that the secretary is standing in for a living body, a person giving up secrets under duress, like Kierkegaard's brooding, guilty father before he died. After he injures the chest, Eremita says that he begs its forgiveness and then goes away to the country. He leaves the broken, hurt piece of furniture behind, but he takes the documents, its hidden contents, its *inner voice*, with him."

"We all have secret drawers."

"Exactly," she said. "And most of the time they're never found. Eremita says that luck usually plays a role in such discoveries, and it's true."

"You're thinking about our father?"

She nodded. "And Max.

"You see, there's another point that Eremita makes. He says that the papers of both men, whom he calls A and B, can be looked at as the work of a single man. He admits this is unhistorical, improbable, and unreasonable, and yet this is what he proposes, either/or, a doubling or internal dialogue, two inner voices in one, the Seducer and the Ethicist combined. Aside from the ironic unveiling—K. coming into the mix—it's true, isn't it, that we're always looking for one person when there's more than one, several contentious voices in a single body. Time is part of it. We have different selves over the course of a life, but even all at once. Max was several people. He had hundreds of masks—all his characters—but day to day, too." She lowered her voice. "When we were in Paris, not long before he got really sick, we left the little movie house on the rue Christine near our hotel. When we stepped out into the bright street, I looked at him and his face had gone gray. He lit a cigarette, leaned against the wall of the theater, looked me in the eyes, and said, 'They'll try to take it all away, baby. But you and I know better, don't we?' I laughed. He sounded like a film noir hero, and we'd just seen one of Jules Dassin's American movies. He didn't laugh with me. His expression was sad, and he looked at me with his gray eyes and his gray face, and it was as if I wasn't his wife. I wasn't Inga." My sister smiled to herself.

"As if he was seeing you for the first time," I said.

"Could be." Inga took a breath. "I've never told anyone this. Certainly *not* Henry. We went back to the hotel, and we made love. The afternoon light in the room was beautiful. Afterward, I went into the bathroom, and when I came out, he was sitting, still naked, on the edge of the bed, turned away from me toward the window. His head was down and he had his hands on his lap. He didn't hear or see me. I stood in the doorway and looked at him. He was signing to himself. He had learned American Sign Language—well, not fluently, but some—when he was working on the script. It fascinated him."

"Did you know what he was saying?"

"I knew only because it's a line from the film. It's when Arkadi is searching for Lili and he finds himself in that strange warehouse full of faceless mannequins dressed in all the clothes she's worn earlier in the film. In a corner of that huge room, there's a chest of drawers."

"I remember. He yanks open the drawers, finds them empty, and starts heaving them onto the floor. When he gets to the last one, he pulls it open, and hears a strange voice say, 'I can't tell you.'"

"Then Arkadi signs the same words," Inga said.

"Max was sitting on the bed, signing, 'I can't tell you.'"

She nodded. "He did it several times."

"So you think he was quashing a desire to confess about Edie or something else, and that's what Edie is hiding from you?"

When I glanced over at Inga, she didn't turn to me. "Erik, I know you sometimes think I don't get to the point, but I started my little story about Max with *Either/Or* for a reason. 'One author,'" she quoted, "'seems to be enclosed in another, like the parts in a Chinese puzzle box.' I stood there in the doorway, looking at my husband as he gestured those words, and wondered, 'Which I and which you? There are too many.'"

"But you didn't ask?"

"He didn't know that I was watching him." She smiled to herself. "Anyway, I wasn't in a greedy, prying mood. That day I had him for my own, you see. I remember distinctly that I walked over to him and put my hands on his shoulders. We both looked out the window at the rooftops and the clouds, and I said to myself: Never forget this happiness." My sister's voice was low and ruminative. "Never forget, because soon it will be gone."

WHEN I WALKED into the house late Sunday, a part of me was still back on the prairie with my father. I took out his well-worn memoir and paged through it. *We were children of the seasons*, he wrote, *sometimes its victims.* He wrote about mud in spring so deep his boots sank into it until he couldn't take another step. He wrote about the grasshoppers, army worms, crows, and squirrels that attacked the crops in summer, and the snows that kept them off the roads in winter. He wrote about how to brew Christmas beer and he wrote about shivarees and square dances and barley beards that stuck in your clothing and clung to your skin and the Hooverville nearby with its hobos and their fires, but I was looking for more, more than descriptions of a way of life that's now gone, more than the story of Lisa and her dead child. I was looking for a path that would take me inside a man.

Father was kind. Many are kind, but often to a select group. Father's kindness drew no lines. Strangers captured it and warmed to him. Those who knew him well took it for granted and of course there were those who exploited his generous nature. He was also a man steeped in regional lore, and he passed on the tales he had heard. His closest friends were also storytellers, but he outlived them all, and there were no replacements. As he aged, he agonized over the distintegration of the neighborhood he had known and once said that one of the most overlooked evils in the world was loneliness.

My father could well have been writing about himself. Perhaps, without knowing it, he was.

"YOU'RE IN LOVE with that woman downstairs," Laura said to me, her voice indignant.

"I thought you weren't interested in anything serious," I mumbled to her from the other side of the bed.

"Erik, whatever's going on between us, it's something important to me and to you, or so I thought." Laura sat up in bed and turned to me, her eyes alive with feeling. "Good grief, we do this for a living. We talk—a little openness might be good." Her voice grew softer. "Listen, I don't know where we're going, but I don't think I want to go anywhere with you if there's some fantasy object hanging over us."

I sat up slowly. Laura had folded her arms across her naked breasts, as if to conceal them now that our conversation had taken on a dire tone. I looked down at her round belly and the curls of her pubic hair, took her in my arms, and kissed her neck, but she pulled away.

"Well?"

As I looked into her eyes, I knew all at once that I didn't want to lose her and that's what I said, but my earlier comments about Miranda had obviously been more revealing than I had intended, and rather than spend the night with her as I often did, I walked out into the cold night and made my way home.

AS I OPENED the door for Ms. W., I noticed that she looked more strained and wooden than usual. After she sat down, she said to me in a cool voice, "By the way, I saw your photograph at the opening of a show."

"A show?" I said, completely thrown off.

"The photography show in Chelsea. Jeffrey Lane."

I heard myself inhale as the words hit. It was now. November.

"I take it the artist is one of your patients."

I had to tell her then that I hadn't seen the show and that Jeffrey Lane was not a patient of mine. I added that whatever photograph or photographs were there had been taken without my permission.

Ms. W. sat up straight in the chair. "I've been wondering if talk, talk, talk does any good, you see."

"Did viewing the pictures make you wonder that?" I asked.

"You looked so different," she blurted out.

It's hard to describe the loss I felt at that moment. It was as if I had been robbed of something very dear to me, and without even having seen the image or images, I felt the burn of humiliation. I was silent then for at least half a minute, trying to find an honest response that would not derail our work together. Finally I said,

"It seems that a picture or pictures of me have been used in a way I probably won't like, but we should talk about what you feel and why the picture was so strong it made you doubt the therapy altogether."

Ms. W.'s voice had the clear, mechanical quality of a recording. "I don't know you. You sit here and listen."

I explained that I was at a disadvantage because I didn't know what the image was.

"You look furious," she said, and then, more softly, "Deranged."

I understood. The idea of losing control, of madness, terrified Ms. W. Her mother had been agoraphobic, and for months we had talked about her fear of erotic feeling, her attraction to and anger at her father and me, her dread of "cracking up," and now she had seen a picture that embodied her fear. When the session was over, I watched her leave the room. She walked like a person in a suit of armor. I put my head down on my desk and fought the tears I felt welling up in my eyes. If I hadn't had another patient, I'm sure I would have sobbed.

WHEN I RETURNED home from work, I found Miranda's letter and drawing. She had slid them under the door, just as Eggy had delivered her little objects to me when she was trying to get my attention months earlier.

Dear Erik,

I saw Jeff's show this morning. The opening was last night, but I didn't go because I felt sure I'd find myself in it, and with so many people around it would have been too much. He's been so secretive about the big unveiling that I stopped talking to him about it. There are lots of photographs of Eggy and me. Most of them are harmless. Some are embarrassing to me, but there's one of you that will probably offend you. I've been calling him all day, but he isn't picking up his phone. I've left him messages. The wisest course may be to simply ignore it, but I want you to know I feel bad and regret having brought all this down on your head. Eglantine and I are spending the weekend with my parents. Call me anytime.

With affection,
Miranda

The drawing had been done in ink and colored pencil. In the upper third of the image, two small figures, a woman and a child, stood with their backs to the viewer on a street that looked like ours—a row of Brooklyn brownstones with tall trees, gas lamps, parked cars, and a fire hydrant. This level of the picture was black and white with some grays, and it made me think of a photograph. Without a distinct border, the colorless street scene turned into a blur of dark greens, blues, and muddy reds. Looking more closely, I saw a parade of smoky monsters with huge or tiny noses, gaping or absent mouths, flapping ears, bulbous eyes, and bestial teeth. One demon held an enormous phallus. Another had a hairy tail. Yet another appeared to be bleeding from his rectum. These grotesque bodies mysteriously became the tops of peculiar houses that grew upward at an impossible angle, part of another street that took up the bottom of the page, this one brilliantly colored. Lush foliage that bore curious-looking fruits covered doorways, windows, and steps. The woman and child were depicted again, somewhat larger in scale, but this time, they were in profile, facing each other as they sat on pink steps outside one of the houses. The little girl had wings.

ON SATURDAY AFTERNOON, I entered the gallery, wearing an old baseball cap and a scarf in an admittedly absurd attempt to hide

my identity. As I looked from one wall to the other, I felt relief that
I did not immediately see any prominent pictures of myself. The
show was called Jeff's Lives: Multiple Fictions, or an Excursion
into DID. There was more than one room in the gallery, and despite my urge to rush around looking for myself, I decided to move
systematically through the exhibition and started with the first
room. The initial images were no images: four blank rectangles
under which stood the caption *No documentation of Grandparents*.
The two works that followed were large black-and-white photographs about two feet by four feet. They looked like old snapshots
that had been blown up to many times their original size because
they had lost much of their definition. A young woman in a flimsy
nightgown lay on her side asleep, her face toward the camera.
Dark makeup smudged the skin beneath her eyes, and scattered
around her on the rumpled blanket were several open bottles of
prescription pills. *Early documentation of Mother* was inscribed beneath the picture. Beside this was a photograph of a man in a suit
walking toward a car with his head down. The caption read: *Early
documentation of Father. Early documentation of Me* showed Lane as a
boy of about seven sitting on the floor with a toy soldier in one fist.
He appeared to have been caught unawares by the photographer,
to have just turned his head and lifted his eyes. Despite its blur, the
picture caught his wrinkled brow, clenched jaw, and hostile gaze.
This large black-and-white photo was framed by color snapshots
of ordinary size, all of Lane as a child, their contents banal, but
somehow fascinating. A fat baby, a grinning toddler, a boy swing-
ing a bat, sticking his tongue out at the photograher, wearing a
rubber monster head, blowing out candles on a cake. A television
screen ran a home movie. The boy, perhaps three years old, was
seen opening a package. Just before the present was revealed, the
screen went blank and started over. On the opposite wall was a
wrinkled divorce decree from 1976, mounted over the mouths of

the people I recognized as Lane's parents, which in turn were mounted on a giant photograph, so blurry that the two figures looked like mere shadows. When I turned the corner and walked into the next room, I first saw a giant color photograph that had been subjected to some kind of digital distortion. It was Lane as a Francis Bacon painting, but in neon colors, his impossibly long chin dragged to a sharp point, his mouth undulating in a howl. The caption read: *The Break*.

Two large photographs hung on each of the adjacent three walls. It took me a moment to realize that they were all identical: an elegant black-and-white headshot of an adult Lane, obviously done in a studio with sophisticated lighting and equipment. The man looked like a movie star. All that changed were the titles: *Good Student, Druggie, Lover, Stalker, Patient, Father*. The video screen in this room played and replayed a typical crash from some Hollywood movie I didn't recognize. A car drove to the edge of a cliff, fell over it, and burst into flames, upon which the film reversed. The car stopped burning, flew up the cliff, and backed up, only to surge forward again and reenact its destruction. Mounted under the screen was a newspaper article that reported the deaths of Lane's parents in a crash.

I walked into what turned out to be the last room. The titles I had just read were repeated, this time in large black letters inscribed directly onto the wall over what first appeared to be collages of some sort—long thin rectangles of combined pictures. I walked past *Good Student* and *Druggie*, but stopped to look at *Lover* when I saw Miranda. There were pictures of her both in color and in black and white. They varied in size and quality, but it was all Miranda: a younger Miranda with long hair in tiny braids. Miranda eating, sleeping, and walking, Miranda at a table drawing and standing in the middle of a room, laughing. As I continued to look, I began to feel the invasive nature of the project: Miranda crying, an angry Miranda waving her fist at the camera, Miranda dancing in some nightspot, Miranda reading a book, Miranda on a swing, Miranda in a nightgown looking tired, Miranda showing her slightly pregnant belly, Miranda waking up in a large bed. The place beside her was empty, but it was obvious from the sheets and the pillow that someone had slept there. The pictures made me sad. I was looking at the documentation of a real love affair. These were intimate pictures of a Miranda I didn't know, someone who had been passionately connected to this strange photographer. At the bottom of the rectangle were twenty or thirty pictures of the empty bed. I thought they were all the same, but as I looked more closely, I saw that the sheets were configured differently. After she left him, the man would wake up in the morning and photograph the empty bed.

In the *Stalker* series, I found not myself but a blank where I should have been, a white cut-out that walked with Miranda and Eglantine toward the park, made my way to the office, and picked up the newspaper from the steps in the morning. There was also a series of pictures taken of me from above as I turned the key in my lock, but all that could be seen were the contours of my absent body. I remembered the sound of the shutter and realized that Lane must have been lying on the roof. I saw several pictures of the house, its number obscured, close-ups of the photos he had piled on my steps, our mailbox, the red sign he had painted on the tree and Miranda had removed, the unsettling image of Miranda without eyes, and many of Miranda and Eggy without me. Some of the pictures had captions. I recall reading *Ex-Girlfriend*, *Daughter*, and *Excised Shrink Boyfriend*. But I still hadn't seen the picture that had upset Ms. W. and prompted Miranda's warning.

When I walked over to the *Father* section, I spotted it right away. It was an eight-by-ten photograph, mixed in among many other pictures with the caption *Head Doctor Goes Insane*. But in that first moment, I wasn't sure who I was looking at. Anger had contorted my face to such a degree that I was almost unrecognizable. Like a rabid dog, my eyes bulged and my teeth shone. I was dressed only in a threadbare pajama top unbuttoned to the waist and a pair of boxer shorts. The cowlick jutting from my hairline stood at attention, my Adam's apple protruded, and my long naked legs and bony knees glowed pale in a dim light that had an unreal glint. In my lowered right hand, I gripped the hammer I had hastily retrieved from my closet. As I looked more closely, I noticed that the picture appeared to have been taken outside rather than from the stairs above the second-floor hallway. I saw the fuzzy outlines of parked cars, a sidewalk, and the street. Lane had altered the setting. Ms. W. had been mortified, not only by my vengeful expression and the sight of her analyst stripped of his dignity, but the photograph made it appear as if I had been raving half naked in the street, wielding a hammer. Beside it was an image of Lane with a large bruise on his forehead. Could I have caused it? No, I thought, he looked fine when he left. Near my own image, I saw one of Lane's father, a photo of George Bush, the Twin Towers, a hospital corridor, and war images from Iraq. But I didn't stay to study them. I backed away from the pictures, suddenly nauseated, and staggered out into the bright light of Twenty-fifth Street, where I squatted on the sidewalk for a moment with my head lowered to prevent the oncoming faint. *Fathers.*

When I felt more stable, I began to walk east toward the subway. Lane had taken a calculated risk. I didn't know the law, but I felt I had grounds to sue him. And yet, he must have believed I wouldn't take any action. I had lied to the police that night. I had pushed him into the mirror. A suit would be expensive and potentially make things worse if word got around. As I walked, I imagined other patients and colleagues standing in front of the photograph laughing. *He knew*, I thought. *He saw*. He wanted to humiliate me. He had. I felt lacerated with shame. I remembered him inviting me to the show, his use of the acronym "DID," his laughter when I'd lifted my briefcase, my hands on his back, his head hitting the mirror. Confusion clouded my trip home. I couldn't understand what Lane had meant by the pictures. Why had I been removed from most of them? A wish, perhaps, that I would vanish? Miranda had advised ignoring it, but when I thought of Ms. W. and my other patients, that possibility seemed intolerable.

I left a message with Allan Dickerson, my lawyer. The threat of legal action alone might be enough to get the offensive picture removed. I called Magda and explained what had happened. I needed to consult with her about Ms. W. I needed advice. "Perhaps you could use some for yourself, too," she said quietly.

BY THE END of the following week, Al had managed to have a black square put over the face of *Head Doctor Goes Insane*. Because street photography is broadly protected in the United States, Lane had changed the picture's background to create the illusion that it had been taken in a public rather than a private space. Despite the fact that it was a matter of my word against Lane's, the gallery made the compromise.

The photograph lived on, however, in Ms. W.'s head, as well as in mine. She was stuck on it, and its meanings multiplied. I had explained the circumstances, which she accepted and had offered her sympathy, but the humiliating image of me became an assault on her, a distorted mirror of the violent, mad person she felt inside herself. My interpretations failed at every turn. I had become convinced that at some level I was protecting myself.

"My mother hated ugliness of all kinds. Ugly vases, ugly rugs, ugly, vulgar furniture . . ."

I listened to this excursion in silence.

"She liked cool, smart things."

I didn't intervene. I just listened, and as she continued to talk, I didn't feel bored so much as cloudy, which I attributed to Ms. W.'s vocal meandering from her mother, to me, to an irritable colleague, to a pile of papers she had to go through, to the weather, which was cold, back to the photograph.

She stood up, walked to the window, and looked outside. I thought about Lane for an instant, the photograph. Hidden fury made apparent. "Health is not a flight into sanity; health tolerates distintegration." *We all go to pieces with our patients from time to time.*

I spoke to her back. "Sometimes looking in the mirror can be frightening."

She turned around and then she said, "I had a dream. Somehow, I didn't want to tell you, but after what you just said, I do."

I made a sound of encouragement. Ms. W. almost never remembered her dreams.

"I was in my parents' old house. The floor was greasy, which was odd. I walked in expecting to find my parents, but it was empty, abandoned, and then, all of a sudden, you were there sitting in your chair." She paused. "Naked. Then I had a hammer in my hand, and I started to hit you on the head. I was so angry, much more angry than I've ever been when I'm awake. I was bashing you like crazy."

I noted the word "crazy" and felt a pull within me, a distinct dread.

"But," she turned around, "your skull was soft, pliable, and when I hit it, it didn't bleed or anything, it just popped back into shape." She paused again. "You were calm, just like now."

A tremendous relief came over me. I felt as if I had been spared.

She held her hands out, palms up, and her brown eyes had lost their usual dullness.

"You took the hammer from me in the photograph," I said, "to use against me."

"What hammer?" she said.

"The one in the picture we've been talking about."

"I didn't see a hammer. Are you sure there was one?"

"Yes."

Ms. W. was silent. "Not long ago, I read an article about unconscious perception. Sometimes we don't even know we're seeing something, but we are." The timbre of her voice had changed. It was warmer and lower.

"Something's happened," I said.

Ms. W. smiled. She sat down in the chair and leaned toward me. "Why is that? I feel alive for some reason. I feel like laughing."

"Go ahead," I said.

She chuckled. "It must be the hammer. Somewhere, at your house, I suppose, there's a real hammer you use to pound in nails. That nutty artist broke into your house and took your picture when you were trying to defend yourself. The photo became part of an exhibition that I happened to see. I hated the picture, your face, especially, but I didn't look at it long, and I didn't *see* a hammer. Then it reappears in my dream. I don't know why, but it feels like a magic hammer."

"And after you dreamed that you smashed me with it and I didn't die or even get hurt, it returned here in this room as a *word* in the dream story you told me."

Ms. W. was still smiling. "Reincarnation," she said.

The word passed through me with a tremor.

After the session ended, I remained sitting in my chair and looked outside. The bleak view of drab buildings, gone gray with years of the city's filth, had taken on a slightly foreign air that surprised me. Through a bleary windowpane, I saw a woman stand up from her desk, lean over, pick up what must have been her purse, and march toward the door. It all happened in a matter of seconds, but as I watched her determined step, I felt a shudder of awe. The simplest things, I thought, are not simple at all.

WHEN WE MET for dinner at the Odeon that Sunday, Inga informed me with a smile that she was busy "rearranging her past," and she wanted my help. I was good at putting pasts in order, I said. For me, it was just another day at the office, but as soon as I had said it, my sister's jocular tone changed to an emphatic one. It was time for resolution, truth-telling, and confrontation. She wanted me to accompany her to a meeting the following Thursday with Edie and Henry and the redheaded journalist we had long referred to variously as the "Burger woman," "Cheese Burger," and "Burger with Fries." I was to be a large rock of sorts, behind which Inga could take refuge if the winds blew too hard. "I'm afraid of those letters, but what can I do?" she said. "If Joel really is Max's son, he deserves something from his father's estate." The meeting was imminent because Sonia had agreed to a DNA test. The results were due on Wednesday. Inga believed her daughter's resistance had vanished for a single reason. My niece had fallen in love. "*Finally*," Inga said. "You know, she's messy now, positively grubby in her habits. Of course it happened gradually over time. For a couple of years I've felt a slow and steady relaxation of her standards, but it seems to me that after her explosion on September eleventh, she's let go. When she comes home, she throws her clothes on the floor and leaves her bed unmade. I find ashes and makeup on the floor. It's wonderful." My sister grinned. Sonia's beau was a tall, skinny college senior with a French father and an American mother. "A lot of hair," Inga told me. "Other than that, I can't tell you much about him. He writes songs. She said she'd bring him by tonight to meet you. They might be there now."

My sister leaned forward. "My life has changed, Erik. The days aren't hard. I work. I read. It's the evenings that are hard to get through. I watch old movies, but often I can't pay attention. Even when Sonia came home late or was in her room, even when she barely spoke to me, it was different. She was *there*. I had to be the mother. I love being the mother. Without Sonia in the apartment, I lose track of myself. I have bad thoughts. I remember Max dying, then Pappa dying. I see Lisa's baby in the ground. I imagine Sonia in a car accident, that she's dead, that you get cancer like Max, and I'm sitting by you in the hospital. I imagine Mamma's funeral, then my own. Nobody comes to mine, of course. I'm forgotten. Nobody reads my books. They're out of print." Inga's expressive face took on a tragic look. "When I was a girl, every once in a while, I would have a sudden thought or image in my head that some beloved person had turned into a monster. I would see the horrible face for an instant. It's happened again a few times." Inga's voice got louder. I looked at the table next to us. They weren't listening. "It's as if I can't help what's coming," she said. "When I'm very sleepy and I've worn myself out with all this nonsense, I sometimes hear Max's voice. It's mean or tired or neutral." My sister sniffed loudly and put her hand to her mouth. "It's never *kind*." On the word *kind*, her voice broke into a small wail.

I found myself smiling.

She looked hurt. "You think I'm an idiot."

"Just a little bit," I said.

She stared at her decaffeinated espresso, then raised her chin and smiled at me. "Isn't it funny," she said. "I feel much better now that you've called me an idiot. Let's go see if Sonia and her Romeo are at the loft."

After the mysterious lump of arms and legs on the sofa had disentangled itself, it turned into my niece and her beloved, a lanky boy with wild dark hair and sincere eyes who shook my hand firmly—a good sign, I thought. Sonia hugged me, and when I looked down into her face, I had the odd impression that she looked younger, that her soft cheeks and mouth had the sweetness of a baby's. It occurred to me that she had emerged from her adolescence rounder, that the sharp angles and razor edges of that bitter time of life had now vanished.

She was flushed and shining when she spoke to her mother. "I've told René everything, so you don't have to worry, but the Hamburger lady came by about an hour ago. Mom, she was rambling. She might have been drunk. I don't know, but she was talking about some bag lady who'd hit her with an umbrella. 'The city's not safe!'" Sonia imitated the woman's voice. "Then she said to tell you that Edie's sold the letters."

Inga clasped her hands in front of her. "To whom?"

I watched René reach for Sonia's hand and fold it into his own.

"I asked her," Sonia said, "but she refused to say. I'm not sure she even knows. In fact, I don't get what she wants. Why does she care?"

Inga shook her head. "I don't know. I've never understood it."

"It's personal," I said.

Sonia looked at me. "It's such a strange word, *personal*. I've often wondered exactly what's *impersonal*."

In the cab back to Brooklyn, I thought about Sonia's words and my sister's face when we parted. Inga had seemed calm, but her skin had turned a flat white.

AT AROUND SEVEN o'clock Monday evening, Eggy knocked on my door. She was wearing a ski mask with holes in it for her eyes and mouth. She looked up at me, her lips moving. I couldn't hear what she had said, so I asked her to repeat it.

"I've come on a mission," she whispered.

"Does your mother know?"

Eggy nodded. I had left a message for Miranda, thanking her for the letter and the drawing and telling her about the compromise with the gallery. She had called me back and left her own message to say she was glad, but we hadn't spoken. I began to hope she would come upstairs to collect her daughter.

Eggy took several long, toe-first strides into the room, holding her hands tightly behind her back. Then she stopped, looked both ways, as if she were crossing the street, and revealed what she had been hiding: a large ball of white string. She took my hand, led me over to the sofa, and gently pushed me down onto it. As I watched, she began to unwind the string. Once she had several loose feet, she tied the end to the coffee table and looped it around a chair and then the sofa's legs, making comments like "Hmm, that's very good," "Good line," and "Excellent." And so it went. I couldn't see her face, but I noted that her eyes, which had been shining with mischief, became more concentrated as she worked. By the time she had used all the string, she had made a vast web that connected every piece of furniture in the room, and I was part of it, since Eggy had bound my two feet and hands to the table as part of her creation. Then, she slid back the mask to the top of her head, crawled under the string, and sat beside me on the sofa.

"That was my mission," she said, "to tie everything together."

"I see that, and it seemed to me that you had a good time doing it."

Eggy sat very still. "This way nothing's away from anything else. It's all tied."

"It's all tied," I repeated.

Eggy lifted a piece of string behind her neck, leaned back in the sofa, made a large noisy sigh, and squeezed her eyes tightly shut. "Why do you know about children when you don't have them?"

"I used to be one, you know, a long time ago."

"When you peed in your bed."

"Yes, I peed for a while, and then it went away."

"But you were a bad, messy, wet boy." I could hear the excitement in her voice and was wondering how I should answer her when all of a sudden Miranda was standing in front of us, and I remembered that I had left the door to the apartment open.

"Oh my God," she said. "Not again."

"Dr. Erik said it was okay. He likes it," Eggy piped.

Miranda shook her head, but she smiled. "You'll have to undo it. You can't keep Erik tied up in there forever."

"No, not yet, please, please, please, Mommy, let it stay for a while, *please*."

I told Eglantine that we'd leave her "artwork" intact for a couple of days, but because I needed to go to work in the morning, she'd have to let me go. This seemed to satisfy her, and once it was all decided, Miranda helped release me from my fetters. As she pulled at the mess of string, her hand brushed my ankle. Her touch made me stupidly happy, but I thought of Laura then and remembered I had promised to call her the next day. My turmoil had begun to seem ridiculous, even to myself.

Because there was nowhere to sit in the living room, I went upstairs to the library and read for several hours. After finishing a badly written article in *Science*, I had taken one of Winnicott's books off the shelf, *Thinking About Children*, and opened it to a place where he was writing about his work as a pediatrician, how he liked treating the bodies of children, that examining people physically can be important for their mental health: "People need to be seen." I remember the sentence, not only because it struck me as true, but because I had just read it when I heard a person on the stairs.

I thought of Lane, but I knew that my front door was locked and that the hatch to the roof was also locked. Nevertheless, I froze as I listened to the soft tread on the steps. It turned out to be Miranda. She was standing in the doorway, her eyes on me. It was her second appearance that evening, but this time she was dressed in a white bathrobe, and I could see the bare skin just above her breasts. She walked into the room, sat down in a chair opposite me, and said, "There's something I've been wanting to tell you. I think it's because I've been hiding it for a long time and somehow I don't want to hide it from you."

"All right," I said, without suppressing the surprise in my voice.

"Remember my uncle Richard? I told you about him once."

"Yes, he died."

Miranda nodded, and her eyes grew thoughtful. "He was a gentle person and rather shy. Sometimes he hesitated when he talked, but he had a good sense of humor and was very smart. My father always said, 'Richard has the head for numbers.' My little sister Alice once asked Dad if we could see the numbers in Uncle Richard's head. My father's parents were both dead, and we girls were all close to Richard, but I was the one who made him drawings, and he took them very seriously and made comments about them. He framed one on his wall—a portrait I did of him when I was nine. I remember working hard on his clothes because he had nice clothes, beautiful shirts in soft colors. He used to take trips to Miami sometimes and come home with presents for us. Once, he brought me a book of Degas's drawings. That gift made me feel more important and grown up than I'd ever felt before. On May 7, 1981—I was eleven and a half." Miranda hugged herself and her voice dropped. "The phone rang. My father answered it, and he just said 'Richard' in this awful voice. His body had been found that morning in West Kingston. He'd been stabbed and beaten. There was an investigation, but nothing ever came of it. The police didn't make any arrests." Miranda took a large shuddering breath and continued. "At Richard's funeral, an American man was there, a person nobody knew. He was tall and handsome, and I remember his suit made me think he must be rich. He came up to me and said, 'Miranda, I was a friend of your uncle Dick's. He told me you're a very talented little girl.' I wanted to talk more, but my father came over, and without really being impolite, nodded at the man and pulled me away. Dad didn't break down at the funeral. It happened later. That night. I heard him with Mum in the other room. He said, 'You can't know what's in your own family.' Then he sobbed.

"When I was thirteen, we went back to Jamaica for my great-auntie Yvonne's funeral, and there was a boy there, older than me, supposedly a relation, but I didn't know him, Freddy. I said something to him about Auntie Yvonne being old and Uncle Richard young, and that it's much sadder to die when you're young. He looked at me, and I saw his face turn ugly. He said one word, 'Battyman.'"

I shook my head.

"It's a nasty word for gay. It shocked me, Erik. I'd never thought about it, I mean, when it came to my uncle. I told him it wasn't true. And then Freddy said something else." Miranda was almost whispering. "He told me that Uncle Richard had tried his 'wickedness' on a teenage boy he knew. I can't believe that . . ." A tear slid down Miranda's cheek and she wiped it away. "We didn't know who he was. He had to hide."

"Did being gay have something to do with his death?"

Miranda rubbed her arms with her hands. "I don't know. They took his money but left his wallet. My father can't talk about it. I've tried a couple of times, but he won't go into it. The shame is thick. Dad's a liberal-minded man, but it's as if he can't, just can't address it.

"I sometimes think that it made me—the murder, I mean, that I can't ever get past it. There are days when I don't think of it and then it's there again. I imagine his terror when they come after him, imagine him bleeding and dying in the street. But there's also the secrecy. It's against the law to have same-sex relations in Jamaica, and the hatred is terrible." Miranda looked up at me. "You know, I always wanted to be a boy, the son my father didn't have. I played the boy in games with my sisters, and I imitated the way boys walked, that swagger, you know, and their tough talk, and then for a couple of years I thought maybe I was like Uncle Richard. Sometimes, I had feelings for girls." She paused. "As time went on, that faded away, but I was really tormented for a while. I've been thinking of drawing something about it now, doing research and making a series. I'd like to track down that man in Miami. I'd like Eglantine to know about it, about Richard. My parents already find my work, well, rather shocking, so they'd be hurt, I'm sure."

"Are you looking for permission?"

"Maybe I am."

"It's not for me to give," I said quietly.

"I know the picture in the show upset you."

"It did. I felt exploited, and one of my patients saw it and was badly shaken."

"Jeff wanted me to tell you that he used it as an image of the dangerous father, not you as you. He said, 'Tell him it's transference and that it's the fathers who make the wars.' He's interested in anger, in explosions. That photo was a violation of your privacy, but it was powerful, and I understand why Jeff wanted it in the show. I can get really angry. Sometimes it's like a fire inside me, and it helps when I'm drawing, helps to push me ahead and not be frightened of what I'm doing. Jeff's father was an angry man. He used to yell and bang his fists on the table. It scared Jeff to death when he was little. His dad was a doctor, too. A cardiologist with a bad temper. Jeff doesn't even know why his parents were in that car together. They had been divorced for a long time. He tried to find out, but none of their friends seemed to know, and Jeff was on bad terms with both of them. Sometimes, he thinks his father crashed the car on purpose, but there's no evidence for that."

"You wanted me to know all this?" I said.

Miranda looked me in the eyes. "I know it sounds silly, but I think it was the string, seeing you all tied up in that string. You just let it happen and didn't stop her, and then you looked so funny and serious when I came upstairs, sitting there calmly in Eggy's net as if nothing had happened to you."

"Seeing me tied up made you want to come upstairs and tell me these things?"

"Well, it doesn't make any sense, but yes."

Miranda had brought her legs up into the chair and folded them under her and she looked younger than usual. I realized that she had never been so open with me, and it made her vulnerable.

"Well," I said, "Eggy's trying to repair what's been broken by tying everything together. Maybe you wanted to tie things up with me."

"I've seen the way you look at me. I know that you like me, but I've sometimes wondered if it's really me you like."

I found it difficult to look at her.

"Jeff's been so jealous, and I didn't want to take advantage of your feelings, even though I'm drawn to you. But tonight I wanted you to know more about me." She paused. "I feel safe with you. You're a good person."

Safe and *good* reverberated powerfully with *tameness*. Miranda stood up and walked toward me, sat down on the sofa, and leaned her head against my shoulder. I put my arm around her, pulled her closer to me, and there we sat for a long time without saying a word. I understood that Miranda had offered me the story of her uncle Richard as a gift. Through it, she had meant to explain not her uncle, but herself. *Maybe you've kept a secret in your heart that you felt in all its joy or pain was too precious to share with someone else.* The murder had become a wall that divided her life into before and after, and I guessed that her childhood had been left on the other side. Shame, no matter how unjustified, had muddied the purity of the family's outrage and left its sting in all of them, especially her father. *He's interested in anger, in explosions. They died instantly.* Maybe the violent deaths in their lives had bound Miranda and Lane together. She had said it was the string, seeing me all tied up in the string that made her want to speak to me. Telling always binds one thing to another. We want a coherent world, not one in bits and pieces.

Then she turned to me, put her cheek against my chest, and said, "You know, it's hard being a mother all the time, having to take care of everything. Even at work, I feel like that sometimes. Ask Miranda. Miranda will do it. Good old, competent, in-charge Miranda. Jeff's always needed attention, too. Sometimes I wish someone would take care of me just a little bit." I felt some tears through my shirt.

I stroked her head and her back, felt the rough texture of her hair under my fingers and then the small protuberance of each vertebra down her spine beneath the white terrycloth and experienced a subdued erotic pleasure. I was playing the mother, after all, not the lover. I had finally taken hold of what Laura had called my "fantasy object," a woman I had lusted after for months, only to find a child in my arms. It started to rain then. We listened to the drops hitting the windows in the room and battering the skylight one floor above us, and I remembered Lane running across the roofs. It's a miracle when the passions of two people actually collide, I thought. So often they dart off in unexpected directions, and there's no chasing them down.

I don't know how long I held her or what time it was when she left me and walked down the stairs to the apartment. I think it was around one. I do know that when she gave me a last hug it had stopped raining.

IN THE MORNING, I woke to an erection and the confused, discomfiting fragments of a dream about a strange woman in dishabille, her naked breasts entangled in the limp spaghetti that had mysteriously enveloped my kitchen—a translation of Eggy's umbilical string, no doubt. It was only as I emerged from that woozy, liminal state that I remembered Miranda coming into the room in her white robe to tell me the story of her uncle Richard's murder and to find some consolation in my arms. During the day, as I listened to my patients, the memory of her voice intruded a few times. *I played the boy. Good old competent Miranda. He said to tell you it's transference.* I also imagined a man lying in a street bleeding and broken and wondered what West Kingston looked like, because the street I conjured belonged to no real place. Mr. T. came to visit me that day. After two weeks in the hospital, he had been in outpatient care at Payne Whitney. I was pleased to see him more coherent and thinner now that he had dispensed with the olanzapine. His new regimen—carbamazepine, risperidone, a low dose of lithium, the antidepressant bupropion, and zolpidem for sleep—had helped him.

"There are wobbles and lurches," he said to me. "But it's better, no glooming, dooming death thoughts, hardly any voices, and they're not loud, kinda fuzzy in the background, receding not impeding. Dr. Odin doesn't talk much, though. A nodder, a scribbler, a grunter. I thought maybe I could see you."

"Will your insurance cover it?"

He shook his head. "Don't know."

"We could make an arrangement—ability to pay."

Mr. T. rubbed his hands hard. His fingernails were thickly lined with dirt, and his expression was soft. "*Herz und Herz,*" he said. "*Zu schwer befunden. Schwerer werden. Leichter sein.*"

"What's that?

"Paul Celan. 'Heart and heart. Deemed too heavy. Heavier become. Lighter be.' My translation. He drowned himself in the Seine."

"He was a poet. Like you."

Mr. T. smiled. "Yeah," he said. "Like me."

Late that afternoon, as I walked to the subway, I thought about Uncle Richard again. *I sometimes think that it made me—the murder, I mean.* I thought about Mr. T., about his father and grandfather and my father and grandfather and about the earlier generations who occupy the mental terrain within us and the silences on that old ground, where shifting wraiths pass or speak in voices so low we can't hear what they are saying.

ALTHOUGH EGLANTINE AND I dismantled the string sculpture the following evening, Miranda didn't come upstairs to fetch her daughter. Instead, she called for Eggy, and the child, after a few minutes of dawdling, took to the stairs. My evening with Miranda had reconfigured that vague country we refer to as the future, a place inhabited exclusively by fears and wishes. Jeffrey Lane had penetrated one of my wishes with uncanny speed, had seen it before he even spoke to me. I had hoped to "win" Miranda and lead her and Eggy up the stairs into the domain of family happiness. But I had begun to understand that the woman couldn't be won by me or by anybody else. She had come to me with her confession and her desire to be taken care of "a little bit," but there was resistance in her character, too, and a will to independence that meant no one would be allowed to tell her story for her.

"IT'S TRUE," SONIA said in a firm, low voice. "Dad screwed that woman and gave me a brother. I don't understand why Mom's so calm about it, almost like a robot. 'The truth is what it is,' she keeps saying. Like I don't get it. I get it. I just don't *like* it. She thinks I should go to that meeting with Henry and Edie and the Hamburger."

As she spoke, the gray light from outside the Greek restaurant on Church Street illuminated her defiant face. Her eyes and her expression at that moment are cut into my mind with unusual precision. Although I had been prepared for the possibility that Max had another child, the fact jolted me, and that shock is surely behind the power of the memory. "Whatever you decide," I said. "I'm glad you're talking."

I thought about Joel, whom I'd never seen, a boy who would have to struggle with a father who had become a tall stack of books and four movies. I wondered if he had seen his young mother as Lili, with her bright eyes and beautiful grin, the elusive sylph of an aging man's fantasy. Would Joel get lost among these fictions? Would he find a place for himself as the son of Max Blaustein and move on?

"Why couldn't Dad just have stayed loyal to Mom?" Sonia's voice broke on the word *loyal* and ended my reverie.

I shook my head. "All I know is that he loved you."

Then she leaned forward again and said, "It's strange, you know, my father is dead, and still, I don't want to share him. I want to be the only child."

"Joel never met him," I said.

Sonia looked at her hands. "You know that I haven't read any of Dad's books."

"You have time," I said.

"I've been afraid of them, Uncle Erik."

"Why?"

"I think because I wanted to keep him safe as my dad. Maybe I really didn't want to be in his head, to know what was in there. I was scared of being burned, that the world would fall apart, that the world I wished for would fall apart. It's all gone now anyway. It's been gone for a long time."

"Since September eleventh?"

"No, since I saw Dad with *her*. Nobody died, just an illusion of the perfect father." Sonia leaned forward and put her hands on the table. "At night it was always the same—the falling people. Waking up to howling in my ears, and I couldn't breathe or speak."

"Is it better now?"

"It's gone. I have nightmares sometimes, but I don't have that dream anymore. I hope it never comes back."

"And now you're in love."

Sonia looked up at me and blushed. "I never was before. It's all new."

"New is good."

"Yes," she said. "Dad's books are new, too. I've finally started to read him."

AFTER SEVERAL LONG and tortuous dialogues on the telephone that took us in and out of our various hopes, weaknesses, and illusions, Laura and I mutually agreed not to stop *whatever it was*. In honor of our unnamed but significant relations, she cooked me a meal, which, by the looks of her kitchen, must have taken all day to prepare, if not longer. She was still wearing an apron over her tight black dress when I poured the wine and we sat down to eat. I was about to taste her first course, spaghettini with scallops, parsley, and red pepper, when I looked across the table at Laura and saw that she was watching me with great seriousness, waiting for a verdict from my face. For some reason, I found her expectation unbearably poignant, and I paused, my fork suspended between plate and mouth.

"What is it?" she said. "You can't eat scallops?"

"No," I said. "It's the way you look."

"What about it?"

"You look generous."

Laura raised her eyebrows and laughed. "What kind of a compliment is that? You're supposed to tell a woman she looks beautiful or sexy, not generous. *Generous* sounds fat."

I didn't let her laughter derail me. "Generosity is something I admire very much," I said.

Laura leaned toward me, her brown eyes tender. "Thank you, Erik," she said in her warm voice. "Now eat your pasta before it gets cold."

We ate the pasta and we ate the veal and we ate the arugula salad and we drank the wine and we laughed, and I paid close attention to her animated, generous face throughout the eating and the drinking and the laughing, and I felt as if I were seeing it for the first time.

INGA HAD TAKEN a suite at the Tribeca Grand for what she called "a gathering of the letter mongers." She had wanted a neutral but private place. Both Henry and the Burger woman had signed legally binding statements that they would not make public anything that was said in the room. No doubt their curiosity had been piqued enough for them to come despite the ban. Sonia had reluctantly accepted the invitation, and I had confirmed my job as bodyguard and well-intentioned observer. In the hours before the peculiar round-table event, I became aware of a mounting sense of anxiety, accompanied by the now familiar feeling of breathlessness.

I hadn't seen Edie Bly since her actress days, and although she remained pretty, Burton was right: her face had been touched by hardness. A new severity had sharpened her once soft features, especially her chin and nose. The recovering alcoholic, the still-smoking, coffee-drinking real estate agent wore a version of the hip New Yorker's all-black uniform, a sweater and a pair of pants that showed off her breasts and narrow hips. She also emanated an invisible cloud of spiced perfume that summoned the doctor from Bombay I had slept with twice, years ago, during my residency, an erotic association which, although irrational, somehow affected my opinion of her. Inga had moved all the available chairs and arranged them in a circle around a small coffee table. Edie sat down next to me and immediately began to jiggle her right leg. I knew she wasn't aware of the restless tic and this augmented my sympathy.

"It's cold out there," she said to no one in particular and received no answer.

An inscrutable Henry arrived, greeted everyone politely, and sat down next to Inga, who, to my relief, appeared equally sanguine. The Burger woman came next, tightly wrapped in a coat and scarves, which she proceeded to undo over a period of several minutes, and, after being introduced to me, she took the only remaining empty chair. I had seen her once on the stairway, when her smile had chilled me, and perhaps a second time when only her back was visible. Except for her red hair and something in the deliberate quality of her gait, however, she wasn't recognizable. After all I had heard about her, I must have been anticipating a larger woman in all respects—more hair, more body, more nastiness. The person who sat across from me looked ordinary. Her round face with its small eyes and rather flat nose seemed as innocuous as her middle-sized body draped in a loose sweater and long skirt.

Inga folded her hands in her lap and began to speak in a professorial manner that reminded me for a moment of our father. "I thought we should air our differences and find a way forward. There is now no doubt that Max is, or rather was, Joel's father, and as I've already told Edie and Sonia, I know that Max would not have wanted me to ignore his son. That would be unconscionable. He will be cared for and will share in his father's literary estate, but that's not why we're here."

Sonia sat frozen, looking down at the floor.

"We're here to discuss the letters," Inga said steadily. "I have questions for all three of you. First, Edie, what compelled you to sell those letters without consulting me when I had already offered to buy them? You know that I have the sole right to make them public." Then she turned to the Hamburger. "As for you, Linda, your motives for harassing me are completely incomprehensible."

After she had uttered the woman's first name, I realized that I couldn't recall her last name, despite the fact that Inga must have said it during the introduction. It was buried under countless facetious references to the great American beef patty.

"Why do you care about my husband's love letters or his past?" Inga continued. "Does the press give a damn about literary lives? Does it give a damn about literature at all? This isn't London. Even I know there's no big story here. It's frankly bewildering to me. Why do you bother?"

Under Inga's direct gaze, the redhead smiled, and then I recognized her; it was the same sheepish, uncomfortable smile I had seen on the stairs.

Inga turned to Henry and said quietly. "I wanted you to be here because you care so much about Max. I mean, what happens to his work, and those letters, well, whatever they are, they're part of him. Sonia knows why she's here. We've kept too many secrets from each other."

Inga turned toward Edie and waited. The silence that followed was thick with emotion, as if every person in the room were emanating some viscous airborne material. I wondered if I should say something but decided to keep quiet.

Edie finally spoke. "I had the right to sell those letters to anyone I wanted. You all know that. You think it's easy bringing up a kid now that I'm by myself? Joel's got reading problems. I'm doing homework with him every night for hours. I'm so tired when I go to bed, I can't believe I have to get up the next morning. I don't give a shit about Henry's *literature*." She gave the word a posh British enunciation, as if to underline that she, unlike the rest of us, was consumed by the problems of *real* life, not snooty literary business.

"But I was willing to buy them," Inga said. "And to help you both. You knew that."

"You think I don't have any pride?" Edie said, her jaw set.

Inga leaned back and opened her mouth in disbelief. "You think this hasn't hurt *my* pride?" She looked baffled for another second and then said, "Maybe that's the problem. He threw himself at you, and you rejected him, but I wanted him so much. I always wanted him." Inga's voice cracked.

"I was in bad shape back then. I'm clean now. I . . . I found myself."

"Whatever *that* means," Sonia said abruptly. "I hear that all the time. You'd think there were selves lying all over the place just waiting to be picked up."

Edie ignored her.

As I listened, I realized that Edie Bly was at a disadvantage with her clichés. She didn't really know what she was saying. "Pride" was code for her need to be seen and understood, and the hackneyed expression "I found myself" had helped her leave behind her addicted self and embrace her sober self. Despite my concern for Inga, I felt compassion for the former actress with the strong perfume. Inga became more, rather than less articulate with anger, and I had heard her bark perfectly formed paragraphs of vituperation in defense of a dearly held idea or person. I was relieved to see that she had fallen silent.

"Who bought the letters, Edie?" Henry asked in a deliberate voice, his face apparently imperturbable.

"I don't know," she said.

"You don't know!" the Burger woman nearly shouted. "Are you crazy?"

"That was the deal, no name. The man paid cash."

For the first time, Henry looked ruffled. He stared at Edie. "Why, you little idiot," he said. "Those letters are part of a literary legacy. They belong to posterity, to all of us . . ."

"A stranger has them," Inga said in an awed voice. "Edie, is there anything in those letters that I should know about?"

An image of Max in a light-filled hotel room came to me then, a mental picture I had seen when Inga told me the story of that day in Paris after they went to the movies. I saw his fingers moving: *I can't tell you.*

Edie's face looked strained. "I'm going to smoke," she announced, and with an unsteady hand removed a pack of cigarettes from her purse, shook out a cigarette, and lit up. "He sent those letters to me, to *me*," she repeated, her voice rising.

"I know," Inga said quietly. "I know, and if you'd wanted to, you could have burned them or cut them up or blackened out what you never wanted a soul to read—all that was in your power. Don't you see, Edie, we have to try to come to an understanding, because my daughter and your son are sister and brother. You've sold the letters to an anonymous person who could do many things with them, and I think it would be fair to tell me, to tell us, if there's something in them that might hurt Joel or Sonia someday."

Edie's bottom lip began to shake, her mouth contorted, the tears fell, and I heard a deep noise break from her throat.

I reached over to her, placed my hand over hers, and patted it for a moment.

Out of nowhere, Linda erupted, "You think you're perfect, don't you?" she said, leaning toward Inga, her face suddenly animated. "Look at you, playing the noble mother in order to wheedle the dope out of Edie. It's revolting. Glamour-puss Ph.D., writing those pretentious books showing off how smart you think you are, how truly special and superior: Ms. Perfect with the perfect daughter and the perfect Tribeca apartment, widow to the Late Great Cult Hero Max Blaustein. I knew I'd find some dirt on you. You needed taking down a peg or two. You want to know why I bothered? That's why I *bothered*." This speech was delivered through clenched teeth with an unmistakable snarl accenting her final word.

My sister's mouth opened, then she put her hand to her chest, as if the verbal assault had hit her body.

"You don't remember me, do you?" Linda continued.

Inga continued to gape. In a small voice, she said, "Remember you?"

"From Columbia. I knew your friend Peter."

"Peter?" Inga said. "You knew Peter?"

"I was in journalism school. You were in *philosophy*." She spat out the word. "We had coffee together three times with Peter. *Three* times. I might as well not have been there. You two were rattling on about Husserl. I said something about it and you laughed." The woman's eyes didn't leave Inga.

"I'm sorry," Inga said. She leaned forward. "I'm terribly sorry."

"Mom doesn't laugh at people," Sonia said. "She laughs a lot, but not *at* people. She can't remember everybody she meets. And I can say one thing for her, she doesn't go through other people's garbage."

Inga could barely get the word out of her mouth. "Garbage?"

"Why don't you tell my mother what I never told her, that I found you going through our garbage. There she was"—Sonia pointed her index finger in Linda's direction—"with the bag open, rummaging through our eggshells and coffee grounds, fishing out papers and letters."

Linda didn't answer this. She sat tight-lipped in her chair.

Inga hugged herself. "It's awful to be forgotten and ignored. It's happened to me, too." She looked confused, reached both her hands toward Linda, and said, "You've taken it awfully far, haven't you?"

Henry interrupted. "I should say so." He turned to Edie, who was still sniffling.

"They belonged to me!" Edie said before Henry could speak. "I told you! He sent them to me! And then all of a sudden, everybody wants them." The tears were running hard down her cheeks. She gasped. "Seven stupid letters. So *important*. A whole lot more important than I am, for Christ's sake. Or Joel, or any *person*. Just some crapola on a few pages. I mean, the whole thing is disgusting."

"That's what you think of my father?" Sonia yelled these words, stood up, leaned toward Edie, and began to shake her hands in the air. "You didn't give a shit about him, did you?" Then Inga stood up, reached for her daughter, and grabbed her by the arm. Sonia turned an angry face toward her mother. Edie cried more loudly, and Henry leaned back in his chair. He looked genuinely distraught.

"Okay," I said in a booming voice. "I think . . ." But before I could continue my sentence, Henry gave a small gasp, and I heard the door behind me slam against the wall. Startled, I wheeled around. Moving quickly toward us was a big disheveled woman with bright pink lipstick and rouge on her broad fleshy face. She was dressed in a huge gray coat, thick green socks covered only by slippers, and a red-and-white stocking cap that partially concealed what appeared to be a curly blond wig. She was carrying two large Macy's bags and an umbrella, and she had a wild look in her eyes.

"Dorothy!" Henry said, "What on earth are you doing here?"

Linda raised her hands. "You're the one," she shrieked. "You're the one who hit me!"

Edie lifted her head, and her eyes, now blackened by smeared mascara and running eyeliner, widened in a look of puzzlement. "I've seen you," she said, "I know you from somewhere."

Dorothy held up one of the bags and said in a clear deep voice, "I have them."

I suddenly knew who it was, but it was Inga who said it: "Burton?"

It was Burton all right, skin shining with perspiration and in need of a shave. The man's disguise was hardly brilliant. As I gaped at him, I wondered how anyone could mistake him for a woman, and yet an instant earlier, he had been someone I didn't know. He removed his coat in a single gesture and then, with a flourish, pulled off his hat and wig. His makeup was still on, however, which gave him a clownlike appearance. Either he had forgotten this or perhaps the ghoulish paint didn't matter to him. From one of his bags, he withdrew a manila envelope and handed it to Inga, who had remained sitting in her chair.

"It happens," he said to Inga, bending over to speak to her, the hem of his blue dress brushing against her shins, "that an opportunity presented itself to me in the form of an inheritance, and in this new financial state, I asked myself whether any good might come of it, aside from my own enjoyment of the greater comforts I am able to afford now that I am, shall we say, slightly flush, and it seemed that I might make up for that Thursday evening many years ago when I"—Burton took a deep breath—"when I humiliated myself in your presence."

Inga lifted a hand to Burton's rouged face and stroked it. "Don't say that. It doesn't matter. It never mattered."

"Open it," he said, and then, in a voice more excited than I had ever heard him use, he burst out, "I bought them. The letters. They're yours. That's my gift, my . . . my atonement."

Inga glanced down at the slender envelope in her lap. She turned it over. "I'm scared to read them." She grimaced. Looking up at Burton, she said, "Should I be?"

"I'm afraid that I'm not in a position to answer that question," he said. "I am ignorant of their contents."

My friend, the cross-dressing amateur detective, had spied, snooped, shadowed, eavesdropped, and deceived, but his code of honor had kept him from reading the letters he had spent good money to procure. When he turned to me, I gestured toward my breast pocket and then my own cheeks and mouth to encourage him to wipe off what he could of the now very moist and gleaming pink stains on his face. He dutifully pulled out the omnipresent handkerchief and began to push it up and down his cheeks and across his mouth.

With trembling hands, Inga withdrew the seven letters from the envelope. She removed the first one, looked down at it, and a bewildered look crossed her face. From where I sat, I could see Max's tiny handwriting. She took out a second and a third, casting a quick glance at the top of each, then continued to the next until she had briefly looked at each one. She inhaled deeply and spoke to Edie, "They're all addressed to Lili, not to you."

"Well, *I'm* Lili," Edie said. "I *was* Lili, anyway."

Henry's lips parted in amazement. "Seven letters to his character.

Seven," he said. "There are seven sightings of Lili early in the film; each time she's different. Did you ever ask him why he wrote to Lili, not to you?"

Edie's eyes widened. "No," she said, shaking her head. "They're all different. I mean, it's like he's writing to different people."

Henry shook his head. "The wily devil."

"Seven incarnations," I said.

"So *that's* the big secret you strung me along with?" Linda barked at Edie. "The big scoop is that Blaustein wrote letters to someone who doesn't even exist?"

Sonia looked at me and then at her mother. When she spoke, her voice was strangely hoarse. "He used to tell me that he heard them talking, his people. Even when the book is over, he said, they're still there. It's like he didn't want the stories to end. He wanted to keep writing them. I think he hoped they would keep him alive."

Henry left first. He hugged Inga, and I noticed that she withdrew quickly from his embrace. Inga shook Linda's hand and reiterated her apology, upon which the woman grabbed her multiple outer layers and escaped through the door. Inga, Sonia, and Edie left together. "The three of us are going to talk at home," Inga told me. "I have the room until tomorrow. You two stay on and have a drink."

And so Burton and I stayed and ordered single-malt Scotch and settled in beside each other in two soft chairs. My plump companion in a dress and slippers excited no interest from the waiter, who served us in a polite, bored way that made it clear he had better things to worry about, probably his acting career. It was then that Burton told me about the many hours he had spent in the streets as Dorothy, his second self, a homeless woman he had named after the girl from Kansas who travels to Oz. He had considered naming his alter ego after another Baum character, the princess he first

introduced to his readers as the boy Tip, later revealed to be
Ozma, princess of Oz, who has been enchanted into the other sex.
While we talked together, I understood that my friend had whole
territories within him I had never known about. He didn't think of
Dorothy as a disguise anymore, he told me, but as aspects of himself come to light, both mad and feminine. "There is a delectable,
yes, positively chewy pleasure to be derived from raving, Erik,
from a lunatic discourse that swells up from God-knows-where,
my manic features, I suppose, once suppressed, have been released
into oratory of preposterous grandeur, delivered to any and to all.
I reveled, Erik, in my false bosoms and preponderant behind, in
my big, fat, uninhibited woman-ness roving the city streets. And
even in the sorrow of it. Oh yes, in the lugubrious, doleful invisi-
bility of my station, yes, that's it, the Nobody effect, I call it. So
few people look at you," Burton said. "Blind and deaf public
hordes with shopping bags and briefcases and backpacks pass you
by—that is the lot, my friend, of the unseen, the unknown, the un-
signified, and the forgotten."

When I asked why Henry had called him by name, or rather by
his other name, Burton told me that while he was staking out the
professor's apartment building, Henry had stopped Dorothy on the
street a couple of times and asked if she needed help. Burton confessed to some guilt about those incidents. He had turned down
Henry's change, he said, but was touched by his generosity. As for
Edie, he thought her life was hard, an ongoing penance for her wild
days. Her son had struck him as a delicate, sullen, difficult boy, and
after making the deal with her, he felt confident the cash would
help Joel, too. It may have been my Lutheran queasiness about
money, but I refrained from asking how much the letters had cost
him. All in all, his vigils had made him kinder toward those two, but
he reserved his wrath for the journalist and admitted that Dorothy

(he did not say "I") had once "weakly tapped" the redhead with her umbrella.

It was darkening outside when Burton and I left the hotel, a little tipsy in the twilight as we stood together on the sidewalk. The Walrus and the Carpenter, I said to myself. While we waited for cabs, we looked downtown, and I know we both thought not about what was there, but about what wasn't, and neither of us said a word as we gazed at the empty sky above lower Manhattan. I watched Burton stop a cab. Dorothy had been mostly dismantled by then. Without the wig, makeup, and breast-and-buttock padding, his masculinity had been restored, but as he lifted his leg to enter the taxi, the long coat swung open, and I glimpsed his blue dress swish beneath it for an instant. I had a thought then, which as soon as it had passed through my mind, made me smile. It was this: The man is really coming into his own.

THREE DAYS LATER, when I came out of the subway, I thought I saw Jeffrey Lane walking along Prospect Park, but I wasn't sure. When a person occupies a subliminal presence in my mind, any number of strangers can take on his or her form. I saw Miranda several times in the two weeks that followed, but Eggy was always with her. Something had changed between Miranda and me, however, a thickening of knowledge that nevertheless kept us apart. We weren't awkward or shy together. It was as if Miranda's confession were locked up in a room that had become inaccessible by ordinary means, a sealed chamber we remembered but couldn't return to. I knew that she was working hard, drawing into the night. When she spoke about the pictures, her voice grew vehement and her eyes took on a feverish glaze that made me deferent and quiet in her presence. When I asked to see what she was doing, she told me to wait.

Eggy carried her ball of string everywhere, "just in case." Her teacher at P.S. 321 let her keep it inside her desk during school hours, and Miranda had allowed her daughter to hang string in her bedroom that connected the ceiling lamp to the bedposts and chair. "It can't be dangerous, that's all," Eggy told me. "I can't trip in the night. I have to be able to get out in a fire, you see. That's what Mommy says." The child was sitting beside me fingering her ball when she spoke. "I don't want to burn up." Eggy clutched the ball harder. "Sometimes bad people turn into fire just like that. They don't even need a match."

She turned her fierce, small face to mine, as if she were challenging me.

"No, Eggy," I said, "people don't just burst into flames without a match. Did somebody tell you that?"

"Frankie's babysitter said that God makes bad people burn."

"I see, but it's not true."

Eggy brought the ball to her nose and pressed it against her face. Then she whispered, "I'm bad."

We talked for a while about bad feelings and good ones. I stressed that every person has both, that having bad feelings didn't make you bad. I don't know if these therapeutic platitudes did any good, but by the time Miranda called her, Eggy seemed relieved. I know that what's said is often less important than the tone of voice in which the words are spoken. There is music in dialogue, mysterious harmonies and dissonances that vibrate in the body like a tuning fork.

AS THE ANNIVERSARY of my father's death approached, I returned home from work in the dark November evenings. On the lined pages of my notebook, I recorded one dream after another, in which my father, whom I believe to be dead, is still alive. He sits across the room at a neuroscience lecture on East Eighty-second Street. I see him from behind as he writes in his study, but he can't hear me when I speak to him. I find him wooden and inert on a sofa, and yet when I get close to him, he blinks. Every time I woke from one of these nocturnal sightings, I would remember the others, which had brought with them the same discomfort, an ambivalence so highly calibrated I felt that each side of the emotional strain could be mathematically measured into a perfect half. Unlike the ghostly presence in Minnesota, these paternal figures said nothing. They were mutes, dummies that barely breathed. When I spoke of them to Magda the day I went to see her, she said that my descriptions made her think of the word "deadlock."

Many of my childhood hours were spent with my father as he went about his work. I sat on his lap when he plowed, on top of the drill when he seeded, and trotted behind him and stumbled over clods of soil when he dragged. In winter, to the weak light of a kerosene lantern, my father milked in the barn while I sat beside him and asked him questions. Could a cat win in a fight with a weasel? Why did skunks invade chicken houses? Why were bulls dangerous while cows were not? How many rattlesnakes had my father killed and what was the safest way to do it?

"Pappa, how can you tell it's going to snow?"

"Pappa, why is tobacco juice coming out of the grasshopper?"

"Pappa, how come burning grass stings you?"

I loved to ask my father questions. I was curious, but I wonder now if I didn't also know that he loved to be asked, that he loved the adulation he felt from me when I asked, that the asking was a repetition of what he had loved as a child and had become: the incarnation of the gentle father who listened and answered during milking sessions in the barn. The answer was less important than the question. My father's answers were often long and involved and I didn't understand them, but I liked to be near him, liked the smell of him, the feel of his beard. *It was hard for him when you grew up.* "He has black moods," Tante Lotte said once to my mother. "You'll see."

"I wish I could remember more," I said to Magda. "There's a haze over things." My father is in the garden, the garden that was far too big and bore many times what the family could eat. I heard my mother say, "I don't know what to do with all these beans." "They'll go to the neighbors," my father always answered, as if we were back on the prairie where there was rarely enough, where they canned and stored what they had for the long winter when the roads were blocked for weeks, sometimes months on end. I watched him weed with a fast hand around the cornstalks, saw the fields and the horizon behind him. "The garden was the farm," I said to Magda. "He was doing it again, and doing it right." I saw him stop weeding and stand up, saw him turn toward the woods, his hands deep in his pockets, and I saw a look of grief cross his face. He didn't know that I was watching him from the garage, and I couldn't go to him. We didn't intrude. Intrusion would mean that I knew, and I couldn't know that he suffered. "He never left the farm," I said. "He was always trying to repair and restore and redo."

The Depression never seemed to end. In addition, there were years of drought, crop failures and dried-up pastures. When rain finally came, only weeds grew. High-velocity southwest winds brought dust from Nebraska and South Dakota and perhaps from as far away as Oklahoma. The sun disappeared for days. Dust, layers of it, covered everything everywhere. The farm animals got sores in their mouths from eating grit-covered grass. People spat black and said things were worse farther west.

Magda was listening as I read the passage to her; her old face had wrinkled into that concentrated look I remembered from the years we had spent together.

"It's as if I'm looking for something," I said, "but I don't know what it is. Something that will release me."

"From the depression," she said.

I looked at her.

"And the guilt and the black moods when the sun disappears for days, and from your father who refuses to die."

I wanted to weep then. I felt the tension in my chest and the pressure in my nose and eyes and the tightening around my mouth, but I had a sense that I wouldn't stop if I began to cry and closed my eyes to press down the emotion.

"In one of his essays," Magda said, "Hans Loewald wrote, 'The work of psychoanalysis can turn ghosts into ancestors.'"

I TOOK NO notes the day Eggy fell, but I remember the alien cadence of Miranda's voice on the message she left me and exactly where I was standing in the cold rain on East Fortieth Street. "Eggy fell at Jeff's. She hit her head. She's in pediatric emergency at Bellevue Hospital. They put a tube in her so she can breathe. They're doing a CT scan." She stopped talking then, and I heard nothing for a couple of seconds. "Erik, she's unconscious." Miranda didn't say good-bye, and she didn't ask me to come. *At Jeff's. Eggy fell at Jeff's.* As soon as I heard those words, an unformed accusation against Lane rose up in me, and the cloud of sinister possibility that had always hung about him thickened. Stalker, thief, poseur. I remembered Miranda's bloody finger, Lane's face in my hallway mirror as he delivered his soliloquy. I remembered the break-in, the photograph, the hammer, and my heart began to beat faster. I saw Eglantine on the floor, unconscious, saw paramedics leaning over her body as they intubated her. When I stepped into the street to hail a cab, I continued Eggy's story in my mind, and although I knew it was irrational even to imagine an outcome until I knew more, I saw her in the ICU dead, saw a woman with a clipboard sit down beside Miranda and explain in a hushed voice about organ donation. The decision had to be made now. In the taxi, I rehearsed everything I could remember about the Glasgow Coma Scale and its relation to recovery rates, the possible impairments after head injury—seizures, cognitive deficits, memory problems, personality changes. I wasn't an expert. Once I knew what had happened, I would call Fred Kaplan—that's all he did, head injury day and night.

As I walked through the doors and marched down the corridor, I realized I was praying—the automatic, half-hearted prayer of a nonbeliever beseeching the lost deity of his childhood to intervene on his behalf. *Please let the child live. Please let her be okay.* I had walked through hospital doors hundreds of times. I had seen hundreds of patients in dire need, but one of the secrets to good care is to not empathize too much, to keep your head, to remain calm. I wasn't calm, and it was more than alarm for Eglantine. There was rage in my step, rage in my belly and chest, and the prayer changed to a chant against Lane. *Monster, bad father, shit.* I strode down the hall, rhythmic fury pushing me ahead. Completely absorbed, I knocked into an old woman, who was slowly propelling herself forward in a wheelchair. I leaned down and apologized. She lifted her wizened face to mine, smiled, and said in a thick accent I couldn't identify, "Never mind, child."

Her voice stopped me. She had called me "child," as if I had suddenly lost many years and about thirty inches. I found the nearest men's room, ducked into it, and retreated to a stall for several minutes where I sat down, put my head in my hands, and listened to a man's piss gush into the urinal outside. My anger turned to despair behind that door. I felt broken. Even now, I can't interpret with any accuracy the overwhelming sadness that flooded me. It was not the pain of compassion; it was shame and misery for myself, and a doomed sense of repetition brought on by the vengeful phrases that had propelled me, one foot after the other, toward the pediatric E.R.

WHEN I SAT down beside Miranda, she barely moved, and when she told me the story of Eggy's fall, she spoke to the floor. I gazed at her tense hands in her lap, with their long fingers and short nails. Lane had picked up his daughter after school and taken her to his apartment, as he did every other Friday. He was on the telephone talking to his dealer, while Eggy played with her string in the next room. Because of the excessive heat in the building, he had left his bedroom window open. While Lane talked, Eggy must have been tying things together. He heard her scream, ran into the other room, saw the open window, string knotted from bedpost to fire escape, and his daughter lying below. The drop from Lane's first-floor apartment on Avenue A wasn't far, but the child must have hit her head and lost consciousness immediately. Miranda lifted her chin and spoke to the wall. "He wasn't paying attention," she said. She paused. "How many times have I not paid attention." Her voice sank at the end of the sentence. It was not a question.

"Where is he now?" I asked.

She shook her head. "He was here. I promised to call him. I don't want to look at him right now. I know he didn't mean to. I just, just can't take him right now." She squeezed her hands more tightly together. "Erik, I signed a paper saying they could put something into her skull. They wanted to know if she was allergic to iodine."

Everything was being done. That was the word. As I sat there in the waiting room beside Miranda, I found myself on the inert side of medicine, where neither heroism nor failure is possible, where time expands and ordinary numbers on a clock can't register it. With every hour of coma the prognosis worsens. There are exceptions, even miracles, but they're rare. And so we waited. The mostly blank walls, the stale odors, the unintelligible chatter, the sounds of beepers, the round face of the man with dreadlocks in the chair opposite me, and the queasy artificial light of the hospital had an almost hypnotic effect as we waited. For a while I stared at a torn, crumpled blue-and-yellow potato chip bag that lay beneath an empty chair, and then at the red cylinder of the fire extinguisher. The awful accumulation of meaningless sensory information became a leaden presence in my body that would have been boredom if it weren't for my underlying hunger to know. Miranda's parents and two of her sisters had arrived by the time the neurosurgeon, Dr. Harden, appeared, but he couldn't tell us what would happen, only what had already happened. Eggy's coma score was 10. Her pupils were normal. She had no broken bones, just a few bumps and bruises. She had been given Rocuronium, a paralytic drug, to keep her quiet, which had already worn off. A ventilator was helping her breathe. The CT scan had shown no contusions or hematomas, an enormous relief, but there was some edema, some swelling. Mild, he said. Still, he wasn't sure what it meant. They wanted to err on the side of caution and keep checking, so they had inserted a catheter to measure her intracranial pressure, which at the moment was normal. He looked about my age and had the brisk, confident manner of an expert in his field. His tone was sympathetic, and yet I felt irritated by a bland quality in his eyes, which I later realized may have been simple exhaustion. Nevertheless, I knew the man saw what he was trained to see.

When they let her go in to Eggy in the ICU, Miranda saw something else. She saw her six-year-old daughter lying at a thirty-degree angle on a gurney, with a partly shaved head, a red-brown mess of Betadine around the hole that had been drilled through her skull. She saw an array of nameless monitoring equipment, lines and tubes and machines attached to her child's face, arms, chest, nose, and throat. She saw the scrapes on Eggy's forehead and the bruise on her naked arm, and she saw that her daughter lay in a wounded sleep, from which some people never wake. When Miranda returned, she was walking very slowly, her lips pressed tightly together, and as she neared us, I saw her list suddenly to one side and reach out to the wall to regain her balance. I stood up, but her father rushed in front of me and helped her into a chair.

Lane arrived a few minutes later. His face was red and swollen, and when his eyes met mine, I saw no flash of recognition. He walked straight past me and then kneeled in front of Miranda. She didn't look down at him. He was whispering to her in a desperate voice, "I'm so sorry. I'm so sorry." I turned my head away and found myself looking straight at Miranda's father.

Then I heard Miranda say in a commanding voice, "Get up and sit down."

When I looked back in their direction, I saw that Lane had obeyed and was sitting slumped over beside her, his head in his hands.

And so we held vigil in an eerie space of the ongoing present, an interval drained of all significance, except that it was suspended between a child's fall and some future moment when we would know.

MIRANDA RETURNED TO Eggy in the ICU, and so she must have heard them say there was lightening, improvement, that Eglantine was coming out of it. Miranda was there when her daughter recognized her, and she was there when Dr. Harden announced his opinion that things looked good, very good, better than he had expected. I saw Jeffrey Lane weep with happiness when he received the news and Miranda's parents embrace each other and then their daughters. I knew that it wasn't over, that even if she recovered fully, Eggy would live with the story of the fall inside her. She would be changed by it.

WHEN I LEFT the hospital, it was snowing—large wet flakes that would whiten the sidewalks and streets only briefly—but the snow was beautiful, and as I paused to watch it fall, illuminated by the building's lights against the darkness of the evening, it struck me as a moment when the boundary between inside and outside loosens, and there is no loneliness because there is no one to be lonely. *After the first major snowstorm*, my father wrote, *we were snowbound until spring*. I remembered the great drift against our front door, the hoarfrost on the window with its complex patterns, my nose against the cold glass, and the vast white dunes formed by the blizzard overnight. Dunkel Road was invisible. The known world had disappeared. "When Lars died, it was snowing," my mother said. "I watched it fall through the window. It fell straight down, and it fell steadily. A change, like a shadow, came over him; it seemed to crawl up his body and then it reached his neck and moved up to his chin, his nose, his cheeks, his forehead, over his head, and then I knew he had died." The night Eglantine woke up, it was snowing. Ingeborg was so tiny, my grandfather said, they buried her in a cigar box. Somewhere on the twenty acres out there in the country, *out home*, the bones of a stillborn infant lie buried. My father digs the grave. An unborn child speaks from inside his mother on Cut Hill, and the English slaver falls to the ground dead. Uncle Richard is lying in a street in West Kingston. My great-uncle David hobbles down Hennepin Avenue in the snow with his stumps in his specially made shoes. He manages to get inside the lobby of the hotel and then he collapses. It was his heart, not the cold. *King Edward and Mrs. Wallis Simpson.* I see Dorothy expounding on the street, pontificating on the state of the world, the preposterous orator. Dear, old, sweaty Burton, memory man, rescuer of ladies in need, lady himself, mourning his mother, the one before the stroke, the woman of "yore." My father is speaking at his eightieth birthday. He begins with the little ad in the paper: *Lost Cat. Brown and white, thinning fur, torn left ear, blind in one eye, missing tail, limps on right front foreleg. Answers to the name of Lucky.* I hear them laughing in the room. I see Laura laughing across the table and I feel her warm ass under my hands in bed. Miranda's head is on my shoulder. I see her dreamed streets and her house with its disquieting rooms and curious furniture. I see a woman lying beneath a man struggle for an instant under his grip. I stand in front of her chest of drawers, and I want so much to look inside, to touch her things. A man slams his desk with a hatchet and finds manuscripts inside. *Like the body of his father giving up secrets.* I see my father's orderly desk: paper clips, ammo, unknown keys. Sonia's closet is messy now. She throws her clothes all over the room, and Arkadi pulls open the chest of drawers in the vast room and finds nothing but a voice. He gets on the train and sees a woman who looks like Lili but isn't Lili, someone else who will capture his imagination, a creature of his invention. When was it, I think, just three days ago, Inga read the first letter aloud to me, her voice shaking. "Dear Lili," Max wrote. "I write to you now in that other person, the one who has written all these years to live. He didn't live to write. He wrote to live. There are days when there are no stories left in him, when he feels he can't do it anymore. There are days when he feels dead. He can't say this to anyone else. He says it to you because you have the armor he gave you, because you can't see him, because you don't know who he is. You don't know he's dying." But Edie must have known that Max was chasing a figment, that he was writing to someone else, to a woman in a movie, a woman he would never find.

Perhaps you loved Miranda because you knew you couldn't

find her, I said to myself, and that kept you from moving forward and left you shivering like Ms. L. on the steps outside a locked door. *Deadlocked. People need to be seen.* Mr. R. looks up and sees the rug on the wall in my office. Something has broken inside him. *The Depression never seemed to end.* I see my father walking across campus with his long strides, and he doesn't recognize me. He passes his son, but he's not looking for me at that moment. He's too sad to see me, absorbed in old sorrows that return again and again. *It's something about Dad.* Inga is talking about Max. *We have different selves over the course of a life.* My father is telling his story about the farm, his army days, his travels, and his work, about people he knew and loved, and about us, about my mother, Inga, and me. The speech seems to be over. My father pauses. His eyes are gleaming with humor. "And that's why," he says, "I answer to the name of Lucky." It's new, Sonia says about being in love. It's new. The New World. A dugout on the prairie. The vanished. *His vacant corpse had lost the man I knew.* Joel will never know his father. *Kyss Pappa.* My young mother bends over the body of her father. The war is still going on. The wars are raging. Men and women are raging. My father sleeps in a hole on the beach as the rocket fire booms above him. *Our brave young men and women in uniform fighting for freedom.* A log house goes up in flames. A little girl is rescued from a burning house. *We cleaned up them graves real nice, didn't we?* The towers are burning. *Bad people burn up. No they don't.* My father cuts down trees. His fist slams into the low ceiling above his narrow bed. My grandfather cries out in his sleep and his small son shakes him awake. Lane saw it in me. He saw the violence, the violence my father wanted to walk off but couldn't. The road isn't long enough. A Japanese officer falls over in the long grass. Sarah jumps, falls. Eggy falls. Sonia watches from the window. People are jumping, falling. They're on fire. The buildings fall. *Wo ist mein Schade Star.* The dead are speaking and Mr. T. is listening.

We hear voices. I hear my father saying my mother's name. He says *Marit*. He says it again. I see him as he leans over his coat in a narrow room in Oslo, methodically picking the pale fluff from the dark material. "*If I could have one memory . . .*" I stand and watch the snow, and it is all happening at once. It cannot last, I say, this feeling cannot last, but it doesn't matter. It is here now. In the drawing the little girl has wings. The coma is lightening. My sister is lying in the grass. Kiss me, kiss me, so I can wake up. And then I see Ms. W. at the end of our last session. She is smiling at me, and she uses the word again: *reincarnation*. "Not after death, but here when we're alive." She puts out her hand and I take it. She says, "I will miss you."

"I will miss you, too."

Acknowledgments

There are many people who in one way or another contributed to the writing of this book. David Hellerstein, Daria Colombo, and Ann Appelbaum gave me insight into the working lives of psychiatrists. Monica Carsky spoke to me about her experience as a psychotherapist. Rita Charon, head of the Narrative Medicine Department at Columbia Medical School, kindly allowed me to sit in on her class for medical students and then included me in the department's lecture series. I want to thank Frank Huyler and Richard Siegel for their expertise in emergency medicine.

Mark Solms introduced me to the world of neuropsychoanalysis, first through his books, and then in person. He invited me to the monthly neuroscience lectures at New York Psychoanalytic Institute and to the small discussion group that followed. I owe a debt to all the researchers, psychiatrists, and psychoanalysts who came and went in that group, but I want to mention some of the regulars: Maggie Zellner, David Olds, Jaak Panksepp and, in memory, Mortimer Ostow. I thank David Pincus, also a member of the group, for his ongoing e-mail conversation with me about minds and brains.

George Makari's knowledge of philosophy and medical history, as well as his experience as a working psychiatrist and psychoanalyst, were invaluable to me.

I want to thank Dawn Beverle, my supervisor at the Payne Whitney Psychiatric Clinic, where I work as a volunteer teaching writing to the inpatients every week.

I am grateful to all the people who came to my classes. Teaching that workshop has been a powerful experience for me, and without my students, I wouldn't have felt nearly so close to the stories of people who are fighting the pain of mental illness.

Jacquie Monda and Edna and George Thelwell deserve my gratitude for helping me find material on Jamaica, as well as sharing with me their own stories from that country.

My greatest debt, however, is to my father, Lloyd Hustvedt, who died on February 2, 2003. Near the end of his life, I asked him if I could use portions of the memoir he had written for his family and friends in the novel I was then beginning to write. He gave me his permission. The passages in the book from Lars Davidsen's memoir are taken directly from my father's text with only a few editorial and name changes. In this sense, after his death, my father became my collaborator. The story of my great uncle David is also true, and the newspaper article about "Dave the Pencil Man" is quoted verbatim. Despite these direct borrowings, I have throughout the novel freely mingled imaginary stories with real ones.